# Ever and A Apocalypse

## Chapter 1 Beginning

April 30, 2013

Staff Sergeant Richard King was running for his life, on a Long-Range Reconnaissance Patrol, his squad had just crossed a river when they were spotted by the Viet Cong. They were deep in Laos, there was going to be no helicopter rescue. They were on their own. The sound of bullets cutting through the jungle canopy was followed by the chatter of AK 47s, a lot of AK 47s.

The trim young man in his tiger stripe camouflage with its hand embroidered patches ran with a long loping stride which covered the ground quickly. His thoughts were; disengage, evade. Nothing else mattered.

Rick felt a sharp burning in his arm, but he kept going without looking. His squad was in front of him, so he knew they were okay so far. The lead man disappeared; Rick at first thought he was down, but in turn each of his squad went out of sight. They were going down a small embankment to a stream which gave them some cover.

The six-man patrol stopped at the bottom awaiting his decision. They could dig in here and hold off a similar size group or keep moving. If it was a larger group, they were in trouble. "Empty a 60mm belt to hold them and then move downstream," Rick rasped as he brought his M16 to bear. Without hesitation, his orders were followed. The linked belt turned smoothly around a B3A can without any kinking. As the last man started to go out of sight, Rick followed.

"Watch out for that crazy old guy he is going to knock that lady over with his walker the way he is thrashing around."

Rick rounded a bend in the small stream and smelled meat loaf. "*Meat loaf*?" he thought.

"*Damn, I have done it again.*" I am in the Rest Home.

"Hey Rick, calm down it's okay, you just had an episode."

"I know what I had," screamed Rick in anger and frustration.

"You think I want this?" He pushed his walker/M16 away.

Marsha Wren was having a nice day shopping; she had found the most perfect looking dress in Macy's window when a rude man bumped into her. A passing gentleman caught her, just as she started to fall. She grabbed him for support and caught his stethoscope.

"*Oh no,*" she thought, *"I am in the Rest Home. I enjoyed shopping more."*

The Doctor helped her down the hall. She chatted with him all the way. It was a shame no sound came out.

As they went into the room, she smelled meat loaf.

"*Oh good, I love meatloaf day in the school cafeteria,*" Marsha thought.

"*My homework is done, and I passed my spelling test. There is that cute new boy. I wonder whether he will notice me.*"

A still irate Rick King asked no one, in particular, "Why is that toothless old bat smiling at me?"

Worthington Manor Rest Home, Columbus, Ohio
September 9, 2016

"Doctor, this is Mrs. Hansen the night nurse at Worthington Manor. I am sorry to report that Mr. Glenn passed away last night."

Pacific Care, Seattle, Washington September 10, 2016

"Dr. Jansen this is Clair over at Pacific Care. I am sorry to let you know that Mrs. Johnson died last night."

South West Rest Home, San Antonio, Texas September 12, 2016

"Dr. Jackson this is the South West Rest Home. Mrs. Rowland died last night."

Eastern Shore Rest Home, Berlin, Maryland September 12, 2016

"Dr. Purdue this is Mrs. White at Eastern Shore Rest Home. I am sorry to tell you that Mrs. Lovy Leonard passed away early this morning."

Baltimore Maryland Johns Hopkins Hospital, September 15, 2016

Research physician Dr. John Parsons took his feet off the side of the mahogany conference room table and tilted his leather chair forward, while taking a sip of his rapidly cooling coffee, before bringing up the next protocol to be discussed.

"This one is really disappointing; it looked so good on the animal tests and passed Phase 1 safety protocol with no problems in the healthy people tested."

"Of fifty volunteers tested, the few adverse health effects were of the mild allergic reaction level. This was to be expected from the outcomes of the previous animal tests performed."

"Now that Phase 2 with actual sufferers of advanced Alzheimer's underway, it's killing instead of curing the patients! The fifteen blinds are doing well on the placebo but thirty of the thirty five being tested have died in a three-week period."

"All of these deaths in the first reporting period! These are the worst results I have ever seen. No way can we continue this test."

"As a side note we must find a way to be notified of an exceptional number of problems early in a study rather than to wait for the first thirty-day summary"

The pharmaceutical representative, Sharon Nielsen doodled squares on her notepad as she thought. "*This drug is a loser.*"

"Yes, we have to stop it right away."

Better to pick the drug studies to battle for, and this isn't the one.

Parson directed his assistant, Barbara to notify the National Health Institute, and the FDA that the study was being halted pending their review. He had no doubt on the outcome of that review. He also asked her to draft a memo about the need for an early-warning system for failures like this. It had never happened before, but the lesson has been learned.

"Also have the Repository up in Towson return the drugs to Benton Pharmaceuticals for disposal. Have them send the originals of the test results for our files, put test samples in long-term storage and immediately send a letter to the various doctors who have patients in the study that it's discontinued."

"Though at this rate, there will be no patients left alive. On second thought send emails followed by the official letter."

He shook his head slowly; this really looked like a promising path for halting if not curing Alzheimer's.

The Repository in Towson administering this particular study took the notice in stride. They handled dozens of studies of this nature every year. Most ended in failure; that was the nature of pharmaceutical drug development. They were provided the drug in the correct dosage format by the developing drug house.

The pharmaceutical company developing the drug would provide a list of the Doctors, who had enrolled patients in the study. The drugs would be shipped to these Doctors for administration to the test study patients.

Previously each Doctor had been notified of the profile of patients that were needed for the study. In this particular case people of both sexes, between the ages of seventy to ninety five, in physically good health exhibiting signs of advanced dementia who had been diagnosed as Alzheimer's were the target.

The Doctors had been recruited by trade journal advertisement, internet postings, or by trade representatives from the Pharmaceutical firm during office visits. The interested Doctors submitted the health history of patients who they thought qualified. Once accepted, the medication would be sent to the Doctor for dispensing.

In turn the Doctor would send to the Repository whatever information was needed for the study. This study required results of a monthly physical, along with the results of cognitive and neuropsychological tests. Brain scans had been run prior to the start of the medication to establish a baseline, and it was intended to perform them again at six months.

This information was all passed on to the supervising physician to interpret; Dr. John Parsons acting as a paid agent of Benton Pharmaceutical, an acknowledged expert in the field. That was all out the window now.

Benton representative Nielsen spoke up.

"On a more positive note, there were several variations of this drug. They have all passed animal testing. Depending on this outcome, we were intending to apply for permission to start new Phase 1 tests for safety. This will accelerate that, but we will be very cautious about moving them to Phase 2. Fortunately this pathway is not closed."

"Let's hope Sharon. It feels like you guys are going in the correct direction."

Baltimore WBAL nightly news September 16, 2016

Newscaster Abi Jackson's attractive face took on a solemn look that also included a hint of anger as she continued.

"We have a further update on the alleged patient sexual abuse incident at the West-Side Nursing home. There are five patients with full-blown AIDS along with complications, and another seventeen have tested positive for HIV. These are all advanced Alzheimer's cases."

"The male nurse Carl Howard being charged is in custody, but his lawyer is not allowing any comments.  District Attorney Dave Mathews reports while there can be no testimony from the victims, the DNA evidence is very clear, and he will be pressing charges."

"In other news…"

West Side Nursing home Baltimore September 17, 2016

The small conference room's warm feeling from its cherry wood furniture was at total odds with the cold business discussion.

"I really don't care what your Profit & Loss sheet will suffer," Attorney Bill Watson retorted.

"The publicity on the sexual abuse is so bad you have to get these people out of here. Can you get those with AID's into a different facility?"

"The Oaks Hospice Group has a facility for those who really do not have a home, but don't want to die in a hospital. They have to charge a lot, but it would look good for us, and get them off site. With their complications, none will live very long, and all have the paperwork which indicates they do not want extra-ordinary measures taken to keep them alive."

The General Health Insurance company representative frowned as he thought this through, and then supported this position by pointing out that this would actually be the least-cost path for them in the long run.

"Even though we do in house Hospice care, and even if it does cost more by having them out of here, it will quiet matters down, and the patient loss will stop. People just don't want their loved ones in danger, especially those who feel guilty for dumping them here in the first place."

The Nursing Home Director, thinking of her Board of Directors reaction to the cost was about to object to this line of reasoning, but stopped as she realized she couldn't win this discussion.

"I will contact the Oaks Hospice Group; it has an excellent reputation and looks good, so when it's shown on TV, it won't look like we are just getting rid of them. We should be able to get all five with full-blown aids out of here this week. They need extra attention, so they would be hard to hide."

"The others will look like any other patient, but we can move them into the back wing, and redirect the traffic flow so people won't know they are still on site. Two of those being shipped out could have been an additional problem since they were also involved in an Alzheimer study, but their Doctor just notified us the study has been discontinued. Sometimes things work out for the best."

Baltimore WBAL Nightly News - September 16, 2018

Abi Jackson wearing a lady's blue pinstriped business suit and light make up, continued in that non-accent of professional reporters.

"The jury has found sex abuser Carl Howard guilty of multiple counts of rape and murder for the West-Side Nursing home deaths in 2016."

"Stay tuned for tonight's editorial for our thoughts on providing patient safety, and how that lack contributed to the bankruptcy of the West-Side Nursing home. Now let's turn to Bill for tomorrow's weather."

Oaks Hospice Group, September 27, 2018

"Attention to orders," "Purple Heart third award," "$101^{st}$ Airborne" "Distinguished Service Cross," "Company F, $58^{th}$ Infantry," "Howling Commandos."

Rick heard the voice drone on. The morphine which kept the pain at bay kept him from understanding what was occurring. He thought he should get up, and kept trying, but he was not strong enough.

"Mr. King is sure restless tonight," described the night nurse after her bed check rounds in the Hospice.

"Not as bad as Mrs. Wren, she keeps trying to get up to go to school. She is afraid she will be late. She thinks I'm her mother, and keeps apologizing that she can't get out of bed."

Oaks Hospice Group, September 27, 2018

"This man and woman, Richard King and Marsha Wren have now been here two years and are still alive," Todd Spencer told the hospice staff committee.

"This is very good for them, but not for our mission. Against all odds while having advanced Alzheimer's and AIDS they still live on. While we try to run a clean facility, and follow all the rules, you would think something would have got to their immune systems."

"Todd, as Medical Director what is your suggestion," asked Matt Kennedy the portly Chief of Staff.

Todd in his usual deadpan manner joked.

"Matt, I suppose we could shoot them for not following the normal path, but I really think they should be returned to a traditional long term care environment."

"Ouch, don't think we could stay in business very long if we started shooting people, look into moving them."

“To move them, we will have to have the agreement of whoever has been paying for their support. I do not remember exactly which insurance company, but they were part of that West-Side Nursing Home scandal several years ago.”

“Oh yeah, I remember that. I just heard on the news that sick sex abuser got mixed in with the general population at the penitentiary.  He was literally hacked to pieces by a group of prisoners, who all just happened to have gloves and masks. No surprise on the knives, but surgical quality masks and gloves? It makes you wonder.”

“Anyway, they seem to be hardy enough that we cannot justify holding the beds for them while others are waiting. I will contact the insurers, and see what they’ll do.”

Oaks Hospice November 2, 2018

“Todd, General Health Insurance covers both of the long lived, and they want to send them to the center city indigent home. I raised a stink over that, told them I would go to the press.  Both have an extended care policy with GHI.”

“GHI is required to pay for rest home support, not put them in indigent care with the city. They finally agreed to have them transferred to the Northeast Rest Home facility up on Loch Raven Boulevard.”

“Good for you Matt, those slime balls would do anything to avoid paying.”

General Health Insurance headquarters, December 8, 2018

"I see those two people who are at Oaks are being moved."

"The Chief of Staff over there wants them out as they aren't in a rush to die. The cheapest thing to do would be to send them to Schaefer, but they think that is dumping. So they have demanded Northeast Home.  Rather than fight them about it we are going to send them to Northeast."

"Then let Northeast know they are only in transient care until beds open up at Schaefer. Fortunately, we checked, and beds are open so it will only be one days cost at Northeast."

"Also I have arranged for their charts to be delayed with their full diagnoses. That way we won't be charged for AIDS procedures. They won't be there long enough to cause any problems. The real charts will catch up with them at Schaefer, and they will take the proper steps."

"Good work Norm."

Northeast Rest Home facility December 9, 2018

The Head Nurse ordered, "Put them in the transient rooms. We just got a call from their insurer that they have coverage problems, and are going to be moved tomorrow to the center city indigent center."

Northeast Rest Home facility
December 10, 2018

"The charts are missing on these two patients we're about to transfer to Schaefer, what should I do?"

"Here is one of our charts showing they have advanced Alzheimer's. That should do until their real charts catch up."

Northeast Rest Home facility December 11, 2018

"What do I do with these charts that just arrived?"

"The patients are no longer here. Hold on to them until they are requested. If they are not requested in thirty days send them out for archiving."

William Donald Schaefer Memorial Rest Home March, 2018

The William Donald Schaefer Memorial Rest Home was where Baltimore's indigent ended up. It was staffed by people, not good people or bad people, just people. Not at the top of their profession because of the abysmally low pay scale but sincere in their efforts.

The facility itself was jokingly referred to as the "Outhouse", a mostly forgotten reference to a poorly chosen remark of their namesake. It was not really filthy, but start with a building that is over one hundred years old, turn it into a rest home, don't update it and never provide the funding needed for proper maintenance, it's not going to be the best place in town.

The floors covered with brownish grimy linoleum that never looked clean even after being mopped. The walls a dingy institutional green are forever appearing to be ready to peel, and flake off, but never quite make it. The ceiling tiles have water stains, but aren't rotten enough to replace. Almost all the fluorescent light fixtures work, but enough flicker slightly that one has the feeling of being in a third world dungeon.

Only the most lost hopeless cases ended up warehoused here, with no one to care for them, much less love them. Most suffered from years of drug and alcohol abuse, and their actions and appearance made them hard to invest any emotion in, even if the staff had the time or energy to do so.

There are two patients to a room in institutional metal beds that were hold overs from World War II. Ninety percent of the patients just lay there, unless being led to the lounge or dining room. The lounge and dining room were actually the same room. To avoid bed sores and the additional attendant care required, whenever possible patients were led down to this main area, and settled in for the day.

Their only exercise was to walk them back to their room to change their cheap diapers. Occasionally a patient would get up and wander around, and if they caused no commotion were allowed to do so.

If they fell they were transported to a local hospital from which they seldom emerged. A broken hip, years of self-abuse, along with advanced age was not a recipe for recovery.

In room 34 bed A, an eighty-three year old shriveled man was lying with his eyes wide open, but not really seeing. If it was not for the slight rise and fall in the sheets, one could not tell he was alive.

Peggy Tapp the assigned caretaker entered the room. She was a fiftyish overweight black woman of medium height, and whose face showed a lifetime of cares.

“Well old man time for dinner.”

She said this cheerfully, knowing full well, there would be no response other than the automatic swallowing as she spooned the soft food into his mouth.

When done, she made a note on his chart which when full would go into storage without further review. No one had the time to review it, and there was never a change, why bother.

In room 42 bed B, a similar event occurred except the bed’s occupant was an eighty-two year old woman. Her caretaker was not as cheerful, and as she fed her patient grumbled to herself that the recent rise in bus fares might make her working impossible. The grumbling did not matter to the patient as she just lay there and swallowed the mush as it was fed to her.

## Chapter 2 Waking Up – April, 2021

William Donald Schaefer Memorial Rest Home April 13, 2021

In room 34 bed A, in a back corridor Richard "Rick" King slowly became aware of his surroundings. He felt like he was waking up from a sleep that was far too deep. He was disoriented and was not processing his environment. It did not match what he thought he remembered, so he just lay there trying to get his thoughts together.

As Rick laid there a black lady who he did not recognize at all came into the room.

"Time for your dinner handsome," a cheerful Peggy Tapp announced.

Rick tried to ask where he was but all that came out of his dry throat was a croak. A very startled Peggy Tapp stopped and looked at him carefully.

Rick tried again, "Water," came out as a dry rasp.

Peggy left the room rapidly and returned quickly with a cup of water. She lifted it to his dry lips, so he could sip it. After several sips, he tried to talk again.

"Where am I and who are you?"

"You're in the William Donald Schaefer rest home, and my name is Peggy Tapp," she told him.

"Figures," he said in his raspy voice, "I'm a Republican."

Peggy chuckled as she picked up his chart. It confirmed what she remembered. This was a patient listed as having severe dementia due to Alzheimer's disease. There was no way that this conversation should be happening!

Peggy thought rapidly, *I have to report this so a doctor can look at him, but first dinner.*

"It is dinner time now, are you hungry?"

Rick didn't have to think.

"Yes!"

The smiling attendant said, "Let me raise the bed and put the tray in place."

She was raising the bed as she spoke. Swinging the table stand into position, she placed the tray in front of him.

"Dinner is served," announced the almost giddy black lady.

Peggy had never seen a patient so far gone make this sort of recovery. After many years of nothing but the unremitting gloom of watching people pass this was a brief ray of hope. She had no illusions that it was nothing but a brief step back from the abyss for him, but it still felt good.

"Looks like mush," Rick commented.

"A step above, but that is what we have had to feed you for the last several months. Now do you need help?"

Rick got a rather stubborn look as he said, "Been doing it for eighty some years"

Rick tried to raise a spoon in a shaky hand but could not get it to his mouth. After letting him try, Peggy spoon fed him.

"Is there any dessert?" he asked.

"Not right now, but I will see if I can find something before I come in to tuck you in for the night."

"It will be appreciated. I'm still hungry."

Later Peggy was at the nursing station and was talking to Liz Herring the night nurse on duty. She described what was occurring with Rick King.

Liz looked thoughtful for a minute.

"This sounds extreme but possible. Alzheimer's is a funny disease. There is the disease, and there are secondary factors such as environment or another illness such as diabetes."

Liz went on, "These secondary conditions make the dementia appear worse, if the condition improves there seems to be remission in the Alzheimer's. I wonder what changed. I will put him on the list for rounds tomorrow."

William Donald Schaefer Memorial Rest Home April 14, 2021

Doctor Charles Meyers, a youthful looking resident at Baltimore East Hospital cleared his throat.

"This is one of the stronger cases of dementia appearing worse than it actually is because of secondary causes."

"The real puzzler is that from the limited medical history we have there are none of the common secondary conditions present such as diabetes, anxiety drug use, depression, urinary tract infection, a thyroid imbalance or vitamin B12 deficiency. There have been no recent environmental changes."

"About the only thing that can't be ruled out is recovery from a series of mild silent strokes."

The recent graduate in Geriatric Medicine continued, "Because of the patients advanced age and known length of Alzheimer's, there is really nothing that would be achieved to confirm this by diagnostic testing. Continue care as before, but realize that for a brief time, you have a more aware patient who needs to be treated as such."

"Thank you Doctor, that is what we thought, but we needed it confirmed," stated Liz Herring the night nurse attending the conference after Doctor Meyer's rounds.

Lisa Hawkins the head nurse followed on with, "As long as he is aware we will work with him to get him out of bed and more involved with his own personal care and interaction with others."

"Sounds like a plan, now I need to get back to East to perform my rounds there. They keep talking about reducing our eighty-hour workweek, but nothing happens. How in the old days residents put in one hundred and twenty hours without killing everyone I will never know."

Both nurses chuckled at the never changing complaint of all resident intern physicians.

Same day

"Good afternoon Mister King, how are we today," bubbled Peggy Tapp.

"I am fine. I don't know about you," replied Rick in a fake crotchety manner.

"It is so good to hear that. Dismal is the norm here, so it is uplifting when something nice happens."

King asked, "What did the young kid have to say about me this morning, He certainly asked enough questions."

"Now don't be mean, Doctor Meyers is trying his best."

"I know, but everyone seems like children!"

Peggy grinned, "I hear you, and twenty to thirty year olds are beginning to look that way to me. I can see how that would be a problem for someone as ancient as you."

"Wait a minute, I am not ancient. I just look that way," King retorted.

Okay then, Old Man, let's get you out of this bed and take a walk."

"Not in this damn open gown I'm not!"

Peggy got a stern look, but then blew it by giggling,

"Get your boney white butt out of bed. Anyway, I have a gown for you."

While talking, she opened the cabinet which served as a closet and pulled out a threadbare men's nightgown.

"We have a collection of the finest men's clothing."

"Better than this gown," grumped King.

He struggled to sit up. Peggy raised the head of the bed then helped him bring his feet around. As he started to lean forward to stand he grabbed her arm and sat back down.

"Dizzy."

"Well what do you expect after being down for the most of two years? Sit there for a minute and let things settle."

"Peggy, what is the date?" King asked.

"April 14, 2021."

"The last I remember is August 2016."

Peggy nodded sadly, "Doesn't seem fair does it, five years of your life gone, just like that. Then again, you are here now, be thankful for what you have. Now lay down again. We have a lot of work to do before you will be able to get out of bed."

Rick snorted, "There's that We again; you going to be doing this work?"

"As a matter of fact Mister Smarty Pants I will be helping you with your therapy. I should be paid extra for all the whining you will be doing."

"How do you know I will be whining?"

"Cause, that's what all you boney butt white guys do!"

"Okay," a pale Rick gasped, "I have sat up too long, now what?"

"Uh, lay down," the rotund Peggy asked?

"Only for you, my dear," Rick said as he collapsed.

Peggy with an evil grin said, "Well done boney, now sit up again."

"What?"

"Yep up and down five times is what the therapist wants, that's one."

"Maybe being out of it was not so bad," as Rick shakily tried to sit up again.

"Now back down. Two." Ricks painfully looking thin arms were shaking as he forced himself up a third time. At his fourth attempt, his arms could not bring him up.

"Well done honey child," Peggy cried, "We did not think you would be able to do three."

Rick grinned weakly as he asked, "What did the Doctor really have to say. I didn't understand him when he tried to explain my condition."

Peggy now very serious, told him, "Mr. King it was thought you had severe dementia, but you don't, some other problem which we think was a series of small strokes made it seem worse than it was. The way you are acting right now it appears you're at a mild stage of Alzheimer's, and that is very good news for you."

"Where do we go from here?" Rick inquired.

"YOU will be doing your ups and downs twice a day till we can actually get you out of bed. As for ME, I am going home, it's the end of my shift," laughed Peggy.

"Got me," Rick laughed right back. "I have so many questions about what has happened in the world, and my last five years. When can I get some updates?"

"As soon as we can put you in a wheel chair and get you down to the lounge"

"Blackmail," Rick complained.

"Yep, therapy has it down to a science." Peggy chortled, "See'ya tomorrow," as she left the room.

Rick sighed as she walked away. "*This is not how I expected the end of my life to go. A quick heart attack or losing it in, Never Never land, but not this, go away then come back. Wonder how long I will be here this time?*"

At the same time in room 42, night shift Nurse Linda Klima was taken aback when the patient in bed B asked, "Where am I?"

William Donald Schaefer Memorial Rest Home April 15, 2021

Head Nurse Lisa Hawkins looked around her utilitarian office as if wondering how she came to be here. To have one unusual medical occurrence was noteworthy. The same occurrence twice was weird. Shaking her head, she pushed the speed dial for Doctor Meyers.

After two rings, she received his voice mail. Leaving a message about another patient appearing to recover from severe dementia, she hung up. She heaved a sigh of relief; she didn't want to speak with him directly.

This relief lasted for about two minutes when her phone rang. "Lisa this is Chuck Meyers, what's this about another case like Rick Kings?"

Lisa spit out, "Marsha Wren, another of our patients who has had severe dementia for several years, suddenly is awake and aware!"

"Slow down Lisa," Chuck told her, "when did this start and how solid is this?"

Wrapping the phone cord around her arm nervously Lisa told him, "During last rounds she asked where she was. Since then she has been conversing rationally as though she has never had Alzheimer's. This has continued this morning, and I have spoken to her. She is puzzled where her last five years have gone but seemed normal."

"Wow Lisa that is unreal. I can't get over there until my scheduled rounds tomorrow, but she and Rick King have to be my first visits."

## Chapter 3 Getting Up

Same-day Rick King's room

"Rick, I am Emily Sheetz your therapist. Let me explain what we are trying to do. You have been bed ridden for two years that our records show. This has left almost all your muscles atrophied."

"We need for you to get into good enough shape that we can get you out of bed and into a wheel chair to make your life more interesting."

"Emily, why should I bother? I am almost eighty six years old, and I will kick off anytime."

"Rick, that isn't an accurate statement. Actuarial tables show that a healthy eighty-five-year old white male lives on the average another five to six years."

"That's the kicker isn't it, healthy."

"Rick except that you have Alzheimer's you're in good health. Now what should we do, let you rot here for five years or try to improve your quality of life."

Peggy Tapp who just walked in added, "And I won't have to wash your boney white butt!"

Rick gave a snort replying, “Well that is the closest I will ever come to a sexual adventure again.”

Peggy came right back with, “more like an appointment with a cold colonoscopy tube.”

“Ouch, you have convinced me, exercise it is.”

All three of them winced at Peggy’s outspoken thought.

Emily was quick to take advantage of this opening. “We’ll start you off with a series of Abdominal Pulls, Leg and Arm Exercises.”

Rick’s voice was alarmed when he said, “Sit ups?”

“In a reduced fashion, pull both knees up as much as you can.” Rick pulled them up, so they were pointing straight up.”

“Rick, touch your butt with your heels.”

He strained, “This is it.”

“No problem, raise your head off the pillow a couple of inches, now put your hands behind your head.”

Again he tried but his head flopped down quickly.

“Sorry Emily this is all I have.”

“No problem, pull your stomach muscles in, and hold for several seconds.”

Rick could do this.

"Repeat pulling them in five times."

"Great, your goal is to be able to do these ten times in a row with your heels touching your butt, and head held several inches off your pillow. This will strengthen your core muscles."

"Lie on your side, gently kick your leg out straight and lock your knee. Very good now hold for several seconds while bringing it back slowly, do this three or four times and then switch legs."

This Rick was able to do four times each leg, with strain but doable.

"Flat on your back now, pull your legs to your chest as far as you can and hold your knees."

"Emily, are you trying to kill me?" Rick panted.

"No pain, no gain."

"Aarrgh, I hate that saying, my drill Sergeant used it all the time. I think his name was Sheetz also."

"Really," Emily asked?

"No but it should have been."

Emily looked a little crestfallen. In spite of her quick mind, she had always been a little gullible.

While she may be slightly gullible, she also believed in paybacks.

“Tomorrow I’ll bring a weight bar and dumb bells.”

Rick turned pale, “You are kidding, aren’t you.”

“You had better behave or you will find out.”

Peggy said, “Where do you store them. I might want to use them on him.”

Rick had learned one thing in all of his years, when two women were against you, just go with the flow.

“How long do you want me to hold my knees here?”

“That is long enough. Ten seconds should do it. Do this for five reps, then work your way up to ten repetitions.”

“Next squeeze your shoulder blades together pressing into the bed but don’t arch your back. This is for your arms. Hold there for five seconds, release and repeat. Start at five reps and work up to ten.”

Rick could do these five times but was panting at the end. Rick’s thoughts flashed back to basic training in 1953.

*“My god what have I come to.”*

Unaware of these thoughts Emily concluded with, “Last hunch your shoulders up to your ears, hold for several seconds and release slowly. Again start at five reps and work up to ten times.”

“Peggy you’re to help him sit up at every meal.”

"Emily, how often should I do these exercises?"

"Do them every other day until you work up to ten reps of each, and then we will review your progress. Only do them with Peggy present, and she will record your progress on your chart."

"So be nice to me Boney or your progress will be very slow." Peggy cracked.

Another lesson learned over the years was when to keep your mouth shut, Rick practiced that one now.

"Okay Rick I will see you next week to see how you are progressing. Be nice to Peggy," Emily said with a grin.

Five minutes later in Room 42

"Hello Marsha, I am Emily. I will be your therapist."

At the same time

Doctor Meyers slowly signed the charts. He was buying time trying to figure out what to do about two such rare occurrences at once. He already wrote in the orders for continued physical therapy. Now what steps to take to find the root cause of why the dementia appeared to recede?

"*Blood tests and a review of their medical histories at their previous institution would be a good start,*" he thought.

As Meyers was thinking of these, a cheerful Peggy Tapp came into his cramped tiny office.

"Doctor we need you in the lounge for a few minutes; it is urgent."

When they arrived, he saw a cake and ice cream waiting. There was a banner hung on the side of the cafeteria like table. **Congratulations Doctor Meyers on completing your residency!**

The staff and patients present burst into applause as he appeared. For a few minutes, there was a minor celebration of another step in life. The usual gag gifts were presented and commented on with laughter abounding. As with all celebrations it was over all too soon.

Head Nurse Lisa Hawkins approached Chuck Meyers, "Doctor there is a patient in 29 A who is developing some breathing issues."

"Let's go check them out."

So the day went. After his rounds were complete Doctor Meyers headed back to Baltimore East. He was looking forward to the end of his shift and the party after that. There was this cute nurse he had his eye on for a while.

He avoided dating anyone seriously all through school. He was not going to be one of those Doctors who married early for the support through school, then upgraded later.

There is a study showing that going through a doorway will cause the mind to reset for the next series of events.

That is why people will show up in a room and forget what they are there for. The mind cleared the immediate past.

It hasn't been proven beyond doubt, but it may explain why mankind lost its chance to find out why two people who had AIDS and advanced Alzheimer's were now showing no symptoms at all.

Baltimore East Hospital April 18, 2021

Doctor John Towers, Director of Baltimore East Hospital was not pleased to have to deliver the news he had, but there was no choice. Not that he cared about the news; he just did not like confrontation. From her body language, Lisa Hawkins knew bad news was coming and was not reacting well.

"Lisa I am afraid we will not be replacing Doctor Meyers."

A startled Lisa Hawkins drew her breath in. She knew it was not good, but this was a disaster. She managed to ask Towers calmly, "Why not?"

"With the city budget cuts we don't have the resources to provide for everyone. We have to back off on routine health those over eighty care for chronic conditions. If they contract additional illnesses they will be treated within the guidelines."

Towers continued in his sonorous voice, which was irritating at the best of times, "We have a fiduciary responsibility to the city taxpayers. Since the federal or state governments will not support this effort, we will have to discontinue the program."

Lisa could not help herself as she retorted, "Has anyone asked those city taxpayers if they want to be left to die just because they are old. You know full well we only have Medicaid patients," she said in rising tones.

"Lisa I must ask you to maintain your professional composure."

Lisa pulled herself back from voicing her true opinions at this point. "Very well under what conditions can we ask for a Doctor to come to Schaefer?"

"We think it is best if an emergency arises you call 9-1-1 and arrange for transportation to our ER. They will determine at that point if life-saving measures should be taken within the guidelines. Now I must call this meeting to an end. I have lunch with the Mayor at his club."

Lisa numbly walked out of the plush office.

*"What has happened to that world where I went into health care to care for people she wondered. In one day, our facility has gone from a rest home where people would be given an acceptable quality of life with medical support to a warehouse of people waiting to die. We never had the money to do it well but we did our damnedest. Now that has been taken from us. I wish I could retire but even that keeps getting pushed back."*

William Donald Schaefer Rest Home same day

“You have got to be kidding,” shouted Peggy Tapp.

“Routine health care includes testing for high blood pressure, cholesterol not to talk of Oncology treatments.”

“Calm down Peggy, none of us like it, we HATE it, but that does not change the facts. The City has effectively cut us off.”

Lisa hesitated while tugging on her sleeve.

“The directive has not come down yet, but there will be personnel cuts. If we are not providing routine medications our need for a pharmacy will be limited, occupational therapy will disappear.”

Peggy angrily added, “Only cooks, janitors and diaper changers will be needed.”

“Crudely but correctly put Peggy.”

“Emily, what are your thoughts,” asked Lisa?

“I am going to work as hard as I can and push everyone possible to be ambulatory before the axe falls on my group. That at least will give some of them a chance. Those that receive no therapy and left in their beds will be dead within a year.”

“That’s what they want,” spit Peggy.

Until this point, Emily kept her composure, but now she bursts into tears.

Peggy who had been venting her anger, switched to Mother mode and put her arms around the young lady.

"Now, Now Honey Child it will be alright in the end."

How it could be she had no idea, but the words had to be said.

William Donald Schaefer Memorial Rest Home May 16, 2021

"Well done Rick," cheered Peggy Tapp. The full-bodied nurse almost bounced in place in her joy. Sitting low in the wheel chair Rick King could see her bare belly as her smock bounced with her.

"*I could have passed on that,*" he thought.

His words though were spoken sincerely. "Peggy I would never have made it this far without you and Emily. You have pushed me beyond belief, but it has been worth it."

He wondered about the hard look that crossed her face as she replied, "It is our job." Then the irrepressible Peggy broke through.

"It was fun pushing your boney white butt!"

"Not as boney as before," Rick came back, "I don't know how much but I have put on some weight."

“Yeah I am the one that has had to move you around; we may have to change your name to Lard Ass.”

“Be nice Peggy,” he warned.

“If I must,” Peggy said with a mock sigh. As she pushed the wheel chair out of the room, Rick realized it was the first time he had been out of it in two years.

As they turned the corner to proceed to the lounge area, she chuckled as she told him. “You know there is a young lady waiting for you. This is your first date with her,”

“Huh?”

“Marsha Wren the other person who they thought had severe Alzheimer’s but didn’t, beat you here. She has been out of her bed for two days now. Women are tougher than men.”

Rick using the hard-won knowledge of his eighty some years did not rise to this bait.

## Chapter 4 First Meeting - May 16, 2021

Rick was wheeled up to a table in the lounge.

Peggy locked his wheels in place and said as she left, "You kids behave yourselves." Rick was left facing a wheelchair across from him containing a little old lady.

*"No other way to put it, she is little, old and a lady,"* he thought. Marsha's height may have been five feet four inches at full growth was now a bent 4 foot ten inches at the most. Her face showed the wear and tear of eighty odd years. Not the raddled lines from smoking, just wrinkled lines from a life fully lived.

Her false teeth did not seem to fit her comfortably, like they had not been worn for some time and had been put in for a special occasion. However, through all this there was evidence of the elegant lady from her prime. Bent from age, her posture still had an erectness formed by a lifetime of standing straight and keeping her shoulders level.

Add to this were grey eyes, which viewed him with a level gaze. This person was not careworn or bitter. She had the confident look of someone who was very comfortable with herself. Even her ragged old house coat hung well on her thin frame.

In turn Marsha saw a man. He was old and wrinkled yes, but still a man. His body type reminded her of a race-car driver or an astronaut. He was of medium build and medium height, maybe five-foot ten inches in his youth, now less than that.

His body was erect and eyes direct. He didn't wear false teeth, and his gums had shrunken in, but not to an extreme degree. Only if he opened his mouth could you tell he had no teeth. Even through all the lines in his face she still could see the grin of a little boy.

Their first meeting wasn't love at first sight, not even like at first sight. It was two normal people checking each other out like all people do no matter their age. Many would snicker at these octogenarians for doing this. Those that snickered would be fools because there is no age limit to the human possibilities of life and love.

"Hi, I am Rick King, and you must be Marsha Wren. I understand that we are both Alzheimer's oddities."

"That's what they tell me," Marsha replied.

Rick asked, "What is the last you remember before you became aware again?"

"I was in a rest home. I would fade in and out, and I remember being angry all the time."

"Same here but suddenly it is like a fog has lifted," Rick stated.

"Exactly," Marsha replied. She went on to say, "I remember in 2013 being diagnosed with Alzheimer's, and my life seems pretty clear prior to that."

"It's the same here. From everything I can remember about the disease, this is far from normal."

Rick went on to say, "It was explained that I must have had some other condition that was making my dementia appear worse than it was. However, I'm not certain that I have any dementia at all."

Marsha laughed, "You are not crazy, the voices in your head tell you so."

"Right," Rick chuckled, "How would I know?"

Marsha continued, "But seriously, I know what you mean. I feel the same way. I can remember the feelings I had when I was descending into that nightmare. Now they are all gone."

"Time will tell, and it appears that is all we have," Rick replied.

The two continued their conversation inquiring about the other's background.

Rick found out that Marsha was born on May 28, 1936 so that would make her eighty-five years old. She was married when she was eighteen years old and had one child who died in childbirth. She had never conceived again. Her husband of fifty-two years, Max, died in 2006 at age seventy six. She spent a career of thirty years as a secondary school teacher. Max a stockbroker didn't leave her wealthy but well off. She had no idea of her present financial state since the onset of dementia.

In turn Marsha found out that Rick had been a Quality Assurance Manager after a career in the military. Rick was born February 21, 1935, so he was eighty six years old. He had enlisted in the US Army as Infantry in 1953, too late for Korea but had several tours in Viet Nam as a Sergeant. He got out after thirty years in 1983 and went into industry.

He was married twice, the first time in 1956 for five years. He divorced her in 1961 when he found out she was cheating on him when he was overseas. His second marriage lasted from 1971 to 1995 when she died of breast cancer.

While he had gotten over her death, he had never felt the urge to marry again. He had a series of live in girlfriends until his mid-seventies. After his last girlfriend gave him an ultimatum of marriage or leaving, he lost interest in women and lived a bachelor's life.

He had no idea why he was not under the care of the VA or what had happened to his money. Ricks wealth was in the form of his military pension, industrial pension, 401k and a house.

Marsha's was in her pension, mutual funds, a 401k, her house and several other properties. They both agreed that they needed some answers and would help each other.

As they were talking, Emily came up to them and discussed their therapy programs. She explained that her work was being phased out June 30, which was the last day of the State of Maryland's fiscal year. This gave them about six weeks to be able to get up and about unaided.

Emily went on to explain, "We will have you walking with a walker within a week. In six weeks you should be able to take care of yourselves. Then I will leave you with a program to continue with, also my email if you have any questions or need further directions."

Marsha exclaimed, "What is going to happen to you?"

"No worries," Emily explained, "I have already lined up a position with the Northeast Rest Home, and it's a really nice facility. Since it is private care government cut backs should not be as much of a problem."

She went on, "People, who can afford it, will always get the best care. I have heard that if things get really bad, and everything will have to be 'Equal', there will be ships set up off shore for short term care for those that can afford it"

Rick asked, "Has it really got that bad?"

"Almost Rick, the politicians from both parties keep kicking the debt problem down the road. We keep trending towards socialist controls, though they are not called that. Right now fifty-six percent of the population that should be working is now on some form of subsidy.

"The dollar has to share world currency status with the Chinese Yuan so even more manufacturing jobs have left the country. Furthermore, the wide-spread introduction of industrial robots has cut down on the jobs available." Emily continued, "Sorry to be the bearer of such grim news, but that is the way it is."

Rick became very silent, obviously in deep thought.

"I remember a lot of talk about hyperinflation, how is inflation now," asked Marsha?

"It has not gone hyper, but it has been in the ten percent per annum for the last couple of years," answered Emily. She continued, "There is constant talk of it taking off if there is a 'Black Swan' event, but it has not happened yet."

Marsha asked, "What is a Black Swan event?"

"A Black Swan is an unforeseeable event which becomes a world game changer. Of course, there are so many pundits out there nothing is truly unforeseeable. Someone always gets the credit for their prediction," Emily replied.

"People claimed the tech bubble of the 1990's, or the housing bubbles in the 2000's were Black Swans. The real ones were the Black Plague or the Spanish Flu. I suppose the dinosaurs would call a giant meteorite a Black Swan. All were scientifically unpredictable at the time and couldn't be stopped."

Emily laughed, "The next event is not a Black Swan, even though you haven't predicted it, and you cannot stop it. It's time for some more physical therapy!"

"Oh Crud," said Rick, "there for a minute, I forgot you were part of the Inquisition."

Using her best evil grin (which was really cuter than evil), Emily wringed her hands together in mad scientist fashion and stated, "We like to surprise our victims. They never know when it is coming."

"Marsha giggled, "I will show you the surprise if you don't get me to a bathroom real soon, or you will be the victim!"

"Oh my I did not realize how long we have been sitting here. Let me get you to a restroom and get Rick some help to the workout area."

"No hurry," grinned Rick.

The workout went as most workouts. Rick complained the whole time in a humorous way as he did everything asked. Marsha did not complain but just did the work.

At the end, Emily stated, “Well, you both did very well today. If Rick had saved his breath it would have even gone better.”

Marsha added, “This was expected. He is a man.”

Once again, Rick used his long experience with women and kept his mouth shut.

Emily noticed this and said, “Well he seems to have been well trained in when not to speak.”

“Yeah,” said Marsha, “Kind of nice that he is trained, he may be a keeper. I wonder if he is house broken.”

At this point, Rick got very interested in the nonexistent pattern of the paint on the wall. Any male of any age should know better than to charge into this conversation.

“It is now lunch time so let’s wheel you back.”

“Thanks for your help Emily,” Marsha said.

Rick interjected, “She enjoys helping us too much. She likes inflicting pain.”

The two women just shook their heads over this typical male attempt at humor. It was so bad it did not even rate as poor. Rick really was feeling out numbered.

At lunch, they were put at a table with other people who were alert. It did not help Rick's out-numbered feeling as there were five more women and only one other man. The other man who was never introduced just shoveled his food in and did not speak.

The women were just the opposite. They wanted to know all about the new comers. It also became apparent that they wanted to know more about Rick than Marsha.

Rick thought, "*I am the new male, and apparently the Alpha Male, why couldn't this have happened to me in High School?*"

This became the pattern for the next six weeks. After two weeks, Rick and Marsha were using walkers. In another four weeks, they used tripod canes.

Emily could not believe their progress.

They were both hard workers, but this was almost unbelievable. The Friday Rick came walking down the hall with his cane casually slung over his shoulder, Emily about lost it.

"Rick! What are you doing? You need the support in case you lose your balance!"

Rick just grinned and said, "Surprise." He then proceeded to stand with one leg raised, and with his arms held out for balance."

“I have been practicing this for a week.”

“Oh my god,” Emily exclaimed, “I would not have thought it possible.”

Rick just grinned. He did not want to ruin Marsha’s surprise. They continued down the hall to outside of room 42. Now Emily really did just about have a heart attack. As she rounded the corner Marsha tossed an object like a bean bag towards her. It did not go very far before landing.

That was when Emily noticed a pattern had been taped out on the floor. The bean bag landed in a box with a large number 4 chalked in its center. Then Marsha started hopping on one leg through the boxes labeled 1-4 and picked up the bag.

She was playing hopscotch! Emily stood there with her mouth open. Every time she started to say something she just gasped for more air. She was in danger of hyperventilating.

Marsha finally stopped as she was laughing so hard. Peggy Tapp who was also there found it much harder to stop laughing but she finally settled down.

Emily finally got out, “Eighty-year old women do not play hopscotch!”

“Why,” asked Marsha?

"It's, it's. It's undignified that's why," weakly retorted Emily. Marsha started to laugh some more at Emily, but she realized that the young lady's world view was so shaken that she was about in tears.

"Emily I am sorry. I just thought this would be a funny way to show you how well I can move. The work you have done with us has helped so much. I have little joint pain now and can move very freely, why I feel like I am only seventy-five! I must admit that 4 is as far as I have been able to go."

Rick chimed in, "A very sexy seventy if you ask me."

This gave Emily pause; looking at Rick and Marsha, she did not see two people in the depths of old age. She saw two people on the verge of true old age but not there. She had a hard time accepting that exercise and mobility could change appearances so much.

She wished that a Doctor would make routine visits, so they could have thorough exams. This was not normal. However, that and several other things were not to be.

"Marsha and Rick I have come to say good bye, I just got notice that they are shutting down the program two weeks earlier than we were told."

"Oh no," said Rick, "are you going to be okay missing pay or can you start early at Northeast?"

"Fortunately, I can start on Monday, so I will be okay. I just came down to give you guys and Peggy a hug."

It quickly became a hug fest for all four.

Peggy then said, "I also have an announcement, my husband and I are retiring to South Carolina to be back with our families. I put my papers in yesterday, and they want me out now to save a few bucks."

Now it became a tear fest as the ladies all hugged again. Rick would have denied it but if one watched closely he wiped at the corners of his eyes several times.

Emily said, "We have to have a going-away party. It is a beautiful day outside let's walk down to McDonald's and get some ice cream."

Marsha piped up, "Emily I don't have a thing to wear, and I don't mean stylish or appropriate. I mean I don't have anything to wear. All I have is this thread bare robe, slippers and gown with my butt hanging out."

As she said this, she half-slapped at Rick. "No comments about my butt hanging out either."

This time Rick dumped all his hard-won experience of keeping quiet when the women were on a roll. "But it is such a nice butt!"

"Well true," Marsha said with a little pirouette.

Peggy chimed in, "Not like your boney white butt."

Peggy said, “I have an idea, come with me.” They all trooped after Peggy as she explained. “We have bags of cleaned and fumigated clothes that have not been turned into one of the charities yet.

They are from clearing out the effects of the recently deceased. Let’s see what we can find if you are not too squeamish.”

From a storage room they hauled out several bags of clothes. There were about ten more bags, so they would have plenty of opportunities.

After half an hour spent sorting clothes, both Rick and Marsha had an outfit. High fashion it was not. None of the clothes were a perfect fit, but they would do. This even included a pair of sneakers for Rick and sandals for Marsha.

## Chapter 5 Outside – May 28, 2021

They walked out the door and came to a halt. How many years since they were outside unaided? It was at least eight years for both of them. It felt both wonderful and scary at the same time.

It was a sunny spring day in Baltimore with the temperature around seventy eight degrees. The air had that big-city perfume of automobile exhaust, garbage, the smell from the Chesapeake Bay and a Baltimore special, a mixture of spices from the large spice company located at the docks.

All in all, it was wonderful to the shut-ins. It smelled of life.

"Times a-wasting there's ice cream to be had," said Peggy.

They turned right out of the door and walked one short block and across the street to a McDonald's.

Needless to say Rick and Marsha were thrilled with the ice cream even though it was plain vanilla.

As they sat eating their dishes of ice cream, Rick noted. "Things have changed. The menu is different and it shows the calories on every item."

"The food police are out in force now days," said Emily.

"Pressure was being brought on companies to do this. In New York City, the mayor got into the act. Now the federal regulators are talking about linking your outside dining to your health records. If you eat the wrong foods and have related health issues, they don't want to cover you."

Emily continued, "The federal budget is in such bad shape, they are doing everything they can to deny benefits. At the same time, they cheerfully add to the dependency roles to gain voter support. It is a mess."

"Why Emily," said Rick, "You sound like a Republican."

"Oh no they are just as bad since they rebranded themselves to get the Hispanic vote," she replied.

Rick said, "The strangest thing about that is most Hispanics I know are hardworking conservatives."

Emily went on, "I am not sure if I have a political home in America anymore."

Marsha broke in with, "That is sad. You are so young and cynical already."

Emily then laughed with her funny little sound, which sounded like she was going Hut, Hut, Hut. There was no real way to describe it, but it was a pleasant sound.

"It's too nice of a day to be sad and serious. The world will go on," she said.

They trooped outside but on the way Rick picked up a job application.

Peggy joked, "I can see the old geezer now. Do you want fries with that?"

Rick replied, "Have a nice day."

For some reason, this broke the group up.

On a more serious note, Rick brought up the fact that both, he and Marsha seemed to be well on their way to a real life.

"The only problem is we are dead broke and have no idea how we got to where we are, much less what happened to our funds and who to talk to about getting them back and how to get out of the rest home."

Rick brought this out all at once, and it left him gasping for some breath.

Peggy thought for a moment, "You both should check your Schaefer records. They should have some sort of a trail. I would do it for you, but I am out of here in less than an hour."

Emily added, "So am I, but I'm local so if I can help I will."

They strolled back to the rest home. Both Rick and Marsha were showing the strain of their longest journey yet. They hugged both ladies good bye one more time and went to their respective rooms for a nap before dinner.

When they went to dinner, Marsha said, "Let's sit at a separate table tonight, we have a few things to discuss."

"I agree," said Rick.

"Besides it will give those old ladies something to talk about."

Marsha giggled as she replied, "The rumor mill will be going crazy. However, we need to have a serious discussion about what we are going to be doing."

Later, as they sat down, Rick brought up the elephant in the room.

"We are different aren't we? Our minds are clear, and we now seem to be in exceptional good health for our ages. Then there is the fact that we both have a mystery of how we got here in the first place."

"Right Rick, now what are we going to do about this?"

"Well I don't think either of us wants to spend the rest of our life in this joint. We can't predict our future so let's plan our lives like everyone else, that things will be fine until life tells us differently."

"That works for me. That means we need to get out of here. We also need to find out what happened to our money. I suspect if we can find how we got here we will be well on our way to getting our money back if it is still there."

"Marsha you had to say that, but I worked awful damn hard for that money."

"Like my husband and I did, but we have to be realistic. So I understand our long-term goal is to get out of here and retrieving our money, if we can. I assume we are doing this as a team."

As she said the words, 'as a team,' Marsha had a funny feeling. She looked up at Rick and saw a different person, she saw him as a man she could be interested in.

"Marsha being a team is about the only way I can see this happening. Now let's talk short term. We need some seed money for this enterprise. I had been thinking along these lines when I picked up that application at McDonald's. We will need far better clothes to be taken seriously in any legal events. However, to get a job, I will need identification and the freedom to walk out of here unaccompanied."

Marsha said, "Then we will have to be perceived as self-sufficient by the staff. So we take care of our rooms, clean and feed ourselves and generally are independent here. That will make us the only two doing it in the building."

"What about ID," Rick asked?

"We need to look into our files here. If any ID accompanied us, it will be stored there. Part of my task will be to volunteer to help in the office. They are so shorthanded I think they will gladly take me up on my offer. In the meantime, look through all the clothing bags for better outfits."

"Sounds like a plan or at least the start of one," replied Rick.

The next day they started on their project. They went to housekeeping and volunteered to look after their rooms. After being looked at like they had two heads each, they were shown where the linens and cleaning supplies were.

After jointly making their beds and cleaning the rooms, they went their separate ways. Rick went to the room with the clothes bags which was fortunately unlocked.

Marsha stopped at the office to see if she could help with anything.

Rick hauled all the bags out to a table and started going through them. He did it methodically and neatly. It never occurred to any of the passing staff to question his actions. He looked and acted like he had an absolute right for what he was doing. The staff were all so stretched they were not about to get involved in anything else.

As he sorted the clothes he thought about Marsha. She was quite a woman. Hmm, he hadn't thought about women like that in many a year.

Marsha entered the office area which looked entirely too cluttered to her. She announced to the two ladies there that she was bored and was there any filing she could do. Silvia the office manager immediately took her over to a pile of folders that needed to be put away. It took about two minutes for her to explain where they went.

It took her several hours to bring order to the files. When she was done it was close to lunch time. She announced she was leaving but would be back the next day to continue helping.

Silvia nodded and said, "Thanks for the help. Lord knows we can use all we can get."

At lunch, Rick and Marsha reviewed their progress. Rick was a little down because he could not find any clothes that made him look better than a street person.

Marsha laughed, “The way you’re dressed you could beg on some street corner.”

Rick got a thoughtful look and said, “That just might work. I am going to check some things out tomorrow.”

Rick and Marsha went to the kitchen in the morning and picked up breakfast treys instead of waiting to be served. No one commented, after eating and returning the trays and sorting out the dishes and silverware they left to clean and straighten their rooms.

It was a bit of a struggle for both as they regained their strength, but they managed.

From that point, Marsha’s day followed the same path as the previous day. The only difference was her pleasantly answering a phone call and taking a message while the other two were out of the office. She passed it to Silvia on her return.

Silvia said, “Thanks.” That took care of that, now Marsha could answer the phones. She was one step closer to freedom of the office.

## Chapter 6 on the Street – June 15, 2021

Rick's day was more adventuresome. He dressed in his only outfit and walked outside. Again, he did this like he had every right, and once more no one second guessed him. He walked around the block slowly taking note of the panhandlers. Most of them appeared to be burn outs with nothing on their mind but the next fix or drink.

One very rough looking black man in his forties seemed more ambitious than the others. Most stood with a cup and handwritten sign hoping for change from cars at stop lights.

This young man (at least to Rick) had a rag and spray bottle. He would walk up to a car and spritz the windshield. The driver would then have the choice of turning his wipers on or letting the man use his rag. It was often a race of rag versus wiper.

When the rag won, the man would hold a Styrofoam cup up to the car window. About seventy-five percent of the time he received some change and occasionally a one dollar bill.

Rick watched this for half an hour then approached the man when the light went green and traffic was moving. "Do you mind if I ask how do you get a job like this?"

The man gave him a bitter look.

"Easy, do twenty years of hard time for a stupid mistake, and no one to help when you get out."

"Ouch," said Rick, "I don't think I want to go that path, besides I don't think I could last twenty."

"The man laughed in his booming voice and asked, "What's your name."

"Rick and what is yours?"

"Charles, now what is your real question?"

"Straight to the point Charles," replied Rick. "I need to raise several hundred dollars, so I can buy some clothes to apply for a real job."

"It should take you about a week to do that," Charles told him.

"A week, you make several hundred dollars a week?"

"Yeah and I only work about six hours a day and never in the rain."

"Well I can see why never in the rain," Rick said dryly.

"So I just set up on a corner and do what you are doing?"

"Rick my man, it is not that simple. You have to be careful not to take someone's territory, or it could get bad real quick. No disrespect, but you don't look like the man you must have been."

"You have that right, how do I avoid that?"

"Simple watch an area several days, if no one shows up it is yours. It wouldn't hurt if you scouted who was working the area. Then go the Salvation Army Mission next block down at dinner time. Ask them about the area you are eyeing and see if they have any problems."

"Rick you will be surprised, but most of the people out on the street aren't the wastes that people think. They will appreciate your asking and trying to avoid trouble. Some of them will even tell you good areas to try. Once you have decided who to approach, point them out to me, and I will tell you if they are safe. There are several that are truly insane and dangerous to be near. You usually can tell but not always."

"Charles, I cannot thank you enough," Rick replied, "I am going to follow your suggestions."

"Keep in touch, let's do lunch, have your people call my people," Charles said in his deep booming voice.

Rick chuckled back, "Right. Thanks again and see you soon."

At dinner that night Rick shared what happened with Marsha. She was not thrilled with him being a street beggar, but thought it was as good of a plan as any. She refused to believe the amount of money Charles said he could make.

“Rick, the man was bragging but even so, if in less than a month you could buy some decent clothes to work at McDonald’s it could work out.”

“I don’t see any other options right now, so I’m going to give it a try.”

“Enough about me, how did your day go?”

“Not bad Rick, I have been filing and answering the phones. I think I am being accepted. Silvia and Ruth asked me to join them on their coffee break.”

“That’s good Marsha, well done.”

Marsha smiled at the compliment. It had been a long time since a man had complimented her.

The next week was spent in their daily routine of being self-sufficient inside the rest home. As they did this their strength improved.

Silvia even joked that Marsha was doing so well that she might put her in for a pay raise. She was thinking of doubling her salary, of course twice zero was still zero. The women had a good laugh at that.

Rick explored the area and found one street two blocks over that seemed to be okay. It was a surface road with four lanes, two in each direction with a turn lane on the main road. The traffic light cycled every two minutes.

He would have to hustle to get one car in two minutes. Since there were two minutes of red and then green he would have a row of cars every four minutes or fifteen tries an hour for money. He discounted yellow for his simple estimate.

If he could average fifteen cars an hour at fifty cents a car, it would be seven fifty an hour times six which worked out to forty-five dollars a day or two hundred and twenty-five dollars a week tax free.

He knew that at McDonald's he would get at best twenty hours a week and could never make that sort of money. This did not seem right but what are you going to do about it?

Once Rick identified his target area, he watched it for several days while walking the surrounding area to view competition. There were really only three that were there every day, and they seemed to be well established at their corners. The important thing was that his traffic flow did not cross theirs. This should not give them direct concern about him taking money from them.

Rick took to heart Charles advice about talking to the men at the Mission. It would be safer than approaching them alone on a street corner. After three days of watching, he went to the Salvation Army Mission that night and lined up with the others.

The staff at the Mission was very polite to him and not pushy. He sat through their service and actually enjoyed it. He had never been religious, but it didn't mean he couldn't listen and enjoy the temporary community that was brought together by the sermon.

After the sermon, he was relieved to see Charles there. He went up to Charles with some apprehension, but was quickly relieved when Charles not only high fived him but said, "Rick my man, good to see you."

This immediately told the others, that Rick was acceptable at least until he proved otherwise.

Rick and Charles moved off to the side, and Rick described the location he had in mind. Charles approved and told him that he had also considered that area, but the one he had was an easier walk. It also had a covered bus stop for the short fast storms that could occur, the corner Rick had in mind didn't.

Rick laughed, "Like anything, there is some science to it. I wonder what else I have to learn."

"Rick, I will tell you something serious you have to learn. You will be on the street; you will be known to have cash on you at the end of the day. The street punks will know this. Carry an eighteen-inch length of rebar. I lay mine down while I am working and no one ever looks at it."

"In the afternoon when I leave, I have it up my sleeve cupped by the palm of my hand so the cops can't see it, but I can slide it out quickly. This can save you if there is only one or two of them."

"What do I do if there are more?"

"Give them the money and pray."

Rick decided this was part of the job that Marsha didn't need to know about. He would carry his stuff in a plastic bag and not let her see the rebar. He asked Charles, "Where can I get a section of rebar?"

"Over on twelfth, there is a construction site. Ask the foreman politely, he knows the score. It would be hauled to the dump anyway."

Now Charles asked Rick, "Who is working your area?"

Rick pointed out the three men, and detailed how the traffic flow wouldn't interfere with them. Charles told him that was good thinking, and he might grow up to be a decent beggar yet!

Rick started to sputter, and then laughed, "I am glad there is hope for me."

Charles gathered the three men and introduced him, and explained what Rick had in mind. Each agreed that it would not interfere with them. They then floored him with their next thought.

“Good,” said the one introduced as Bill, “You can get in the rotation.”

“Huh?” Rick brilliantly replied.

Bill went on to explain that they found that if one of them was out sick (in this world, it could be ill, hung over or strung out,) for more than two days it was harder to retrain their customers. Furthermore, it might open up their corner to an interloper. So they watched out for each other. If someone was missing for a day, they would cover for him for one week, or until known dead.

As the new guy each day, check each of us and cover for us the next day if one of us is missing. Be certain to let me know as I follow you. Rick had a chuckle. Even in street begging the new guy had to pay his dues.

## Chapter 7 Going to Work – June 21, 2021

It was Rick’s first day to work the street. At seven-thirty in the morning, he set out as this seemed to be the best time to catch the going to work crowd. He dressed in his old, but clean clothes.

He was armed with a plastic bag which contained several hand towels, a spritz bottle with a water vinegar mixture, a handheld squeegee all borrowed from housekeeping, an umbrella found in the storage room, and an eighteen-inch length of rebar he had bummed from the construction site.

His first step was to swing by the other three beggars where he found them all to be on the job. A small wave let them know he was holding his end of the bargain. After that he proceeded to his intersection.

He set up on the island in the middle of the road, so he could work the turn lane. One of the things he noticed was the vehicles turning here looked more prosperous then those stopping in the straight-through lane.

His intention was to work this lane for the week, then change if needed. With squeegee and bottle in hand, with a towel hanging out of his back pocket, he approached his first car. Instead of charging in, he raised his bottle and looked at the driver.

The driver a young man shook his head no. Rick did not fuss, gave a small smile and moved onto the next vehicle. This driver was more proactive as they had their windshield wipers turned on. Rick gave a small wave and smile and moved on to the next car.

The windshield on this one was pretty nasty looking, and the driver nodded his head yes when Rick raised his bottle.

Rick went right to work spraying the window and squeegeeing it down. He hustled around to the driver side and held his cup out. The driver dropped some change in the cup. He turned to the next car and got a no. The light turned at that point and the cars moved forward.

Rick checked his container and found he had one dollar and fifteen cents. The man must have emptied his change without counting it.

The next cycle went the same. It took six cars to get a yes, and he was barely finished when the light turned. He got a dollar bill this time. After the first hour, he had nine dollars and eighty cents.

Not bad! He had found that it wasn't worth going past the sixth car in line. If he tried to clean any windows after that he couldn't finish or worse yet, finish and not have time to collect.

Half way through his second hour he realized that he was tired. The work wasn't that much and the walk short. He just was old and out of shape. He finished the second hour and instead of doing the planned three hours headed back to the rest home.

Once at the home, he trudged to his room and lay down. After an hour's nap he freshened up, and then counted his money. He made twenty two dollars in his two-hour stint. He went down to lunch and ran into Marsha. She had taken to eating with the office ladies, so he did not see her at lunch every day. It was obvious that she was waiting for him.

"How did it go Rick," she asked?

"Very good," he replied, "I got twenty two dollars in two hours."

"Wow, I didn't think it would be that good."

"I meant to put in three hours, but it was just too much. I am going back later and spend another two hours. I need to know the best times to work my corner. At the same time, I have to pace myself until my endurance is built up."

"I have had the same problem in the office. I am now up to four hours a day."

Rick asked, "Have you made any progress on finding our IDs?"

"I think so; those files are kept in a locked cabinet by Silvia. She has to lock it to maintain patient confidentiality under the HIPPA rules. I am not sure how I am going to get into them. I am hoping she will leave them unlocked one day while she goes on an errand."

"Well it isn't as we have any time constraints," Rick said. "Be careful because if you get caught, we will really have a hard time getting to them."

"I will," Marsha replied.

Later in the afternoon, Rick went back to his corner and netted another nineteen dollars and seventy eight cents. People would just give him all their change. He kept this up for the rest of the week. On Friday night, he went to the Mission to check up with Charles and the gang of three as he thought of them.

Charles gave his normal booming hello and high five. He asked Rick how his first week had gone. Rick told him he had brought in one hundred and eighty seven dollars.

The gang of three joined them and told Charles, that Rick seemed to have his act together. They had been watching him off and on. They were impressed with how few wipers he had turned on.

If you aggravated people that was what they did. For someone really obnoxious there would be six or seven cars sitting at the turn signal with their blades going on a sunny day.

Rick explained that he really did try to do a good job and his technique of holding the bottle up and giving them the choice. The guys thought this was radical, but would think about trying it that way.

As Bill put it to Rick, "I'm not sure if I want my customers to expect that level of service. Next thing you know, they will want me to wash their side mirrors."

Rick laughed at this then got a thoughtful look. He shook his head and asked the guys how their week had been.

They replied same old, same old. They then wandered over to get in line for dinner.

Charles told Rick. "They will never tell you how they are really doing. It is like gold miners not talking about their claim or even lying about it. They don't want anyone getting ideas about jumping it."

Walking home later, Rick wondered how someone like Charles ended up where he was. He seemed intelligent and helpful, not as bitter as he was the first-time Rick had spoken to him. Something about the picture did not add up.

The next Monday afternoon Rick noticed two teenage kids hanging across the street. As he finished up and started back to the home they followed. As he turned the corner on a less busy street, he heard.

"Wait up old man, we need a buck."

"*Right*" Rick thought as he let his section of rebar slide down. He stopped and faced them.

One of the kids said, "I will take the whole thing old man."

As the kid stepped forward so did Rick. He remembered his Army days. Decide, don't hesitate and end it NOW. Rick punched the kid in the solar plexus as hard as he could. The kid folded in half.

As he was going down Rick slapped him in the side of the head with the rebar. It would leave him with a cauliflower ear for life. He turned quickly to the other kid who was just standing there.

“Get him out of here, or I am going to work you over like him,” Rick growled.”

“Shit man, we didn’t mean anything.”

“Well I do, now get going.”

By this time, the uninjured kid was helping the other one up.

Rick said, “Pass the word, I am an old man, and I know I can be taken, but there will be a price for that taking.”

“You are a nasty old bastard,” the kid told him.

“See you have learned something today. Now go.” Rick watched the one help the other down the street before he turned and went to the rest home.

At dinner, Marsha asked him how his day went.

Rick replied, “Same old, same old.” He then started laughing quietly.

Marsha asked him what was so funny, so he told her about the gang of three and their gold chains. She thought that was a hoot, but also knew he was holding back.

Oh well, men did that. It was funny men claimed they would never understand women. Women would never understand men, so it was even. The only difference was women knew this; men didn't.

The rest of the week Rick tried something different. He had a damp towel, and he wiped down the driver side mirror. He was now up to three-hours sessions as his stamina improved. His walk was feeling more like a walk rather than an old man's shuffle.

Put that together and his take was now averaging fifty dollars a day. He even had people snapping their fingers in aggravation when they missed the light.

Rick had a smile on his face, from his days in quality assurance; he had learned that prompt, good cheerful service paid off. He was reproving that old lesson as a beggar!

That Friday he was talking to Charles, when Charles asked an odd question.

"Hey Rick, have you seen drug deals going down around your corner."

"Not that I have noticed, but I wouldn't even know what I was looking for."

"It would be a guy hanging on a corner. Guys pull up to him and give him cash. He then tells them where their pick up point is. He will call on a cell phone to someone tending the point. They pull the drugs from their stash. They place it behind a bench or something.

The guy picks up the drugs. The only time the dealers are at risk is when they move the drugs from their stash to the pickup point. They usually have some punk kid with no record do this. If he gets picked up, it's a slap on the wrist for him, and then they hire a new kid."

"Can't say I have ever seen the like, but if I do, do you want to know?"

"Yeah if you think of it," Charles replied. He tried to sound nonchalant, but there was a little too much intensity for Rick to be fooled. Charles had a real interest. Now was he an undercover cop, or was he watching for gangs on his territory? Rick thought about it on the way home, but decided it had no real impact on him. If he saw anything, he would let Charles know, then watch to see it play out.

The following week had an event that shook Rick up at first. He was washing the window of a car when he realized he was looking into an unmarked police car.

Oops! He had no idea if what he was doing was legal, but he suspected not. After his first panic, he just gave a two-finger salute to his forehead, and didn't raise his jar to the cop.

The cop smiled, waved and pulled out. From then on that was Rick's procedure with marked and unmarked cars. Not once did he get the evil eye from the police.

## Chapter 8 Things get Strange – August 2021

Rick went down to dinner with Marsha that evening. She once more inquired how he was doing with his finances.

He replied with a grin, "I have over sixteen hundred dollars from the last six weeks. That is pretty darned good. I am turning out to be a decent street person. Don't think I will be asking if you want fries with that."

"That is excellent Rick, where are you keeping your money," she said?

"It is on the top shelf of my wardrobe cabinet, beneath my underwear."

"That is too risky. It would be easy to steal. You should get it into a bank account."

"Marsha I can't open a checking account without some form of ID. How are you doing at the office?"

"Not very good, unfortunately Silvia has excellent work habits and never leaves the files unlocked. I'm getting desperate and about to do something radical."

"Marsha, really be careful," Rick exclaimed. "We don't get to many shots at this; if you get caught, they will never trust us again."

Marsha said with a small smile, "I have an idea that is so radical I don't know why we didn't think of it before. I am going to ask her!"

"What," Rick spluttered, "What do you mean."

"I am going to ask her if we had any ID accompany us. All she can tell me is she won't look, or if she finds them, not give them to us. I have been working there for five weeks now and don't see any other way."

"Hmm, the only downside is that if she says no, she will be more conscious of locking the files. Since she is so good at that now it makes no difference. Go for it."

The next morning Marsha did exactly that. She asked Silvia if she could have a minute during their coffee break.

"Silvia, do you know if Rick and I had any identification like a driver's license when we were admitted? As you know, Rick has been out and earned some money, too much to leave lying around. It should be in a checking account."

Silvia thought for a second, "I don't know Marsha, but if you do it is in your files let's take a look after break."

Marsha didn't know if she should shout for joy or cry because it took her so long to do the obvious.

She settled for a mild, "Thank You."

After their break, Silvia led her to the files and unlocked them, pulling Rick's and Marsha's files out. Both files contained their social security cards and long expired driver's licenses.

There was also a transfer form from Northeast Rest Home.

Silva said, "There is no reason you shouldn't have these, we only retain them if the person isn't competent, both of you certainly are. Here are yours, I have to hand Rick's directly to him."

She then said with a smile, "Of course the way you two have been acting lately that might become moot."

"What do you mean," asked Marsha?

"You don't fool me girl. I see the way you look at him."

"Silvia! I do not! And besides we are too old for that."

"You are still breathing. You're not too old," rebutted Silvia.

"It's really not like that," Marsha replied half-heartedly.

"I just admire the man for the way he has gotten his life back and is out trying to do things instead of whining about it."

"Right," said Silvia, "and you just lie around doing nothing all day. I'm not certain who is in my office helping me for free every day."

At that point, Marsha realized that she was on the hook to work in the office or Silvia would know what she had been trying. Her face must have given her away.

Silvia laughed, "I wondered how long it would take you to ask. Ruth and I had a bet going. She thought it would be two weeks ago, I said last week. So the bet is off. You do not know how hard it was for me to remember to keep those files locked."

Marsha looked at Silvia and started laughing (it would never do for an eighty-six-year old woman to giggle), "Okay you got me, but I would still like to help in the office."

"Thanks Marsha, we need it, and you have really taken a load off of us."

While this conversation was going on Rick had been walking to work. Since Charles asked him about seeing any drug deals he varied his walk to check out the surrounding area.

On his fourth day of doing this, he saw a man loitering near a street corner. A car pulled up, and a man handed what could have been cash out the window. A brief conversation ensued. The car pulled away, and the loiterer made a call on his cell phone.

"*Bingo,*" Rick thought. He continued on his way.

Every day for the next week, he used this route, several times observing cars pull up and the same routine happening. He was careful to use an old man's shuffle and kept bent over.

The more non-threatening he looked the better. He hadn't given it any thought until then, but his walk had become a much younger man's stride, and he was standing taller.

On the fifth day, there was a difference, when he was almost up to the man, a car pulled up, and in a reverse of the previous stops the man handed an envelope to a passenger in the back seat. As the car pulled away Rick took note of its license plate.

It was a vanity plate so was easy to remember. He kept on like he had not seen anything.

The next Friday he approached Charles.

"Charles you asked me if I have seen any drug deals going down, I think I have." Rick then went on to explain what he had been observing and the license number.

"Thank you Rick, I will take it from here. I don't want you to go near that corner again. You have probably figured out I am working undercover to watch this area. You have moved us up the food chain with this plate number. We will handle things."

Rick was relieved. He had figured Charles was an undercover cop, or from a rival drug gang, but not which. A man he considered a friend had asked a small favor, and he had helped. He was still glad that he was on the side of the angels.

Marsha was very excited when he returned to the rest home later. "It worked! Silvia gave me everything of mine she had. She will give you yours directly. She can't give them to me because she does not have a HIPPA permission slip from you."

They both had a good laugh over Silvia's and Ruth's bet. She neglected to tell him Silvia's other comments about how she looked at Rick.

"I'm not sure how this helps that much, a social security card and an expired driver's license won't be enough to open a bank account."

Rick replied, "I have been thinking about that. I will just have to renew my license."

"Won't you need to take the actual driving test again and can you pass the eye test?"

"Yes and yes," Rick said. "My eyes have always been good. I think I can get the use of a car for the test."

"How would you do that?"

"Well the Baltimore police owe me a little," Rick told her, knowing full well the grief he had coming. After telling his tale, grief it was, Marsha felt like he was taking too many chances out on the street.

To her surprise, Rick agreed with her.

"Marsha, the longer I keep going out there the higher the chances are that something will go wrong. I know that, I just have not figured out how to break the cycle. I could work at McDonald's. It is certainly honorable work. It just would take about ten times as long, and I'm not getting any younger."

The next-day Rick saw Silvia and got his license and social security card. She seemed to be very curious about his and Marsha's plans for after they had established themselves.

Rick wasn't aware that they had any plans. They were just working as a team, so they could get back to a normal lifestyle as long as their health held out.

Silvia just said, "Oh," to that piece of information. She thought, "*Who am I to disillusion him; Marsha has plans, even if she hasn't thought it through.*"

Rick asked Silvia about his admission form. She made him a copy. It was the same as Marsha's, same date, from Northeast. This was a little strange. Whatever happened; it happened at the same time to both. He said nothing to Silvia about what he had just read.

That night they discussed it at dinner.

"Marsha there is something funny about this. Why would both of us be transferred in, without records from Northeast the same day?"

"Rick you're getting to be a conspiracy nut," Marsha teased.

Rick looked at Marsha sharply, "I have never had a conspiracy thought in my life."

Rick stopped what he was about to say as he looked at Marsha.

"Marsha, what is your age?" he asked.

"You know it is eighty five."

"Will you do me a favor, walk over to the mirror and look at yourself; as a matter of fact, I will join you."

They walked over to the mirror and stood side by side looking into the mirror.

After several minutes, Marsha said, "What is going on? Neither of us looks in our mid-eighties, we appear more like seventy."

Rick slowly said, "It is not only our facial appearance it is our carriage. We are standing taller."

"Marsha I don't know what is happening, but for now we had better think conspiracy. Who or why I have no idea, but I do not want to end up in a laboratory somewhere."

"Well I don't either, but it couldn't be worse than here," she joked.

"We can walk out the door here," Rick said darkly.

Marsha said, "I am sure there is a simple explanation, but no sense in bringing this to anyone's attention."

"Since we are seen here every day people probably don't really look at us anymore."

Marsha replied "I think that must be, but I would be more comfortable if I knew what was going on."

The next evening Rick went to the Mission to talk to Charles, but he wasn't there. It took two more trips before he caught up with him. He explained to Charles about why he and Marsha needed identification, and the fact he needed a car to use for their driving test.

Charles thought for a minute and said, "Yeah we can do that. Meet me here at ten o'clock tomorrow morning."

At ten the next day they met at the Mission. Rick introduced Marsha to Charles.

Charles said, "Rick you old dog, I did not know you had such a pretty girlfriend."

Rick and Marsha did not argue the point about their relationship. They were both anxious to get on with it.

Charles had an old beater of a car. "This is from the impound lot, but it runs. I don't want you connected with any official cars, or even any personal ones. I have made an appointment for both of you with a friend who works in the MVD so it should be an easy in and out.

On the way to the MVD Rick drove and practiced parallel parking along the way. Parallel parking was no longer a Maryland requirement, but Charles didn't say anything as it was good practice. Rick had been driving for almost sixty years, so it was only blowing the rust off.

Charles made the comment, "You sure don't drive like an old person. There is smoothness with your driving that you do not usually see in older drivers."

Rick shrugged his shoulders, "Seems normal to me."

When it was Marsha's turn, she performed similarly.

The driving test went off without any problems. Both Ricks and Marsha's eyesight and depth perception proved to be as good as anyone on the road. Both certified that they were not insane, on drugs, illegal or anything like that.

Of course Rick thought, *"I wouldn't tell them if I were."*

The driving test went smoothly with the exception that the examiner said the car smelled pretty bad. Soon Rick and Marsha after paying in cash had new driver's licenses with their pictures and were on their way back to the Mission.

Marsha said she noticed that smell on the way over. What do you think it is?"

Charles thought a moment, "It probably has something to do with the body they found in the trunk."

"What!" Rick screeched.

Charles let out his booming laugh, "Gottcha. I have no idea what caused this smell."

Rick had the grace to laugh and admit he had been had.

"Charles, I sincerely want to thank you for your help and guidance in all of this."

"No problem my man, this duty I have sucks, it is usually dealing with the losers and the bottom feeders. It feels good to help someone who isn't."

They arrived back at the Mission, and Charles let them out with a cheerful, "See you around."

Before leaving the Mission Rick went into the front door, he put a one-hundred dollar bill in the red kettle that always stood there.

He felt he owed a debt to the Mission and couldn't leave it unpaid.

## Chapter 9 How Did it Start? - August 2021

The next day he and Marsha rode a bus to a chain store where they bought some reputable looking clothing. They changed at the store, and put their old clothes in the store bags. From there they traveled by taxi to the White Marsh Mall, spending six hundred dollars each, on much better apparel.

This included a business suit for Rick, and appropriate dresses for business wear for Marsha. This along with shirts, blouses, ties, hose, shoes, socks and underwear along with other items gave them a good start on a professional wardrobe. They also bought several casual outfits. By careful shopping, achieved their objective and had a little money left over.

They took a cab back to the rest home. They both went to their rooms, and put their purchases away. At dinner time, they dressed casually and went down for their meal. Silvia was just getting ready to go home and saw them. What she saw brought her up short. She was seeing two people who looked to be in their healthy seventies if it wasn't for their wrinkled faces.

Neither was stooped over. They both looked taller because of this. This wasn't the frail look of eighty-year-old's. Rick was tanned from all his time outside. Marsha was delicate looking with a pale complexion. Her eyes looked large because of the skillful application of makeup. These weren't the people that she knew two months ago.

"Rick and Marsha, I don't know what's happened to you, but it's for the better. If only we could bottle it."

Marsha replied, "I think it is the clean living and good food here."

That little joke resulted in several comments about institutional food. At the end, they did agree the food could have been a lot worse. It was also enough of a change of subject that Silvia forgot about their appearance.

Over the next several days, Rick and Marsha had many serious conversations. They centered around two points. They had to obtain their records from Northeast without anyone being the wiser. They needed to get out of William Donald.

As Marsha put it, "I am tired of sleeping in a room with a smelly person in the next bed. Since I have woken up, I have had three roommates, they have all died, and not one of them ever spoke a word."

After some discussion, Marsha realized she had the power of the office! The rest home was not running at full capacity, so she would make certain that the second bed in their rooms would only be used as a last resort. Later discussion with Silvia found easy agreement with this solution.

They agreed that Rick would keep working his corner even though they knew the risks. They needed the seed money to find and obtain their funds and restart their lives.

As far as the records went, Marsha now knew the proper forms and procedures, so she ordered them from Northeast, sent to her attention. It took a month for them to arrive. There were two packages each about six inches thick. The City of Baltimore at that time was using a delivery service which arrived just before noon every day.

Rick who always returned to the home after his morning stint made a point of being friendly with the messenger. Marsha provided herself and Rick; William Donald Schaefer Rest Home badges which they wore on lanyards around their neck. Silvia's only comment was, "Good, new people won't question you."

Head Nurse Lisa Hawkins was friendly to them but never questioned them. Marsha asked Silvia about Lisa's attitude.

Silvia replied, “She is just going through the motions. She has put in for retirement. When we lost the support from Baltimore East, it took the heart out of her. She will be gone at the end of the year.”

Lisa’s attitude worked in their favor, if the Head Nurse and Silvia the Office Manager did not question Rick and Marsha, then why should anyone else? With their identification on their lanyards, most of the staff thought they worked there. It was obvious Marsha was office staff. Rick seemed to come and go, but no one questioned what he did.

Rick got into the habit of meeting the messenger near the front door and signing for the day’s deliveries. The messenger knew that was okay, Rick had the proper identification, and it saved him the steps to the office. The day the packages arrived from Baltimore East was no different; Rick signed for them and set them aside in a hall closet while he delivered the rest to the office.

He then returned to the closet and retrieved the packages, and took them to his room placing them in his wardrobe. Since they had bought their clothes, maintenance had installed a simple hasp to make the wardrobes lockable.

All it took was a work order issued by Marsha in the office. Rick chuckled and thought to himself, *“Maybe she could get us on the payroll. Nah, better not try that, though we are getting pretty good with gaming the system. James Bond, eat your heart out.”*

The thought of James Bond made him think of the beautiful Bond women. This gave him a twitch that he had not felt in years. He shook his head and went back up front.

That night they discussed what to do about the files they had. There was too much to lie out on a table in the lounge without Silvia asking questions. During their discussion, Marsha kept rubbing her jaw. Rick asked her what was wrong.

Marsha replied, "Nothing my gums are sore. I have not been able to put my teeth in all week."

"Let me see." Marsha opened her mouth.

Rick peered in and said, "Oh my god. Marsha run your finger over your gums and let me know what you feel."

She did so, and her eyes got as big as saucers.

"Rick, I am teething!" For all their talk about their bodies looking younger, nothing brought it home to them like this. What was going on? Rick tested his gums and could feel nothing, and they were not sore.

However, they did not feel as sunken, as though the gums were filling out. They discussed this in circles until they realized they just had one more piece of the puzzle, or they had another mystery. There was no way to tell at this point.

They talked about how the files could be reviewed without anyone knowing. It was decided that Rick would buy a brief case and carry them to the Enoch Pratt Library branch several blocks away. He would review the files there; no one would question what he was doing. He would do this after lunch before his afternoon shift on his corner.

The next-day Rick took a bus to Wal-Mart and picked up a cheap briefcase. Upon returning to the rest home, he locked it in his wardrobe along with some pads of lined paper and pens that Marsha had got from the office supply cabinet.

Rick got into a routine, up early for morning shift at the corner. He was back to the rest home by nine. Then spent time with coffee and newspapers; The Baltimore Sun, The Wall Street Journal, and The Washington Post.

He would then go online in the small work area set up for patients. That was a nice area but he was the only one who ever used it. It was set up by a volunteer group to help the patients.

Rick thought that was funny. The patients were not in condition to use the computer setup; hell most of them weren't even conscious. It did make the volunteer group feel good. He saw them as liberals, and he was using it to read the Drudge report. Talk about your irony.

He would have lunch with Marsha sharing his thoughts on the news of the day. Marsha usually agreed with him but was careful not to let him know she thought he was a bit of a conspiracy nut. He was not extreme with secret cabals; he just thought there was more organization to forces pushing America towards European Socialism than she did.

Marsha felt it just was human nature in action. Not necessarily the best of human nature but still normal.

After lunch, Rick would take his briefcase to the library and go through the files writing copious notes. He would return to the rest home a little after three o'clock and proceed to his corner for his afternoon shift.

By this time, Rick had realized that Bill was correct, he did have customers. Most people were regulars going to and from work. In the morning, he would be in the left-turn lane going south. In the afternoon, he would work the curb side lane going north. This avoided trying to sell the same crowd twice in one day.

After several months, he recognized cars and drivers who would never let him wash their windows and those that usually did. He got into the habit of giving all cars a cheerful wave and a smile. It did not get him new customers, but at least stopped the wiper blades.

Later in the day, he would return to the rest home for dinner with Marsha. They even took to using the bus on weekends to go to restaurants in the mall area. As they walked to and from the bus stop, they would hold hands. They never discussed this. It just occurred.

On some days at his corner the weather was nasty, so he had purchased cold-weather gear.  As it approached Christmas, he took to wearing a Santa Claus cap. It was a strange life but a good life.

He was surprised that the week before Christmas, he started getting tips. By Christmas, he picked up an extra three hundred dollars. Rick realized that he had connected with his customers. By being there with a smile and a friendly wave everyday he became part of their lives. He was totally flabbergasted when several people who never let him wash their windows gave him a tip.

On Christmas Eve, Rick was working his corner, and he noticed a WBAL TV van parked on the side street. He was amazed when his favorite newscaster Abi Jackson came up to him followed by her camera man.

"Are you Rick?" she asked."

"Yes, I am," he replied with a puzzled look on his face.

"If you don't mind we would like to do a human interest story, man working the street's Christmas Eve and all," she explained.

"There are some questions that I won't answer but go ahead."

Abi asked him the normal pre -on - the - air questions. Name, where from, how long had he been doing this, did he like it, what was he trying to achieve.

Rick in turn asked, “Why did you select or even know of me?”

“The wife of our producer comes by here every day. She mentioned you to him, and he thought it would work well with our people segment.”

His answers were; my name is Rick. I’m from around here. I have been doing this almost two years, if I didn’t like it, I wouldn’t be doing it, and I am doing it to make money. In other words, the answers that you would expect and make everyone wonder why the reporter even bothered.

“You seemed to have developed a following, you’re not looked on as a street bum,” she told him. This was emphasized by the cars honking and waving as they went by.

Several even rolled their windows down and yelled, “Way to go Rick.” Rick could not figure out how they knew his name until he remembered the sign he had previously taped to the light poll on the corner. It stated; Merry Christmas and Happy New Year, with many clean windows to you next year. Rick.

When Abi asked him how old he was, she was amazed when he said eighty-seven. She knew this segment would make the air. When she tried to pin him down on where he lived, and why he didn't appear to have social help, he deliberately played the slightly crazy card. It wasn't enough to scare her, but enough to shorten the interview. Everyone knew most street people were crazy didn't they?

Rick was excited when he reported back to Marsha what had occurred. They watched the eleven o'clock news that night. The interview made the air but had been cut to less than thirty seconds. They both agreed that it was short and generic enough that no one would recognize him or take note.

Of course on Christmas Day during the staff gift exchange, half the people present recognized Rick. Most of them did not know what he did during the day. They thought he was on staff. When they found out he was a patient, no one got excited or made a deal out of it. They thought it was cool.

Rick and Marsha had each taken one hundred dollars to buy Christmas presents for each other. They stayed practical and gave each other clothes. During Christmas week, they did splurge with cookies and eggnog for the office area and the staff.

Between Christmas and the New Year they had a serious conversation. Rick had opened a checking account with fifteen hundred dollars. He also prepaid five hundred dollars on a VISA card. That with five hundred in cash was enough seed money to start trying to retrieve their funds.

Rick had gone through their files several times, and he felt he understood the chain of events that got them to where they were:

1. They each were committed voluntarily to the West-Side Nursing Home.
2. While there they had deteriorated to the point, they were declared incompetent and the court appointed a trustee, Burns and Burns was given charge of their finances.
3. Their stay at the nursing home was to be paid for by General Health Insurance Company with whom they each had a policy. This had been arranged by their trustee Burns and Burns.
4. They both had previously signed cards stating they would participate in an Alzheimer's study if their conditions deteriorated.
5. They were in the study, but it was discontinued because of a high death rate. They appeared to be the only known survivors.
6. They were victims of sexual abuse, which resulted in them having full-blown AIDS.
7. They were moved to The Oaks Hospice.
8. After being there for two years it was decided they were not in a hurry to die, so were to be moved to another rest home.
9. GHI wanted to put them in an indigent center, but that would be in violation of their insurance policies.

10. The Oaks Hospice forced GHI to admit them to the Northeast Rest Home.
11. This stay lasted for one day when GHI had them moved to William Donald Schafer.

\+ Now they knew how they got to where they were, they knew who had their funds, and that they had a possible law suit against GHI.

They had no idea why they did not have AIDS anymore or suffer from dementia.

They had no idea how to be deemed competent, and not raise questions about their strange medical histories. They were at an impasse and decided to let it sit for a while. Their living conditions were stable, Rick was accumulating funds. This was too important to rush into.

## Chapter 10 - Black Swans? - August 2021

Marsha got Silvia's agreement on removing the second bed from her room. She and Rick bought a small love seat, chairs, coffee table, and a TV stand along with a thirty-two inch flat-screen television. Rick had wanted a fifty inch but was talked out of it. All but the TV was obtained from the Salvation Army Mission.

A few dollars on the side got the furniture delivered to their room. Another extra payment to maintenance had cable run into the room. Silvia had a long conversation with the new Head Nurse, so she was on board. The Head Nurse was not sure what was going on. Silvia may have left the impression that they were in the Witness Protection Program.

On Tuesday August 22, 2021, Rick and Marsha were watching the nightly news on WBAL. Rick's favorite news caster came on with the news before the show started.

"This is Abi Jackson with an amazing wonderful story. There has been a breakthrough on Alzheimer's. Benton Pharmaceuticals has announced that their newest drug has passed Phase 2 testing and has been fast tracked for approval by the FDA.

This wonder drug apparently not only prevents clumps of protein forming in healthy people but dissolves them where they are already formed. This has the potential of 'returning' many people who have Alzheimer's from their dementia.

Our understanding is that this drug will have to be taken on a continuing basis by the 'returnees' and is probably why Benton's stock has shot up almost one hundred percent on afterhours trading. The SEC is already talking about halting trading to keep an orderly market. The next story is just as amazing."

Monks Pharmaceuticals has announced they have been fast tracked by the FDA on a vaccine for HIV. This is a preventative vaccine and not a cure for those in advanced stages though it should lessen the severity of even that. When asked for their reaction the head of the Baltimore Gay and Lesbian Alliance responded, "Party Time."

Marsha yelled, "Rick that is it, we are now returnees! We were in an Alzheimer's study. Actually, it may have been very similar. The only difference it has been six years since we had our last doses. All we have to do is imply that we were in the study, and that will explain our lack of dementia."

"What about the HIV issue," Rick asked?

"What about it, let them think we have AIDS and are on the medications. All we have to do is prove we are competent, and they will have to release our funds from the court-ordered trust."

Rick said, "I'm not certain that it will be that easy. We will have to be examined by a Doctor, the evidence submitted before the court. The judge will either decide we are competent or order further testing. I will do some Internet investigation to see what the procedure is in Maryland."

During this conversation, Marsha was almost bouncing around in joy.

This gave Rick pause, "Marsha I think we should keep looking old by walk, make up and clothes. If I did not know better I would think you are in your mid-seventies. Especially since your teeth have come back in. I wish mine would hurry up and break through. They are driving me nuts."

After work the next morning Rick went up on the Internet and confirmed his line of thinking. They would be tested for; thought, awareness, perceptions, judgment, mood, and memory. Rick thought with a chuckle, *"I hope my political leanings do not count against me."*

There was one interesting clause, if their incompetence had been temporary, caused by a stroke or something of that nature, after one year they could present evidence to the court and be declared competent. That might be an easier route if they could take it.

The next question was where to start. His initial thought was to hire a lawyer, but that could get expensive real quick. Then there was the matter of trust. Even though they would have a lawyer client-relationship this would be a very delicate dance. The last thing he and Marsha wanted was to be put into endless studies to explain their condition.

After thinking for a while he realized they had very few people that they really trusted. It was a short list, Silvia and Charles. Even though Silvia and Charles did not know the whole story they knew enough that it would not be difficult to explain what they were trying to accomplish. That evening he and Marsha discussed the situation and decided she would talk to Silvia and him with Charles.

Rick donned his latest set of rags and went down to the Mission. There he found Charles and went through the high five ritual. Once they had walked aside Charles started first, "Man I am glad you are here tonight. In two weeks, I start my new duty and will be off the street. I will be working a desk. My wife will love it, and I will have more time for my kids."

"Charles, I never knew you were married much less have kids," Rick stated.

"A six-year-old boy, Charles Junior, and a four-year-old girl, Condoleezza, we call them Junior and Condi. I wish I had some pictures to show, but I don't dare while undercover."

"That's okay, maybe one day you will be driving by my corner, and we can catch up."

"That would be good, Rick. You and Marsha are certainly different than anyone else I have met down here. Tell me what is up with you and Marsha, you're getting together?"

This gave Rick the perfect opportunity to explain that both he and Marsha had both been declared incompetent and needed to find a way to get that reversed, but only wanted to work with a lawyer who they could trust.

Charles broke out into his big smile and said with a laugh, "I have just the lawyer for you. My baby sister would be glad for your case. She was in a large law firm but has recently gone out on her own. She is the best of all worlds for you. She is experienced but hungry."

"That sounds good, when could Marsha, and I meet with her," Rick asked?

"Let me make a quick call," said Charles.

He said, "Phone call Clarisse. He waited for what were probably two rings and said, "Hi Sis this is Charles.  I may have some business for you. Two friends of mine need a competency hearing. No the other way, declared competent. Yeah I know that is backward, but that is what it is. When can you get together with them?"

He looked at Rick, who mouthed, "tomorrow at two."

Charles repeated this to Clarisse, who was fine with the appointment.

Charles handed one of Clarisse Bowden's business cards to him while saying, "Can't carry my kid's pictures but a lawyer's card is okay, what a world."

Rick thanked Charles and went back to the rest home. He updated Marsha on their appointment. She told him that Silvia had been out on a sick day, so she had not talked to her.

Rick told her, "That may be for the best, let's see what the lawyer has to say before we bring her in to it."

The next-day Rick and Marsha took a taxi to their appointment. They had dressed up with Rick in a suit and tie while Marsha wore a woman's business suit with a conservative blouse. Both of them had taken efforts to make themselves, look as old as they could, but it was getting harder all the time. Rick shuffled along using his cane while Marsha walked as stooped as she could. They still looked in pretty good condition for their ages.

Clarisse looked nothing like her brother Charles; she was petit with a light complexion compared to the large framed and dark-skinned Charles. Rick and Marsha made no comment as the introductions were made.

Clarisse smiled and said, "Charles is my half -brother if you have not figured that out."

"I hadn't got that far but there is a difference. I bet you are glad he is the big one," Rick said, in his normal not quite politically-correct manner.

Clarisse laughed and replied, "You got that right. Now what is this about you wanting to be declared competent?"

At this point, Marsha took over and gave a brief explanation that they were probably the first returnees from Alzheimer's. They had been declared incompetent but now their minds were clear they wanted to regain control over their estates.

Clarisse said, "Well from the way you present yourselves, I think you could win your case. Are you in a position to give me a retainer?"

"How much would you need?"

"Can you do five hundred dollars?"

"I thought lawyers worked with a one dollar retainer?"

"In your dreams, sure if it is a small matter for friend or family you might, but this is my protection that you will pay your bills. Think of it like a security deposit on a rental."

Rick glanced at Marsha then said, "We can do five hundred. Is a personal check okay?"

"Certainly," Clarisse replied.

While Rick wrote out the check, Clarisse asked, "How long have you two been married?"

Marsha quickly replied, "We aren't, yet."

Rick about fell off his chair, this was news to him!"

Clarisse replied, "Oh, sorry about that, it's just that you two seem so comfortable with each other like you have been married forever."

Rick replied, "We are a team because we have the same problem. Though I think the definition of team is undergoing a change." With a quick grin at Marsha, he said, "It might be a very good change."

Both Marsha and Clarisse got large smiles; women and thoughts of weddings were almost always pleasant thoughts.

Rick was more serious in his thinking, "*Well boy you should have seen this coming. Why fight it, she is a good-looking woman, we know we are a team. We are at the same place in life, and most importantly I love her. It is not a youngster's infatuation but a mature comfort with her that makes me want to spend the rest of my life with her.*"

These thoughts went through his mind quickly as he said, "We need to have a serious talk Marsha."

Both of the women's eyes light up at these words.

He continued, "My eyes and hearing aren't as good as they used to be, I think we really should have got that fifty-inch screen."

If looks could kill he would have been a puddle on the floor from the sets of laser beams directed at him.

Clarisse said, "Marsha your case should be easy. I'm not certain about him."

"I can understand that," said Marsha glaring at Rick.

Clarisse wisely changed the subject; she didn't want to lose her clients. Let me do some research and get back to you.

Rick and Marsha both gave their prepaid cell phone numbers. They purchased them at Wal-Mart the previous month. They had joined the twenty-first century. Rick only used his for phone calls; Marsha did text messages, took pictures and even twitted whatever that was.

They thanked Clarisse for her time; she called a taxi for them.

Instead of giving the rest home address Rick said, "White Marsh Mall."

Marsha looked at him as if to ask what was going on.

Rick answered the unspoken question by saying, "Marsha Wren, I am too old to get down on my knee, but will you marry me?"

She was in shock. She had been angry with the way he had changed the subject in the law office, but she also regretted saying what she had. She felt she had pushed too hard.

"Yes Richard King I will be glad to take your hand in marriage, and yes, you would look silly trying to get on one knee on the side walk."

The next part Rick knew how to handle as he took Marsha in his arms and kissed her.

The cab driver coughed and said, “This is nice folks and congratulations, but the meter is running.”

## Chapter 11 - Marriage and Competence - August 2021

They broke away from the kiss and got into the taxi, instead of sitting apart like they usually did Marsha slid over next to Rick.

Rick said, “I want to go to the Mall to buy an engagement ring. It can’t be the most expensive, but I want to do this right.”

Marsha sighed in contentment, “Whatever you want dear.”

Rick chuckled inwardly, “*I am glad I am old enough to know the rules, whatever I want is what she wants.*”

Marsha elbowed him in the ribs, “Stop those thoughts right now!”

“I was not thinking anything wrong,” he protested.

“Of course not dear, I’m starting your next phase of training,” Marsha giggled.

Rick’s survival instincts cut in, and he shut up. When they got to the Mall, the Taxi driver rushed to shake Rick’s hand and congratulated them once more. At that point Rick felt compelled to give a larger tip than usual, but realized he did not mind at all.

He started to walk away from the cab when the driver chased him down and said, “You forgot your cane, though you don’t look like you need it.”

Rick replied quickly, “Unless the weather changes then my knees get bad.”

“I’m beginning to learn that,” the cab driver said as he got in and drove away.

Once inside the Mall Rick and Marsha spent time in a chain jewelry store. The lady helping them thought they were such a cute couple and really liked the idea of a December romance.

She told Marsha this who replied, “This is really a fall romance we are not in the winter of our ages yet.”

Marsha had looked over several rings, and one had obviously caught her eye, but it cost fourteen hundred dollars. It was small with today’s pricing, but she still thought they couldn’t afford it.

Rick watched for a while as she looked at even lesser stones then told the saleslady, “I think we will take this one, pointing to the ring that had caught Marsha’s eye.”

Marsha protested, but her protests were weak as it turned out the ring fit her perfectly with no adjustments needed.

Rick said, “I do love you, you know. It just took me a while to sort it out. It snuck up on me.”

This led to another kiss, but the saleslady was used to this, and she didn’t have a meter running.

Rick purchased the ring on his credit card.  He recently had prepaid it to two thousand dollars. They went to the Mall food court and talked over a cup of coffee.

Rick asked, “When would you like the wedding to be?”

Marsha replied with a grin, “I think after we are declared competent, or you could weasel out of it.”

“I never thought of that,” Rick exclaimed. “Is it too late to use that excuse now?”

“Yes dear, you’re all mine now,” she replied.

“Okay,” Rick easily agreed, “just checking.”

“Your checking days are about over my dear,” Marsha twinkled.

Rick said tentatively, “You know there are no doors on our rooms.”

“That is no problem dear, until we are married there will be no need for doors,” she said sternly. Marsha relented after seeing the look on Rick’s face, like a kid whose candy had been taken away.

“You are so easy. We certainly will have to figure out where to have some private time.”

After seeing the look of relief on Rick’s face, she no longer could hold the whoops of laughter.”

The next-day Clarisse called Rick, and told him the first step would be to find a friendly Doctor to evaluate them for the initial filing. Rick thanked her and after discussing it with Marsha, they decided it was now time to bring Silvia in on it she should be able to help identifying a Doctor.

Marsha told Silvia, about them retaining a lawyer to guide them through the steps to becoming declared competent. She explained that they needed a Doctor to do their first examination. If this was thorough enough, and their paper trail back to the original Alzheimer’s study held up, they may be able to avoid a second evaluation. The simpler it could be the better.

Before Silvia replied, she happened to notice Marsha’s left hand. Since Marsha had been waving it ever since they sat down it was hard to avoid. The engagement ring led to the inevitable hugging and squealing.

The other office lady Ruth had to get into the act. The new head nurse Barbara Johnson walked in so the party continued. Before it was over most of the ladies on staff were part of the mini-celebration.

The ladies had many a comment after they heard that she and Rick had to be declared competent before they could get married. They varied on a theme of men and competence, especially those they were married to, but it was all in good fun. After things settled down Silvia told Marsha she would make a phone call. She had a Doctor in mind.

Several days later, Silvia told Marsha on their coffee break that she had talked to a friendly new Doctor who specialized in Geriatric medicine, who would be pleased to examine them, and that there was a Psychologist in his practice who specialized in the competency of the elderly. The Geriatric Doctor was Dr. Charles Meyers who had left the city hospital. The other Doctor who they had not met was Dr. Robert Heinlein.

Later when Marsha shared the names Rick's eyes got big, "I wonder if he is any relation."

"Relation to whom," inquired Marsha.

"The science fiction author," replied Rick. "Oh, I have never been a fan of that," she said. Rick thought, "*Oh my, our first major difference.*"

At the same time, Marsha thought, *"I had better do some research on the field, at least know the major authors and their themes. Don't want to disappoint my man, now that is a nice thought, my man."*

They let Clarisse know who their potential doctors were. She made some phone calls checking them out, especially Dr. Heinlein. She called Rick back, and let him know that they would be good to work with. Dr. Meyers was new to the field so didn't have much of a track record, but there was nothing there to show any bias against the elderly. His prior knowledge of them should work in their favor.

Dr. Heinlein had been practicing for ten years, and had a reputation of usually siding with the patient. This was important as some Doctors always seemed to decide that the patients were incompetent. This was especially true if there were large estates with hungry heirs.

Appointments were made, and kept. Both got a clean bill of health from Dr. Meyers. They were careful not to show the actual amount of flexibility they had developed. Fortunately, Dr. Meyer hadn't had a chance to give them physicals in the hospital, and they were bedridden the last time he had seen them.

Rick and Marsha brought their very carefully edited files. The files showed nothing of the AIDS condition. They left in the fact they were in a discontinued Alzheimer's study with Benton Pharmaceutical. Dr. Meyers was very excited by this.

"You may be the first Returnees," the phrase coined by Abi Jackson was going into general usage.

Their sessions with Dr. Heinlein went very well. Their sessions were back to back, taking several hours each. They had no chance to talk between sessions. Both asked the Doctor, as they introduced themselves, "Are you any relation to…"

"No but you have passed the first test," laughed the Doctor.

The Doctor proceeded to give them a series of short tests and interspersed this with what appeared to be general conversation. They realized the gentle conversation gave insight to their; thought, awareness, perceptions, judgment, mood, and memory.

At one point in each of the conversations, Dr. Heinlein got pushy with them, with Rick it was about his politics.

With the more even tempered Marsha, it was about her lack of a temper! He tried to call her a milk toast mild mannered nothing with no backbone.

In their preparation, both she and Rick were ready to be pushed as to their moodiness and short term anger. Wasn't the Internet wonderful?

Neither of them rose to the obvious bait the Doctor presented them. Doctor Heinlein had been around this block several times.

To each he inquired, "So you did some preparation to know what to expect."

Both answered yes to this.

"It is nice to have a lawyer to help you prepare," he chuckled.

In their own words, they both told him this preparation was done before they approached a lawyer. They had done this to tell if the lawyer they were using was up to the task. The lawyer would either know, or honestly explain they didn't know what to expect, but do their homework.

Clarisse had done her homework.

Doctor Heinlein pushed this conversation. Both told him that Rick had the first thought of checking it on the Internet, while she had conversations with the nurses at the rest home.

While saying nothing Heinlein thought, "*Most competent people I know wouldn't have done this amount of preparation and forethought.*"

The result was that both Doctors wrote reports stating they were in excellent physical and mental condition for their age, and that they were both mentally competent to handle their affairs.

Of course, Rick had to make a comment about handling his affairs. Marsha was not amused.

As they were about to leave the office after half a day spent there Dr. Meyers asked to speak to them. They went into a small conference room right off the lobby. He asked if they would like some coffee which they both accepted.

After it was delivered, he stated, "You do know that you shouldn't have been at William Donald Schafer, that GHI was conducting fraud, when they had you sent there.

According to your files which you brought with you, you each have a policy with them for rest home care. You shouldn't have been in a home for the indigent.

Marsha broke in, "We do not want to get into any public fights, we just want to be declared competent and get on with our lives.

"It is not that simple. I would have to talk to my lawyer, but I have now been made aware of a crime and have responsibility about reporting it. This may not be covered by Doctor Patient confidentiality, because it is only indirectly related to your health.

Besides continued Dr. Meyers, "This may work to your advantage; they have also committed fraud against the City of Baltimore. They should have been paying for your care; instead, they foisted you off on the city. I suspect if the right parties brought pressure to bear they would be willing to settle quickly and want to keep everything quiet."

Rick asked, "Who do you see as the right parties?"

"I would start with Dr. Towers at Baltimore East. The rest home comes under his primary direction. I would think he would be very happy to get his hands on some of GHI's money. He isn't the sort to do battle for you, but for his domain and budget, Katie bar the door."

Marsha said, "These things have a way of getting out of hand and could go public which we don't want."

Marsha didn't say that they had no desire to end up as laboratory specimens. She and Rick had talked this through many times and kept coming to the conclusion that with the combination of the failed Alzheimer's study and full-blown AIDS that their condition would never be repeated.

There was something in their genetic makeup that made this possible. With the recent breakthrough in Alzheimer and AIDS, no one would be interested in studying them for those diseases.

They would be interested in studying them for their amazingly improved health. While they had no objection to the rest of the human race to enjoy health like they had, they weren't willing to do it at the price of losing their freedom.

Their qualms about their good health and sharing it with humanity were put to rest later that day.

## Chapter 12 - A Real Black Swan - 2021-22

"This is Abi Jackson of WBAL with what may be the most important story that I will ever be able to report. There has been a breakthrough on aging. Upton Pharmaceuticals announced they have FDA approval of a drug which will prevent aging. The studies have been ongoing for the last ten years."

“It was decided to keep everything as quiet as possible because of the potential for disruption if it failed at the last testing stages. If nothing else the impact on the stock market could have been devastating.”

“The study was conducted on people whose ages ranging twenty-five to ninety-five and it stopped aging in its tracks. Whatever physical age the person was when they started the trial they have maintained. They haven’t aged while taking their daily dose of this medication.”

“There is no way to tell how long a person will live with this drug called, ‘Live’. Only time will tell, it has been explained that people will still contract disease’s, it won’t cure any health issues that are present. It just freezes the body, if you will, at its current physical age. Upton has been manufacturing and storing doses for the last year in preparation for the demand.”

“’Live,’ works by extending the number of times telomeres may split. It has been known for some time that aging and deterioration set in when the ends of cells known as telomeres don’t divide cleanly. It has been compared to the eyelet protecting the end of a shoelace. When the eyelet is worn away the shoelace will fray and fail.”

“Tests on earthworms have been able to extend their lives over two hundred percent. Previously when this was performed in mammals, the telomeres would split so frequently they were working the same as a cancer. The breakthrough that Upton has made is combining the telomere extension with a small-molecule drug known as TIC10, which activates a gene call TRAIL (tumor-necrosis-factor-related-apoptosis-inducing ligand), and yes, I did practice that before we went on the air."

"This combination extends cells, but then tells the body to kill off the excess cells. It is a delicate balance. Each person's dosage will have to be monitored and adjusted for them. It will be generally based on sex, age, and weight but other factors may appear later. That is why it will be a daily gel capsule with a timed release. Upton predicts with further study they can develop a once in a life time capsule."

"Trading on Upton stock has been halted by the SEC. The SEC announced that it would allow trading to restart in forty-eight hours but will halt it again if the market requires it. Now on to more mundane news…."

Any worries Marsha and Rick may have had about revealing their stories were now put to rest.

They discussed the ramifications of this event. Rick based on his science fiction reading pointed out that the effect on the earth's population could be dramatic. A quick search on the Internet revealed the earth's population had now surpassed seven billion.

If things had stayed the same in the next ten years, it would reach seven and half billion, and UN studies actually predicted population decline, as the economies of third-world countries improved.

However, if people only died in accidents, the world's annual death rate of one in one hundred thirteen people would result in nine billion people in ten years. With the sharp increase in population, the economies of the third world wouldn't get ahead of this curve. Starvation and unrest would follow.

Rick realized this simple arithmetic was based on everyone receiving the 'Live' drug.  That wouldn't happen but would cause other problems. The wealthy of every country would receive it, but not the poor. In some countries, it would be rejected for religious reasons. It looked like some major problems were fast coming at the world.

What about the people in their own rest home? There were patients already on a regime for the Alzheimer drugs. They were starting to show signs of returning. This still left them in very poor health. Would they be eligible for the life extending drugs? Since they were indigents, they were at the mercy of the government.

Patients in for-pay rest homes would present a dilemma for their loved ones and lord help those whose heirs were waiting on a fortune. If they had signed a 'no special measures to extend life' form would this prevent them from receiving the medications? The ethical questions were frightening.

He and Marsha realized the sooner they had control of their funds the better off they would be. They didn't know where or how, but their inclination was to find a hole and crawl in it.

Again after days of conversation, they approached Clarisse with the matter. She was all for going after GHI for every dime they could get. This might have been influenced by the potential fees she would receive. Rick and Marsha informed her they had no objection to a large settlement, but they didn't want any publicity.

Any settlement had to be out of court with everyone bound by confidentiality agreements. She couldn't understand this requirement, but after a long conversation, they allowed her to use the threat of going public, but to yield to the inevitable insurance company request for an out-of-court settlement with no publicity.

It was now December of 2021. Rick had been working his corner every weekday for over a year. He had made over thirteen thousand dollars tax free. There was a little over nine thousand dollars in his checking account. They had a lawyer lined up; they had Doctor's examinations in hand. It was now time to petition the court.

The first obstacle that Clarisse ran into when filing was that while there were many forms for declaring someone senior or a juvenile; voluntary, or involuntary not competent there was no form for declaring someone who was incompetent now competent.

The Clerk of Court, who she went to, was not trying to be an obstructionist. It just didn't fit into any of the boxes she had to work within. She finally told Clarisse, "File the forms that people use for a temporary incompetence. I know that your clients were filed as permanently incompetent but let the judge sort it out. This will at least put your people in front of the judge."

Clarisse went along with this and filed the paperwork. A hearing was scheduled for Friday January 18, 2022. After all their preparations and planning the hearing was anti-climactic. The judge already read the submitted Doctors reports. He commented that he was amazed and pleased at the returnee situation. He told them how depressing these hearings usually were when he knew that he was deciding that people's lives were over. His biggest concern was that new forms would have to be designed.

In the meantime, he ordered the Clerk of Courts to prepare a letter of competency. Mr. Richard King and Mrs. Marsha King nee Wren had been examined by the Court and deemed competent. He also requested a copy to be sent to Burns and Burns their court-appointed trustees with instructions to dissolve the trusts and return the proceeds immediately.

Clarisse set up an appointment the following Friday with Burns and Burns. Again, it was cut and dried. Burns and Burns had been waiting to receive death certificates for Marsha and Rick, so they could turn their trust over to the

State of Maryland. While they received a fee for handling the trust, it was not large enough to cause any thoughts of corruption.

Their pensions and social security had been going into the trusts, and their mutual funds and Ricks 401k had appreciated. The cash portion of their income along with the proceeds from the sales of their respective houses was placed in Maryland tax-free bonds. The income wasn't great, but since they were about to take a large tax hit every little bit helped.

Clarisse brought a tax attorney from her church on board. Since this was a one-time deal with him, they had agreed upon a straight fee of two thousand dollars. After inquires they found this to be a great deal.

It was set up for the funds to be dispersed on April 10th. It would be like a closing on a house except, there would be representatives from the IRS and Maryland Comptroller's office present. It took so long because it was the middle of tax season and difficult to get everyone together.

Again, it was anti-climactic. The conference room at Burns and Burns was small, but comfortable, very much like a real estate office. There were pens scattered for signing everywhere. Marsha's session went first, after signing her name what felt like fifty times, but was only twenty-three times, she was ready to be done. After an hour a half, the last paper signed was for a wire transfer into her newly opened checking account for two million three hundred forty seven thousand dollars and fifty seven cents. Separate checks, to the state and feds were written for the taxes owed.

Rick's session lasted the same amount of time, but his gross was only one million nine hundred fifty five thousand dollars and thirty two cents. Rick thought about joking that he now could marry Marsha for her money.

Fortunately, he thought before he spoke and came out with, "Honey now you can make me happy by marrying me." These were the right words as he got a quick hug and a kiss from his bride to be.

They had discussions about their wedding. Well, Marsha had discussions with Silvia, Ruth and Clarisse. Rick was informed that they would be getting married at city hall. They would be inviting; Silvia, Ruth, Clarisse, Charles, Emily and Peggy and their respective spouses or significant other. They did not know if Peggy could make it up from South Carolina, but the others were local and should be there.

Rick and Marsha decided to rent an apartment in Delaney Valley. They could now afford it. They also purchased two vehicles, Rick a Toyota 4Runner and Marsha a Camry.

After renting the apartment it had to be furnished. It was a three bedroom, two and half bath, kitchen with attached dining area, family room with fireplace and a living room. It also had a two-car garage attached.

Though it was expensive, they could now afford it. Rick dreaded the thought of furniture and decoration shopping. They were currently living in a Hilton Garden Inn suite near the White Marsh Mall, but while nice for a short stay it was not set up for long term living.

Rick was very surprised when he got into the shopping. Since he had to participate, he decided to put a good face on it, this quickly turned to enjoyment. It turned out that his sense of what colors would match was a little better than Marsha's. She would defer to him, which enhanced his enjoyment and insured his participation.

It only took several weeks to pick out everything and have it delivered. Rick hung the drapes and pictures. They had their first home.

The wedding took place on January 24, 2022. Everyone invited was present, including Peggy Tapp; she had driven up from South Carolina, and would spend the weekend with a sister who still lived in Baltimore. After the brief ceremony in judge's chambers, they went back to the William Donald Schafer rest home for their reception.

After the cake cutting, and not jamming it in each other's faces they received the usual wedding gifts. Most were in the form of small appliances like toasters or sets of linens. There were no duplicates, or any items that they already had. It was like someone had coordinated the gift giving. Silvia was quite pleased with herself.

Marsha and Rick shared that they had no honeymoon plans at this time. They would be retiring for their first night at their new apartment. The conversation centered on old times at the rest home.

Silvia delighted in telling how she kept the cabinets locked and frustrated Marsha. Charles told how Rick got his start on the street corner and also wondered if he was going to keep it up.

With a serious look, Rick replied, "I think I am going to franchise it out." This brought the house down. For once one of Rick's jokes worked.

Since not everyone knew about the pending law suit this wasn't brought up. Everyone present assumed Rick, and Marsha would now enjoy a quiet life waiting for their time to come. Of course with the exciting new medication, 'Live' who could tell how long that would be?

The reception broke up shortly after the last good old day's story had been shared. This diverse group didn't actually have much in common other than their acquaintance with Rick and Marsha. Rick and Marsha went home to their apartment for their first wedded night. They proved very quickly their health had improved. Even though they still looked their ages they now felt and acted like their late sixties.

## Chapter 13 – Justice

After taking a week off, Rick and Marsha had a meeting with Clarisse. They decided it was time to proceed with General Health Insurance. Clarisse would file the forms to start four law suits.

There would be one each by Rick and Martha against GHI, then separately against a Mr. Norman Thompson, the insurance company representative.  The grounds would be for fraud as their policies were to provide rest home care in a for-fee rest home.

Their policies actually were initiated by Burns and Burns as part of their trust arrangement. Each suit was for one million dollars in actual damages and ten million pain and suffering on each.

Their game plan was to try for an out-of-court settlement for a total of five million each with a non-disclosure agreement covering all parties. They wouldn't bring this up because they knew the insurance company would. Their announced position was that they were ready to go public.

Clarisse even would let them know she was considering taking out advertisements for other people who may have been dumped by GHI. This would then become a class action law suit.

The papers were served to Mr. Norman Thompson at GHI, since his was the only name on the paperwork. He was served four sets of papers, those that Rick and Marsha had filed against the company and those against Mr. Thompson. This was a total of forty four million dollars. They had no expectation of receiving this amount, but they wanted to get their attention.

They did.

GHI Headquarters February 2022

"Norman, what the hell are you telling me," screamed Ed Billings Vice President of the Rest Home-Care Division. Ed had only been with this division for a year, so he knew nothing of what went on under Sam Evans the previous VP.

"If you calm down I will explain it," said Norm Thompson.

"You damn well will," came back a very upset Billings. Billings then got up from the couch where he had started the meeting.

Ed was of the mindset that employees should be at ease, so he didn't put the barrier of his large desk between him and them. Instead when they asked for a meeting, he started in the living room area of his luxurious office with the couch, end tables, coffee tables and wing back chairs.

For working meetings he had a conference room table with eight chairs around it. Only if it was a serious personnel issue did he retreat behind his desk.

He now retreated behind his desk and said in a calmer tone, “Let me see if I can get Sam Weber in here.” Weber was the staff corporate attorney. This was the last person Thompson wanted to see, but he knew he had no choice and that his days at GHI were probably numbered.

While waiting for Weber, Billings had his secretary make three copies of the four sets of papers. There was one for each of the three of them, and one for his secretary’s files. The originals against the company would go with Weber. Thompson could keep his.

Upon arrival, Weber read through one set of papers and asked, “Can I assume for now that the other three sets say the same?”

“Yes, you can,” said Thompson in a low weary voice.”

“Okay, first of all does this case have any truth to it,” Weber asked?

“Unfortunately, it is all true,” Thompson replied.

“How did that happen?” inquired Weber.

“Sam Evans was always pushing us to avoid paying when we could,” Thompson replied in a subdued voice.

Billings said sarcastically, “Well now that is going to be a little hard to prove since he is dead. Why are you named separately in this suit?”

“If you look at the appendixes you will see my name and signature on the order to Northeast to move them to Schafer because they didn’t have coverage,” Thompson said.

Thompson then blustered, “I’m not going down alone on this. If you check the files, you will see there was a pattern of this occurring before I was in this office. Every underwriter here has one or more case like this. Evans really was the force behind this.”

Billings was getting red in the face and about to explode again when Weber interrupted with, “We will be interviewing everyone in this office and all recent employees of this division.

Weber continued, “The important thing here is to establish our exposure and come up with a plan to limit the damages. Norm you are suspended with pay, starting immediately. We aren’t leaving you high and dry, but if this gets out of control we have to show some good faith actions up front.”

“In the meantime, I recommend you hire an attorney to represent you. The company can’t represent you in this action. We will try to get plaintiffs to drop their suit against you. If this thing spreads it would include all the employees individually. We could never re-staff the department. ”

“I’m so glad you care,” Thompson said dryly.

"Hey we are trying to help you," said Billings, "watch your mouth."

"Yes Sir," Thompson quickly said. "I do appreciate how this is being handled so far; it's just that I felt like I was following company policy."

"Well you weren't," said Weber.

Weber continued, "I will contact their attorney of record, Mrs. Clarisse Bowden. I will let her know we will respond after we complete an internal review. I will also tell her Norm, that you are retaining your own attorney, and that they will be in contact."

Ed Billings asked, "I thought we tried to do these things as slow as we could, that way they run out of funds quicker than we would?"

"Normally, I would say yes, and we will slow walk them later in negotiations if we can't get a dismissal."

"We will definitely perform a slow walk on any payments due. Right now, we want to keep them from going public. After we get them to sign a confidentiality agreement, then we can slow things down."

Billings said, "I like the way you think Sam."

Thompson said, "It is exactly that sort of thinking that got us here."

Billings and Weber both glared at Thompson, but said nothing. That hit too close to home.

Clarisse to Marsha – February 2022

Clarisse called Rick and Marsha's, "Hi Marsha. It has started. We have a letter saying they are doing an internal investigation, and that we will be hearing from Thompson's lawyer soon."

"Clarisse I'm comfortable with going after GHI, but we will destroy that Thompson guy. I don't mind the company, but he will have family, and it will ruin their lives."

Clarisse responded, "He didn't seem to mind destroying yours, but it is only a ploy to get them bothered. If this really is an ongoing problem they will have a lot of employees vulnerable."

"They can't afford to lose them all, so they will offer more to get him taken out of the suit. That or they will say that he is the sole cause and sacrifice him. The problem with that will be trying to prove that he individually could benefit."

"In the meantime, I have some really good news. A case settled in civil court that they thought would take months. We have been moved up to May 16 of this year. I was going to feel good if we could get any date this year. Of course, they will say they don't have enough time to get ready, but with what evidence we have submitted from

Northeast and Schafer; I don't think the judge will cut them any slack."

GHI Headquarter - March 2022

In Ed Billing's office, Ed and Sam Weber the corporate attorney set at Ed's conference table with case files scattered.

"As you can see Ed, it was as Norm told us, it was prevalent through the department," Sam told him. "The biggest danger we have now is Norman and his attorney. I'm surprised that they haven't subpoenaed our records to help their case."

"From some comments, I have heard I think they are about to do that. They have been talking to employees in the department and explaining to them how they have to stick together on this."

"Not good Ed, I think we are going to have to pay and pay through the nose on this. The only damage mitigation will be to keep it from the public. If we can get them to take an out-of-court settlement, sign a confidentiality agreement and drop the case against Norm, we will have done the best we can."

"How much would it take," asked Ed?

"I would like to start at three each, go to five if we have to," responded the attorney. "I will call Clarisse and see how that would be received."

Sam Weber found out very quickly how it would be received.

Before he could make his offer Clarisse brought up, “I’m glad you called Mr. Weber, I wanted to tell you in advance we are about to start advertising in all the local media for other victims. We might as well get it all done in one class action suit don’t you think?”

This is not what Weber wanted to hear.

“How soon do you intend to do this?” he inquired.”

“I have an appointment at a studio tomorrow; just think I will be a big time ambulance chaser. It is kind of exciting. My husband is already calling me, “Rainmaker.”

This gave Weber instant heartburn.

“Mrs. Bowden, are you going to be in your office for another hour,” he asked in a strangled voice.

“Yes I am I will be expecting your call.” As she hung up, Clarisse punched the air, “YES!”

Weber quickly rounded up Billings and the Division President. He explained it was going to hit the fan if they didn’t settle today.

The Division President said, “Give them everything to keep it quiet. Buy Thompson out of it. We can’t afford for this to go public, there is something going on I can’t share at this time, but we can’t have this in the public eye.”

Sam Weber to Clarisse Bowden same day

"Mrs. Bowden thank you for letting me check on a few things. We would like an out-of-court settlement."

"What sort of settlement are you thinking of," she asked?

"All four suits total forty four million dollars. We will settle for all of that if you drop the suits against Norm Thompson, and sign confidentiality agreements for all parties."

"I will have to check with my clients, but I can't see why they wouldn't accept that," she replied.

"In the meantime please don't proceed with your advertising."

"I will put it on hold," Clarisse replied.

This time when Clarisse hung up she didn't celebrate, she collapsed with a huge sigh. If Rick and Marsha cooperated, she had just made almost fifteen million dollars. Since their takeaway would be about thirty million dollars, she couldn't see them rejecting the offer.

When she called Rick and Marsha with the news, they were dumbfounded.

Rick was able to push, "We will take it," out of his suddenly dry mouth. Marsha stood there and flapped her hands up and down. After they both settled down they discussed the details with Clarisse. So no games would be played, they wanted the money in hand at the same time as they agreed to dismiss the case.

Furthermore, it had to be within the next two weeks, or they would allow Clarisse to release her ads. They all agreed that they needed to keep the pressure on GHI for a complete and quick settlement, or they might regain their nerve and slow the process down until they went broke. They weren't aware that GHI had other concerns.

√ Clarisse to Sam Weber March 2022

"Mr. Weber I have talked to my clients, and they are agreeable to all terms if this can be cleared up in the next two weeks. That means all parties have signed the agreements, and funds deposited."

"Mrs. Bowden this is very quick. I don't know if we can do that. I will have to talk to our Management."

"I expected that, I must let you know if it isn't completed by that time the class action advertisement will run."

"Please Mrs. Bowden don't be hasty I will try to get back to you by tomorrow."

Sam Weber to the GHI Division President same day

"Todd, they are playing hardball on this. I would like to fight them. I think we can drag it out enough that they will run out of funds."

"We don't have the time Sam. What I didn't want to say in front of Billings the other day is that our Division is being sold. The buyers will be here early next month to start due diligence. If they find this hanging over our head it will raise concerns that there might be other issues, and you and I will be out the door for messing up a two point six billion dollar sale."

"That is a game changer; put that way, the sooner I can get this behind us the better."

Weber to Bowden March 2022

"Mrs. Bowden we are prepared to settle everything, including payment in one week if that is agreeable."

"It certainly is. Will my office be an acceptable venue?"

"Agreed Mrs. Bowden, and I would like to thank you for your professional conduct during these proceedings. It hasn't been easy, but you have kept it on a much higher level than most attorneys would have."

Weber continued with a chuckle, "As a matter of fact, the ambulance chaser club might kick you out. On a more serious note, we did check you out thoroughly, and you have really started your private practice out with a winner. I expect to hear more of you in the future."

"Thank you Mr. Weber and I wouldn't be surprised if you heard more of me."

Weber didn't know how to take that statement and wasn't going to pursue it.

The settlement went down with no interference or setbacks. Rick and Marsha now held almost thirty-five million dollars in their joint account. Clarisse gave her brother Charles a million-dollar referral fee.

After taxes, he was able to buy a new house with no mortgage. Clarisse herself found that though she couldn't talk about her case, the grapevine knew she had won a big one. As a known winner, her practice started growing overnight.

Rick and Marsha had one last conversation with Clarisse. They all agreed it was time to proceed to the next step of justice for victims of GHI. They were bound by confidentiality agreements, but not everyone in the know was. While they were still together Clarisse made a phone call to Charles.

"Hey Charles you ought to follow up on your idea of having Abi Jackson do her own follow up on where Rick is today. It would make a good human interest story, and I know Rick would love to see her again."

This comment by Clarisse drew Rick a sharp elbow from Marsha.

## Chapter 14 - The Bigger They Are - 2022

"This is the voicemail of Abi Jackson. Please leave your name, message and number. I will get back to you as soon as I can."

Charles left a message to the effect he had a follow-up story on Rick the Windshield Cleaner Man. When reviewing her messages she had a hard time remembering the story, when she did think of it, she wondered how a follow-up on that story could be interesting. Even with her doubts, one thing she had learned was to follow up on leads.

"Charles speaking," he said as he answered the phone in his deep voice.

Abi identified herself.

"Glad you called Abi; I thought you might be interested in following up on Rick. He now lives in Delaney Valley."

"How did he get that sort of money," asked Abi?

She knew that it was one of the more expensive areas of the Baltimore suburbs.

"You need to start at the William Donald Schafer rest home to get your answer," replied Charles.

"Don't you know," asked Abi?

"I have a good idea. It appears to involve insurance fraud on the part of an insurance company, but I don't have proof."

"Charles, I have your name and phone number, so I can find out more about you. What is your role in this?"

"I'm an undercover cop with the Baltimore Police Department."

This was the beginning of a mutually beneficial relationship that would rock the political and criminal worlds of Baltimore for several years.

Abi decided to go straight to William Schaefer to see what would develop by dropping in. There was no one at the front desk when she entered the lobby. There wasn't evidence of human occupation for years if the three-year-old calendar was any clue. The sign in book hadn't been used in seven years. She decided not to bother signing in.

As she entered the next area, which was the wide-open common area used for meals and general meetings, she saw a harried member of housekeeping wiping down a table.

"I am looking for someone who can tell me about Richard King," she inquired.

The lady looked blank for a moment. "Oh you mean Rick, Marsha's husband. Silvia in the office would know them best. Marsha worked there."

The housekeeper pointed her to the office area. Abi walked into the open office area.

A lady looked up and said, “May I help you? Oh, you’re Abi Jackson, what are you doing here?”

Abi was pleased that she had been recognized though it would change her tactics slightly.

“I am flattered that you recognized me,” she replied.

“We watch your noon newscast every day. Rick got it started. I think he has a crush on you. Even though he and Marsha have moved out we still watch your show.”

“What’s your name,” Abi asked, as she held out her hand.

“Ruth Richards, and I am pleased to meet you,” was the reply as they shook hands.

“I understand that Rick and Marsha now live out in Delaney Valley. That is a real jump from working here.”

“Oh they didn’t work here. They were both patients, though Marsha did volunteer in the office while Rick worked his corner.”

“That seems to be out of the ordinary.”

“Very, but you know they were among the first returnees from Alzheimer’s. It is such a blessing we have six other patients more alert and getting up now.”

“No I didn’t know that Ruth.”

“I think that they had to do with the big law suit they won. Well at least, I heard they won a large law suit. I don’t know of any of the details.”

“Who would know?”

“Silvia our Office Manager might,” replied Ruth.

“Where would I find her?”

“She should be back any minute. She just went to the restroom.”

Abi asked a few back ground questions of Ruth, how long she had worked at William Donald, until Silvia returned. She also recognized Abi. Abi had no complaints about having a fan base. She was still young enough to enjoy the recognition.

Abi caught Silvia up on her basic story. She was considering a follow up on Rick, one of those, where are they now stories? She was very surprised to learn that he was living in Delaney Valley.

“How did that happen,” she asked Silvia. Silvia hesitated then remembered something Marsha had said not that long ago.

“If any member of the media asks about us, answer their questions, as long as they don’t conflict with your professional ethics.”

Silvia thought, *"William Schafer wasn't involved in that law suit so that isn't a problem. Our former patients have released us from our confidentiality responsibility, besides it isn't a HIPPA issue, so why not."*

She was careful to explain that reasoning to Abi. She continued on to explain.

"They sued GHI insurance and had an out-of-court settlement with them. I don't know what the law suit was about or for how much, but it must have been quite a bit."

Abi had a few more general questions about Rick and Marsha's stay. She was also interested in the fact that they were considered to be Alzheimer's returnees, but wasn't able to develop anything other than that they had severe dementia, came out of it and then judged to be competent.

This gave Abi two lines of investigation. First, the legal records of their competency judgment, second was the law suit filed against GHI. It didn't take long at the courthouse to find, and purchase copies of all the relevant documents. This was much more interesting than a follow up on a guy who washed windshields.

Abi took this to her producer, before she could spend more time; she had to have his buy in. After laying out what she knew, the producer was eager to follow the story. He also came up with the thought that they should do a local story on the other returnees at the rest home.

The major networks were all over the returnee story, but a home segment would go over well locally. If they followed some of the local returnees and reported their progress once a month it would help ratings.

Abi was able to build on that by adding, “You should let sales know. I bet there would be some health care types that would be glad to sponsor those segments.”

The producer went on, “I hate to say this, but the patients at William Schafer have no one to return to, check at places like Northeast. It would be good to have families with loving grandchildren. It would be much more photogenic.”

Abi sighed, “You are right, but in the meantime I am going to follow up on this GHI story. I will start with Rick and Marsha.”

Silvia had given her their phone number, so she returned to her cubicle and made the call.

“Is this the King residence,” she inquired when a woman answered the phone.

“Yes it is who is calling?”

“This is Abi Jackson with WBAL, I was wondering if I could come to your house and ask a few questions.”

“You are that lovely young newscaster whom Rick always listens to. When would you like to come over?”

"Now if it is not too soon."

"Oh dear I will have to hurry and clean up our apartment."

"It will take me almost an hour to get there, is that alright?"

"Yes that will be fine, what needs cleaning the most is Rick. I have to get him out of those grubby old clothes he likes, into something decent. When he hears it is you coming that will help."

She gave the address before hanging up.

Abi went to her station provided car with WBAL in large letters and spoke the address to the built in GPS. It took her fifty five minutes to get there, so she went right to the door.

The door was answered by a lady who looked to be healthy mid-seventy. She was dressed in a pair of green slacks and brown sweater with a long necklace with copper disks. With her low-cut heels and light make up, she looked very elegant.

A man also in his seventy's was standing back slightly. He wore light tan chinos, with a blue-button down collar shirt. He had on a tweed sport coat with elbow patches.

Abi looked at them and said, "Are you Rick and Marsha."

Marsha replied, "That's us."

Abi responded, “Well you certainly look better than when I interviewed Rick last Christmas.”

“Exercise and good food really help,” replied Rick.

“I must say my pay was much better on the street when I appeared to be older.”

Abi thought, “*This story just keeps getting better.*”

“That is very interesting, but what I was interested in was the law suit you just won against GHI. What was the fraud they perpetuated against you?”

Rick and Marsha exchanged glances.

Rick replied, “I wish I could tell you but part of the settlement was that we wouldn’t talk about our suit.”

“You say ‘our’ suit like there could be others.”

“As I said we can’t discuss how we were admitted to William Donald Schafer.”

“Could I talk you into an interview of how your life has changed since you have got off the street?”

“I don’t see how,” replied Rick, “It would bring up questions of how we got our money. I don’t want to be accused of welfare fraud.”

“Well thank you for your time,” said Abi.

"Uh, before you go could I have your autograph," asked Rick. Marsha just barked a laugh and said, "Boys."

Abi thought about it on the drive back to town. It was like they were trying to say something without saying it. There would be other law suits if people knew how they were admitted to Schafer. How were they admitted, and how could she find out? Then she remembered that the law suit mentioned they had been admitted from Northeast.

She gave the voice command to the GPS, "Northeast Baltimore rest home." She arrived in fifteen minutes.

This lobby area was completely different from the other rest home.

As soon as she entered there was a cheerful, "Hello may I help you?"

The lobby was bright; there were fresh flowers at the desk. There was clean carpeting instead of dingy tile. The calendar was current and she was immediately asked to sign in, as she explained that she would like to speak to the director if it was convenient.

No, she didn't have an appointment. When told that Abi Jackson from WBAL was in the lobby the Director immediately found time for her.

Unfortunately for Abi, that was almost the last thing he found for her. After settling her in a comfortable fabric-covered chair in his office, and her declining coffee, he had to tell her that he couldn't share the contents of the files of Marsha Wren and Richard King. It would be in the violation of the HIPPA laws.

He seemed to be sorry that he couldn't do so, but he couldn't violate the law, surely she understood. A disappointed Abi said she understood then brought up the secondary reason for her visit.

"Another story that my station would like to follow is the returning of Alzheimer's patients. We know that nationals are covering it, but we would like to do some local segments as people come back, and how their families react."

"That we can help with, if the patients and their guardians agree, how often?"

"We would like to have a two-minute segment once a month. It would follow three people as they make the transition. We would interview them, the staff and their families. If it is possible we would like to talk to some of them first so we have the most likeable ones."

The Director Paul Douglas laughed, "Yes people are people and not all of them should be returning if you ask me, but please don't quote me."

Abi grinned, "No we won't. I suspect I will know which ones you are talking about very quickly. Is there anyone on staff that I should be working with?"

"There are several but starting with Emily Sheetz, head of physical therapy, would be best. She is well-spoken and very outgoing. She will represent Baltimore East the best I think. Let me call her in and introduce you."

Emily came into Paul's office in a short while. Paul introduced them and said, "You look like sisters!"

The young grey-eyed blondes looked at each other and said, "Nah."

It would have been better if they had not said it in unison like sisters. They quickly established they were no relation at all.

The Director told Emily what Abi was there for and asked if there were any patients who would interview better than others.

"Yes there are several that I can think of," said Emily. "Would you like to meet them Abi," she asked.

"Briefly if I can, what I really need to do is get this written up as a program that we can share with those families we would like to participate and obtain releases from them," replied Abi.

The two young ladies left the Directors office to meet some of the people. Emily mentioned, "It's a shame you aren't doing this over at William Donald Schafer, there are two people there that would have been great."

Abi asked, “Would that have been Richard King and Marsha Wren now Mrs. King?”

“I was at their house earlier today.”

“Why were you there,” asked a surprised Emily.

“I was trying to follow up on a law suit they filed against GHI for fraud conducted on their care.”

“Oh I saw that in their file, they were sent from The Oaks Hospice center to here for one day. After they arrived, GHI said they weren’t covered, and had them sent to William Schafer.”

Abi kept a straight face, but now she knew what happened. This could be big.

“I wonder if there are any other people in that situation.”

“I have no idea Abi,” replied Emily.

After that, Emily took Abi around to visit several patients whom Emily thought would be good to follow. Each of the two women and one man were pleasant, out spoken and had family support. Abi thanked Emily for her help and returned to the studio.

Abi and her producer Jack Rowland decided that the best place to start on the GHI story was to get official support from Schafer to identify patients who had been covered by GHI.

They would then try to trace back and see if they had been in other rest homes, and for how long. Abi would return to Schafer the next day and start with Silvia.

The next morning Abi met with Silvia. After explaining what she looking for, Silvia thought it best she set up a meeting with Dr. John Towers the Director of Baltimore East Hospital who also had jurisdiction over the William Donald Schafer rest home.

A call by Silvia along with a brief explanation got them onto the Directors afternoon schedule at 2:00. He loved media attention.

At 2:00, Abi and Silvia were escorted into the Directors office. The way he made them welcome and comfortable in his plush office left Abi cold.

She knew this type well. All for themselves and the power they could grab. She compared this office to the lobby of Schafer and knew his priorities. It would be easy to get what she wanted.

"Dr. Towers, thank you so much for meeting with Silvia and me quickly," Abi gushed."

"*God I hate myself when I have to do this,*" she thought.

"No problem at all," said the flattered Doctor. "How may I help you?"

"To recap what I have learned without any HIPPA violation occurring, we are pretty certain that GHI has been conducting insurance fraud by declaring people that they covered, no longer covered without legal reason, and then dumping them onto your budget at Schafer."

"How do you know that," asked Dr. Towers?

"We know of a couple that found out about it, sued GHI and received a settlement, but had to sign a non-disclosure agreement."

"What do you propose to do about this," inquired the Doctor?

"With your permission, we would like to follow the story as your attorneys go through your patient files of those who have suffered dementia and identify those who were originally insured by GHI. Then with court orders issued follow your people back to their previous rest home and see how long they were there. That will give the evidence for Baltimore East to file a suit for all your losses."

"That sounds very good, and if it's as you have said we certainly need to recoup these funds for the city."

Abi smiled inwardly as she thought, "*Gotcha, I knew the appeal to your budget and the good publicity you personally will get would hook you.*"

"We would have to hire an outside attorney to handle this as I know our attorney does not have the expertise. Towers certainly knew the attorney didn't have the expertise, as he was his son-in-law.

Abi said, "I know the attorney that won the other settlement. She couldn't talk about that case, but she certainly would know what buttons to push at GHI."

"That would be excellent," replied Towers.

Since there was so much money at stake it took two years to settle the case.

Clarisse Bowden's firm received thirty percent of the one hundred million dollar settlement. This time since WBAL followed the story from the start, there wasn't a non-disclosure clause.

The buyers of the GHI division moved and renamed the policies to their company. The GHI division headquarters was closed down, and the entire staff let go.

The City of Baltimore received sixty-five million dollars as their part of the settlement. None of it went to upgrading William Donald Schafer rest home.

Dr. John Towers was put in charge of the entire City of Baltimore Hospital system.

WBAL later was able to document that five million dollars was diverted as consultancy fees to the law firm of Dr. Tower's son-in-law. One million of this was paid out in bonuses to the son-in-law.

Another million was contributed to the Mayor's re-election campaign through several different avenues.

The Mayor won the election. Abi Jackson became ever more cynical even after winning both an Edward R. Murrow and a Polk award for the story she had broken.

## Chapter 15 Conversation between Rick and Marsha – 2022

While the city's suit against GHI was in process, Rick and Marsha were having several conversations about their lives and where they were going.

It started with Marsha stating, "Rick it is obvious that something is very different about us. Our teeth have come back in; our eye sight is perfect. We have none of the aches and pains that we have suffered from the last twenty years. We are more flexible and in general excellent health."

"I know Marsha. I have given this a lot of thought. It must have something to do with the failed Alzheimer's study and then having AIDS. We are the only ones who had both events, and I know of no others like us."

"I wonder how long these improvements will continue. It isn't daily, but I feel younger than I did last month, and certainly not as old as six months ago."

"We both look younger also," said Rick. He continued, "I even feel like I think faster all the time."

"So do I."

"What if we are retrogressing in age?"

"I don't know, those people on Live are bragging about no longer aging," said Marsha.

"We are different. I hope we don't retrogress back to diapers."

"I wish that was one of your bad jokes, but I have wondered the same thing."

Rick continued, "If we are retrogressing and there is no cut off, we will continue until we are infants and can no longer care for ourselves. Then what, do we become embryos? It makes no sense to me, and if so nothing can be done about it. I think we need to plan as though we will come to a point where our body ages stabilize; then will we start aging again?"

"We will just have to wait and see about the aging again. When would we stabilize," asked Marsha?

"I don't know," was the reply. "I will do some Internet research," stated Rick."

It only took a simple search string of, when does the human body start aging, to come up with an article. It surprised Rick to learn that the organs of the body aged at different rates. The first was the skin, lungs and brain in the early 20's; then the muscles, hair, breasts, bones, and fertility in the 30's; followed by the eyes, heart, and teeth in the 40's; kidneys, prostrate, and hearing in the 50's; bladder, voice, taste and smell in the 60's; with the liver last in the 70's.

He shared this with Marsha, who thoughtfully said, "If that is the case we are in our 40's right now. That is why our skin still looks eighty plus, but our teeth and eyes are fine. I have never really had hearing problems, what about you Rick?"

"Huh," Rick asked? This earned him a swat on his ear from Marsha, who was standing behind Rick while he sat at his computer.

"No, my hearing has been fine for all my life," he hastily added.

"Well I look forward to my breasts not sagging anymore. I don't have much, but they will look better."

"They are fine as they are," Rick stoutly stated. He hadn't survived around women for most of his life without learning some of the right answers!

Marsha was silent for a minute then said, "I think I had better go back on birth control until we know for sure where we and our are bodies are."

"I hadn't thought of that at all," Rick replied.

He continued, "With the uncertainty of our bodies and the condition of the world I do not think now would be the right time to have children. Then there is the fact that we don't know if this change is considered a mutation that we can pass on, or just a change to our bodies. If it isn't a mutation, it means any children we have will age and die while we might continue. I like the idea of us having children together but don't know if I could stand outliving them."

Upon that note, Marsha hugged him mourning for the death of her unborn children. As they hugged, one thing led to another until they were practicing making children on the living room couch. Old people can have fun.

The next morning, Rick and Marsha were sitting on the balcony of their rental condo having morning coffee. It was a beautiful spring day in the Delany Valley. The grass on the rolling hill sides had turned a lush green; the daffodils were all in bloom. The temperature was in the mid-seventies, so it seemed like a perfect day.

Both wore shorts and polo style shirts. Other than their grey hair, looking at them from behind one would think they were in their forties. Their faces were a different story. They had the wrinkles of eighty year olds.

While sitting silently enjoying the view, Marsha suddenly straightened.

“Rick, following the news hasn’t been encouraging. I remember back around 2013 the world was coming to an end because our national debt was seventeen trillion dollars, now it’s almost thirty trillion. The rest of the world is in the same condition. Something has to give. I know they used to talk about some banks being too big to fail. Now it is some countries are too big to fail. How much longer do you think they can kick the can down the road?”

“I have been wrong on the doom’s day prediction so many times I should give it up. There is one thought that has been coming back to me time and time again. With Benton’s ‘*Live*’ drug on the market, the population of the earth will be increasing.

If the drug works on everyone and is made available to all, then the earth’s population will increase by thirty percent in the next ten years. I don’t see that happening, but I would think there would be serious repercussions. Say for religious reasons it is forbidden in a country, it would lead to eventual unrest and war.

In a country like the US, the population would expand dramatically. What will be the effect on the food or water supply? Can it be expanded fast enough, if it can’t it will lead to price competition for food. I do know for a fact that inflation is the one can that can’t be kicked down the road, no matter what the politicians think.”

“The world economy has been the Emperor with no clothes for many years now. Once inflation hits, it will end up causing the most horrible depression the world has ever seen. I once read that the dark ages in Europe were three hundred years of falling prices. I am afraid this will rival that."

"Do you mean that civilization will collapse," Marsha asked?

"No, just like the real dark ages there will be pockets of enlightenment. Think of the monasteries, they preserved knowledge. Some of what they preserved shouldn't have been like the Aristotelian view of the world. It took until the Renaissance to change that. I suspect it will be better than that as knowledge is now more diffuse."

They paused in their conversation while they refreshed their coffees. The day which seemed so full of the promise of spring seemed darker around the edges now.

Marsha said slowly, "If the inflation runs wild. How will people keep up?"

"Many won't," Rick said harshly. "There will be civil unrest, translate that to looting and maybe civil war. Those out in the country that are fairly self-sufficient should be okay. Even in Germany during their terrible inflation period, farmers managed.

Those who live in the cities and are dependent on the government will be in big trouble. Our federal government has been in some form of gridlock for twenty years now.

Do you see them be able to increase the amount on peoples EBT cards?"

"I know I would do what I had to, to feed my children. There will be riots and looting. Food will run out in the cities, and the death toll will be incredible. Right now, the average city area has a three-day food supply. Collapse will set in before anyone can react. That is just on the national level. What happens to the world when the US policeman isn't on the beat? Who will stand by the Israelis; or between India and Pakistan, North and South Korea, China and Taiwan, the list goes on and on. The nuclear genie is out of the bottle. It will be ugly."

"Rick," asked Marsha, "do you really think all of this is possible?"

"Dear I just don't know. I think of it as a bell curve. The body of the curve is the highest possibility. Outside either end is the outlier. In this situation, the body of the curve is that we just keep on muddling through. The extreme outliers are a wonderful world or a horrible world. I think we just tipped more towards a terrible world outcome."

"If you think we are heading for a terrible outcome, and we might live for a long time. What should we be doing?"

Rick stared off into space for a while before answering. "We should step aside. Not go into hard-core survivalist mode living in a bunker with years of freeze-dried food. Move to where the urban problems can't walk to us.

Ensure that we have a food supply. Become members of a community of self-sufficient people rather than trying to go it alone. Look at it as a change to a rural lifestyle rather than a retreat from civilization."

"If I am wrong we will spend some years as small farmers rather than city dwellers. That doesn't seem too large of an error to make. That is unlike the hard-core people who are prepared to repel the entire human race."

"Rick, those hard-core people you talk about scare me, with them the underlying theme seems to be survive then be the lords of whatever remains."

"Marsha it depends on what type of people they are. The good ones could end up as your Lords by default, as the only ones that preserved a higher lifestyle. The bad ones would want to be the Lords by conquest. I bet there would be some of each."

As they had been talking, the nice spring day had yielded to storm clouds. Now the sky let loose, and they had to scramble into the house. They left the seat cushions and their coffee cups.

As Rick closed the doors Marsha said, "And that is how it will be, sunshine one minute and scrambling the next, leaving our coffee behind. Except, it will be people dying while we flee for our lives, leaving everything we have. Let's think and talk about this some more, but I think we should decide what to do."

She went on, "I agree that with people living longer, food prices will go up enough to cause inflation. Inflation will wreck the economy that we have. Violence will not be far behind. I would rather be wrong and live in the country than be right and living here. We have the money to make a choice. We shouldn't waste it."

Marsha and Rick repeated this conversation several times over the next week. They went back and forth on what they thought might happen and then what they should do about it.

Finally, they sat down at the kitchen table with pencil and paper and listed those items they felt were mostly probable: a) they were different from everyone else, and had no idea how long they might live; b) with a large portion of the world population living longer, there would be food shortages; c) food shortages would lead to some sort of trouble; d) and they didn't want to be in the heavily populated east coast when the troubles hit.

While they knew none of the above was the absolute fact they felt it was probable enough that they would have to take some action. If you see the train coming you get off the tracks. The only problem was they didn't know where to go once they got off the tracks.

Once again, Rick took to the Internet to try to figure out where they should go. After doing site searches for several days he threw up his hands in despair.

“Marsha I keep finding so much conflicting advice it is the same as no advice,” he groaned.

## Chapter 16 – Let’s Volunteer- 2022

“I was waiting for you to come out of the computer Dear,” she smiled. “I have made a list of the criteria we had talked about and added several of my own; would you like to see it?”

“Darling I would love to see anything that helps make sense of this mess.”

Marsha’s list was very short; a) not within walking distance of a large city ‘at least twenty-five miles’; b) near a small community; c) viable farm land available, not subjected to drought; d) not near a hard-core survivalist area; e) no hard winters. The last was Marsha's addition.

Marsha handed Rick the list and then picked up a copy of a National Geographic road atlas which she had lying on the floor.

"Where did that come from," inquired Rick.

"I picked it up yesterday at Barnes and Noble."

"I didn't even know you went out."

"Well you have been in that computer for the better part of the week, and I got tired of sitting around. I didn't think you would miss me."

Marsha said the last with a grin, but Rick got the idea that he'd better start paying some attention to Marsha.

Rick perused the list while Marsha flipped some pages open on the Atlas.

"Marsha you have captured our thoughts well, and I whole heartedly agree with no hard winters."

Rick actually was neutral on the hard winter's requirement, but he knew he had some ground to make up with Marsha. Besides the more he thought about it, he wasn't really a fan of snow and cold.

The Atlas had an annual snowfall map; it revealed that to have less than six inches a year of snow they would have to live on a line formed by the border of Virginia and North Carolina. It would extend across Tennessee and Arkansas dipping south diagonally across Oklahoma and Texas. It did not include the mountain country of Virginia.

The same area on the map had acceptable average rainfall except the necessary areas of Texas and Oklahoma were smaller. The number of day's sunlight varied from 2400 to 3200 hours a year, but the lower number was acceptable. This was what was considered the southeast portion of the United States.

They ruled out Florida because of the water shortages brought on by population pressure. This would only get worse according to their theory.

The entire eastern Seaboard was ruled out by population.

Texas and Oklahoma ruled out by their concern for water. For some reason, they weren't comfortable with those states in the Deep South, there was a cultural difference. Not that they had a problem with the culture, just could they move there and fit in before bad times started. Especially when they thought, those hard times were only five years away.

Rightly or wrongly, this left them Tennessee and Arkansas which they knew little about.

As they winnowed the states down Rick remembered a web site he had visited. It was a survivalist site that listed what they thought were the best places in the United States to live. What was interesting was that it considered many of their criteria.

The web site's goal wasn't to find a place for a mountain fortress, but to locate a community where you could live. It showed two areas Mountain Home, Arkansas and Pikeville Tennessee. The land wasn't expensive as elsewhere.

Pikeville was more attractive because it was an hour away from Chattanooga with large city facilities while there was nothing near Mountain Home that would qualify as a metropolis. They wanted the best of both worlds. They wanted to be out, but not too far out.

This logic indicated that somewhere near Pikeville, Tennessee was their starting point. Rick used Google Earth to check out the lay of the land around Pikeville. After a half-hour of searching, he was excited.

"Marsha this looks ideal for our needs. The town is in a valley with limited access. The main road runs north and south up the valley. The valley dead ends about ten miles north of town as the two mountain ridges merge. There is a small road going north, but it looks like it would be easy to control access to the area.

"There is a main road that cuts east and west at Pikeville and a few back roads over the ridges, but it is very limited access to that area. From the fields, I can see it is a good growing area. The many ponds in the area reveal plenty of free-flowing water, so maybe we could have a hydroelectric power generator."

Using a city data web site, he found that Pikeville's population had been dropping for years. It was now around fifteen hundred. There was also an imbalance in the sexes. There were nine hundred women, three hundred men and three hundred children. Most of the women were retired widows who had never left the area.

The average income was well below state levels. The only chain store in the area was a Tractor Supply, and it appeared to be on its way out. Land prices were well below the state average. If one had to depend on the area to make a living it wasn't good news. This wasn't a problem for Rick and Marsha. With their investments and recent increases, they were now worth forty million dollars.

After much discussion, they decided a trip to Pikeville might be in order. Rick made flight arrangements with Delta from Baltimore to Chattanooga, reserved a rental car with Hertz and made arrangements for three nights at the Coachman's Inn in Pikeville.

In the meantime, Marsha had performed her own Internet search and found several properties for sale in the area. She found a Century Twenty One realtor who worked out of a home office in Pikeville and made arrangements for her to show them some properties.

Marsha and Rick hadn't firmly decided what they wanted, other than it had to be more than four hundred acres for privacy, have some area that could be farmed, flowing water preferred and up close to one of the mountain ridges. From their price searches on available land, they felt that two million was a reasonable upper limit.

Their public reason for buying would be for a country retreat. The agent Hope Popule assured Marsha that there were at least a half-dozen properties for sale that fit the description. As a matter of fact, there were several that weren't on the market currently, but for the right price they could be.

On Monday June 20, 2022, Rick and Marsha flew from the Baltimore airport. Rick still insisted on calling it Friendship airport even though its name had been changed in 1972 to Baltimore/Washington National Airport. Somewhere in there it was also called Thurgood Marshall.

Most people called it BWI.

They landed in Chattanooga a little before noon after changing planes in Atlanta. Everyone from the southeast knew if you were going to Hell you had to change in Atlanta.

By the time they retrieved their luggage and picked up their car from Hertz, they arrived in Pikeville a little after 3:00 in the afternoon. The drive was uneventful. The car drove itself with no drama. During the first few years of self- driving cars there had been some real incidents and many speculative stories, but now they were a fact of life.

Upon checking into the Coachman's Inn they asked where the restaurants were located. They were told that the Pikeville Family Restaurant wasn't only the best in town; it was the only one in town. The McDonald's closed three years ago, and Campbell's shortly thereafter.

The nice elderly looking lady behind the Inn's front desk told them they couldn't leave it too late as it closed at 6:00 pm during the week. It opened for breakfast at 5:30 am every day.

After freshening up and unpacking in their room, which apparently was last redecorated in Western style with wood paneling about 1950. They dressed casually and drove the three blocks up Main Street to the restaurant.

By this time, it was 5:00 o'clock so they weren't surprised to see the place half full when they opened the front door. They were surprised when a waitress doing double duty as the hostess said, "Hello strangers you just passing through?"

"No," said Rick, "We are looking for some land with the possibility of moving here and doing some light farming."

This might have been the funniest thing in the world to say for everyone in hearing distance broke out laughing.

The waitress said with a smile, "You have never farmed before have you?"

Rick was wondering what he had got into as his comments passed along to those that were too far away to hear. As each group passed it along new laughter would break out, especially those wearing John Deere or Ferguson ball caps. From the confused looks on their faces, the waitress who wore a badge which read, 'Mary', took pity.

"I did not mean to make fun of you, but there is no such thing as light farming. If you are farming it is heavy dirty work most of the year."

This was said in a thick Tennessee accent which they had to listen to very carefully. It was a pleasant sound, just hard for them to understand.

Once he got it Rick broke out laughing.

"You got me there," he grinned. "I guess I am a farmer wantabe."

Marsha chimed in, "I never said I wanted to be a farmer. I just agreed to live in the country."

Mary looked them up and down, "Oh my God. We have Green Acres here."

This took the house down as many of them were old enough to remember the television show from the mid to late 1960's.

After this comment, Mary got serious and asked, "Two for dinner?"

"Yes ma'am," replied Rick.

After getting them settled in a booth and taking their drink orders and a little more grief from Mary about Yankeefied unsweetened ice tea, they studied their menus.

They were relieved to see regular American food. They were getting a little concerned about where they were. After they ordered a hamburger and fries, they looked at the people around them. They seemed to be friendly and several even nodded and gave them a, "Hello Y'all."

After dinner, they took a drive up East Valley Road and while it was very pretty looking along the way they didn't know what they were looking at so they called it a day. Returning to the Coachman's Inn, they were glad to find that either the walls were very solid on the old facility or that there was no one on either side. While it was still early they went to bed with their E-readers and had a pleasant evening.

The next morning they had breakfast at the Pikeville Family Restaurant, but it was a much lower key meal. The place was busy, but they weren't picked out as strangers and joshed.

This was fine with Rick; he was never at his best when he first got up. Marsha normally had a better disposition in the morning, but was happy to sip her coffee as she woke up. They shared a copy of the Chattanooga Times-Free Press to get an idea of what was happening locally.

They did learn that there was no news out of Pikeville. This was a good thing as they wanted quiet and laid back.

At 9:00 o'clock, Hope Popule came in as they had agreed to meet at the restaurant. She came right to their table, which was no surprise as she appeared to know everyone else. Hope was a tall thin lady about thirty years old.

She had dark-brown hair and large brown eyes. The most striking feature about her was how her normally, solemn face lit up when she smiled. She went from an attractive lady to a beautiful woman.

Marsha hit Rick lightly in the side as she said, “Down boy.”

Rick chuckled as he said, “In my dreams.”

Hope was dressed as she had advised Rick and Marsha, comfortable jeans, long-sleeve shirt and stout looking walking shoes. This wasn’t to be like looking at houses in the city. She also carried a three-ring binder that zipped up around three sides, which presumably contained information on properties she thought they should look at.

Rick rose as she approached the table and shook her hand. They introduced themselves. Rick offered her a cup of coffee which she accepted. They then had a general conversation about what they were looking for.

Hope smiled at Marsha and said, "That is exactly what you told me when you first called me. So often people tell me one thing, show up with their minds completely changed, and it is my fault, that I'm not prepared with the right properties."

Marsha replied, "We aren't like that. Excuse me for asking, but your accent doesn't seem to be from around here."

"I grew up in Florida and my parents were both from the North, so I really don't have a southern accent. However, I can y'all with the best of them, and drink my ice tea sweetened. Unlike you Yankeefied light farmers."

"Oh boy," said Rick, "I have heard that news travels fast in small towns, but this is incredible."

Hope giggled a little as she said, "My Aunt Mary knew I had an appointment today with two people from Baltimore, so she called me last night. She really got a kick out of the light farming comment and hopes she didn't offend you."

"No," replied Marsha, "it was actually funny when you think about it, what Rick meant was we wanted to have a garden."

"That's different; that's just gardening, not farming."

Rick replied dourly, "Yeah I figured that out."

Marsha using a fake whisper to Hope said, "He's had his heart set on a full-sized tractor so it rained on his parade a little."

Rick could not really hear what Hope whispered back, but it sounded suspiciously like, "Boys and their toys."

Hope continued on in a normal tone, "Let me show you what we have for sale right now," as she unzipped her binder."

Marsha was still laughing as Rick eagerly went for the subject change.

The five properties that she had listings for were all between four to six hundred acres; all but one had been working farmland. That one was still forest covered and had been used as a hunting preserve by a club from Chattanooga. Hope had a map of the area and showed where each of the farms was located.

One that immediately caught Rick's eye was right at the base of Hinch Mountain. It was on the backside of the mountain and there were no roads over or around it. It also was the furthest up the valley, so was set in a dead end, several miles from the one road that left the valley going north.

The farm immediately to the south of it was also for sale. Its southern border was a creek not big enough to call a river. Hope told him it was a combination spring fed; rain run off creek.

Rick and Marsha's eyes both lit up when told its name was King Creek.

"Let's go look at them," Rick said.

Marsha added, "It would be fun having a creek with our name, even though it isn't really named after us."

Hope gave her wonderful smile as she said, "After living there for five years or so people would forget that it wasn't."

*"I can't get too excited about this but this sale is looking good,"* she thought.

"If you guys are about ready I suggest we make a restroom stop and hit the road."

Outside they got into Hopes SUV, a silver Toyota 4Runner and headed north.

They stopped first at the property which was bounded by King Creek. The Creek itself was in half flow as the last of winter snow was long gone from the mountain ridge. Because of the flow, it looked to Rick that it would support a micro-hydroelectric generator.

He asked Hope about that, and she told him that there were several in the area but didn't know how difficult it would be to get the permits from the Tennessee Valley Authority and the Army Corp of Engineers.

There was a small unoccupied house on the property, but one look told Rick and Marsha this wasn't for them. It looked like an old share cropper's shack from the 1800's. The barn and sheds weren't much better.

This was the property owned by the gun club. When the members visited they had brought their own RV's or campers with them. They had not trashed the area, but they had done nothing to keep the buildings up. There was a five hundred-yard gun range set up out back. It used the side of the mountain itself as a backstop. This was serviceable, but nothing fancy.

Hope had a sinking feeling about the sale." *"You should know better than to count your chickens."*

"Let's look at the other property," she said.

"Yes let's do," replied Marsha.

Rick just nodded as though he had something on his mind. The next property had more land that had been under plow and while the house was much newer, it was a small two bedroom one bath house that looked as though the plumbing and electric would never meet code.

The owners were not home, so they had the full tour. While very clean and neatly kept it wasn't the sort of house that Rick and Marsha would be comfortable in. As they were walking back to the SUV, Rick went over to the edge of a corn field. He picked up a handful of soil and let it drain between his fingers.

Marsha asked him what he was up to.

Rick replied, "I don't know, but I see the farmers do that in movies so thought I should"

Marsha and Hope just looked at each other.

Hope had all but given up on a sale; she could see that neither house would be acceptable to the Kings. While they hadn't made disparaging comments like many people would have, you could tell they were not thrilled.

She was very surprised when Rick asked her, "Refresh me, what are the sizes and prices of these two farms?"

"This one is five hundred and forty acres, and they are asking one million two hundred and fifty thousand dollars. The King Creek property is six hundred and twenty five acres, and they are asking a million six."

Hope who had learned never to quit selling until they drove away, made sure she worked that King Creek reference in.

"Mind if Marsha and I talked for a minute," Rick inquired?

"Of course not," Hope said as her hope renewed itself. As she watched Rick took the lead in the conversation but Marsha quickly started talking. Both became animated and arms were waving as they talked, but it seemed to be a good animation. They talked for the better part of ten minutes until they wound down. They seemed to come to a decision and headed back to Hope.

## Chapter 17- Lets Make a Deal June 2022

"Sorry we took so long, we would like to make an offer," Rick said.

Hope asked, "On which property?"

“Oh, the both of them,” Rick replied, “a million four fifty on the King Creek land, and a million and a quarter on the north lot.” Thus the two northern-most farms off of East Valley Road were renamed.

Hope shook herself and told them she thought that would work. As they were driving back to Hope’s home office, they had to ask her to slow down three times.

She had a hard time keeping her mind on the road. She had obtained both listings and was now selling them. That calculated out as her share to be over one hundred and fifty thousand dollars, more than she had made in the last five years. It was not even lunch time yet!

They got to Hope’s home in Pikeville in less than half the time it took to get to the farms. Now that they had made their decision to proceed, Rick and Marsha were almost as excited as Hope. Almost, was the key word as they kept asking her to slow down.

This was ironic as in her younger days Marsha had been known to drive over ninety miles an hour on road rallies on regular highways that weren’t limited access.

They shared with Hope that their plan was to build a new house near the property line of the north lot and King Creek farm. They intended to file with the county commissioners to re-deed the land as one plat for tax purposes. This would save them some money and of course the name would be King Creek Ranch.

When Hope asked why Ranch and not Farm, Rick told her that Ranch just sounded cooler than Farm.

Hope thought, *"For old people they sure are lively."*

Hope's home was a nice three-bedroom brick house. She had an office set up in one of the bedrooms. When they went into the office, they were both distracted by a whirring sound. Looking in the corner, they saw a cage with two Guinea pigs, one of the pigs was using the wheel at a furious rate.

Hope laughed, "That is Cookie; she gets very active when someone comes into the room. I think she is trying to get away."

"They are cute," said Marsha.

"I have had them for a long time now; they are very old for Guinea pigs."

While Hope was fond of her Guinea pigs, she also remembered why they were here. It took over an hour to fill out the paperwork. Along the way, she was thrilled to hear that these were to be cash sales.

She said, "The hunting club will be glad to get this wound up as they haven't used King Creek for several years. The Johnsons will be ecstatic to sell their property; they have wanted to move to North Carolina to be nearer their grandchildren.

Your building a new house will be a boost for us locally. I don't know how much money it will bring to the area, but we have been going downhill for so long that any building will be taken as a positive sign. The only new people who have moved here in years are that survivalist group south of town."

This last statement caught Rick's attention.

What is this about a survivalist group?"

Hope realized she may have put her foot in it, so she immediately downplayed the group.

"We call them that, it's actually a group of families that have bought a farm. They use it mostly during the summer as a vacation spot for their families. They have set up a shooting range for the guys, and seem to haul in a lot of goods, including food. I guess they would be more preppers than survivalists."

"They might be worth getting to know," mused Rick.

They tend to keep to themselves, but since they are only here during the summer their kids don't go to the local schools, and they aren't church goers, so they don't have many opportunities to meet people."

The conversation turned to the logistics of closing and transfer of funds if their offers were accepted. Hope felt that she had seen a clue as to why Rick and Marsha wanted to move to this area. They were nice people and had the money so why not?

Besides, for this amount of commission, she would probably broker a deal for the devil if he showed up. They signed the last papers. Hope started with her phone calls to let the Johnsons and her contact at the gun club know there were offers on the properties. She let both parties know that the buyers had two properties in mind, to push them along.

The Johnsons were joyous to hear from Hope and told her they would be glad to look at any offer she had. The gun club representative had to present it to their Board of Directors, but he felt they probably would accept the offer.

Hope made an appointment with the Johnsons for later that day for them to review the offer. She scanned and emailed the gun clubs paperwork to them.

Her contact told her he would call a special meeting of the Board as soon as possible, as they didn't want to miss this opportunity to sell.

Rick and Marsha returned to the hotel while Hope drove out to the Johnsons to deliver their offer. Rick called their bank in Baltimore to see what they had to do to transfer funds or to obtain certified checks.

It turned out to be a lot easier than he thought it would be, BB&T; their bank had branches in Chattanooga. It looked like the one on Broad Street was the closest.

They also had a branch in Athens, TN which was technically closer but when Rick and Marsha reviewed the map on Mapquest, they realized they wanted no part of the hairpins on Route 30. It may be closer, but they would get seasick on the drive.

They went down to the diner for an early dinner. Mary was on duty again. Apparently Hope had been on the phone because Mary was completely up to date on events.

Rick was at first concerned about their business being shared, but Marsha let him know that this was a small town. Very little was secret and get over it!

Rick knew this was a losing battle, but it was a lesson learned on conducting business in a small town. He really wasn't upset with Hope; he could understand why she was so excited.

As they were ordering some chicken-fried steak; Rick's cell phone rang. It really rang. He had no fancy tunes; his went ring, ring, ring. As he explained to the young lady at the phone store, phones are black, they go ring, and they weigh about five pounds. She could not change the weight, but she did give him a black phone with a traditional ring. At the time, Rick ignored the muttered, "Old fart."

"Rick King here."

"Mr. King this is Hope Popule. The Johnsons have accepted your offer. They felt like God had answered their prayers."

“I am not certain about me and God, but I am glad that they are happy.”

“Ecstatic is more like it,” she replied. From the excitement in her voice, Hope wasn’t far from that condition herself.

“How long will it be before we can close?”

“It should be a quick closing. The land has no debt. It has been in their family since before the Civil War; or as Mr. Johnson called it, the War of Northern Aggression”.

“Hmm if I meet him, I had better not tell him one of my ancestors Rufus King was a Union General, and that his son Rufus Jr. won the medal of honor at the battle of White Oak Swamp in Virginia.”

“Good thinking, I’m not sure how serious he is but some of these old families around here haven’t forgotten. The important thing is the title search should be easy, but I just hope the boundaries aren’t described by this Oak tree near that Cherry tree next to the Creek.

Those deeds were mostly from the Revolution or before, but they are a real pain to clear up. Sometimes miles of land have to be surveyed from a known point to straighten things out.”

“I guess that will be as it is, not much we can do about it,” Rick said in a calming voice.”

He asked Hope if she was driving. She told him she was just getting ready to leave the Johnsons.

"Hope, please slow down. You're talking a mile a minute. You had better pay attention to your driving."

It got quiet on the other end of the call.

"I guess you are right. I am very excited. This is by far the biggest deal I have ever had. Being in the million-dollar sales club around here is a really big deal. Plus the money looks really good. I will let the car drive, to be safe."

"Okay young lady calm down a little, maybe you should borrow Cookie's race track when you get home. We planned to be here for a week, but I don't see the need for it now. If there is any negotiating to be done on the King Creek property, we can do it by phone and email."

"Okay I will certainly keep you posted."

In the meantime, their dinners were delivered.

Marsha said, "Well that was an exciting and expensive few minutes."

"Yes," said a buoyant Rick, "it certainly was. I didn't realize how much I wanted this to happen."

"Well it's not a done deal yet, and we have to get the other offer accepted," said a grinning Marsha. "I guess I wanted this also, this is an entire new departure for me; I have lived in towns and cities all my life. I will be able to talk about going into town, and out on the farm and all that good stuff."

Rick whose grin was getting bigger said, "I can complain about the weather and getting the crops in."

"Now you are getting silly," said Marsha. "You never told me about any famous relatives before."

"It's not a big deal," said Rick.

"Rufus Kings grandfather was also named Rufus, and he was a signer of the United States Constitution, a US Senator and failed presidential candidate for the Federalist party in 1816 if I remember right.

He had another member of the family that was a confederate general who was killed at the battle of Petersburg. Furthermore, a remote cousin was Admiral Bull Halsey."

"Wow your family helped found the US," Marsha said admiringly.

"What about your family, any famous Americans?"

"My husband was a descendant of Christopher Wren the English Architect. However, what I think is funny, my maiden name is Monroe, and my sixth great grandfather James Monroe beat yours in the election of 1816."

Rick got a shocked look on his face, "Really?"

"Gotcha," said Marsha. "As far as I know I am no relation."

Rick laughed, "You had me going."

"It is nice you know so much about your family,' she said. "It is good to know, but it won't pay for the coffee here."

Hmm, hey Mary, did you know that Rick here is descended from a Confederate General, who died at Petersburg?"

"Wow; that is impressive, of course everyone around here lost people in the War Between the States."

"Will being a descendant of a Confederate General get Rick a free cup of coffee?"

"Not a chance," Mary replied.

"Told you so," said Rick.

Marsha thought, *"I don't think that I will rain on his parade today. Someday I will let him know that I am about the thirty-fifth hundredth in line to the British Throne. That changes every time a new royal is born, and they are a prolific bunch. Especially now that Elizabeth is taking life extending 'Live', she could be on the throne another hundred years."*

They finished their meal and went for a ride around the area.

When they got back to the Coachman's Inn Rick changed their return flight to Baltimore to the next day.

They returned to Baltimore late Thursday after a day of flight delays. They missed their first leg because of a work action by the TSA security screeners. The TSA union was now saying that besides having limits on work hours, they should also only have to screen so many people per hour.

In Chattanooga, they decided on six hundred people per hour. Rick and Marsha were about number six hundred and fifty, so they had to wait thirty minutes in line while the screeners just stood there. After the hour turned they started screening again, just in time for them to see their plane pull away from the gate.

The next flight to Atlanta was on time, but the flight out of Atlanta was on a ground stop because weather around Baltimore. Rick moaned about how bad air travel had gotten compared to the good old days of the 1960's and 1970's. He finally shut up when Marsha asked him about the inflight service at Kitty Hawk.

The next several days turned into the weekend, and time seemed to stand still as they waited to hear on their second offer. Finally on Monday afternoon, Hope called with news.

"They have accepted your offer," she squealed.

"That is fantastic," said Marsha, who answered the phone.

“What now?”

“We can close in three weeks. The title searches will go right through. The King Creek property had to get the land surveyed when the gun club bought it so it has modern markers,” Hope explained.

“The North lot is bounded by King Creek on the south, so that is taken care of, Hinch Mountain and the National Forest boundaries take care of the North and East. The West is defined by East Valley Road so the title search shouldn’t take too long.

## Chapter 18 – A Walk in the Park July 2022

They returned to Chattanooga for the closing on both properties on Tuesday July 19, 2022. They had Ricks 4Runner drive them as they now had to move two cars to Tennessee. They read and napped most of the way.

The closings took place in the Century Twenty One offices in Chattanooga. Rick and Marsha had been told what checks they needed to bring. They arranged to pick them up at the Chattanooga BB&T earlier that day. The signings were back to back so both Rick and Marsha were suffering from writer's cramp.

Rick had contacted the TVA and explained what he wanted to do with a micro-hydroelectric generator. He was amazed at how friendly and helpful they were, as they explained the red tape, he would be drowning in.

They had the flow and drop rates for every piece of moving water in the area. He was told that King Creek would support a generator, but that it would require a pond with a dam. This complicated things as he was now changing the nature of the beast.

He would have to submit engineering studies that modeled his pond and dam with the resultant outflow. Of course, there would have to be an environmental impact study done. These had to be submitted to the TVA and the Army Corp of Engineers.

They didn't want him to cause any flooding or change the area and kill some endangered critter. Never once was it said that the TVA might not want any competition in generating electricity.

It didn't really matter what Rick may have thought of the regulations, it wasn't that he had any choices.

He explained his thinking to Marsha, "I am going to proceed with the permit applications even knowing that they will take several years. At the same time, I think we should dual source our power and put up a solar farm. I want to be off the grid as soon as we can."

Marsha was a little reluctant about solar power until her main objection was answered. She didn't like the idea of all those panels disturbing the nice roof line of the house she envisioned.

Once Rick understood this, he suggested the panels be ground mounted, with a slight rise between them and the house, so they wouldn't be a distraction.

Now all they had to do was go out to their property and select a site. Since the day was hot, they wore polo shirts, walking shorts and tennis shoes. Their drive out to the farm was punctuated with talk of what they wanted in a house and out buildings.

It was now King Creek Farm instead of King Creek Ranch. Marsha finally convinced Rick that it might appear uppity to their new neighbors. Rick backed down but didn't tell Marsha that he had remembered the King Ranch in Texas, which he thought was the largest ranch in the United States. He didn't want to look like he was horning in on their name.

They went up the drive way of the farm bordered by King Creek. Once they got to the old farm house/shooting clubhouse they got out and looked the area over. The house was almost a half mile off the main road.

Rick said, "I think we should build more to the center of the property so let's head north and see what's there."

"I agree," replied Marsha.

That is when their lesson began. This was mountain country. They walked north about half an hour. It wasn't a straight line. There were foot hills and bramble bushes that had to be circled around.

Their bodies were now sixty year olds, but out of shape sixty year olds. They hadn't any real exercise in almost thirty years. They came to a staggered stop at the top of a small hill.

They could see the top of the house from where they started. Rick brought a small range finder with him. It was like those that were used on golf courses to determine how far from the pin the ball was. He had to check it twice because they were only a quarter of a mile from where they started.

Between the hills, brambles and just not paying attention, they hadn't gone due north, but had staggered around the country side, and had no idea of the real lay of the land.

"This isn't working."

Marsha, still trying to catch her breath just nodded. They sat for a while and rested. Marsha was the first to notice, but Rick was quick to follow. They were sitting near an ant hill, and they were getting bitten. They were lucky and didn't know it, they weren't fire ants.

They both jumped up and started clearing ants from their legs and clothes. They then checked each other out.

After they were both cleared, Rick said, “Well that kills that idea.”

“What idea,” Marsha asked?

Rick only grinned.

All of a sudden, Marsha said, “No way,” but at least she was also grinning.

A more serious Rick said, “Let’s call it a day, head back and regroup.”

“I can go along with that.”

Looking at the house they noticed they had turned west and then were apparently going south. It wasn’t very far to the drive way to the house. Instead of going a half mile north like they thought they had gone a quarter mile west by north west.

The hike back to the driveway, and then to the house took less than half the time. They had been walking for almost two hours, and seen very little of their new property.

On their way back to the Coachman’s Inn where they were now getting to be regulars, they saw some dust rising from a cleared field. As they watched a four-wheeled All-Terrain Vehicle came into sight.

“That is what we need,” said Marsha.

“You are right. We will look after lunch.”

They heard it mentioned there was a farm equipment dealer in Dayton that would probably have what they needed. They freshened up at the hotel, then went to lunch at the Pikeville Family Restaurant.

Mary had just come on duty, and the crowd was light, so they had a few minutes to talk. She asked them how they liked their new land.

Rick was the sort who didn't mind a good laugh at himself, so he told Mary about their morning's woes.

She in turn explained they were very lucky they didn't sit on a fire ant hill, and how bad they could be. From now on they were to wear good boots, thick socks, long pants, and long-sleeve shirts, and don't worry about how hot it got!

A man in his early thirty's sitting at the next table said, "Mary is right, wear cotton clothes that breathe but make sure you are covered out there. By the way, I am Mike London. I gather you are the Kings that just bought the Johnsons and the gun club places, that new King Creek Farm."

"That's right," replied Rick.

"I'm Rick and this is my wife Marsha."

As Rick made the introductions, they all stood and shook hands.

"My place is a little south of town on the west side of the valley."

"Oh, are you out near that farm the survivalist group owns," Marsha asked?

"Yes ma'am but they are really standoffish. The only way you know they are there is all the gun fire. I reckon they think they are going to have to fight a war."

Rick felt a little uneasy about that. He had fought in several wars and still had bad memories which he didn't talk about. He decided right then and there that he was going to find out what the goals of this group were.

Mike continued, "Have you thought about ATVs?"

"We saw one on our way back here, and decided to check at the Dayton Tractor Supply Store and see if they carried them," replied Rick.

"I am pretty certain they do."

Mike continued, "That is a lot of land you own, over eleven hundred acres. If I remember right it is about three quarters a mile from East Valley Road to the mountain ridge so you must have about a mile and a quarter of frontage along East Valley."

"That's right," said Rick. "What I can't figure out is how much land is an acre?"

Mike laughed, "An acre is 43,560 square feet. A perfectly square lot of one acre would measure about two hundred and eight feet a side. So if one side of your land is three quarters a mile deep, then the other dimension would be about a mile and a quarter. That is extremely rough arithmetic and remember, while your border on East Valley may run straight, none of the others do.

"Weird but it actually makes sense," replied Rick and then continued. "How was 43,560 square feet decided upon?"

Mike said, "I have absolutely no idea. It is an old English measurement."

Mike went on to say, "Have you folks considered getting aerial photographs taken. It will really help give you a good idea of the flow of the land."

"Mike," exclaimed Marsha.

"That is a wonderful idea, anything to keep me out of those bugs!"

"I know there is an outfit that flies out of the Chattanooga airport that does that," said Mike.

Mike then pulled out his smart phone, and a quick search came up with Chatham Aviation and their phone number. Mike told them they could see what maps the Army Corp of Engineers had of the area, and also the TVA.

He also suggested that since they were going to Dayton, they stop in at the Farm Bureau extension office which had just opened and see what maps they could provide.

Rick and Marsha thanked Mike profusely.

Rick told Mike that he would like to give a tour of King Creek Farm once they were settled in. Mike liked the name they had given the land.

He said, “I would get a sign up quickly or people will just refer to it as the King place, like they do all other farms around here.”

“Who does work like that around here,” asked Rick.

“I would ask Steve Klima. He can make a simple sign and put the name in with a router. With the letters painted it would make a good-looking sign. I know he made some up for the Boy Scout Camp, and they looked very nice.”

“Where would we find Steve,” asked Marsha?

Mike gave them Steve’s phone number which he had in his phone’s memory.

Tell Steve I told you to call him, we are in the National Guard together. Even though I am his Sergeant, I don’t think he dislikes me that much.”

This made Rick laugh as he remembered his military days, Sergeant’s come in all types, good, bad and in between. You respected and depended on a good one, tolerated the one in between and feared the bad ones. They could get you killed.

After lunch, they drove to Dayton. They had avoided this trip before because the road had a hair pin curve which actually looked like a hairpin. The traffic was light so the car kept just to the speed limit, and though the road had many curves, they didn't get sea sick like their original worry. Just in their few drives around the area they had found roads that they would avoid, if at all possible.

In Dayton, they found Nelson's farm store. It bought and sold feed and grain along with the connections to obtain almost any piece of farm equipment you could think you might need.

Jack Nelson met them at the door with a cheerful, "Howdy neighbor, how can I help you?"

Rick explained they had bought property over north of Pikeville, near the base of Hinch Mountain.

"Oh so you are the new owners of Kings Creek Farm, glad to meet you, I'm Jack Nelson."

Marsha said, "It didn't take long for that news to get around did it?"

"You folks don't know how big of news your purchase is, there haven't been many land sales around here in the last ten years, and yours is by far the biggest. The youngster's leave as quick as they can, we've almost got to the point of no return."

He went on, "They are talking about closing schools around Pikeville and busing them here. That will be the only way our schools will stay open. You once had three generations on a farm, for the most part, it is just one now, and those are the grandparents. When they go, no one wants to move back to run the farm so it goes up for sale. The only buyers until you folks have been large companies buying land to hold."

Jack continued, "Everyone likes the name King Creek Farm, first when the news started going around last night it was, 'Did you hear about King Creek Farm' knowing that people would have to ask, 'What is King Creek Farm' so the caller had inside news; then people felt it made the area special because we had 'Named Property.' We have never had any of that around here. It might help land values. I bet the Pikeville Diner this morning had all sorts of people coming up with names for their farms."

"No offense intended, but you aren't youngsters, so I'm not certain people should get as excited as they have been. Kind of sad, when two, fifty year olds moving into area is the big news."

*"If they only knew our true age thought Rick and Marsha at the same time."*

"Anyway, how can I help you today," asked Jack.

Rick replied, “We are looking for a couple of ATV’s to use to explore our farm.”

“Good thinking, “replied Jack, “you have a lot of miles to cover. Most folks with larger spreads use them.”

Jack took them outside to his lot. He showed them new and used ATV’s and explained the pros and cons of each. While it was obvious, he was a salesman they felt he was explaining their options fairly well. They decided early on they wanted to buy new.

Nelsons were a Honda dealership so that took a lot of the decisions off the table, unless they shopped at other dealers. While not talking about it Rick and Marsha sensed that the other would be satisfied to buy here. They had chosen two sturdy four-wheel single passenger ATV’s, when Marsha noticed a larger machine sitting in the corner.

“What is that,” she inquired.

“That is a white elephant. It is also an ATV but it is built for four passengers. If you look, there are two sets of seats, and also a small cargo area in the back.”

“Why is it a white elephant,” Rick asked?

Jack laughed, “Because no one will buy it from me!”

“Rick it would be nice for us to ride around together, and also for when we want to show others our farm.”

"It would, but the others just look more agile and easier to get around on," said Rick.

Jack Nelson hadn't been a salesman for more than thirty years by passing up opportunities. "If you buy all three I bet we could work out a good deal for you."

This took Rick and Marsha aback for a moment, but they looked at each other and saw the other had no objection.

Rick said, "Let us take these for a spin around the lot to see how they handle, and maybe we can talk turkey."

The machines handled very nicely, Marsha pushed her single ATV harder than Rick did, but they both gave them a workout.

As they were walking into the office Jack told Marsha, "You know we sell sport models, and they have off-road races around here."

This got the laugh that was intended though Marsha got an interested look for a moment then shook her head to clear it of wild ideas.

In the office, Jack got down to business. He started out by showing them the suggested selling price of each unit. He wrote down what he would sell each of them for individually. Then he put down a package price.

"Folks you do understand that I am in business to make a profit. The package price does leave me a profit. Not much, but a profit. That four passenger unit has been on the lot for over a year, so I really want to get rid of it."

In the meantime, Marsha was on her smart phone looking up prices. She added up several numbers and showed it to Rick.

"Jack that really is cutting it to the bone," said Rick.

"Yes it is, but at this point I just want to move them."

"I understand and by moving the other two units it will help meet your dealer incentive from the manufactures hold back. That sounds like a winner for all of us. You have a deal," said Rick.

Marsha broke in, "Not so fast Rick. I notice everyone around here wears a ball cap from a tractor store. Are you going to throw in a hat for us?"

Jack laughed, "You drive a hard bargain." He reached into a cabinet and pulled out two ball caps with Nelsons embroidered on them.

"Now you can wear my advertising proudly!"

Rick chuckled, as Marsha grabbed the hats. Marsha then looked at Rick with wide eyes.

"I have a hat for the field and one for town. I wonder if he is going to give you one."

Rick started to sputter as Jack roared. Marsha relented and handed a hat to Rick.

"Have you folks bought a trailer yet to haul these thing's home," asked Jack?

"Not only no trailer; the only vehicle we have here is a car without a towing package," Rick replied.

"Let's complete the paperwork then we will haul them to your place. I also suggest you stop at the gas station across the street and fill them up," said Jack.

"Oh you mean Nelson's gas station," asked Marsha.

"Yes ma'am, my son Paul owns it; just trying to keep the money in the family."

"Works for me," replied Rick.

Jack asked how they were paying for the ATV's. He was a little surprised when Rick asked if a check was okay. Jack had read these people for money, but this was almost thirty grand!

"I have a truck trailer combination you might want to look at," said Jack.

Marsha added, "We are going to need one."

They trooped out to the other side of the building. There were dozens of trailers, but only one truck. It was a pickup truck but what a pickup. It was the largest truck they had ever seen. It was not a monster tire truck.

“What is it,” asked Rick?

“It’s a 2022 International Harvester Commercial Extreme Truck. They reintroduced the CXT last year. They haven’t made any since 2008. Actually, it is made by Toyota since they bought out Navistar. Now that Toyota’s headquartered in the US, they are trying to rebrand their name.

This truck will tow up to thirty tons at highway speed. The cab has every luxury you can think of, and it can hold five counting the driver.

“How much,” Rick started to ask.

Marsha talked right over Rick. “I don’t think we are interested in anything that big.”

“Just curious,” said Rick.

“One hundred and seventy-five thousand,” Jack put in.

Rick looked at Marsha; she just looked back at him.

“Thanks for taking care of my curiosity, probably more truck than we need.”

Jack replied cheerfully, “It’s here when you are ready.”

As they turned away Marsha was mumbling something about dead bodies.

“Where do you folks want your quad ATV’s delivered?”

You know the entrance to the old Johnson place?”

“Yep, I have been out there several times.”

“There is a barn there we can keep them in.”

“I think we might be setting up house there for a while till we have a new place built.”

“Will it be okay if we drop them off tomorrow,” Jack asked.

“Sure but can we have the owner manuals now?”

“No problem folks; let me put them in this folder along with your paperwork. I will make certain they are gassed up.”

“Thank you,” said Rick.

Marsha also thanked Jack but she added, “If you try to puppy dog that truck on Rick, I will be after you with a shotgun.”

Jack grinned and roared his large laugh. “I hear you.”

On the way home Rick asked Marsha, “What is puppy dogging a truck?”

“If you have a puppy you want to get rid of. You take it to some one’s house that has kids, and you leave it overnight. The kids will adopt the puppy; the parents won’t be able to fight it. With a truck like that they would park it in our driveway and let you drive it several days, one truck sold."

"But we don't have any kids," said Rick.

Marsha just snorted, "Yeah, right."

Rick laughed as he said, "I had never heard of that sales technique before, but I can see where it would work."

## Chapter 19 – Reminders of By Gone Days July 2022

Over the next two days, Marsha and Rick made arrangements for aerial photography of their land, and signs to be put up at the gun club and Johnson Farm entrances. They were simple pieces of plywood supported with two-by-fours. The face of the sign painted white said, King Creek Farm in large blue letters.

They then flew back to Baltimore and let their landlord know they were moving out of their Delaney Valley apartment. They made arrangements for their furniture to be packed, and put in storage in the mover's warehouse in Chattanooga. Marsha contacted their few friends and gave them their new forwarding address.

They were getting ready to drive Marsha's Camry to Tennessee when they received a call from the Burns & Burns Trust company. They were asked if they could come downtown sometime. They had a box of personal effects for each of them.

While doing a periodic clean out of their long-term storage, they came across boxes with their names on them. The boxes contained items like their high school diplomas, baptismal certificates, wedding announcements, and a small package labeled US Army and old passports.

The next morning on the way out of town they detoured to Burns & Burns. They took receipt of the boxes and hit the road. It was a good thing the boxes were only the size of several shoe boxes as the car was loaded with their clothes.

They didn't bother to look through the boxes, but just headed west on I-70 to join up with I-81 on their way to Tennessee.

It was interesting to have the self-driving car pull into a gas station, have a reader check the cars credit, use a robot to fill the tank with the manufacturers recommended fuel. While this was happening, another robot mounted on the roof of the canopy above the pumps cleaned their windows. The station also scanned the car's data, but all fluids were within norms and there were no faults on any equipment.

As Marsha said, "The only thing it can't do for us is get out and pee."

They didn't intend to do the ten-hour trip in one day. Even though they did not have to steer and were feeling better all the time they did not want to push it. After spending the night in Lynchburg, VA they continued on to Pikeville. They reached the motel about nine o'clock that night, after stopping for dinner in Chattanooga. A quick shower and they were soon sound asleep.

The next day over their morning coffee at the diner they discussed their coming moves.

"Rick would you consider getting a double-wide mobile home for the farm until our new home is completed. I can't stand the thought of living in either of those old farm houses."

"I think that is a good idea Marsha.  It is going to be a year or more before construction is completed, and I agree about those buildings. The Johnson house could be made livable for us, but it doesn't seem worth the effort. The gun club building is about to fall down."

"I have been thinking about this for a couple of days now. We could place the double wide in the open area in front of the gun club house. I noticed a place selling them as we came out of Chattanooga."

"I noticed it also, though I hadn't thought about us getting one," replied Rick.

Just then Rick's cell phone rang. He took a short call and announced, "Our aerial pictures are ready, looks like we were meant to go to Chattanooga today."

The weather was pleasant, so the drive to Chatham Aviation to pick up the aerial map of their land went well. The owner Mr. Chatham explained how to interpret what they were looking at in a clipped British accent. Rick understood what he was looking at from his Army days but appreciated the refresher.

He pointed at a level area right at the base of Hinch Mountain and said, “It looks like this area is flat enough for our house and any out buildings we may want. It is near the center of the property and far back from the road.”

Marsha added, “If I read this right, we could put a winding road around these hills without having a steep driveway.”

“Those hills would be perfect for observation posts,” stated Rick.

Marsha looked at him like he had grown a second head, while Mr. Chatham smiled and said, “You remind me of another bloke I used to work with.”

Rick looked at Chatham but all he got was, “That was a long time ago and far away, almost like another world.”

Rick let it go.

Marsha said, “We will talk later.”

On the way back to Pikeville they stopped at the mobile home sales lot they had both noticed. It didn’t take long for a salesman to gravitate to them. In short order, they had discussed what they needed.

They started with two bedrooms and a bath. With only a little help from the salesman they had talked themselves up to three bedrooms, two baths, one of which was a master bath, dining room along with a family room and living room.

They managed to run the price up to fifty thousand dollars, which put to lie the signs out front which proudly flaunted nothing over thirty thousand. When Rick brought this up to the salesman, he didn't even have the grace to blush.

"That is if you don't go with any options, and I don't think you missed any."

Just about then Rick got a gentle elbow from Marsha, so he let it go.

The salesman did get a painful look on his face when they described where they wanted it.

"Have you folks thought about sewage, water and electricity?"

Rick replied, "There is electricity to the house it's near. There is also a well and septic system, and I thought we could just hook into those. I know they are okay because they were checked as part of the home inspection of the property when we bought it. The home is a tear down is why we need the double wide while we're having our new house built."

*"Damn,"* thought Rick, *"I shouldn't have told him about buying this for temporary quarters, no price reduction for us. Oh well, what is done is done."*

From the glare he got from Marsha, he knew his big mouth had got him in trouble again.

The very helpful salesman was glad to arrange for their premium display unit to be moved out to their property and set in place. They would even arrange for the foundation to be put in and hook ups made by their people. Just another mere twenty-five thousand dollars!

Rick started to open his mouth then looked at Marsha. He realized that he had used up all his attaboys, and asked how he should make out the check.

The salesman was thrilled when he realized there would be no price negotiations or credit problems. He would receive full commission. He even threw in a couple of ball caps with the company logo. It was arranged for the unit to be put in place the following Friday.

After shaking hands with a very happy salesman they started back to Pikeville. Rick had been watching the gas tank and pulled into a small convenience store to fill up. It was an older station without the window washing robot. He got out of the car to go to the restroom while the car was fueling its self.

As the tank was filling he walked towards the station. He noticed a car and driver sitting with motor running near the front door of the store. The passenger door was open like someone had just gone in to quickly buy something.

It just didn't look right to Rick, so he looked for the license plate number. There was no plate. Just as he was thinking old blue, two-door Ford pickup about 2014, he heard a noise like a gun shot.

Reacting more than thinking he grabbed a window washing squeegee with a hard plastic handle. As he ran to the front door of the store a man burst out.

Rick reversed the squeegee and thrust it into the man's stomach as hard as he could. With an explosion of air, the man went down, not even gasping at first. The hand gun which he had been holding went flying.

The car which had been waiting took off with the open door slamming closed from the acceleration. Rick saw that the robber was down for the count, now gasping for breath, as though he was going to die.

Rick kicked the hand gun further away. Then he rolled the robber over and knelt on his back. This guy was going nowhere.

By this time, Marsha had gotten out of their car and headed into the store. She was afraid of what she would find. Her fears weren't quite realized. There was a small Indian man there who had been shot in the side.

He was in great pain but there didn't seem to be any arterial bleeding. It appeared that a bullet had grazed his ribs and probably broken one or more of them.

There was a first-aid kit behind the counter which contained a large sterile pad. She placed it on the wound and had the man, a Mr. Patel according to the Manager on Duty sign; hold it tightly to his side to staunch the blood flow.

She then called 911. She had a little trouble telling the operator where she was at but when she said, "Patel's convenience store," it was quickly worked out.

The Tennessee Highway Patrol car must have been very close because it was there within two minutes. The officer got out of the car with handgun drawn as a robbery with gunfire had been called.

The officer, Sergeant James Weselis a fifteen-year veteran didn't take long to figure out who the bad guy was and cuff him. About that time, two sheriff cars pulled into the lot, and you could hear other sirens in the background.

Rick gave a description of the car that had driven away. Officer Weselis radioed the description to the dispatcher. The Sheriff's Deputies took him and Marsha aside separately and took their statements.

What Mr. Patel had to say verified their story, so the Deputies were satisfied that they understood what had gone on. They Mirandized the suspect, exchanged cuffs with the Trooper and locked him in the backseat of a cruiser.

An ambulance had pulled up, and it didn't take long for the EMT's to re-bandage Mr. Patel and transport him. He had called a family member who was on their way, and the State Trooper assured him that he would stay until someone arrived.

One of the Deputies came back to Rick and Marsha and said, "Where did you learn to handle a squeegee like that?"

Rick started to answer, but Marsha started to laugh.

"I guess you can say that I have experience with a squeegee," Rick managed to get out before he too went into near hysterical laughter.

The Deputy clearly not understanding the answer nodded his head and walked away.

This time it was the State Patrol Trooper who approached them.

"I thought you folks would like to know, the car that drove away was disabled in a wreck, and we apprehended the driver."

"As soon as they read him his rights, he tried to start a plea bargain, so I don't think you folks will even end up in court over this. Thanks for your help but you might think twice about charging a man with a gun with only a squeegee. It was a cheap twenty two, but he could have killed you."

As the trooper left Marsha said, "That is another thing we have to talk about when we get home."

Rick thought, "*Maybe it would have been better if I had been shot.*"

About that time, reaction set in and Rick started to shake. Marsha's eyes got wide, and she grabbed him in a hug and didn't let go. It took him about fifteen minutes to settle down. Marsha got him a bottle of orange juice from the store. Mr. Patel's daughter wouldn't take any money when she tried to pay.

Rick was sitting in their car when a TV news van pulled into the drive way. A reporter got out followed closely by a camera man. They went straight to the State Trooper who gave them a very terse description of events.

The reporter immediately approached Marsha and asked her for an interview. Marsha gave a proud description of her husband's actions.

By this time, Rick was settled enough that he got out of the car, and was ready for the reporter and camera man. The reporter asked him how it felt charging into possible gunfire.

His reply of, "Different day, same job," confused her, but she kept up the normal inane questions asked at a time like this.

The reporter got their names, and the fact that they were just moving to Pikeville, she showed surprise and asked, "Is Kings Creek Farm yours?"

"Yes," Marsha replied.

"I heard about you from my Aunt Mary. The people up there are all excited; it is the first major property movement in that area in years. They hope it is a sign of better things to come. What are you doing for housing?"

As Marsha started her reply, Rick and the camera man (who had turned off the camera) shook their heads and walked to the store to get another drink. Women discussing housing, this could take a while.

The camera man said, "Different day, same job, were you in the service?"

"Viet Nam," was the reply.

The camera man said, "You don't look that old," then dropped the subject. Even now people weren't comfortable discussing that war.

Rick and Marsha decided they had enough excitement for the day and would just go back to Pikeville and eat at the diner. Rick regretted it as soon as they walked in the door.

A wall-mounted TV was showing his and Marsha's interview at the convenience store. All the patrons were glued to the screen, but the questions started as soon as the clip was over.

Rick was usually a talker, except when others thought what he had done was exceptional. He had seen exceptional, and hitting someone with a squeegee was not the same as jumping on a grenade. He gave a few short answers without being rude. Marsha was proud of her man and talked enough for both of them.

Once the excitement had quieted down Rick was approached by a tall well-built man apparently in his forties. He had a military bearing with a short brush haircut. His casual attire screamed off-duty soldier.

Holding out his hand, he introduced himself as Major Watkins.

"Rick I run the survival camp south of town. I would like to get to know you better. I think you could add something to our program."

"I doubt that," Rick replied.

"I think you could. You adapted a weapon and overcome. Not many people can do that," stated the Major.

"There was not much adapting, that squeegee was the only hard edge item available," said Rick.

"That is exactly my point. Most people would not even think to look for a 'hard edge', much less realize that the squeegee fit the bill."

"That may be, but I am really too old and out of shape for those games," Rick replied.

Watkins replied harshly, "Tell that to the punk who is sitting in jail in Chattanooga."

Rick answered slowly, "I guess you are right. I saw what was happening, identified a weapon and took immediate action. Most people don't do that well."

The Major smirked and said, "You got that right. Now will you consider visiting us, and see what we teach, and if you could help?"

"I would be interested in seeing what is going on, what day would be good?"

"Any day but Mondays would be fine. That is our down day. Just stop by, no advance notice is needed. We run a guard at the gate as a practice exercise. I would like to see if they follow procedures with unannounced guests."

Rick chuckled, "That is fine as long as procedures don't include strip searches."

"Just some form of identification and the name of the person you are visiting should do it," replied the Major,

"Though I would not mind strip searching some of the women who show up."

"Anyway, I think you did some good work today and would like to know you better. Stop by when you can. I need to get back to base now; I hope to see you later."

With that the Major turned and left. Rick and Marsha sat quietly until the Major was out the door.

"Rick, I don't like that man," Marsha said.

"Neither do I, he rubs me the wrong way."

"Then why did you say you would like to see what they were doing," Marsha asked?

"Know your enemy," was Rick's terse reply.

They finished their dinners quietly and retired to the motel for the night.

## Chapter 20 – The new land – July 2022

The next week was busy for Rick and Marsha. They had to arrange for 5G telephone, internet and television service with Bell South. Marsha talked about the bad old days when you had to deal with many companies and a DSL connection or cable was the fastest service you could get. Now that 5G ran at ten or more times the speeds they were in 2014 nothing could beat it. They were talking about 6G but no dates had been set.

They signed up with the electric company at the local Pikeville office. As befitting a small town it was a one-person office and the lady at the desk knew all about their move. She let them know the modular home people contacted them about having a crew available to connect the service to the home.

Rick and Marsha drove out to the home site. There was a flatbed truck parked in the yard and a man digging with a back hoe. Rick introduced himself while Marsha waited in the car. The worker explained that he was getting the water, and septic lines dug up, so they could be connected to the modular home.

He also let them know he surveyed their driveway and let the company know they would have to trim some limbs to get the modular home in, but they were lucky in that no whole trees would have to come down.

They then went over to the barn and found their ATV's as Jack Nelson said he would leave them. They decided to ride together this trip on the white elephant. The vehicle was officially the 'The White Elephant' as the name and a cute white elephant were painted on the side.

They had a topographical map from the U S Army Corp of Engineers for navigation. Marsha drove while Rick gave directions. Their goal was to find and review the area that looked best for their home site from the aerial photograph.

They had to wind around several hills to find the site which was about three-quarters of a mile from their starting point. This didn't seem like much when riding, but they remembered their first trip out. The route they took had a gentle rise, but nothing that would give an automobile trouble in the winter on a cleared road.

Once they went up the last rise, they came to an open flat spot at the base of Hinch Mountain. When they had driven by Hinch on the road and seen it from a distance, it looked like a worn hill. Now they were next to it, and had seen how difficult it was to get around on these small hills, they realized it was called a Mountain for a reason.

The open area was about twenty acres in size. It was surrounded by another hundred or so acres also level, but tree covered. The trees were established pines, so there wasn't much in the way of underbrush. They drove around the area and confirmed its size. As usual with pine needle covered forest floors the sound was deadened to the point that it had a feeling of being in church.

Marsha stopped the ATV, and they just enjoyed the lack of sound. They were far enough from any highway, they couldn't hear any traffic, and there wasn't much in this area anyway. At one point they could hear a small aircraft engine, in the distance, but it soon faded. They sat and enjoyed the environment for a while then moved back to the clearing.

Marsha stopped in the center of the clearing. She looked at Rick and asked, "When you first looked at the aerial photographs you mentioned observation posts on some of the hills. What are you thinking?"

"I was wondering when that shoe would drop," Rick replied. "My thoughts are twofold.

First a simple camera set up, which wouldn't be as visible as a camera at the front gate. It would be wireless with a battery power source. There would be a motion detector set up before it, to an alarm in the house, so we could see who was coming before they were in sight of the house. It would be set up for large sizes like a car. Living this far out I want to know who is coming up the drive way, especially after dark.

Secondly, and it's a distant second if it hit the fan, it would be handy to have firing positions away from the house.

"Do you think it will come to that?"

"If our living a long time happens like it is starting to look, then yes. When is a different question? Will the government collapse in the next ten years, probably not, in the next one hundred a good chance, in the next two hundred, without a doubt?"

"Historically, governments and nations change over time. Seldom have there been major changes without major upheavals. Marsha, as to the direction that this country or its successor will take, your guess is good as mine."

"What about England, they have been the same country for almost a thousand years."

"That is true but there have been many changes in the form of government from Cromwell to Kings by Devine Right to the current parliamentary systems, that does not count the Barons, the bloody additions of Wales, Scotland and Ireland, the loss of most of Ireland, the British Empire, and most of the British Commonwealth. The name may be the same, but that island has changed many times."

Marsha asked, "So trouble is coming from a historical viewpoint, but we don't know when."

"You got it hon. Look at it this way, based on not only history but the world as it is today; the United States is an outlier in the scheme of things."

"Well now, that is enough gloom and doom for today, where should we place our house?"

"Ah, on to the important things," Rick smiled.

"Yes," Marsha replied smiling sweetly. "You can't predict when the nation will come to an end; but if you don't get our house built, I can predict what will happen!"

"Yes ma'am, right away, ma'am!"

They both broke out laughing at this piece of nonsense. An onlooker who didn't know them would have guessed their ages to be in the early sixties or younger. As they continued their light banter, they drove around the area.

It became apparent that they'd miss the sunrise as they were right at the base of Hinch Mountain. Well, the sun would rise at their house around ten am. They decided this wouldn't be a problem for them, but they have to make certain any crops planted were far enough out to catch the morning sun.

The mountain itself made the placing of the house easy. There were two steep ridges about four hundred yards apart going east to west from the mountain. They'd place the house between them with the house facing south. The house would be offset in the pocket formed by the mountain and its ridges. The house was to be situated about one hundred yards from the northern ridge. This allowed maximum daylight to the front of the house.

Protected on three sides with a winding road to get to them wouldn't protect them from a professional assault but could make any amateur's life difficult. Rick had some ideas of how to make it even more difficult for the amateurs. If the professionals came, the events were predictable; scouting and an over whelming force. But then why would they bother?

The rest of July 2022 flew by. Their double-wide trailer was set in place and all the hook ups were made. Their furnishings were pulled out of storage and moved in. On August first, they were settled into their new temporary housing.

In the meantime, they interviewed several architects in Chattanooga. They settled on Smith & Evans. They had excellent references and had a catalog of previous homes that fit within what they had in mind. Rob Smith was the senior partner, and they got along with him and Charles Evans very well; even though 'Charlie' came across a little too liberal for Ricks taste.

The architects recommended Rebel Home Builders as their contractor. They had a long-term relationship with John

Mertz as a builder. In this case the son, John Jr. would be making it happen.

The house that was settled on, at least Marsha's idea of settled on, was five bedrooms, six and half baths, a large kitchen with a breakfast nook, formal dining room, living room, mud room, family room, library/office (Rick), sewing room (Marsha), the master suite included a walk-in closet with all built ins and under the house a full basement.

It would be two stories with a roofed porch around the front and west side of the building. A three-car garage attached to the east side of the house. The roof above the porch with an open balcony around the second floor, and bed rooms opening out onto the porch.

In front (south) of the garage an almost Olympic size heated swimming pool, fenced off with an outdoor kitchen area.

As Marsha reminded Rick, they were building a long term retreat. They had no idea when things or even if they would go bad, they had the money; worthless in the future, so she wanted to spend it on the house she wanted…Now! Rick had been around for over eighty years and he well understood superior logic.

Included in the plans were the black topping of the driveway, a new well, septic field, a solar farm and a five thousand square foot general-purpose metal building with a concrete floor. Even Rob Smith was a little shook up, when he presented the estimate of close to seven million dollars. That was a LOT of money for this area.

In private, Rick joked, “This will take us down to our last thirty-five million dollars.”

Marsha smiled and said, “Well, we will need new furniture.”

Rick just groaned, not at the money, but at the shopping. The groaning was just pro forma, Rick’s dirty little secret was that he enjoyed furniture shopping. So take away his man card, he was enjoying bringing their house together.

It was the end of August till they signed off on drawings and signed all the contracts. The estimated completion was late spring of 2023. Work was started immediately on upgrading the road to the property.

It didn’t take long to have the well drilled, tested, chlorinated, retested, re-chlorinated and finally passed. They were glad they weren’t depending on that well for their immediate needs. It took one day to drill the well and install the pump. It took another three weeks of flushing and re-chlorinating to have the water certified as potable.

The concrete pad for Ricks ‘shed’ was poured and the building was up before the end of the month. The shed was placed to the east of the house across from the garage entrances to limit the amount of blacktop needed. The general-purpose building had its own electrical service panels. Also included was a bathroom, plus a large sink of the mop bucket type. Rick made sure there was room next to the workbench for a refrigerator, microwave, and there was a small television viewing area set up. With a recliner in front of the TV, a man could make a strategic retreat from the house if needed.

The solar farm was put in place, and the batteries had their own small out building. The solar farm was ground mounted facing south and placed to the west of the house towards the back, almost at the base of the ridge. This gave maximum sunlight, and out of the line of sight for most of the house. The area was set up as two separate sets of one hundred panels each. The site quality was rated at 1145 so each field could produce almost 22, 000 kWh or almost more than twice their estimated annual usage. There were also two separate sets of batteries for redundancy.

The basement digging started immediately. Heavy equipment was brought in. When Rick saw the excavator, he knew he had to have one, why he wasn't sure, but had to have one. Maybe he didn't have to surrender his man card after all.

When he mentioned his desire to Marsha, she just shook her head and walked away. Rick thought he could hear mutters about, "Boys and their toys," but he wasn't about to go there.

Very shortly after the basement was started a major problem emerged, just three feet below the surface was a solid chunk of bedrock. The only way the basement could be dug was with explosives.

Marsha wanted a basement, and Rick was certainly going to give her, her wish. Besides he could help couldn't he? It was quickly made clear to Rick by the experts brought in, that while he may have blown-up people in Viet Nam, that didn't make him qualified to blow out a basement.

The first thing Rick learned was that they would be using water gel explosives not dynamite. They would be pumping the liquid slurry into bore holes. He did learn that he could obtain a license to use explosives and keep them, as long as he met the requirements of Federal Regulations in 27CFR Part 555 subpart K. Further research found that he could order a ready-made magazine set in place. They would even register it for him, and set him up with the required record keeping.

Rick was warned that since this was going to be a newly registered site, the ATF would most likely check it out quickly, followed by homeland security keeping an eye on him. Since he had no plans to do anything illegal as long as the laws of the United States of America were the law of the land, there was no problem.

Unfortunately, he saw a time coming where this might not hold true. In the meantime, he had a lot of tree stumps to remove and rock to penetrate. He decided this was important enough that he would proceed out of petty cash.

For a mere one hundred thousand dollars, he could be in business. Since Rick wasn't terminally stupid, the cost also included a class on safe usage and storage. The unit would be delivered in September, and the class the same month, so he had plenty of time to prepare Marsha for the good news.

## Chapter 21 – Rick's Misspent Youth – July 2022

In the meantime, things just kept getting better and better. The Kings received notice from the county that they had to clean out the drainage ditch beside the long road or the county would do it for them.

The cost would be twenty-five dollars per foot. Since their frontage was just about one mile long the cost would be about thirteen thousand dollars, or amortized in their property taxes for ten years it would increase their taxes by thirteen hundred dollars a year.

Or they could hire someone to dig it out for them, or do it themselves. Rick checked and found that the outside cost would be almost the same, except it would be due half up front and the rest on completion.

Or he could buy a used John Deere 2013 model 60G mini-excavator from Jack Nelson for fifteen thousand. The job would almost pay for it, and they would have it for future use, what could be better?

Rick made up a small presentation of his homework to Marsha.

She just about floored him when she asked, "What would a new one cost? That way, you wouldn't have to worry about any hidden problems."

It just so happened that Rick had that information. One should be prepared.

"We can get a comparable model new, for thirty thousand; they have gone up a lot in the last ten years."

"I still think you should buy a new one."

"Yes dear," Rick rushed to reply.

Marsha started laughing at him, "I knew this was coming ever since you said you wanted one, even though you didn't know what you would use it for. I have had a lot of time to think, new or used. It probably will need a heavier trailer to haul it. Then the question is will your truck pull the weight? I bet Jack has that International still sitting on his lot, you better check all that out. Don't want to under buy."

To say the least Rick was flabbergasted, "What have you done with Marsha," he asked?

It was her turn to laugh. "You have let me build the new house exactly how I have wanted, that is in the millions. Your equipment will not come to a quarter million, and it's not as though we don't have the money. Besides, I love you."

Rick hugged Marsha and replied the same, "I love you to, dear."

The next morning Rick was up early. He asked Marsha if she wanted to go with him to see Jack Nelson. She declined, saying she wanted to go through her boxes from

Burns & Burns. Rick asked her to take a look in his while she was at it, he hadn't any idea what might be there.

Rick didn't break the sound barrier on his way to Nelson's, but he did speed. Lucky for him the State Patrol was elsewhere. While Jack Nelson wanted to be neighborly and talk to who was rapidly becoming his best customer, Rick wanted to get the deal done. You would think that he was afraid Marsha might change her mind.

Rick's worries were for naught. She didn't call or come walking through the door. It was arranged to deliver his new truck, with trailer and excavator, in two weeks. The delay was getting a new excavator delivered to Nelsons.

When Rick got home, Marsha was waiting for him but the subject wasn't his newly purchased toys, eer, construction equipment needed for important projects on the farm.

"Rick, I didn't know that I was married to a hero," Marsha stated.

"Huh?" was Rick's brilliant reply.

"Your box from Burns and Burns contains the usual documents one collects throughout their lives. Your baptismal certificate, birth certificate, five expired passports, and your high school diploma are here. What are interesting are your Army records and medals. I didn't know what they all meant so I looked them up on the Internet."

"They were so impressive that I also did a search for Viet Nam and Rick King. I found out that you were one of the most decorated soldiers of that war. Your ending rank of Command Sergeant Major was the highest enlisted rank. I think that qualifies you as a hero."

"Marsha, all that happened a long time ago. Like everyone else, I was doing my job. I did long range patrols for most of that. It put me in interesting situations at the wrong time and places. Most of it was spent running for my life and trying to keep my squad alive."

"Put it another way I was unlucky to be there; and those that lived were very lucky. The flash backs have lessened over time, but I do remember the real heroes. The rank was what they gave me when they didn't know what else to do with me."

"Somehow, I think there is much more to the story than you are telling me. The only thing that matters is I now know that my man will take care of me to the best of his ability, and that ability is very impressive."

"Most husbands would do that."

"Yes, but you would do it better than most. Now I understand how you could handle that punk kid in Baltimore and robber in Chattanooga."

"Hitting people in the stomach isn't the stuff of heroes!"

“Having the reflexes and will to take those actions at the right time says a lot. However, I have just started to embarrass you, now let’s look at all the pictures that were in the boxes. You were cute as a child.”

“Oh God, will those pictures never go away?” Rick moaned.

That little trip down memory lane got Rick thinking about the old days. Not the fighting in Vietnam; that didn’t need to be remembered. He thought about how young and dumb he was in 1953 when he first joined. The army was a different place then.

His trainers were blooded in World War II and re-blooded in Korea. There was no such thing as political correctness or worrying about his self-image. The only worry his instructors had was how to keep these dumb fucks alive long enough to learn.

He had to know his equipment inside and out. It wasn’t high-tech and he would have laughed himself silly if he had to carry any battery’s other than D cells for his flashlight. The M-1 he carried was a World War II left over, and it shot just fine.

Later, when the fighting did start they introduced the M-16. It jammed a lot and was a bitch to keep clean. For a year, he forgot to carry it; instead he used a Winchester Model 12 shotgun.

This shotgun didn't have a trigger dis-connector so you could fire its six shells as fast as you could pump the action. Man could he pump that action when scared in combat.

A counseling session in training would be a trip behind the barracks. The army hadn't gone to a professional model yet, so there were many of life's misfits; bitter, scarred, drunken misfits. Rick learned very quickly to not get in a fight with these people. They killed many times and didn't really see a reason not to do so again.

Kipling understood these men. Before his career was finished Rick also understood them, and thanked God that he never became one. It was close several times.

By the time the first troops went into Vietnam on a combat basis Rick was as prepared as anyone could be. At least, he thought he was, as a young sergeant he thought he would have plenty of support. Then the draft got serious.

He had officers and troops that had been civilians ninety days previously. President Johnson prevented the call-up of experienced NCO's from the Army Reserve and National Guard units. He thought he would be a junior NCO being trained, instead he was the trainer. It didn't take long to become a Staff Sergeant.

Fighting the enemy at times seemed to be easy; at least, you could shoot them! How he managed to keep the drugs to a dull roar and his green as grass second lieutenants from being fragged he never knew, but he did it.

Since they were doing long range patrols, the unit lost men, but not on his watch. This was because of training, attention to detail, leadership (Rick hated to admit it, but he had been a good leader), and a butt load of luck. Anyone who had been in combat knew there was no answer to why him, why not me?

That luck expressed itself in several ways for Rick. While dinged up enough to rate Purple Hearts he had no disabilities. While he had seen people dismembered and mangled it didn't live with him. Most of all he didn't become one of those embittered soldiers who had no respect for themselves or life. He had been tested in the fire, and the slag burned away, but he remained strong.

That was probably why after the war in 1976, he was called to his commander's office at Fort Campbell. He was introduced to a one star general whose name was Robert King. His commander a two star named James Craig had his top kick set them up in a conference room.

When they were alone General King took off his jacket and took a sip of the coffee that had been provided.

"First of all, I would like to say Hello cousin."

This really puzzled Rick because he didn't have many cousins, and he thought he knew them all.

The look on his face must have reflected that because the General laughed. "Third cousin four times removed that is, let me start by saying you have permission to speak freely."

This really confused Rick, he had heard of second and even third cousins but third cousin four times removed?

"How do you figure that, Sir?"

"I didn't. A genealogist with the Society of Cincinnatus did," replied the General.

"We are both direct descendants of Rufus King. He was a signer of the Constitution of the United States. Most people think full members of the Order of Cincinnatus are all direct descendants of George Washington's officers. He and his direct descendants were elected as honorary members."

"Like the descendants of Washington's officer's only one member of the family who is a serving officer can be an active member of the Society at a time."

"I have heard of the Society," said Rick, "but I really don't know what it is or what it does."

"Simply put after the Revolution, Washington's officer's wanted to make him King. This would also put them in line for Noble titles. He forestalled this by creating the Society of Cincinnatus.

Cincinnatus was a Roman general who won the war then went back to his farm rather than be Emperor. How he sold that idea I have no idea, but he did."

"That probably was as pivotal moment in American history as any, but it is very little known. It is probably what set in place the loyalty of the military to the Constitution and not any party. One of the most notable achievements of the Society is its lobbying and getting reasonable retirement benefits for the military."

"Today I am here on another mission. You know as well as anyone that the Army is a huge mess. The public thinks the Army lost in Vietnam. We know that it was the Politicians who walked away due to public opinion."

"There is even the thought in some circles that public opinion was swayed by useful tools of the KGB. Only history will answer that one. The troops we have left are the dregs of the draftees. This is worse than the aftermath of most wars. You saw what was left after World War II and Korea, how would you rate the current troops against those?"

Rick thought for a moment, where the hell is he going? Well, he had permission to speak freely.

"Sir, those left after Korea met Kipling's description of Tommie's. These meet Wellington's definitions."

The General chuckled, "Well said."

"That brings us to the point of this meeting. Army Command recognizes this problem. The Army will be reorganized in the next decade; we have to rebuild it almost from scratch. The chain of command will have new layers built in. Things are simply too big as they are. We are also moving from a draft to an all-volunteer force. You saw the mess we were in for trained NCOs when Nam first started."

The General continued, "While never official the Army does use the resources of the Society. They asked them to find descendants of Washington's officers in the ranks. It is felt that they would be loyal to the bone. Once a list was built records were reviewed. Your name came up. That is why I was selected to approach you."

"We need people like you to start up a Noncommissioned Officers Education System, later there will be an advanced version and there is even talk of a Sergeant Majors Academy. Would you be interested? The only possible downside is that we would ask for a full thirty-year enlistment."

"I had planned on that anyway," said Rick, "I have twenty three in right now. Yes, I would be very interested in NCO training."

At this, the General stood up and held out his hand, he had made the sale,

"Your new orders will be cut immediately, Congratulations Sergeant Major King."

A very startled Rick King was able to pull himself together, shake hands and salute the General.

"Thank you Sir; and this promotion is more than I thought would ever happen."

"Here is my card cousin, if you ever need to talk you have permission to speak freely as a family member, just don't expect me to solve your problems. I don't think I would make a good NCO."

"Yes Sir and Thank You Sir, we people who work for a living are used to solving our own problems."

Both Rick and Robert cracked up at this time-honored NCO statement; it probably was considered an old saying in the Roman army.

As Rick flashed through those old memories, his thoughts were on how strong he was in those days, not only physically but mentally. Now, he was old and worn out. No sooner had he had that thought than he realized that it wasn't true. While he was not forty five anymore he did not feel his eighty seven years, he was getting stronger every day. Where would it end?

## Chapter 22 – Marsha's well spent youth – July 2022

While Rick was remembering his youth, Marsha was thinking of hers. She had to chuckle to herself. Today's definition of youth started at eighteen and went until the early sixties. Age gave a different perspective on things.

While certainly not as exciting as Rick's, it was rewarding. Starting as a teacher in 1957 was a lot different than today. While the school provided textbooks, each teacher got to flesh out their class. There was no standardized testing and no political or religious groups trying to take over the curriculum, other than the eternal argument between creation and evolution.

She continued her studies while teaching, so ended up with a PhD in Education. Part of this drive was to give meaning to her life after she lost her first child, and couldn't have more. This many years later, she still remembered her grief, but it was a distant memory to be brought out and thought about, rather than a dark grinding pain.

She and Max, her late husband were best friends. His earnings as a broker didn't make them rich, but did allow them to travel the world. They both were active in their professions. Neither had close family, so they kept their friends. Unfortunately, as time passed, friends either moved or died. After Max died in 2011, Marsha was left alone. She did well living by herself. She had a social circle of friends who all exercised at the YMCA doing water aerobics.

She and her friends went to lunch several times a week. For a while, they formed their own Red Hat club. It was fun going to the Inner Harbor in Baltimore on a weekday and getting tipsy; then shop the clearance racks at all the stores. The treasures found were saved for birthday and Christmas gifts for each other.

This went well until Alzheimer's raised its ugly head. This led to the entire fiasco with the Alzheimer's study and the HIV infection. Thank God she wasn't aware during these episodes.

Now like a miracle, she was aware, getting healthier and stronger all the time. It wasn't an all at once turn around. If she thought about how she felt three to six months previously there was a positive difference.

Now she had a husband she loved dearly and enough money that they should never want. What more could she ask for? One thing occurred to her. In her many conversations with Rick, they had discussed how far their bodies would retrogress.

Also, along with getting younger it seemed to be a healthier younger than their first time around. If that proved true could she have children? Only God knew, and she wasn't talking.

In the meantime, Marsha had found a project she could get into. At the diner Mary and she were talking one evening, and she learned that there was a local group of home schooler's that were having problems with the state because their curriculum didn't meet standards. This was right up her alley.

Within a month she had met with the group, after explaining her background, they asked for her help. There were four families involved. Marsha not only met the young mothers but their mothers, mothers in law and even several grandmothers.

This in turn led to her joining a card club and a group that home gardened, not that it was the time of the year to start a garden, but she would like to get a good start for the next year.

It only took her a couple of weeks work and a redesign of their home, so she would have an office of her own as her life calling was renewed. The state officials not only were pleased with her work, they asked if she would be interested in working with several other problem groups around the state.

Within six months, she became the go to person for home-schooling curriculum and student activity issues. She also made it very clear she wouldn't be involved with any religious or political problems. She didn't have the time, the expertise or the energy for these.

Marsha was also very involved in the design and construction of their new home. She was scouring the internet for furniture and decorating ideas. If she didn't do this, she would have to turn in her Woman Card! At the same time, she was investigating the economy and what was going to happen. The doomsday's crowd had been calling for the economic collapse of the world for many years. The can always got kicked down the road.

Marsha didn't see how this could continue with the Black Swan event that had occurred. The drug "Live" had changed too many equations. No government or central bank would be able to steer through these waters without big problems. They had been living in a house of cards, and now it would tumble down.

At her urging, she and Rick invested five million dollars in gold and silver. It was a mixture of coins, one-ounce gold eagles, one-ounce silver dollars and junk silver (US coins prior to 1965 were 90% silver, now called junk silver.) They arranged to take delivery at Jack Nelson's store.

The containers were labeled excavator attachments. Jack was a little put out they didn't order the attachments through him but took delivery, and called Rick when they were in.

Rick asked Jack when he could pick the boxes up, Jack told him he could pick them up any day, but that he wouldn't be there on Wednesday, but the store would be open. So of course Rick picked the cartons up on Wednesday.

Jack's yard helper loaded them into Rick's big IH pickup with a forklift. When Rick got back to the farm, he then had the question of what to do with their treasure. The age-old solution of pirates came to mind.

Rick dug a ten-foot deep hole with his excavator, lifted the cartons with the bucket; and then filled in the hole. He had dug out the sod first so was able to put the grass back. He thought about watering the grass to hide all evidence but then decided to park the excavator on top of the filled-in hole.

This should keep any human critters away from their treasury. While the house was being built, they were having a true vault installed. It would be built into the area where rock had to be blasted out, so should be very secure.

As Marsha reviewed all these thoughts, she also tried to sort out what was happening in the world in general. While the construction was proceeding, a national debate had started. People were now going to live a lot longer in excellent health. They would be essentially kept at their present age in good health until they reached around two hundred years then it was predicted that they would go down rapidly. The changes that society was about to undergo would be far reaching.

The life insurance industry's actuarial tables had just gone out the window. However, the industry wasn't rushing to change. When your policy was based on someone living to be eighty and they would now reach two hundred your profits would be sky high.

The regulatory agencies were trying to sort these out, but with all the state and federal hearings by a multitude of groups up to and including the U. S. Congress, there wouldn't be a quick regulatory resolution.

While the regulators dithered, the public was making decisions. They were dropping their life insurance policies. Forward looking insurance companies were rolling out products that involved accidents and the recovery from them.

The issue of Social Security was threatening to tear the country apart. There was no way that the system would support a person retiring at sixty five for this length of time.

There was also the reality that a person who was now eighty years old while in good health wouldn't be able to perform a labor type of job. How would the transition period be handled?

In the long run, retirement age would be set at one hundred and ninety years if the current predictions held true. This would support people in their final decline. Since they would be paying into the system for almost one hundred and seventy years, costs would go way down.

It was the transition period that was causing the debate. If someone had retired at sixty five recently would they be required to go back to work? It appeared there would be no easy answer to this question.

Then in one of those few times in American history when both branches of Congress were held by parties which could negotiate across the aisle and a reasonable President, the proposal came forward to dissolve the program completely.

The program that would replace it would care for those that weren't able to work. Age played into this. Those applying for this program would be required to take a full physical and if needed a mental evaluation.

The older one was the lower percent disability needed to be eligible. If one was one hundred years old, then twenty percent disabled would meet the requirements. At eighty, it required fifty percent disabled.

These requirements were harder than first glance. The population in general was much healthier. The Medicaid crisis was over. The program was simply dissolved. The largest hue and cry was from the dislocated bureaucrats and their unions.

It set off a game of musical chairs in the state and federal governments. The average state budgets went into the black for the first time this millennium. States like Texas were reducing taxes.

The lobbies that would have supported Social Security and Medicaid had their own problems. Those that pretended to lobby for Senior Citizens, but had turned into insurance companies were running out of funds.

The pharmaceutical industry had its own funding issues. Big Pharma was trying to change its business model from having patients take a medication for long periods of their life to creating medicines to correct genetic related problems.

Even this was tough sledding as 'Live' seemed to address these. Another field was antibiotics for the SAR's family.

SAR's which was related to the common cold kept mutating. It had a nasty turn in Saudi Arabia in 2014, which had spread throughout the mid-east. Strict travel control kept it contained, but at any time it could turn into a pandemic.

The only reason travel control worked for the mid-east was that the US had finally become self-sufficient on petroleum. Fracking had proven to be the solution. A sharply curbed EPA was forced by the executive branch to get out of the way.

The dire predictions of earthquakes, tap water burning and surges in cancer didn't occur at this point in time. What had occurred was an enormous strengthening of the US economy and its worldwide influence.

At the same time, the Middle Eastern oil rich sheiks were no longer rich. Their life styles were based on an ever increasing flow of money. When this flow stopped their power over their populations stopped. The diseased ridden, now poor countries quickly turned to radical Islam.

Meanwhile, the privacy intrusive programs of the NSA cut off the flow of funds from US Muslims to the middle-east. The hatred of the US didn't lessen in those areas but their ability to export terrorism was crippled.

Home-grown terrorism in the US had continued at the same levels for over ten years. As the population grew to realize that there were fewer deaths annually than from deer auto strikes or even bee stings they had less patience with TSA and other invaders of privacy. However, as surveillance technology advanced, it became less obvious so people ignored what they couldn't see.

The one issue that appeared to be heading for a quick resolution was the religious one. Some denominations felt that living to two hundred through an "Evil Drug" wasn't the Lords will. The U. S. Supreme Court was fast tracking a case.

Basically, it looked like separation of church and state would hold. They didn't have to take the drug, but they would live, work and retire under the same rules as everyone else.

The sharp stick in the eye for both liberals and conservatives was the issue of term limits. Prior to this death was a natural term limit. There would have to be changes, so society wouldn't become static. The question that had everyone befuddled was life time appointments to the court system, particularly the Supreme Court.

It would take revisions to the US Constitution to resolve the problems. One group wanted to do it by amendment, others by a Constitutional Convention. School was still out, whatever it was it wouldn't be pretty, as the worse on all sides was coming out.

Worldwide every conceivable option was playing out. The worst was in Nigeria where the Clerics where saying it was evil and don't take it, while supplying it to their families and followers. They used the same logic as they did on the Polio vaccine.

The environmental doomsday crowd was screaming from the roof tops about over-population. The strain on the world's resources would bring it all crashing down.

The economists were expressing concern that people living longer would change the requirement for having children to support you in your old age. Effectively, there would be no old age as such.

The Marketing people realized that with the demographics shifting that all their projections were out the window. They also had to face the fact as people currently reached retirement they didn't consume as they did in their child-rearing years. What would prolonged life do to the world's economy?

The entire health care industry was falling apart. At least the portion that took care of the aging. The young still thought they were invulnerable, and gangs still ran rampant in the cities, so trauma centers flourished while rest homes emptied out.

Pediatrics was still viable, but it was thought as time went by people would be in general more disease resistant. If nothing else they would have many more decades to build up resistance.

Another change in the country was college education. They priced themselves out of the market. Young people and their parents realized that the many trades; plumbing, sales, and the service industry didn't require a college degree. It became very apparent that the only degrees required were those that needed technical competence such as engineering and the medical profession.

The higher-education system was quickly reverting back to educating the technical professions or as a place for the upper classes to send their children to meet each other. In the last five years, fully half of the Universities and colleges had lost sixty percent of their enrollment. States were closing down facilities. Tenure didn't count for much when the entire school was closed.

The byproduct of these closings was less exposure to political ideology and the influence of the teachers unions. This in turn reduced resistance to the requirement that a teacher have an accredited degree in the field they were teaching in, rather than a teaching degree.

There was already discussion on dissolving the US Department of Education.

More and more jobs were being taken over by robots. Robots were becoming more sophisticated in the task they could perform and costs were dropping. This put pressure on the low and middle portions of the labor market.

This pressure accomplished what the completed border fences had not. The illegal immigration flow had almost stopped and there was a net outflow.

Those illegal immigrants in the country now had a means to become legal, but the only drawback was they would have to pay penalties and taxes! In most cases after the illegal immigrant families did a cost comparison, they realized that they were better off staying illegal or returning to their home countries.

If they didn't return to their countries on their own terms and were caught, they now would be deported quickly and at the mercy of their own country. They left their home countries because of the lack of mercy, better to return at night with a plan in place.

The best approximation was now three million illegal's in country and dropping. Some counties in various states would pay with bus fare with no questions asked, to an obscure Mexican border crossing, to make their way home.

The cost of the bus ride was more than paid for by reduced crime and welfare costs.

This was done very quietly, but since the illegals were requesting the trip, it wasn't breaking the law by the counties. However, the outcry of those wanting cheap labor or votes was horrendous, fruitless but horrendous.

Careers were a topic on everyone's mind. You would certainly have to love your job to do the same thing for over one hundred and fifty years! The national conversation on this issue was that people would work a job for thirty years while saving money for re-education and training for their next field of endeavor. A side effect of this would be more saving and less consuming.

The national economy was booming, and it looked like a long run was going to occur.  Those groups which believed in the social progressive movement had less influence, and it would get weaker. It was a good time to be a conservative. A newsletter from Baltimore, if read between the lines showed that all wasn't perfect.

The newsletter from the William Donald Schaefer Memorial Rest Home announced that this would be the last issue as the City of Baltimore was closing the home, as the last Alzheimer patient was released.

What wasn't said in the newsletter that while everyone released was now in good health, they were still functionally old and most had nowhere to go.

On a larger scale, the inner-city slums were a time bomb. They still had no jobs; they weren't qualified for those that did exist. Drugs were still endemic, and the conservatives were in power.

There was talk of 'welfare reform' on a massive scale. This played well on conservative radio, until one took into account the costs in the short term of human lives. Breaking the dependency cycle seemed like a good thing to everyone except progressives and those who were dependent.

Progressives were not concerned about the people; it was their votes that counted. The people were just that, people and deserved better from the country that had created their condition.

Again, the talk shows had no mercy on the inner city 'Culture'. They seemed to forget if you isolated a population, they would generate their own culture. It happened in small farm towns, football teams, choirs and prisons. It was human nature.

If you created the conditions for the culture to exist were you not responsible for the culture? The easy out was to say, the other political party created this mess. The truth is the people of the nation voted.

All of this left Marsha unsettled. The question wasn't, would the wheels fall off. It was when.

## Chapter 23 – Settling In – July 2022 to August 2023

The next two weeks went by in a flash. The Rebel Home Builder's subcontracted crew cut and laid a rough road to the new house construction site. Test holes were dug at the construction site to establish exactly how far the bedrock extended.

The test did provide relief on one issue. It turned out that by shifting the proposed home site twenty yards north most of the basement could be dug out instead of blasted. One of the architect's concerns had been having the basement in a bowl blasted out of rock. This would have given drainage issues. There still would be a sump pump but it could be a standard pump, rather than one used for Alaskan gold mining.

The contractors were surprised when an independent crew came to install the safe vault, but they didn't ask many questions. This was good because Rick and Marsha weren't going to give many answers. It was obvious that it would hold items of great value, but they gave no hint of what it would be. If the workers knew what was buried under that excavator, there would be a hole in the yard in minutes.

The construction of the house took on a rhythm of its own for the next ten months. While Rick and Marsha paid attention to the details, they didn't make pests of themselves or let it consume their lives. They made many trips to Chattanooga looking for furniture and decorating ideas. Though he grumbled, Rick actually enjoyed this as it gave them a mission. It was a mission that bonded them ever closer together as they discussed their likes and dislikes.

Fortunately, their taste in design was very similar, but not surprising as they both came from a Middle American background of a conservative time. Even in something as simple as appliance colors they had common memories. The avocado green of the 1970's which was so chic then was now a cause for laughter.

This led to other old fads. When Rick found out that Marsha wore a mini-dress and Go-Go boots in the late 1960's he got all excited. That was one fashion that never should have gone out of style, at least according to Rick.

Rick also got to try out his new excavator on the ditch beside his property. It was fun and manly for the first quarter mile then it became mainly work, the last half mile was just work. He did get to meet people as they drove down the road. They waved the first time they saw him, the next time they would stop and introduce them-selves, and asked how much he charged. He counter offered, if they filled the tank, they could borrow the infernal device.

Only one person took him up on his offer, Paul Kettler, who owned the property on the other side of the road. He had his son Paul Michael do the work! It turned out Mary who worked at the diner was Paul's wife.

They began to settle into their new area. It seemed strange to say they were going into town, and the town was little Pikeville. Going to the city was Chattanooga. The local newspaper was the Chattanooga news which very seldom covered news from Pikeville. Maybe it was because so little happened in Pikeville.

The most reliable source for events was Mary at the diner. It was from her where they heard about the fireman's carnival. It was the local volunteer fire department's annual fund raiser.

They went to town the next Saturday to attend the carnival. They had never been to any small-town events, so didn't know what to expect. The first person they ran into was Hope their realtor. She almost ran to catch up with them.

"Hello there, it's nice to see you out enjoying yourselves. Everyone is talking about your house Marsha. I hear it is really going to be nice."

"Hello Hope," replied Marsha, "we have given it a lot of thought. It is going to be my dream house."

"Tell me all about it."

Rick left the two talking about the house and wandered the small area of the carnival. There were about eight rides, and ten games to take your money. Rick saw the town had an information booth in case someone didn't know what was going on locally.

He thought they could just have a sign up saying, "See Mary at the diner." Local clubs were selling fried chicken and catfish. The fire department had a hamburger and hot dog stand. They were also selling raffle tickets.

Rick wandered over see what was being raffled. It was an old Browning 725 Citori Grade 5 shotgun. The walnut stock was the most beautiful he had ever seen. He bought twenty of the twenty five dollar tickets.

As he was paying cash a voice behind him said, "You must really want that gun." Rick turned and saw from his uniform the local Fire Chief.

"Yeah it would be nice to have."

"Well good luck. We really need the money, but I don't think this will even save us."

"How so," asked Rick?

"The state has raised the standards for fire departments. We need to acquire another front line fire engine and replace our tanker. We also need a new brush truck and rescue unit. I don't see how we can ever raise that much cash; even buying used it will be close to six hundred thousand dollars.

If we don't do that we will lose our certification and local insurance rates will go through the roof. If it goes on too long the State Fire Marshal will pull our charter and not let us respond to fires."

"How much are you short?" Rick inquired.

"We have a little over two hundred thousand, so we need to raise four hundred, I just don't see it." The Chief chuckled and asked, "You don't happen to have a spare half million do you?"

Rick made a deal of pulling an empty pocket and showing he had no change."

"Well it didn't hurt to ask."

"No it didn't, you never know what might come through. By the way, I'm Rick King."

The Chief held out his hand and replied, Mathew Johnson, call me Matt."

"Nice to meet you Matt, now I had better find my wife."

"Okay and good luck on that shotgun."

"Thanks."

Marsha and Hope were right where he had left them, still talking about the house. He stood there for a minute, and they finally wound down.

He asked Hope, “I hear the fire department has a real problem.”

“Yes they do, with the new regulations it is going to put us into the status of an unprotected region. We may not even be able to get insurance on our properties.”

“What is going on?” asked Marsha.  Hope and Rick brought her up to speed.

Marsha looked at Rick and he just gave her a small nod.

“I agree, let’s go find the Fire Chief,” she said.

“How do you think we should do this?” Rick asked.

“There is not a snow ball’s chance of doing this anonymously in a town of this size. Let’s just write a check and count it as a tax deduction.”

Hope had been listening to this exchange looked back and forth, “Are you talking about donating a large sum to the fire department?”

“Yes, but let us write the check and get on our way before you spread the news.”

“I promise I will tell only one person.”

Rick and Marsha started to laugh so hard they had trouble standing straight, "Your Aunt Mary," wheezed Rick.

Hope grinned and said, "Yep, this will put me up on her in the big time gossip contest around here."

"Let's go see the Chief together." They had no trouble finding the Fire Chief. He hadn't moved ten feet. They waited for him to finish his conversation.

"Matt I would like you to meet my wife, Marsha."

"It's nice to meet you, Ma'am and hello Hope."

"It's nice to meet you Chief," replied Marsha.

"Matt would you believe that I asked Marsha if she had a spare half million in her purse, she said no, but she does have her checkbook with her."

The Chief didn't appear to comprehend what was being said. "Well, anything you can afford will be appreciated. We have decided if we cannot raise the whole amount we will return what has been raised."

"Chief is there somewhere we can go to be private for a few minutes."

"Sure my office is right here." Since the carnival was being held in the field next to the fire station, it was a short walk.

“Rick, do you mind if I ask how much you are planning on donating?”

Rick realized that the Fire Chief didn’t understand what he had been trying to say.

“Marsha and I would like to make up the short fall with a little cushion. You asked for half a million, that is what we would like to donate.”

The Chief stopped dead, now his mouth was open, but no words were coming out. After several tries, he said, “You had not better be joking, my heart wouldn’t take it.”

“They have it,” Hope replied.

“We intend to live here for many years. This is just an investment to keep it a decent place to live. Besides our tax accountant has been on us for not giving any charitable donations.”

This was not really a true statement by Rick, but it seemed to ease the look on the Chiefs face. The real joke was on Rick, because the next time he talked to their accountant, he was asked if they had given thought to some serious charitable donations as it would help their tax position.

When they reached the Chiefs office, Marsha quickly wrote out the check.

Marsha told the Chief, "We know this will get out quickly, but we really don't want to make a big deal of this, if we could do it anonymously we would."

"Would you be our guests of honor at our Christmas dance? We should have the apparatus in place by then. We will present you with a plaque, and that would be it."

"Sounds good," replied Rick.

"Now Hope, you had better find your Aunt Mary before you burst. Just give us a few minutes to get to our car."

The Chief whose grin couldn't get any bigger just nodded his head, "That will spread the news. I need to round up my crew and let them know the good news; this is going to turn into the biggest party this town has ever seen."

The Chief waved the check and said. "In the meantime, I had better lock this up. Will it be okay if we deposit it come Monday?"

"No problem," said Marsha.  They went their separate ways. Rick and Marsha were heading for their car.

"Well that was a quick trip Marsha."

"Yes it was, but I think we've done the right thing."

"Now of course, every group in town will think we owe them funding."

"They will find out differently soon enough," Marsha replied.

"Do you think we were a little impulsive?" asked Rick.

"Most definitely, but at the same time we can afford it. Rick I know you don't pay as much attention to our portfolio as I do. Do you realize that we have almost as much money as when we started?"

"What," a startled Rick replied.

"The market is in the middle of another bubble, and we made the right picks."

"Marsha, you made the right picks. I just listened to your ideas and said go with them."

"You listened," she said as she held his arm.

"Be silly not to, you are the one that is paying attention to our finances."

"I got that from my late husband, he was very good at stocks. We just never had enough money to get really serious returns."

"Well you are apparently getting them now. At the same time, what you are saying is a concern. When will this bubble collapse? I guess I am glad we just spent a bunch on real things. We will benefit one way or the other, from having a good fire department. I wonder what else we should support."

"Why don't we sleep on it and talk about it tomorrow?" said Marsha.

Just as they were entering the parking lot, Major Watkins from the survival place got out of his car and approached them.

"Hi folks, I was hoping to see you today. Rick, you still need to visit The Farm."

Rick could hear the capital letters in the way Watkins said The Farm. Did he think he was the CIA or something?

"To tell you the truth I had forgotten about your invitation. When would be a good time to come out?" Rick asked.

"Any day, but Sunday and Monday this week would be good. We get our weekend warriors on Sunday, and then are down on Monday. It gets kind of hectic Sunday, and I wouldn't have time to show you around."

As Rick and Marsha proceeded to their car she said, "I still don't like him, he says the right words, but I just don't believe them."

Rick took her hand as they were walking and replied, "I agree, but I think I had better go over there and see what they are capable of.

"That's true dear, but you know what I mean."

Rick sobered up, "Yes I do, guys with weapons and a wanna be attitude are always dangerous, if only to themselves. That guy tries to look tough like he has been there and done that. If you have really been there and done that, it is the last thing you want to look like."

As they reached their vehicle Rick held the door for Marsha and said, "It is really weird I feel younger and better than I felt six months ago, and looking back a year it is incredible. I am supposed to be late eighties, and I feel late sixties.

Marsha thought for a moment, "I feel the same. I wonder where this will end."

Rick snorted, "If it ends."

## Chapter 24 – The Farm - August 2023

Between the finishing of their house, moving in and getting over the row caused by the explosive magazine showing up, it was late summer before Rick could go out to The Farm.

The fight over the magazine wasn't really that bad, Rick had just forgot to tell Marsha he had ordered it, and he had been running some errands when it arrived.

For some reason having, five hundred pounds of high explosives show up on the door step of her new home irritated Marsha. She didn't scream and cry. She was a cold straight talker. For the first time in a long-time Rick felt real fear.

After a week of little conversation, they finally cleared the air. It was actually Marsha's survivalist mind frame, which was the breakthrough.

When Rick explained his credentials from the military; and his plans to overstate his use, so it would end up off inventory she saw the light. Before it was over, she wanted to go out and blow up stumps! He did make a resolve not to surprise her again.

He didn't, at least not for a month or so.

He had received an email from his truck that it needed an oil change. Rather than letting it drive itself in, he took it into Pikeville and from there went onto the Farm. Rick would always think of it as The Farm. He had called ahead so he was expected. He was mildly surprised when he turned off the main road and went a quarter mile down the drive.

There was a manned checkpoint. It had a lane of jersey barriers to funnel traffic and slow it down into the checkpoint. There was a barricade to be raised to get past the checkpoint. There were three guards, as he pulled to a stop, he was asked for his name and identification. While one guard examined his driver's license another was putting a mirror on a pole under his car.

He noticed the third guard was to the rear of the truck on the passenger side with a clear field of fire. All were armed with an AR15 variant. The stop was quick, clean and professional. It also brought Rick's antenna up. This operation was more serious than he thought.

He was waved through to the main compound. There the Major was waiting. Watkins was genial in his greeting and said, "Welcome to our compound Sergeant!"

Ricks surprise at this knowledge of his past appeared on his face. "Well now, Major you have been doing some homework."

"Not a lot really, you appeared on a list from Viet Nam as a Staff Sergeant, nothing about your career or even MOS."

Thinking on his feet, Rick replied, "I was a company headquarters clerk, paper pusher supreme.

The Major grimaced a little and said, "There is always a need for paper pushers."

He continued, "We are always looking for recruits for our operation." As he talked, he started to show Rick around. Rick was again taken aback by the number of shops and barracks on the property. The firing range said it all to him.

It was as good as any he had seen in the army and better than most. Of course that was comparing to what was current to when he was in. Who knew what fancy gadgets they had these days? It didn't matter, this was a good place to train troops. As he was thinking that a squad went double timing by.

"Wow you guys are serious; this isn't a weekend warrior get away. It is a real troop training facility."

"I am glad you realize that Rick. I know you are in your eighties, but it is a very fit eighty. We could use a professional paper pusher. Your rank would be Staff Sergeant just like the old days."

Rick attempted a joke, "What's the pay?" The Major laughed and said, "Well we would only charge you a thousand a month. Officers have to pay two thousand for a Lieutenant, up to five thousand for a Major.

So far, I am the only one, but if we get more people I am going to promote myself to light bird and charge myself seven grand a month."

Watkins continued, "It cost a lot to maintain this level of an organization." As he was saying this, they went into a large pole barn structure. There were half a dozen technical vehicles parked there.

A technical vehicle is a truck (Toyota being the world's favorite) that had been armored up, and weapons mounted. Each of these had a pintle in the back for mounting a belt-fed machine gun. They looked like they could take fifty calibers.

Rick whistled, "It just keeps getting better and better. You have the Federal licenses for this?"

“Yes we do. The weapons are kept in the armory. We can field a force of two hundred men on four hours’ notice. With this as backup there isn’t anything in this area that can stand up to us.”

“Now that brings up to the real question, what is the purpose of this force?”

“Rick, you know as well as I do the United States is going to fall apart. When it does we want to control our fate. We will be the power in the area, and people will do what we want.”

“It’s good to be King,” replied Rick.

“You do get it, as part of this you can keep that nice new house you just built and be one of the powers of this area.”

“Sounds attractive,” replied Rick, “can I have some time to think it over or is this join or die.”

The Major gave him a dirty look, “We don’t reach that stage until it hits the fan.”

“Okay I see what you have in mind, and I could play a good supporting role. Let me talk it over with my wife, and I will let you know within a week or so.”

Don’t take too long we only want the committed.”

“I won’t I just need to think it over.”

Rick was really thinking, "*not only no, but hell no, but it wouldn't be really smart to tell him that right now. I will try to think up a good reason to say no later.*"

"Major Watkins I thank you for the tour and the opportunity. I won't take up any more of your time."

The Major said in a hard voice, "Rick I am glad you stopped by. I think you will reach the right decision. Your future may depend on it when things go south."

Rick couldn't get out of there fast enough. This was going to be trouble in the future, big trouble. When he got home and described the visit to Marsha, she also was concerned. They decided not to panic, but to think about it for several days and then revisit the issue.

That Saturday they discussed his Tuesday visit to The Farm. They had both come to the conclusion that this needed to be brought to the attention of the authorities. The following Monday Rick called the FBI office in Chattanooga.

The agent he was connected to was very familiar with Major Watkin's group. They had investigated and found they had no plans against the United States of America. They also had the proper Federal licenses for all weapons.

Rick got the impression the group had been infiltrated as part of the FBI process of checking them out.

The group which Rick learned for the first time was called Watkin's Rangers would only come into play if the United States ceased to exist as such. This wouldn't be against the law because there would be no law!

The FBI appreciated his call but there was nothing they could do under the circumstances. The FBI agent while entirely professional left Rick with the feeling that he was being talked down to.

After that phone call, Rick and Marsha tried to figure out a story for the Major as to why Rick couldn't join them. The problem was taken out of their hands when Rick received a call from the Major.

The call was short and to the point. "I hear you have been talking to the FBI. I guess you have made your decision. Don't come to us for help later. When we save the area after the breakdown you will be taxed appropriately."

The FBI agent had implied infiltration, now Rick understood who had been infiltrated. He didn't think it was a government plot, just a sympathizer in the local FBI office. From the attitude expressed, Rick would bet it was the agent he had talked to.

Marsha was very upset, but Rick was very calm about the whole call. When Marsha asked him why he didn't appear bothered he replied.

"He just changed the game from personal politics to another form of politics which I am very good at."

“What is that,” asked Marsha.

To paraphrase Von Clausewitz, “War is a continuation of politics. I am very good at war. There is nothing overt to be done now, but there are some things I can do to help later.”

“Such as,” Marsha inquired.

“The first thing I need to do is to get up to date on scouting technology. Night-vision devices, long distant cameras to name some, I need to scout their little farm out before I decide anything.”

“You may be getting in better shape all the time, but you are still an old man. Don’t think you are Rambo.”

“Yes dear,” replied one of the soldiers that John Rambo was based on.

Marsha was smart enough not to push that issue, but did ask him how he was going to find out about the latest technology.

“Since the FBI seems to be on his side, I am going to do it very quietly. I have been thinking for some time that a false identity would be useful.”

How do you go about that, meet some guy in a dark alley?”

“I guess that would be one way. What I was thinking was to find an infant that died very shortly after birth about fifty-five years ago, one that had only lived a couple of days at the most; so that a social security number wouldn't have been issued then obtain a copy of the birth certificate."

"Once I had the birth certificate, I would fake letters from two Doctors and the parents saying the child had been institutionalized its whole life, so it never had a social security number issued. Now that the parents were of an advanced age they were doing estate planning, so needed a social security number issued.

With the 'Doctors' supporting letters, this should occur. Next is an address. It will have to be in a part of Chattanooga where cash talks loudest. A long term motel that is just a step above homeless will serve. With an address, social security number I can get a driver's license.

Now I will be able to obtain a prepaid credit card and open a checking account. With these in place, I can rent an apartment at a better address. From there I can obtain utilities, especially Internet service.

I will also want a dead drop mail box for things like Soldier of Fortune magazine, which will have articles and advertisement for the latest toys available."

Marsha thought for a moment, "I only see one thing that you have forgotten."

"What's that?"

"I will need the same."

"Why?"

"We are looking younger and younger; it is getting past the 'Live drug' explanation. I don't want to end up as a lab rat, do you?"

"I never thought of that, you are right. I will get right on it."

It took Rick the rest of the year to make it happen, but at the end of the time they had two fairly solid identities that would stand up to most investigations. Unless someone noticed that death certificates were issued.

This shouldn't happen as none of the states or the federal government had yet started matching birth certificates with death certificates.

They rented an apartment in Chattanooga, which had a nice side benefit, when they wanted to spend a night in town they had a place to stay and did not have to haul clothes back and forth. They had rented a town house, with two garages because they had bought a car in Rick's new persona.

They would park their 'country' car in the garage and drive their 'town' car. They had ended up buying new wardrobes, which were younger and more upscale than what they wore in the country.

When they stayed in town for the weekend, they would attend a show either on screen or live and go out to dinner. Marsha even talked Rick into taking weekend ballroom dancing classes. They were polite to their neighbors, but didn't try to make friends.

Rick started the process of learning what was new in the military scouting world. He found it amazing. If they had this equipment back in the day, it would have been a walk over in Viet Nam. They had been winning the war when the country lost its political will; the war would have been over before the will was lost.

He also started exercising again. No fancy machines, just pushups, setups, pull ups and running. He was feeling better than he had in forty years. Marsha joined him after several weeks. Soon she could keep up on everything but the running.

Marsha could do several miles. Rick could do many miles. They both became more fit and looked younger all the time. Their skin had started to regain its tone and wasn't sagging with age.

While Rick was investigating and buying night-vision gear, Marsha was setting up a second financial plan. If they had to abandon their real identities, they would have reserves in place to continue.

They wouldn't be poor and on the run. Just on the run! They were spending money like there was no tomorrow but the economy was in a bubble, and they were making it as fast as they could spend it.

## Chapter 25 – The Farm April 2024

It took longer than he had thought, but Rick was ready to return to The Farm to establish its strengths and weaknesses, to find out what its real manning was and what its military capabilities were.

Ricks investigation led him to check out their web site. They made no bones about it; they were building a force to control the local area if the United States government fell. If it didn't fall, then they would take no action.

From the comments made by the site's visitors, and the blog run by the Major; Rick wanted no part of their plans. He spent a lot of time looking at topology maps of the region. He had identified a small pass through the mountain that backed up to the Farm. He was considering the logistics of getting there when he hit himself on the forehead.

If going through that pass was the back entrance to the Farm, then the Major would have it under surveillance. As soon as he thought that, it occurred to him that others like the FBI might be watching also.

From there he made the leap that the new technology he had been reading about might be in use. An aerostat balloon kept on station would keep track of a large area. It would hold all the infrared devices and light enhancers needed and would broadcast them to a ground crew.

It would be almost automatic with computers separating out false-positive alarms like deer crossing a trail. Only when there was real human movement would anyone have to review the data. A simple check on the FAA's website for the NOTAMS for the Tennessee Region showed a notice about a 'weather' balloon stationed at ten thousand feet above the Farm.

It didn't matter to Rick if the balloon was spying on the Farm or looking for intruders. It was an obstacle that had to be avoided. It also showed that whatever was going on was very high level.

Now how to go into an area that was under continuous automatic surveillance day and night? He would need to hide his heat signature, also be camouflaged from the air and ground. It would be a slow and arduous approach. His movement would have to be at night. It would help if it were during a period of heavy rain.

This would help hide heat and make his movement harder to detect. With branches and rain, blowing everywhere no pattern interpretation software would catch him if his movements were random enough.

Then a horrid thought occurred to him, what if besides the aerial surveillance, they had cameras on the ground? They were so small these days you would never see them. One man without professional support couldn't do it.

It was a shame he couldn't tap into the feed from the aerostat. Even if he could it would be encrypted. He wasn't even certain which agency was receiving the intelligence take.

The FAA website showed the aerostat belonged to Homeland Security. He reached a dead end after that. He had no way of knowing where the satellite uplink was feeding much less a way to get into the facility.

He expressed his frustration over this dead end to Marsha. It would really be easier if he could get someone else to do the work.

Marsha said, "Rick there may be a way to find out more about the satellite feed. I remember a story from a neighbor who did quality audits to the ISO 9001 standards. He had audited a place that bought satellite band width for the government. The government is required to put out everything to bid.

She continued, "But it is too much to bid on immediate needs, like communication bandwidth. The government let companies bid on the right to place all the bandwidth requests. An agency would contact this company, and they would then find the least-expensive commercial satellite time available for that uplink and downlink."

"So that means I have to find the company that won the right to provide communications. Then establish who they gave the order to; and also find out where the downlink went. Then penetrate the agency receiving the feed."

"That's right Rick," she replied.

"I have a headache all of a sudden," Rick said.

"And I have just the cure," Marsha replied, as she tugged him in the direction of their bedroom.

The next-day Rick was having his morning coffee when a light bulb went off. He checked the Homeland Security Web site. There they proudly told how they were keeping America safe by spying on Americans. One of their projects involved an Aerostat stationed in the Tennessee Valley for the FBI.

"It can't be this easy, can it?" thought Rick. His next stop was the FBI website to look at where their infrastructure was located. He found that the Washington field office is where all satellite communications were sent. This wasn't the headquarters but still the second largest FBI center.

However, he doubted that the take was evaluated there. He found out there was a resident field office in Chattanooga.

This was the office he had talked to. He bet it would be going there, but how to access it?

He decided to check out the field office on Chestnut Street in Chattanooga. It turned out to be in an office building on the fifth floor. Since he wasn't a cat burglar, or for that matter, any sort of a burglar, there was no way he could get inside by breaking in. As far as a Mission Impossible scenario it wasn't on the books.

Brain storming with Marsha, they came up with trying to get at the backup disc for the satellite take. That idea went nowhere real quick. First of all, they wouldn't be backed up in Chattanooga, but at Washington, or some Homeland Security site. Even if they could get at them what software would be needed to run it?

In their session, Marsha asked, "Rick, remind me what is the objective?"

"The ultimate objective is to prevent the Major from taking over this area if things go bad."

"And you are going to do this how?"

"I would destroy his weapon stock pile."

"How are you going to destroy it?"

"With explosives of course, where are you going with this Marsha?"

So you want to scout the place to find out so later you can go back and blow his stuff up?"

"Yes," replied Rick.

"But you know where he keeps his weapons, he showed you the building that contains the armory and his technical trucks," she inquired.

"Yes I do but I have to be able to get in to plant the explosives."

Why not just bomb the place?"

"Uh, I don't have a bomber?"

"Rick, think for a minute, things have changed, how hard would it be to obtain a Drone that could deliver several hundred pounds?"

Rick got a stunned look on his face. He then grabbed Marsha and gave her hug and a kiss. The hug and kiss went on and on, and the outcome was predictable. For some reason, as time went on their love life was getting more frequent and passionate, not like the monthly get-together of almost ninety year olds.

Later, Rick told Marsha that her thinking was brilliant. The target was identified; he just needed a delivery system. He was boots on the ground Army, not one of those Air Force fly boys! He had nothing against them. They certainly saved his life in Nam enough times.

He just didn't think like that. If they could blow up the Major's weapon stockpile, it may not stop him completely, but it would be a severe setback. It would also change the equation with the Feds, whatever that equation was; the Major wouldn't be bringing anything to the party.

If they were against him, they could use the excuse of the explosions to shut him down. If they were for him, they would have to question why they should continue to support him.

If he could get a Drone to work it would really set the cat amongst the pigeons. Marsha was right, Drones were available now, but the ones large enough to carry the payload he would need were still thought of, as organizational vehicles. The Major and the FBI would go nuts trying to find out the group that was after him. This could be fun!

Again, the internet proved its usefulness. He identified the CG-10C Snow goose as the perfect vehicle. It was manufactured by MMIST in Canada. It would haul a six hundred-pound payload two hundred miles. Designed as a UAV to deliver battlefield supplies, it would be perfect for his needs.

In a pinch, it could be operated by one person. It took off from the ground and could be transported in a pickup truck. MMIST was up to a Model F now, and the Model C's had been sold as surplus to other country's militaries, or companies, which worked in remote areas with no landing fields.

Now the question was; how to obtain one, learn to fly it, use it and leave no tracks. The leave no tracks was the hard part. When that bird exploded there would be parts everywhere. The parts would have serial numbers on them. While most would be destroyed beyond legibility, there would be some that could be read.

The FBI was good at that sort of stuff. A serial number on the axle of the truck Timothy McVeigh used was enough to put the puzzle together. So he had to buy the device in a way that couldn't be connected to him.

Once he had it he had to know how to fly it. Rick didn't think that he could do that by reading the manual. He and Marsha had several long conversations on this issue. They settled on two main points, find someone to buy it for him, and buy two of the CG-10C's.

He planned buy one through a false buyer, the exploding bird or EB as it came to be called. The second would be used to learn with, it would legal, traceable and there when and if the FBI came knocking.

They considered who they could get to be the front man in buying the EB. Marsha suggested mercenaries and then they could kill them afterwards.

Rick laughed for a minute and then got a serious look on his face.

“Marsha we don’t want to be around when the killing starts.”

“I was just kidding.”

“I know dear, but that came awful close to kidding on the square.”

“What’s kidding on the square mean?”

It means you are kidding, but that you also mean it.”

“Oh, no I was just kidding, if this was a story, I might mean it, but not in real life.”

“No big deal, for a second I thought you meant it. I would do it if it was a last resort but only as a last resort.”

“So who can we hire that we won’t have to kill,” asked Marsha?

Rick thought and came up with, “How about someone who wants to leave the United States forever? Say from South America who wants to go home but who doesn’t have the money?”

Marsha quickly came back with, “I bet we could find someone like that at the Mission in Chattanooga. We would just be hiring them to pick up the EB, that isn’t illegal in its self, once they leave the country it is doubtful they would even hear about the event much less put it together that they had  a part in it.

Rick and Marsha spent the next month volunteering at the Mission in Chattanooga. They didn't try to force the issue. They helped in the soup kitchen and where ever they were needed. They did look and listen to what was going on.

They finally identified a candidate, Carlos Alberto Cortez. He had come from Columbia and actually had a green card. What he didn't have was the intelligence to hold a good job. His wife's family had helped them come to the United States, but she had died. He couldn't carry his weight in the family business, so they let him go.

He had two small children, and he was desperate to take them back to Columbia to his family support system. He was hard working and honest. They checked and found he had a modest apartment and that the children were well fed, and cared for by a cousin while he worked odd jobs.

He seemed to be a perfect fit for what they needed.

## Chapter 26 – Didn't Expect This - April 2024

In the meantime, Rick got a phone call from the Fire Chief. He asked if he could stop by and talk to Rick. Rick said yes, but hold for a moment. Rick and Marsha quickly talked it over and figured that the Chief would be hitting them up for more money. They would listen. They invited him out for coffee late Saturday morning.

When Chief Johnson got to their house, they went out on the veranda since it was such a nice spring day. Marsha had set up a coffee service with some sweet rolls on the side. They were very surprised when Chief Matt Johnson had an entirely different agenda.

“Folks we have the equipment on order, and most of it will be here in the next month. I must tell you, while you want to remain anonymous people have figured it out, and the word has spread. Telling Mary ended any chance of being unknown.

That being said, everyone will be pretending they don’t know it’s you. You have a lot of good will built up around here. That is all except one fellow, and that’s what I want to talk about.”

“Who do you mean,” asked Rick?

“That Major Watkins isn’t very happy with you; it seems you asked the FBI about him.”

Rick and Marsha were both disconcerted to hear this. “Where did you hear that,” Rick questioned?

“As I said word gets around out here. One of the fellows who is employed as a farm hand at The Farm dates a local girl, he told her and it went from there. Now don’t get me wrong, that Major guy scares all of us. That is what I want to talk about.”

Rick and Marsha exchanged looks.

“Go ahead,” said Rick.

"We are concerned first with the country. Any fool can see we have gone too far down the debt path, and have over half the country on some sort of welfare. This can't have a good end. I know it has been said for the last fifteen years, but someday it will collapse. That's when our second fear comes into play.

It's the Major and his announced plans to take over the area once the country collapses. You aren't the only one who has gone to the authorities and been rebuffed. They say he has broken no laws yet, and if he does after the country is gone, it isn't their problem. Damn fools."

"What are you proposing, putting together your own armed force," asked Marsha.

"That is part of the plan but only a small part. We have a small working group right now, the Sheriff, a Judge, a County Commissioner and me.

Rick we would like you to join us."

"Doing what?"

"We are a Disaster Planning group. If all outside help was cut off what would it take for this area to survive? We know that there is FMEA and the State Agencies with their County extensions. However, they only look at short-term problems. Like a month-long power outage. We are thinking of no power available from the outside, ever. Along with that is food, health care and yes, local defense."

“We figure we need to have on hand almost a year’s worth of food for the valley. There are around nine thousand people living here. We know families will return home if they can, so it will be more like fifteen thousand, we will need to feed before crops come in. Now, this is a worse case, but that is what we are looking at.”

Marsha said, “That sounds like a lot of food.”

“It is. We have to plan on two hundred fifty pounds of flour per person. That works out to almost two thousand tons! Meat fifteen hundred tons, sugar or honey four hundred and fifty tons, salt, thirty tons, vegetables and fruits over five thousand tons. The only problem we don’t have is water. That is based on FDA numbers.”

“Have any idea of the costs involved,” asked Rick?

“Yeah, I have nightmares about it. The flour alone at two dollars a pound is seven and half-million dollars. Cattle at eleven hundred pounds would yield seven hundred fifteen pounds average meat. One cow would feed three people. That means five thousand head. We could buy them as weaned calves at six hundred dollars each. That would be three million dollars. You get the idea, just on food alone we figure it will take fifteen million dollars to feed everyone.

Then there is the infrastructure to support it. Also things like health care. We don’t have a Doctor or a Dentist in the valley. This looks like a seventy-five million dollar project."

"Matt, I hope you don't think we can pay for all this."

"Oh no, we think we can finagle most of it with state and federal grants. We just need some help with coming up with a plan. Like we buy five thousand head of cattle, who is going to raise them, feed them, take care of veterinary issues."

"Then we will need a slaughter house. We won't want all cattle; there will be hogs, chickens and sheep. Where will we store the grain, where we will grind the flour, bake the bread? We need someone to help develop the big picture, so we can fill in the details. We figured with your army back ground you could at least point us in the right directions."

Rick got a very concerned look, "My army back ground?"

"You don't think we check out everyone who lives around here?"

"Never occurred to me, I have always been a private person, and I'm a little taken aback by this."

"No harm meant Rick, just with all these government data bases it is easy to get a quick background check on anyone."

Marsha inquired, "What do you know of Major Watkins?"

"Well to start he never made Major, best he did was Captain in the reserves, and that looks like a political promotion. Literally a political promotion, he was a gofer for that nitwit that was our Governor ten years ago."

"The Governor only lasted one term, but that is when Watkins got his promotion. He had joined the regular forces, but was let go before he made first lieutenant. Don't know why, but when he went over to the reserves, they took him as a first lieutenant, but it took him eight years and the Governor to get to Captain."

From the look on Rick's face, he was thinking hard, "I would like to talk this over with Marsha, can I let you know later?"

"Sure no real hurry, but we really want you on board."

After Matt left Rick and Marsha just stared at each other for a while.

Finally, Rick said, "Well that was out of left field. What do you think?"

Marsha shook herself like she was trying to get out of a deep sleep.

"That certainly was a surprise. We did come here because we wanted to be in a rural area rather than urban if things went bad. If the whole community is thinking along the same lines we would have a better chance."

"Yes it would, and now that we have been invited in, there would be resentment and problems if we opt out and things do go to hell without us giving any aid."

"So at this point we really don't have any choice," replied Marsha thoughtfully.

I don't think so, and actually I think it's a good idea," said Rick.

He continued, "I just question if raising the funds will be as easy as they think. That is a lot of money."

"Maybe I could help write grant proposals," Marsha said.

"Dear, that's a good idea. Actually, the planning part sounds attractive to me."

"Speaking of planning what are you going to do with your plan for Major Watkins?"

"I think it's best to go ahead. It would eliminate a big problem. Besides if he is gone maybe the Feds won't pay as much attention to this area."

Rick stated, "My next step is finding a Snow Goose that is for sale."

"How will you do that?" inquired Marsha.

"I will start with good old e-bay!"

Good old e-bay didn't have what he was looking for, but he found out there was many a site that dealt in used aircraft, there was a CG-10C Snow goose listed for sale in South Dakota by a couple of guys who had tried prospecting for gold in Alaska in some pretty rough country.

Rick opened a g-mail account, using a free Wi-Fi hotspot in Chattanooga and made contact. He was able to keep the price down to seventy thousand dollars in gold. They wanted more, but when he offered to pay in gold, the Dakota Boys jumped on it.

Using his Chattanooga identity, he contacted Carlos Alberto Cortez. He offered him five thousand dollars and expenses to drive a large box van rental truck up to South Falls and pick up the Snow Goose.

Cortez was thrilled with this opportunity. It would get him and his family home. Rick gave Cortez a package for the guys in Sioux Falls. He didn't tell him its contents. No sense in tempting the poor guy.

The trip went off without a hitch. Carlos made the round trip in six days. He met Rick at the Mission. Rick took the truck from there. The Snow Goose was set up on a frame on wheels, so he was able to get it into the north barn at the King Creek ranch.

The barn was on the first property they had bought. There was too much traffic at the old gun club barn for his comfort.

Rick made a point of finding out what flight Carlos would be leaving on. He was waiting for the family at the airport. The little girls were cute with their small wheeled bags in tow. Carlos had his hands full keeping them moving and in a straight line. They wanted to stop and look at everything.

Rick told Carlos how much he appreciated him making the trip and handed him an envelope.

Carlos, don't open this until you are on the aircraft. You need to be sitting down when you read this. It is a bonus for making the trip."

Carlos's mind was obviously on his daughters as he just said, "Thanks."

Rick walked away chuckling, as he thought of the look on Carlos's face when he opened the envelope and found a cashier's check in US dollars for one hundred thousand dollars.

This was over two year's salary in Columbia. Carlos might not be the sharpest person on the planet, but he would figure out that maybe there was a reason that he might never want to come back to the United States. Not that he planned to anyway.

Rick would have been very surprised if he had been with Carlos when he opened the envelope. Carlos just took a look and nodded his head and put the envelope away. It was as though he had figured a few things out. He told his daughters,

"Maybe we can afford a pony on our new Estancia."

## Chapter 27 – Things that go bump in the night – April-June 2024

When he got home, Rick set up the simulator software that accompanied the Snow Goose. He figured he had many hours of work to learn to fly the beast. He figured wrong. It was insanely easy to fly. The majority of the simulation time was for maintenance.

All he needed was the GPS co-ordinates of his target, and it would fly itself. There was a built in camera, so he could view the landing site to ensure there were no obstructions, and then built in radar would set it down.

All he had to do was check the fluids, make certain there were no broken dangly bits, see all green on the control panel, enter the GPS points and hit start. It was so simple that there was an immediate change of plans. They wouldn't need a second Snow Goose to learn on. This simplified things, which was always good. The Snow Goose really was built for soldiers to use on the battlefield.

Next Rick considered its payload.

He had enough explosives in his bunker, but it all had to be accounted for. After some thought, he decided to go with a two-stage process. The first stage would be a shaped charge, which would be set down on the roof of his target.

He would set the charge down, lift up and away, and blow a hole in the roof. He would then lower the Snow Goose into the building and set the main charge off blowing all to hell.

The main charge could be an old-fashioned fertilizer bomb. He had the fertilizer and diesel fuel. The shaped charge would be the problem. Dynamite would do the trick. He just would have to cut some trees, and then dig the stumps up, and clear the ground.

He would then show that he used dynamite to remove the stumps instead of digging them up. He figured that five pounds would be more than enough. Ten trees cleared would do it.

He told Marsha of his plan, and she had one question.

"What about the noise? If you used that much dynamite in one shot most of the valley would know it."

"Oops, I will do twenty trees and actually use a quarter stick on each for sound, it will be loud, but not carry through the whole valley."

"That sounds like it would work. Now why are you clearing the land?" She asked.

"We need more storage close to the house?" Rick said quickly. He obviously had given it no thought.

Marsha gave him a wifely look and said, "That will do, so you had better buy a storage building and arrange for it to be put up."

That project took on a life of its own. He had to identify the building, which ended up four parking bays wide. He planned to put in a small machine shop with a lathe, metal break equipment, drill presses, a welding rig and all the support items that would go with it. He was far from expert with metal working, but he could get the job done.

It took him all of May to find a supplier in Chattanooga for his new out building, and to clear the land. Next he had a concrete floor put in, water, sewage and electricity run to the building. Then the building was erected, and the utilities connected.

Almost as an afterthought, he had a small office put in. It was logical to put in a refrigerator, and to mount a fairly large-screen television on the wall.

Marsha said, “Good, another man cave. It will get you out of my hair at times.”

Rick took this as a license, so a keg cooler appeared then a popcorn machine, several recliners, and a pool table in the corner of the shop.

Between the new garage and the other outbuilding, he had two hideouts. Rick was of a mind that a man never could have enough get away spots. The thrill of having two hideaways was reduced when Marsha insisted that the home security system have cameras watching the interior and exterior of both buildings. It was as though she thought he might try to hide from some chores!

Actually, she worried about Rick working by himself in one of the buildings and getting hurt. This way, she could keep an eye on him.

Mary and Paul from across the way had come over when they heard the dynamite going off to check things out. From that point on Paul was involved in the building of the

Cave as the women came to call it. The Sheriff on one of his routine stops had some good suggestions. The popcorn machine was his idea.

Ricks first real project in his new shop was shaping a one-inch metal plate that was about two feet on a side. At least, he tried to shape it. He found out he couldn't create enough heat or pressure to move the half-inch thick piece of steel plate. The welding rig would heat the plate up, but only in a small area. There was enough of a heat sink effect that he couldn't get the metal to flow.

He played with this for two weeks before it dawned on him that he wasn't trying to create a piece of art work. He then went to an industrial metal shop in Nashville and bought a sheet of half inch steel. He doubted the metal fragments could be traced, but he didn't want to make it easy.

He cut the steel plate into two-foot squares, and then he cut a roundish hole in three of the plates. The first hole was eighteen inches in diameter, the second twelve and the third six inches. He then welded them to the original plate.

The smallest hole was next to the plate with the largest hole being on the outside. This gave him a crude bowl shape. The finished weight would be around one hundred and twenty-five pounds. This would limit his main payload to three hundred and fifty pounds, but that was more than enough.

His next issue was how to attach the shaped charge to the underside of the Snow Goose, then to release it. There were several hard points on the bottom of the drone so it would be easy to drill holes for fasteners. He came up with an eyehook to hang the device from. He could use nylon cable to lift the device.

He then rigged up a simple propane torch that could be radio activated, when the torch came on it would melt the nylon so the charge would stay on the roof when he lifted the drone.

While all that sounded simple, it took him another month and hundreds of tests before he felt that the device was reliable. Of course when he invited Marsha out for a demonstration, the torch had slipped and the flame wasn't directed at the nylon.

It took him another week and hundreds more attempts before it was reliable. He remembered his Army days, when they would get new equipment to field test. He was getting a better appreciation for what the designers went through.

His next step was to select a launch site. Since the Snow Goose would lift off from the trailer, this wasn't a large problem. All he had to do was pull up, undo the bindings; lock the blades in place and go. It would take all of ten minutes at the most.

After practicing a dozen times he had it down to five minutes. Then Marsha informed him she would be going with him. Between them, they could launch within three minutes of stopping.

He used Google earth to pick the launch site. Near Pelham Tennessee, there was a small private airport named, Krashinski Airport. He had to use it with a name like that.

He drove over and checked it out. It was right next to the road. He could turn into it without being seen from the highway. There was no gate. It would be easy to drive into, launch and drive away.

The only problem he could for see was the night of the launch as he turned into or out of the airfield that a sheriff's car might drive by at that time and question what he was doing at the airfield.

Some further investigation revealed between the state police and sheriff, there would be at the most five cars on the road in the entire county at night. One phone call would take care of his problem.

It was June before everything was in place, and the weather was to be clear and dry for several days in a row. On Tuesday of the first week in June, he modified the laptop that contained the simulator software he had been using.

He removed the hard drive and replaced it with another he had purchased for just this event. He took the hard drive with the software and the supporting paper documentation and CD disk into the shop.

Fifteen minutes with a welding torch and there would be no recovery. The hard drive was a piece of slag, the papers burnt to ash and the CD a molten blob of plastic. He placed them all in a trash bag.

Next he put the stolen plates on the truck and trailer. In this day and age, there would be cameras in the strangest places, even in the country. He then changed the tires on the truck and trailer. From high tech cameras to low tech tire tracks, he and Marsha spent many an evening discussing the possibilities. He placed magnetic signs on the side of the truck and back of the trailer.

They were for a horse farm up in Kentucky. He found them in the same junk yard as the extra wheel rims.

He then went out to his excavator and dug a hole in the corner of his compost pile about eight feet deep. He dropped the trash bag in but didn't cover the hole. Rick loaded the Snow Goose which was mounted on its carrying frame onto a trailer.

Wednesday night he and Marsha drove the fifty miles to the Krashinski airport. When they were about five miles out Marsha made a phone call to the Sheriff's office. Using a throw-away phone she reported a robbery with gunshot fired at a gas station across the county from them. This took care of them being surprised by any police at the airfield.

They pulled into the airfield, and their practice paid off. They were out of the truck and had the Snow Goose launched on its preprogrammed course in under three minutes.

It would take them an hour to get home; and the drone that long on a straight line to get to Watkins armory. Rick programmed in loiter time of fifteen minutes. Furthermore, if new instructions weren't given because he wasn't in position to control the bird it would just fly back to its home barn.

The trip home was no problem, and they made it with five minutes to spare. There was one problem that Rick hadn't anticipated and that was when he got home he had to pee so bad it hurt. This took three minutes of his time cushion, but he made it.

He radioed the new instructions to the drone. These were to the GPS location of Watkins armory. After twelve minutes flying time, the drone was in position.

Through the camera, he could see that the drone was almost perfectly centered on the roof of the correct building. It was simple, but nerve racking to lower the drone to the roof.

Next Rick lit the propane torch. It took fifteen seconds in all his tests to melt the nylon. He allowed thirty seconds before he raised the drone back up. He moved it to a height of two hundred feet and offset from the roof at five hundred feet and set the drone to hover.

He then made a phone call that he agonized about. He killed many in war, both in hot blooded fights and cold-blooded ambushes. That had been a long time ago, but he finally decided that he was back in a war. He was just getting in the first blow.

From the burner phone, he called Watkins. "Major you had better check out your armory."

He then set off the shaped charge which was on the roof.

From the camera mounted on the bottom of the Snow Goose, he could see a flame on the roof. It didn't jet straight up. It bloomed out from under the metal plate. When the glare was gone, he could see a gaping hole in the roof.

As he re-centered the drone over the hole from the wide-angle lens he could see a figure running up to the building.

He brought the drone over the hole and dropped it straight down. Just as it was about to impact he hit the ignition device for the fertilizer bomb. His picture went in a flash of white then black with no signal. It was now eleven p.m., for better or worse, it was done.

Rick then unloaded the Snow Goose transportation frame from his trailer. This wasn't the original frame. That was long cut up and sold as scrap. He made a new one almost identical to the original. It didn't have the rust-resistant paint job or nice smooth welds.

What it did have was different metal from the original. They were both steel, but they were of different grades. He cut it into small pieces with his welding rig. He would never be elegant in his welds but elegant didn't count when cutting.

He put the cut-up sections in his junk bin after scorching the exterior of the metal to remove any paint residue from contact with the Snow Goose.

The magnetic signage was actually plastic with magnets attached. It was a matter of minutes till the torch burned the plastic away. The magnets themselves weren't a problem. He attached them to some steel in his scrap bin. The license plate he had taken from a junked vehicle was thin metal which the torch ate right up.

As a decoy, he dug a hole about ten feet deep the previous night in his compost pile. He now filled in the hole, and pushed compost over the top to hide evidence of freshly moved earth.

He then remounted the original tires on the truck and trailer. The ones that took the trip to the Krashinski Airport were removed from the rims and cut up with a sawsall. Marsha then fed the smaller tire parts into a wood chipper.

They knew the steel belts in the tire would dull and then tear up the blade on the chipper, but that cost would be nothing against the cost of getting caught. They placed the now rubber mulch in large plastic bags.

He and Marsha sat on the porch late into the night drinking coffee. There was too much adrenaline flowing for sleep. Contrary to public opinion action let down didn't always lead to wild sex. They knew they had committed murder this night, and weren't thrilled, but at the same time they felt they were in a fight for their lives.

Around three in the morning, they were tired enough to go to bed and sleep, they had to be up and ready by noon. They figured it would take the FBI that long to get to the house. Rick previously had made a call about the Major. This would make him a person of interest.

Marsha had done the research on the Internet of what to do if the FBI knocked on your door. They didn't have to let them in if they didn't have a warrant. If they let them in they would effectively be opening their home to search. They didn't have to talk to the agents without a lawyer present.

There would always be two agents, one to ask questions, the other to take notes. Since it was a federal crime to tell a lie to an agent, the questioning agent would try to get you to contradict yourself in a long question and answer period.

The recording agent would note this, then they would have a federal charge to use as a lever on whatever they were trying to achieve.

The best advice she could find is to let them talk all they wanted about you looking bad for not co-operating. Wait for a lawyer. If worse came to worse, set your own recorder out. This would shut them down fast, as any mild contradictions would come across as mild misspeaking rather than lies.

He who controls the minutes controls history. A true recording wouldn't help the agents, so they weren't interested in questioning you with one present. Somehow innocent until proven guilty had got lost with the FBI.

Rick and Marsha had just finished lunch when the unmarked car with a man, and a woman in it pulled onto the garage area blacktop. They went out onto the porch to meet them. Marsha had a tape recorder in hand, Rick a pen and hard back notebook.

The agents were both dressed in dark suits that were so stereotypical in their look that both Marsha and Rick snickered. The agents walked up the steps and didn't come across in a threatening manner at all.

They appeared to be open and friendly.

"Hi are you Rick King?" asked the first agent to come up the steps.

"Yes I am, and who are you?"

"I am FBI agent Ken Stevens, and this is my partner Tammy Dawkins."

They all spent a moment shaking hands.

Then Rick said, "It is nice to meet you, may I see some identification?"

"Sure," said Ken, with that he and Tammy flipping their cases out and back quickly.

"Uh, slow down partner. I need to read them and get the badge numbers," said Rick.

"Don't you trust us?"

"Sure you are from the government, and you are here to help me. Now may I see your identification long enough to write down whom I am talking to?"

Both agents held out their badge wallets long enough for him to record their personal information.

"Thank you, now what's up?"

"We would like to come in, so we can ask you some questions about a phone call you made several months ago about a Major Watkins,"

Do you have a warrant to search the house?"

"No, we just want to sit down and talk."

"I'm not inviting you in. I know I surrender some of my rights if I do that."

"Mr. King you appear to have something you are trying to hide. You really ought to cooperate and protect your good name."

Agent Dawkins spoke up for the first time, "Let's just take them in. They will talk to us then."

Marsha held her tape recorder out so all could see it.

Hey, it's against the law to record Federal Agents," said Agent Stevens.

We have nothing further to discuss if you want an official conversation, we and our lawyer will meet you at your office, other than that good day."

"Hey, we are the FBI you have to talk to us," blurted out Dawkins.

"No, we don't, good day," Marsha spat out.

Both Agents stood there for a few moments.

Stevens started over, "Folks somehow we got off on the wrong foot. We really do need to talk to you, some bad stuff went down last night, and we need to know why you suspected Watkins of any wrong doing?"

"As I said you can make an appointment for us and our attorney," replied Rick.

"You are making it look like you are involved with this by not cooperating. You were ready with a notepad and recorder when we drove up."

Marsha and I are writing a book, and we try to keep good notes. You just got unlucky that we were about to start a brainstorming session. Now, we have said all we have to say."

"You will be hearing from us!"

The Agents returned to their vehicle and sped away.

"Well that went well," said Marsha.

"I just hope the recorder was on for that whole conversation," Rick commented.

"It was. I loved it when she threatened us with being hauled in."

"Yes that will play real well with the court if needed. In the meantime, let's go into town and have some coffee at the diner. We will get the latest gossip on what happened last night."

Marsha added, "That was a nice recovery about why we were prepared for them, but now we have to start a book."

"Oh God," said Rick, "I can't think of anything that has ever happened to me that might be worth a book, how about you?"

"No, we could block out a science-fiction story and start to write, we just said we were writing, not that we were any good at it."

Point taken," said Rick.

## Chapter 28 – Now what do you say happened? – June 2024

After the FBI agents left, they made certain that the security cameras were recording. Next they locked the house and checked that all barns and sheds were also locked. They then went to the diner for coffee. As expected the diner was abuzz with rumors.

The rumors went from a propane tank explosion to an all-out war with tanks and bombs. They ranged from no dead to over a hundred killed.

All of this washed over Rick and Marsha, the more confusion the better. The item that left them cold was told to them by Mary.

"I hear there is a crime scene unit over at the Krashinski Airport taking tire impressions; I wonder if that is linked?"

"Where did you hear that Mary," asked Rick?

"One of the State Troopers that was on his way off shift mentioned it. He was doing traffic control for the FBI unit."

"It's been awful dry to leave tire prints."

"That's what I told the Trooper. He told me about a new method that picks up the oils left on the pavement by the tires. Some chemicals and a special type of light and they can get pictures of any tire tread less than two days old if there aren't too many tracks."

Rick laughed, "Ain't technology great. What will they think of next?"

When Mary left the table, they exchanged glances. They both knew enough that they calmly finished their coffee, talked to a few neighbors before they left. Rick had to lift his foot off the pedal several times on the way home. He finally gave up and turned control over to the car.

"What are we going to do with that chipped up rubber," asked Marsha?

"I don't know yet. We can't take it out of the workshop, there might be overhead cameras. Burning it inside will create such a stink that it would be weeks getting it out."

They decided it wouldn't be real bright to put the trash bags with the chipped up tires out for the garbage pickup truck. The simplest thing to do would be to use the chipped up rubber as mulch in the flower beds Marsha planted around the house.

They then decided to sacrifice a set of four snow tires they had in the workshop. They had no miles on them. Rick bought them in an overabundance of preparing for any eventuality. Marsha teased him periodically about these, now he may be vindicated.

When he got home, the first thing he did was help Marsha mulch the flower beds with the chipped up tires.

He then cut up the snow tires and placed them in trash bags. He loaded the bags on a trailer and hauled them to the landfill. He was dog tired when he got back to the house but felt he had done all that could be done.

In the morning, Rick couldn't believe how well he felt. He was over eighty, and had no aches and pains. He should be in agony after all that he had done yesterday. He and Marsha talked about the previous day over a hearty breakfast steak and eggs with fried potatoes accompanied by orange juice and lots of coffee.

"This will be interesting," said Rick. "I have heard that the FBI will go through your trash.

This will give us an idea how seriously they are watching us," added Marsha.

"I hope we are being overly cautious, but there isn't room for error in this.

Several days later, they went into town to the Diner to hear the latest gossip. Mary wanted to know right out, why the FBI was asking about them. Rick and Marsha exchanged glances, and both shrugged their shoulders.

"No idea Mary," said Marsha.

Mary let it go at that, but you could tell she wasn't satisfied with the answer.

They had finished their breakfast and were about to pay their check when a suited man approached them. He was middle aged but looking at him; he spelled Authority in large letters.

His suit wasn't an off-the-rack model. His tie, belt and shoes all screamed power dresser. This was someone that had to be taken seriously, or he was the biggest fraud going.

They found out very quickly that he was no fraud.

"Sergeant Major, Mrs. King may I join you for a minute?"

Looking around Rick realized that no one was sitting near them and that there were several men standing near the door. They had come in quietly and had them boxed in without them even realizing what was going on.

These were professionals. Neither of the men by the door had the look of muscle. They looked like competent killers. Rick knew their type from the service.

"Agents Dawkins and Stevens aren't happy with either of you; they spent all day in protective clothing at the dump."

Rick and Marsha said nothing, just waited.

"They are especially hunting for tires, which may match some partial prints, magnetic signs for an out of business horse farm up in Kentucky, some stolen license plates and the metal carrying frame for a CG-10C Snow Goose."

"There are also some upset agents up in Alaska, seems those boys from Dakota are mining in a pretty remote location. One of the agents broke a leg getting there. That's the bad news; the good news is that they have found nothing. The powers to be have pulled the plug on the investigation. It appears it was an accidental propane explosion that started it all."

Rick and Marsha just sat there and waited.

He laid out several photographs, one a side view of Ricks truck, the others parts from the Snow Goose.

"There aren't that many Snow Gooses in the world much less the United States, so it was easy to establish these parts came from one sold recently. That's why we wanted to question the people in Alaska.

The picture of your very distinctive truck was taken by a game camera at the Krashinski Airport. They set up it because of recent vandalism. It was a shame the angle of the camera didn't show either of you or the aircraft.

"You have taken care of an enormous problem for us, and Uncle Sam still needs your help."

Marsha got her breath back first, "What problem?"

"We backed the wrong horse, and it was about to become a major embarrassment."

"Like in Major Watkins," asked a confused Rick?

"Exactly, some agencies in the government realize that the country is about to fail. There is too much debt, too many problems in the world that we won't be able to contain much longer. At one time, we could have, but we just don't have the financial resources or the military in place to control the outcomes.

They are trying to set up in place, areas that won't totally fail so that the country and civilization can be rebuilt. Watkins was going to head up this area. Then he decided that he would rather be the local War Lord.

Add to that some reporter from the New York Times was getting close to figuring out the entire program, and that we had backed Watkins.

That is the problem you have solved. Anything that links us to Watkins has disappeared in the last two days."

Rick's mind engaged again. He hadn't locked up like that since his first fire fight.

"What help do you need from us?"

"Simple, we have done one of the quickest background checks on you two that I've ever seen done. Medically you two shouldn't be here.

We have a glimmer of why you are, but that's not my problem. My problem is that we still have to set up a Civilization Survival Center here. Other than the Watkins issue, you have been sterling citizens. Some might say that even including Watkins you've been sterling citizens. We want you to form a group and continue to develop a CSC."

"Are you aware there is a group that wants exactly that and they have invited us to join them?"

"No I'm not aware, please explain."

Rick and Marsha between them went on to explain what Fire Chief Matt Johnson was involved in and what directions they wanted to go.

"That is excellent; we can build on that in good ways. We will take nothing away from the basic plan: just make certain the resources they need are available. We will be making suggestions as to what additional resources you will need, like an isolated Internet, copies of all major libraries, what sort of skilled workers should be encouraged to move here. That said it really has to be a local effort."

"Why is that," asked Rick.

"Because there will be many questions asked. It would be impossible to keep this a total secret, so the next best thing is to be public to a point. If it was known that the Federal Government was looking at its own demise, there would literally be panic in the streets. Local government or volunteer committees can be passed off as some type of extremist. As a matter of fact, we would encourage you to do that as your 'public' face."

Marsha asked, "If you think the government is going to break down. What about the large cities?"

"It depends on how it breaks down. We are going to try to avoid hyperinflation and food shortages. If we can it will be a soft landing, and the Republic might even survive. The wild card is the rest of the world. If the US dollar fails, which it will, the question is how the Iran's and North Korea's of the world will react.

If they go nuclear the world as we know it is doomed. It will be launch, counter launch until we and Russia are forced to launch, then there will be no cities left."

"Where do we go from here?" Rick asked.

"Go home and get your heads wrapped around this, you will be almost in shock for the next couple of days. I don't know of anyone else coming this close to getting nailed by the FBI for first-degree murder and taking a walk. Don't think for one minute that you can ever get away with something like this again. We will assign a liaison who will be contacting you. The code will be a simple, CSC."

Oh, by the way, Agents Stevens and Dawkins are being transferred. For some reason, they feel like you are getting away with murder. I think they are going to end up as liaisons to the Dominican Republic or someplace similar.

When they got home and turned on the news, they got their answer of how it was going to go.

"This is Abi Jackson of Fox News," opened the young lady they had met in Baltimore. "The FBI has announced that the explosion near Chattanooga, Tennessee, which killed Major Frank Watkins, was the result of a propane tank exploding, which set off an illegal ammunition and military-grade explosive storage facility.

The FBI had been investigating Watkins group for some time, and they were ready to make arrests when this untimely event happened. Watkins followers, a small group have all been taken into custody."

## Chapter 29 – The Beginning of The Fall – July 2024

Rick and Marsha went home and spent the next two days talking in circles. Their lives had just spun out of control. They were now puppets of some group within the federal government. They had supposedly gotten away with murder, but the reality was this is the no knock, no search warrant crowd.

There was also the statement that their strange un-aging was, "somebody else's" problem. When would that shoe drop?

It was Marsha who came up with the conclusion. The way she worded it to Rick was, "When all is in doubt, just soldier on."

This just about floored Rick, the last time he had heard that was from a Korean conflict veteran who had been in the retreat at the Chosin Reservoir.

The following Monday, Rick called Matt Johnson and told him he, and Marsha would be very interested in joining their group. They were invited to their very first meeting that night at the firehouse.

The only people they hadn't met were Sheriff Steve Linn and County Commissioner Bill Wigle. The others were Judge Mark O'Malley who they knew from the diner, Jack Nelson, who had cheerfully taken so much of their money,

Paul Kettler their neighbor, and his wife Mary and local realtor Hope Popule.

They were greeted warmly. Matt started the meeting with the statement; you folks were invited to this group, because Rick knows how to make things happen in a large group and Marsha is a skilled educator. The others of us here know everything there is to know about the Sequatehie Valley.

Rick got a sinking feeling in his stomach.

"Has the mission been defined?"

"What do you mean," asked Matt.

"What is the endgame? You want to turn the valley into a place that can survive the downfall of the United States. Have you defined what that is?"

"Not really, we just know we need to do it."

"I don't disagree, but we have to have a definition of where we want to end up. That is our objective. Then we figure out where we are against that objective, after that fill in the blanks."

"Rick that is why you are here; you have cut to the heart of the matter. We had an idea, but no way to turn it into reality. So the first thing we have to do is decide upon our objective; that sounds easy."

Rick winced at those words, "Maybe not as easy as you think. It is a given that you want the people in the valley and their families who can make it back to survive whatever may be coming. The real question is what level of civilization, do you want them to be at when it is over. A pre-industrial farm economy is very doable. Anything higher becomes more difficult."

Mary Kettler spoke up, "We want to live at the same level we are now!"

"Does that mean you want to be able to use your cell phone?"

"Of course, I would be lost without it."

"Well then we need to set up an independent phone system as we can't count on the large providers to be there. Then there is the equipment problem. What do we do when a cell phone towers circuit boards get fried? We can keep some spares on hand but there are limits. Want to talk about manufacturing pharmaceuticals? It is one hell of a lot more difficult to keep our current levels going than it appears on the surface."

"Then do we just give up?" asked Matt.

"No, it means that it will take more planning than you have originally thought and a lot more resources than we currently have available."

"Well at least, we can think. I don't know about the resources," replied Hope Popule.

"Hope no disrespect but fundamental knowledge is needed here. We can think of all sorts of things, but we need real experts to guide us in what can be done. Especially the logistics required."

Rick continued, "Do we have any specialist setting up a cell phone network in the area? If not we have to import one, then there is their family, if any. That puts our headcount up, which in turn puts up our food requirements. It is like what the army faced in the days of mule trains. You had to calculate how many mules you would need to haul your equipment, then how many mules you needed to carry the fodder for all the mules. Don't even get into the math of replacing mules that died along the way."

Matt Johnson sighed and said, "Rick you understand this more than we ever will." Please take over the chair of this meeting.  Marsha, we haven't elected a Secretary will you please take that on?"

Rick replied, "Why don't we have a formal motion and vote, that way, there is a clear record of what is transpiring so there will be no sour grapes later on."

Bill Wigle spoke up, "I would like to be considered for the leadership role."

Matt looked around, making eye contact with each person, "Anyone else?"

No one kept eye contact or spoke up.

"Okay why don't Bill and Rick speak for a couple of minutes of why they should be the Chair and then the rest of us can ask each of them questions, after that we vote.

Rick started to speak up, but Marsha gave him a sharp elbow.

"Do it Rick, they need you."

Rick once more wondered how wives could read minds. He was about to say that he really didn't want the job and that Bill Wigle could have it.

"Who goes first," Rick asked instead.

"Flip a coin," suggested the Sheriff. Both candidates agreed. Rick lost the flip so the County Commissioner spoke first. His speech consisted of his long association with the area, of how he won office right out of college and has held the job ever since, his knowledge of how a county works and what a general good guy he was. He repeated each of these points at least three times, and you could see eyes start to glaze over.

Rick's presentation was short. I was a Command Sergeant Major in the United States Army. I helped set up the Sergeant Majors Academy. I learned my trade under fire in Viet Nam. I then went on to a career in Quality Assurance in the manufacturing sector. My health is good. I am one of the Alzheimer returnees and have had the Live medication so probably will be around for a while.

There were questions for both candidates, but the conclusion was foregone. Rick was elected by all present. When he saw how it was going even Bill Wigle voted for him.

Marsha's position had no competition, so she had the job. Actually, she had started on the job as soon as she sat down and pulled out a notebook and began recording minutes. No one else brought pen and paper with them.

Judge O'Malley asked to be recognized. He brought up another problem they would be facing.

"What will the laws be after, The Fall?

Everyone in the room heard the capital letters as he spoke in his deep slow southern accent. His question stopped the room for a moment.

Marsha was the first to speak up, "I think you have already put together that the full United States legal code and all the interpretations, rules and regulations put forth by the various departments of the Executive Branch won't work at that time."

"No they won't," replied the Judge. "The complexity would be overwhelming."

Sheriff Linn then brought up the fact that they would even have to define the form of government they would have. They would be working in a legal vacuum at first. Somehow, he didn't think the county commissioner style of government would work for what, in fact, would be a small nation state.

At this point, Rick brought up, "Now you are starting to get it. This won't be easy. Let's meet again next Monday, and I will present a high level plan of what we will be facing. As a group, we will pick it apart. The goal of this step will be defining what we want to be after The Fall."

Judge O'Malley wouldn't go down in history as the man who coined the term but the term would go down in history.

Marsha had a simple question, "What do we call this group? I need something for the minutes." This prompted the most spirited discussion of the evening. It all boiled down to the notation Marsha made in her minutes.

After discussion, it was moved by Sheriff Steve Linn and seconded by Jack Nelson that the working name of this group will be, 'The Valley Group,' at a later date it may be appropriate to change the name. This motion passed unanimously.

Rick brought up several other items. "We have to have coffee next week. Plus this room could use a white board."

The Kettler's volunteered to take care of these details.

After the meeting, Wigle came up to Rick.

“My wanting the office was a politician’s reflex. As I was speaking I realized that your job isn’t only going to be hard, it is going to take a hard man. If this goes down like we think it will, you will have to make life-and-death decisions. The more I thought the less I wanted it; that is why I started to ramble.”

“You are right about that, but I’m going to need your support. You do know the people around here, and make sure we are using our resources as best as we can. And, I think you will have to play a prominent role in whatever government we come up with, if nothing else you will be the ‘good guy, to my bad guy’.”

As Rick and Marsha drove home, they wondered, what have they gotten themselves into?

## Chapter 30 - Help from Big Brother - July 2024

They didn’t figure out the scope of what they had gotten themselves into, but the scenario got worse with a phone call on Tuesday. A man who identified himself as Frank Silverman called about CSC.

He asked to set up a meeting with them on Thursday afternoon. He further stated that Rick had a good grasp of the problems they were facing with his cell phone and mule train examples at last night's meetings.

Rick relayed the conversation to Marsha.

Marsha replied, "So they want us to know they have someone else on the inside of the Valley Group. That doesn't line up with what that FBI guy that we first talked to said. He acted surprised that there is a group thinking about creating a survival center like they were thinking of."

Rick answered, "I'm not comfortable; the government is demonstrating to us, they intend to keep control. If it was the entire government, it would be one thing. But we know it is just a small group within the government, probably Homeland Security. What are their motives? What is their endgame?"

"More importantly what is for lunch," Rick continued.

"How about grilled cheese?"

"Sounds good, I will put on some fresh coffee."

Later in the afternoon, they both spent time in the office at their respective computers. Marsha wrote the minutes from last night's meeting. Rick started an outline of a plan to bring order to their current project.

After their pot roast dinner later that evening Rick discussed where he was at, with Marsha.

"We need to get Maslow's hierarchy of needs covered first; food, clothing and shelter. But we can't do that till we know about how many people there will be."

Marsha and Rick batted that around for a while.

Then Marsha brought up, "There is another entry point, what about power, it is the foundation of a modern society. Until that is guaranteed we are really stuck."

"Hmm, power and knowledge," mused Rick, "after those, raw materials, equipment and skilled workers. Which sounds simple; until you realize that we need materials, etc. for every discipline that makes up a modern society. And that is just the support for the professional levels needed such as health care. I am willing to forgo the lawyers."

"Speaking of knowledge, besides a copy of the Library of Congress, we will need a copy of every document held by the Federal Citizen Information Center."

"What is that? Not the Library of Congress, the information center, though you are thinking big there."

Marsha replied, "The Federal Citizen Information Center is in Pueblo Colorado. It is the group that sends out those, 'How to information pamphlets.' Everything from basket weaving to raising chickens, shoeing horses and lancing boils. Since they are done by the government, they can't be copyrighted. Because of that I'm not sure if they would be in the Library of Congress or not."

"Beyond the library books, we will need a software library. That brings us to a computerized information center that will be a large server farm. This just keeps getting bigger," Rick tiredly moaned.

Marsha said, "Rick I have a better idea of what we need."

"What is that," he replied.

"I think we need to go to bed and make love. The world will be here tomorrow, and if it isn't we will have spent our time well."

"Wonderful thinking!" said a rejuvenated Rick.

The next morning as they were clearing the breakfast dishes off the table, the phone rang.

"I'll get it," Rick said.

"Sure leave me with the washing!"

"Hello; Kings"

“Rick this is Frank Silverman your CSC contact. You will be getting a phone call from an old commanding officer of yours, Robert King.

“He is going to be your go-to-guy in the future. He retired as a three star. He now works for Homeland Security. He has a proposition, we think you will like. We know one of your big worries right now will be power. He has the answer.”

“That will be a relief, when will he be calling?”

“Let me hand him the phone.”

“Rick, this is Bob King, how are you doing?”

“Fine Bob, I am really surprised to hear from you. I thought you were retired and living in Florida.”

“I got bored, my wife passed four years ago. We never had any kids, and I have no other family to speak of, so I decided to get back in harness. This group in Homeland Security seems to be a good fit for me.”

“I’m glad to hear it, what do you have for me,” asked Rick.

“I would like to come to your place and explain it all to you. It is a little much for a phone call.”

“Okay when do you want to do it?”

“The sooner we can get together the better.”

“Where are you coming from?”

"The Pikeville Diner."

"Well come on over, do you know how to get here?"

"That's why God invented GPS," chortled Bob.

"Ok we will expect you in about half an hour."

As Rick hung up, he saw that somehow he stepped in it. Marsha had her hands on her hips and didn't look happy.

"Uh, I will run the vacuum while you clear the table," he said.

"No, I will do that while you take a shower, then I will get cleaned up."

"Yes dear."

Rick had learned something in his many years.

It was a hurried rush around, but they managed to straighten up the house and get cleaned up with fresh clothes. It was a close thing, and they only made it because the General took forty five minutes instead of half an hour.

When Rick opened the door to Bob King, the former General just stood there for a moment. He shook his head, and then Rick's hand.

"If I hadn't read your file, I wouldn't have believed it, Rick you don't look sixty, and I know you are almost ninety."

"It's all due to clean living, General."

"It's Bob and it sure as hell wasn't good clean living!" replied the General.

They both laughed at that as Rick admitted the General to his home.

When the General met Marsha, he just smiled and said it was a delight to meet her. He didn't get to be a General by making comments about a lady's age, even if they were positive. They went into the kitchen and had coffee at the kitchen table.

"Rick I know that the Center for Disease Control, and the Food and Drug Administration have been asked to investigate both of your health issues, or non-issues as the case may be. They were able to get all the records from the courts about the AID's, but have run into a stone wall on the drug trial."

He went on, "Typically of bureaucrats, they are following the paper trail only. They want to find out why you don't appear to have Alzheimer's or AID's. What they don't see is your appearance. I guarantee if they did they would have you in a lab study so fast your head would spin."

"They have talked about taking samples, but their ethical panels, thank God, are saying no because they don't have the drug study results and original inputs."

“Rob what happened to the drug information?” asked Marsha.

“Wow,” said the General, “I haven’t been called Rob since high school.”

“I’m sorry,” Marsha replied, “It just came out.”

“No problem, actually I like it. I’m trying to start my life over since my wife’s death and maybe this is part of new life.”

“Anyway,” continued Lieutenant General Robert ‘Rob’ King, Homeland Security Project Manager. “It appears that drug companies have legal responsibilities to maintain drug manufacturing and test results for so many years. Once that time has passed they destroy all the records, so they can’t be discoverable in a law suit.

“So they can’t reconstitute the drug, they don’t have any samples or records of your physical baseline before and after the drug treatment. The ethics people say they can’t proceed. None of that would mean a hill of beans if they knew that you appear to be regressing in age. Rick doesn’t look a day older than when I first met him forty years ago, and from your age, I would say the same for you Marsha.”

“What are you going to do about it Rob?” inquired Rick.

“Me? Nothing, not my job, my job is to help you set up a survival center. If nothing else and they got their claws on you, it would hold the project up. So we will have to be very careful if they have any interface with the project."

Rob asked, "Have you figured out that Homeland has a spy on your committee?"

"Yes, they pretty well told me as much in my last conversation."

"Do you know who it is," asked Rob?

"Not yet, I was planning to start dropping comments to individuals and see which ones made it back."

"I can save you some time. It's Bill Wigle."

"He was on the list but nothing specific," stated Rick. "Is this just to keep oversight on the project or something deeper?"

Rob sighed and said, "Deeper I'm afraid, I think they want you to set this all up, let the country collapse then waltz in and take over as tin pot dictators. It all started when Wigle came to them about the group being formed. They had him continue on as they planned to take it over at a later date. They brought Major Watkins in to be the muscle."

Rick said, "I think I know your position on this, but why don't we clear the air."

"Simple Rick, I took an oath, and even more than that, our ancestor fought with Washington. That means a lot to me.

The country may not survive in its present form, but I'm not giving it away to some bully boys."

## Chapter 31 – Send the Scoundrels to Congress – July 2024

"Do you have a plan?"

"Only a vague plan at best," replied Rob.

"We can get rid of our spy by offering him something he would sell his mother for."

"What's that," inquired Rick.

"Get him elected to Congress. That way, he is out of our hair. If you get me on your committee, I will be the 'spy', that way we can control the flow of information."

"I like that, promote him up and away. He might even still be some help."

Marsha chimed in, "If we can manage it correctly he can be a lot of help. We could come out in the open with our program to some degree. Advertise it as a Community Bootstrap Program, rather than a survival center. Wigle could be our front man in getting grants from the government and foundations."

Rob got excited, "We could use those grants as guises to funnel Homeland support without it being noticeable. I love it, 'Operation Bootstrap!'"

"Sounds good," said Rick, "How are we going to make it happen?"

"Rick you need to pay more attention to politics. The fourth congressional district is in play this year. Our nine term congressman is retiring. Wigle is a Republican so all we have to do is get him past the primary."

"As I said, how are we going to do that?"

"He is going to be identified as the person who gets Major Watkins land turned into a major homeland security installation. It is going to bring jobs to the area. He will be a hero," interjected Rob.

"Fine," said Marsha, "but that is only the tip of the ice burg. How are we going to prevent this faction of the Department of Homeland Security from taking over?"

"Marsha they have already made a fundamental mistake. They have put me in charge of this area and personnel assignments. Everyone at that base will be one of ours. What concerns me is they may have in place some sort of mechanized brigade to charge in after we are set up."

Rick pointed out, "We will have to have intelligence from inside. Do you know who this group is within DHS?"

"They are the Appalachian working group. I may have overstated things. They have a spy in your group, but I really don't know that they want to take over. Maybe they are just being prudent to make sure that the group doesn't get up to no-good."

"That's most likely. That's the simplest explanation. We tend to see conspiracies where there aren't any." Rob laughed, "What does that say about us?"

Rick replied, "That we're being prudent. If they are only keeping track to make certain we won't impose a dictatorship, no harm done. If they want to install their own, we will have a chance. We need to know their intentions."

Rob said with a small sigh, "Unfortunately, you are correct, and unfortunately I don't have a clue of how we can find out their real plans." Rick thought for a moment.

"See if you can obtain a copy of their table of organization, and any other working groups."

"From the sounds of it, there is more than one. A comparison may show us what we have to investigate. If they are a one-off group, there will be something different. If they're all the same, then we have to assume it is nothing, or nationwide in scope."

"Rick you are correct, and no matter what they will have to have a link to the military. We have a chance to find out what is going on from the military end."

"Right Rob, we both should have some contacts left, even if they are the children of people we served with."

"Now you are making me feel old, but again you hit it."

Marsha said, "Let me get some more coffee and let's discuss what else has to be done. I would like to hear about your plans for the Watkins place."

Marsha bustled around for a few minutes and brought in a fresh pot of coffee and a plate of cookies.

"Fresh baked this morning, chocolate chip," she said as she set them down. Both men poured coffee and grabbed a cookie.

"Hmm good," said Rob, "it has been so long since I have had anything homemade like this. I think your kitchen will be our command center!"

"Sounds like a plan," replied Rick, "An army should never travel beyond its supply chain. Speaking of supply chain, how do you see it?"

"Rick if this is going to work it is going to have to be almost all teeth and no tail."

Marsha asked, "What does that mean?"

"In the army, all teeth and no tail would mean nothing but fighting units, no support units. Normally, you wouldn't want to get into that condition because if things got bogged down they would starve in place," Rob explained.

"One of the most famous examples of the tail saving the day was at the Battle of the Bulge. Patton rightfully gets credit for turning his armored divisions on a dime, but many don't understand that it wouldn't have worked without the Red Ball Express."

"What was the Red Ball Express?" asked Marsha.

"It was the supply chain for Patton's armored division, without food, fuel and bullets, those tanks would have been useless. It started in August of 1944 at Normandy Beach and kept going to the front line. They made the main highways in France one way, towards the front.

He went on, "They were marked with a Red Ball, which came from railway usage. A red ball meant a high-value freight train which would stop for nothing, like hauling fruit before refrigeration. Each truck had a Red Ball painted on its door.

"The trucks were considered high-value targets by the German Luftwaffe. Over seventy-five percent of the drivers were African-American because everyone knew they couldn't handle combat. So they had them drive gasoline tankers while being bombed. It took fifty four hours to get to the front, think about that, fifty four hours non-stop driving by vehicles, which had been destroyed."

"That takes a braver man than I, what those guys went through was the real start of the change of attitude about black soldiers, put them with the Tuskegee Airmen. A fighter escort group for bombers, and they more than proved that blacks were the equal of anyone. Unfortunately, it took till the Korean conflict for them to be fully integrated."

"I have read about the Buffalo Soldiers," said Marsha.

"Yeah that is a funny one, when we saw the cavalry coming over the hill in the westerns when we were kids; they were all lily white. When in fact twenty percent of the cavalry where black. They earned seventeen Medals of Honor during the Indian campaigns."

"You would think that the powers that be would have caught on. They also did very well in the Spanish-American War. Just think about it, they weren't well thought of, weren't invited to the fight, and they still showed up and were heroic."

Rick said thoughtfully, "I saw a lot of blacks bleed in Nam. Their blood was just as red as mine. How did we get side tracked on this?"

Rob shook his head with a start, "We were talking of logistics and how we would be structured. The most important thing we have to have in place is power."

"Have you any plans," asked Rick.

"Yes, after the DHS facility is in place at the Watkins place we are going to put in two small nuclear reactors. They are assembly line built and hauled into place and fueled. They are fast neutron reactors working on the standing wave principle, by design, they can't melt down. They are air cooled so no water problems."

"Each will last for two hundred years and each will power a city of three hundred and thirty thousand people. Most of the structure will be below ground. Maintenance is very simple and only requires a small staff of experts. Now you know everything I know about them."

“Won’t there be political hell about putting them in,” asked Marsha.

“They will be hauled in on trucks, put into position in the dead of night, same with fueling. They will be up and operating within a United States reservation before anyone knows what is going on. That is one reason we want Wigle to be a Congressman. He will be on our side in this. There was discussion of a reactor in the area some years ago, and he supported it them.”

“This is almost overwhelming,” stated Marsha.

“Yes it is, but we have to break it down into chunks that we can handle,” replied Rick.

“There is a lot more help available than I have brought up,” added Rob.

Rob continued, “DHS has commissioned study groups at think tanks and major universities to come up with answers to various questions.”

“Such as,” inquired Rick?

“What is the overall profile of a survival center is the big one, then it breaks down into, what skills, what equipment, what raw materials, and what infrastructure,” answered Rob.

He continued, “What is almost amusing, was that at the universities after a couple of false starts, diversity and political correctness went out the window. It appears, they are a luxury that a society in survival mode can't afford."

"Well duh," replied Rick.

"We aren't talking of the easy stuff here Rick, not equal opportunity employment. What do you do when a family shows up and the father has an arrest record a mile long for violent crime? Do you let the family in? Do you make the father move on?"

"If the family wants to go with him, do you let children go when you know they won't make it, do you forcibly separate the family? Do you let the father move on when you know what he will revert to? You can't maintain a prison system, what are you going to do, shoot the poor loser?"

"Oh," said a suddenly subdued Rick, "Those questions have always been above my pay grade. I just had to implement what was decided."

"Rick this just proves the old adage. The more things change the more they stay the same, the think tanks and schools are going to answer the questions. You are going to implement the answers."

"What do you mean," asked Marsha?

"There are going to be two components, Military and Civilian. Rick is heading up the Military. We won't call it the Army, but that is what it will be. At the same time he will be the Civilian head. The CSC will operate under martial law until things settle, so Rick will be the strong man in command."

"I don't think I want that job," Rick broke in with some force.

"Rick, since you came to our attention you have been under a microscope. Your career and records have been looked at by many people. You are the best person we have for the job. The fact that you are already in place is just icing on the cake."

"The fact that you don't want the job is one of the things that make you the most desirable. There will come a time when you have to step down. That will be the test that few could pass."

## Chapter 32 –We need clarity – July 2024

Rick drawled, "I don't know about you folks, but I am getting confused about where we are going, and what to do next." "

I agree," said Marsha.

"It's getting hard for me to hold it all together also," added Rob.

"Let's adjourn to my office where I have a white board. I just hope it is big enough."

"Sounds like a plan," Rob agreed.

"I will freshen up our coffee. I think we will need a lot," put in Marsha.

"At least someone remembers that an Army moves on its stomach," laughed Rob.

Marsha said tartly, "I don't know about an Army, but I do know about men!"

Rick took his life in his hands when he asked, "Could you also bring some more cookies, the General here ate them all."

Marsha gave him that look only a wife can, "I saw who ate those, and it wasn't the General."

The General wisely kept his mouth shut.

When they were settled in the office and started to put items on the white board, some order began to appear.

“Okay, Bill Wigle being a spy or not isn’t really an issue, and we have a solution,” said Rick.

Since it was his whiteboard, he had automatically grabbed a marker and started making notes on the board. He didn’t give any thought, but it made him the leader of the discussion. This also made him the leader of the group. General King very well versed in group dynamics gave an internal smile; he had Rick right where he wanted him.

“DHS is prepared to provide us ample resources; we just need to bridge between them and The Valley Group. How are we going to explain your sudden appearance?”

“Rick I am wounded,” said thc General, “I would think when you had a knotty problem you would turn to your old commander, who you had heard was working with DHS, thinking he might be able to help. One can only guess at your wonderment and surprise when you found out we were going in your direction.”

“You even kept a straight face, well played,” said Marsha with a smile in her voice.

“Yeah, well played, I walked right into it didn’t I,” added Rick. “I also noticed I am the one at the front right now. I bet I am going to be your fall guy.”

“Now Rick, how could you ever think I could be that devious,” said Rob as innocently as he could.

Unfortunately, he didn’t look innocent at all or even mildly repentant. The fact that he was smirking when he said it was a dead giveaway.

“On a more serious note Rick, you are established in the area, and you have the youth and energy needed to pull this off.”

“Youth?” inquired Rick.

“Well more the middle age competent appearance required by the people you will be leading. Mature enough to instill confidence and young enough to have the required energy. Face it; I look like I may not be here next week. Besides I have to work inside the DHS to protect our backsides.”

Marsha who had been keeping notes all along spoke up, “Here is an outline of what you will need to present at the next Valley Group Meeting. The high lights will be how the General and DHS have become involved. What they are bringing to the party. This includes a base of operations at the old Watkins place, a power supply which will be good for the foreseeable future. We have support from major universities and think tanks for specific needs of a CSC, and our own Congress critter to watch out for us in DC.”

Rick and Rob exchanged glances.

Rob verbalized their thought. "Rick you may be the front man, but I can see who will be running the show."

Marsha looked at them and said, "Where do you think the saying came from, 'Behind every good man, there is a better woman."

Neither Rick nor Rob remembered the saying going quite like that, but you pick your battles and this wasn't one of them. By training they knew you only fought when either forced or when you knew you could win. Neither case applied here.

"Change of subject folks," said Marsha. "I have been thinking of the makeup of The Valley Group. By natural inclination, they will be uncomfortable with the DHS or any other Federal group being involved. How can we counteract that?"

"Good point," said the General.

Rick thought for a moment, "Why don't I put on an act that the DHS is the devil, and we need to sup with a long spoon; that is why we want Bill Wigle in Congress. Actually, it wouldn't be acting. I don't entirely trust what is going on, no disrespect General."

"None taken, I agree with you. I don't think I know the whole story. I hope that I do, but this is definitely a Regan moment."

Rick looked puzzled for a moment, "Oh yeah, Trust and Verify."

"Got it,' replied Rob.

"So Rick is going to bring Rob into the picture but appear to be reluctant about Federal involvement, and demands that we have a Congressman on our side," summarized Marsha.

She continued, "That appears to take care of the possible spy problem, but what if there are two or more of them. We need to feed each member of the committee a specific piece of information that could only come from them. That way if we hear it back we know the spies."

Marsha went right on with, "Also we should insist that we have a liaison in place which meets with their Appalachian working group. Of course that would be Rick. He is the only one with the time and experience to participate. I think we should talk to Paul and Mary Kettler, Hope Popule and Jack Nelson with his wife Olive and bring them in with us."

"We have known them all for a while now, and frankly, they don't seem to be the type to have previously been involved with the DHS prior to this. That way, we wouldn't have to suggest everything ourselves. It also sets us up with five of the ten votes. This should be enough to control the group."

The General looked at Rick and shook his head, and then said, "Yes dear."

Rick who had just taken a sip of coffee almost snorted some out his nose.

After that, commotion settled down the General informed them that DHS had done a background check on everyone in the Valley Group and had found no problems, but of course they would cover up for their people if there were any. They decided to invite their friends over to dinner on Friday evening.

The following Friday everyone showed up but Jack's wife Olive. She had a previous commitment at a Bingo game and wasn't going to be active in the group. It would be nice to say that everyone fell in with their plans at once, but it was a contentious evening.

Paul Kettler was the most vociferous in his objection to the Federal government's involvement, but even he gave in at the end. The project was just too large without their help. The government was going to do something anyway so they might as well use the support, but they sure as hell weren't going to trust them!

They decided that since Paul was the most skeptical, he would continue to be so at the meetings. Mary would appear to calm him down to go along, but it wouldn't look like they were a unified group.

They had nothing against any of the other five members, but they just didn't really know them. Until the others earned their trust, they would view them as potential enemies. It also meant they would all make efforts to get to know them.

Keep your friends close and your enemies closer!

## Chapter 33 –Trust the Government? – July 2024

Trust between the government and its citizens had been falling for the last twenty years. As one late night comedian had put it, it was a draw between the government hating its citizens and its citizens hating the government. They just didn't know how to live without the other. A divorce by violent revolution or other means had been forecasted for years, but things just kept limping along.

The entitlement rate had exceeded fifty percent, but the country didn't fall apart. The national debt kept growing to pay for everything, but it had become a joke. The official unemployment numbers were sky high, but people weren't starving on the streets.

The reason was the underground economy. The consumer Ponzi scheme was finished. People didn't spend a fortune on the latest pair of Air Jordan's. They did barter or use bitcoins for what they made and the services they provided.

It wasn't a life of ease but one of earning rewards for hard work. Because of this, four distinct classes were emerging, the elites who had their fortunes and lived like they always had, the welfare class who were supported by the government debt, the disappearing middle class who had opted out of the aboveground economy and finally those in the middle class still with jobs and treading water.

The last two groups worked hard, lived well but not richly and had become incredibly politically incorrect (at least according to the elites and the government, whom they cheerfully ignored.)

The revolution had occurred, but they forgot to inform the U. S. government. As state legislative and executive branches became more conservative they realized they didn't have to follow federal rules if they gave up federal funds. The citizens were sending money to Washington.

Washington was skimming off the top for their bureaucracy and special-interest groups. Of course the income tax wasn't lowered. However, by the states giving up the federal money they didn't have to spend on federal programs, so they could keep their taxes down or in some cases even lower them. This made the Feds out to be the bad guys and the States the good guys.

Teachers unions hated when administrative jobs disappeared, but few missed the unions when they started to disappear! Unions had their place, but they had become big business interested in the business of the unions, not the wellbeing of the actual teachers.

Texas started it when they upped teacher's salaries, but required them to have a degree in what they were teaching, not a degree in teaching. A teaching certificate became a three-month course. They really got an uproar going when they decided that to teach a business course in a college you had to have run a business!

The federal government was still getting its money. They could pay off their constituents (welfare and big business) so they were happy. Administration types had a choice, join the underground economy or go on welfare. It turned out that most administrators were already in the underground economy, nobody said they weren't smart.

The ones that weren't smart went on welfare and joined the underground economy. They went to jail when caught. The old middle class wasn't in a very forgiving mood these days.

With life expectancies growing all the time, health generally improving, the economy shifting, it wasn't a question if something major was going to happen, just a question of what and when. The whole country was hunkering down to survive it and what would replace the current governments.

During all this, the shining star as usual was the U.S. Military. They did their job and made it very clear, no tin pot dictator would take over the country, as long as they were on the job. They wouldn't interfere with the Constitution and by god, no one else would either. They took no actions, but as in chess, the threat was worse than the execution.

This was the attitude of the members of The Valley Group as a whole and very much the attitude of Rick's inside group. They just referred to themselves as a local working group as they all lived close together. They didn't formalize their group and never made public their minutes.

The General brought and left with Rick equipment to sweep for bugs. When not in use he kept it locked in his enormous safe. The safe itself had little in it. The gold and silver he had bought was still buried!

The following Monday was the Valley Groups regular meeting. All were in attendance. Rick opened the meeting with the Pledge of Allegiance and followed by the Lord's Prayer.

He believed in both, but he also wanted word to get back to the DHS that he was patriotic and religious. Of course, to some people that made him a terrorist.

Previous discussions with the General resulted in him not being present at the Valley Group meeting. They wanted open and free conversation tonight. Rick kicked it off with a recap of his charge, a high level plan of how to achieve survival after 'The Fall'.

“I went back to my old rolodex card file to see who might be around that could help. I made about a dozen calls (he had made none,) and I finally called my last commander, Lieutenant General Robert King.’’

Yes, we are related but the connection goes back to the Revolutionary War, and our only contact was professional. When I explained what I was calling about, he gave a reply that knocked my socks off.”

“The General now works for the Department of Homeland Security in a department that is setting up what they call Civilization Survival Centers. In other words, he is from the government, and he is here to help us.”

That set off the up roar! After rage was expressed loudly by Paul Kettler, others had their say.

Finally Judge O’Malley asked a critical question. “What do you think we should do Rick?”

“Judge, I have given this a lot of thought. There are several possibilities here. Let’s discuss the good ones first. One, they are honest in the program and are going to give us access to the top-level advice from the universities and think tanks the General referred to, then they will fund us and let us proceed our own way. Anyone who believes that hasn’t lived in this country for the last fifty years.”

“Two, they provide the access and funding, then proceed to micromanage us to the point that the program is unworkable. That is the most likely. Then there is the dark side of things. Points one and two are both based on them working in good faith.  In addition, I have a concern of a conspiracy where we set it up; then a splinter group within DHS moves in and set themselves up as rulers.”

Again, the meeting turned into an uproar. Rick let it go on as human nature had to take its course. Each member of the committee had to have their say, it was an ego thing, but very important in group dynamics if the group was to function. Once more, it was the Judge, who asked the key, calming question.

“Rick, you have had time to think about all this, what are your conclusions?”

“I think we had better look this gift horse in the mouth,” Rick replied dryly.

“I think we all can agree on that, but how would you do that,” queried the Judge.

“The first thing I would do is insist that we had direct contact with the schools and consultants, not have the DHS be a middle man. Second, we need someone high powered on our side that can keep the DHS part way honest.”

“Who would that be,” asked Jack Nelson?

“Bill Wigle,” replied Rick.

"Uh, I hate to tell you, but I am only a county commissioner."

"I meant to say United States Congressman William Wigle," Rick restated.

"What, Huh," said an obviously confused Bill Wigle?

"Bill, John Mertz our current Congressman has announced he is retiring. When it is announced that through your efforts, we are getting a DHS center located here, creating over a hundred new jobs, you will be a shoo-in for the primary. Other than that Democrat who won when the District was first formed a Republican hasn't lost an election since the Civil War."

"It takes a lot of money to run for Congress, even in a small rural district like ours, it is close to ten million dollars, I just don't know how to raise that much," a still confused Bill said.

"We will just have to pass the hat," smiled Rick.

He continued, "When it gets to Marsha, she will put in five million, when it gets to me, I will make up the difference."

The Judge broke in, "You know there are contribution limits?"

"I know that bundlers come up with huge amounts, I guess we are now bundlers."

"Oh, as in like the Clinton Chinese bundlers that came up with hundreds of thousands of dollars from poor families that didn't make twenty thousand a year?"

"Yeah like that," said Rick.

Marsha broke in, "Now we don't want to give our money away, so we will hire professional fund-raisers and get as much of it as we can that way."

Bill Wigle had calmed down and was now seriously thinking of the possibilities. "I think we can keep cost down by doing some serious opposition research. It looks like Steve Welles is going to be my only serious competition. If the rumors are true he has some serious baggage."

Rick and everyone present picked up on Bills buy in.

## Chapter 34 –It is real easy – July 2024

The discussion continued with Paul Kettler going a little overboard with his anti-Federal rhetoric. Judge O'Malley asked him a question to clarify his thoughts.

"Paul, I gather that you have two issues, one is that we can't trust the Federal government, and two we can do this on our own."

"You understand it perfectly," he replied.

The Judge then continued, "What will we do about laws?"

"Why we use the laws we have."

"Our laws are based heavily on a prison system, do you propose building a penitentiary. I don't mean a jail for drunks and people awaiting trial, I mean a place to serve out a sentence."

"Could we just shoot them?" Paul semi-seriously asked.

"Are you going to be the one doing the shooting?" asked Sheriff Steve Linn.

Rick could see this conversation having no good direction, so broke in.

"The way I see it, we really will only have several punishments available, the death penalty, exile, fines and probation or combinations of these.

“That’s right,” said the Judge, while Sheriff Linn nodded his head in agreement.

Paul came right back with, “Okay, so the punishments will have to change, but we can still have the same laws.”

Marsha put down her pen and jumped into the discussion. “That’s a good idea Paul; now remind me of your opinion of the EPA? Also Common Core, along with the requirements to be a teacher. Then there is health care. I am sure you don’t want to change any of those laws.”

Paul puffed up, and then just as quickly settled down. “Yeah I guess we will need new laws which could be a very good thing.”

Mary, who had been getting ready to kick Paul under the table to shut him up chimed in with, “What about land ownership laws?”

“What do you mean,” asked the Judge.

“Well, if I own a piece of land here and have a mortgage with an out of town bank that doesn’t make it, do I owe anything? That doesn’t seem fair to the people who borrowed from a bank just down the road, who will still owe. Also, what about land that isn’t claimed by anyone living here, and someone shows up saying it’s theirs, what proof is acceptable?”

“What if someone settles in an unclaimed house and improves it, then someone shows up with a legitimate claim? After it all settles and we expand out of the Valley, who owns that land if it is occupied, or unoccupied."

Rick put his head in his hands and moaned, "This isn't like stories of the Post-Apocalyptic world that I have read. Everything there is simply starting over."

"That's the point Rick, we don't want a complete start-over," answered the Judge.

Rick straightened up and looked Paul Kettler in the eye, "I think your question about new laws has been answered."

"Yes it has, I hadn't given it the proper consideration, but I still don't trust the Feds."

"Oh, you can trust them to be true to their agenda. The question is; what's their agenda?"

Marsha who had been keeping an eye on Bill Wigle the whole meeting saw him sit up sharply, take a deep breath, then slouch back down. It was obvious to anyone looking at him that something had got his attention.

Jack Nelson the businessman brought up a good point, "What will we be using for money? Our economy will be too complex for simple barter and we won't be able to use the U.S. dollar as there will be too many floating around from the 'Badlands."

"Interesting point Jack," replied Rick. We will have to create our own currency."

“What will we back it with,” asked Matt Johnson? He continued, “I would hate to see us fail because we repeated the mistakes of the past with a fiat currency.”

“What is a fiat currency,” asked Hope?

“Italian cars,” Jack Nelson put in quickly.

After everyone chuckled at that Matt Johnson answered her, “To rule by fiat is to say this is the law, and that’s it. A fiat currency is one where the powers that be just state this money is worth so much and it isn’t backed up by anything real, like gold.”

Matt continued, “That works as long as everyone believes it has worth. When people realize all they are holding is a piece of paper that has no real value that is when things go south. So as long as people have faith in their government the currency works, when they lose faith is when the problems begin.”

“We need to make a decision on whether or not we want the Feds involved.”

Rick asked, “Does anyone want to make a motion?”

Per their prearrangement Hope Popule brought the motion forward to have Rick open discussions with his contact at DHS on what assistance they could lend.

Again by prearrangement after seeing how the show of hands was going to work out, Paul and Mary Kettler voted against the motion. The motion passed but it made it look like they weren't in lock step.

After that vote the group returned the discussion to finances for the operation. It quickly started to go in circles.

Rick interjected, "Maybe those groups that will be advising us will have thought about a solution."

"Let's hope so, if not with all the trees around here we could make a lot of wooden nickels," put in Sheriff Steve Linn.

"And on that note I think we should adjourn," said Rick, "All in favor?"

There was a round of ayes from those that weren't groaning.

"The ayes have it, meeting adjourned until next Monday."

When Rick and Marsha got home, she was in a playful mood, a very good playful mood. This had been happening to both of them more often recently. Not only were they feeling better and looking younger, they were acting younger.

The next day Rob King called at the agreed upon time of eleven a.m. and they updated each other. Rick told Rob about the meeting the previous night. He also let him know that Marsha was working on the minutes of that meeting and would copy him when they were emailed to the committee members.

For his part Rob brought up, "Now the Valley Group work begins Rick. We need to set up financing for this operation and establish communications with all our working groups. It will be a natural to have Judge O'Malley work with the law group, Sheriff Linn with the policing and Matt Johnson with Emergency Services."

"We are going to have to buy a lot of land to set up the public infrastructure, everything from a hospital to an airfield so Hope Popule should head that up. There will have to be an expansion of businesses to support the community; that is made for Jack Nelson. Paul and Mary Kettler will be the representatives to the food and farming operations. Bill Wigle of course will be our Congressman."

"Marsha will be in charge of education."

"That just leaves me, what is my role," Rick asked semi-seriously? The answer took him aback considerably.

"You will be in charge of the military end of things and also the entire Valley until we can relax martial law. That won't be for the foreseeable future."

"What," exclaimed Rick! "How do you figure that I am qualified to do either job?"

"Right now you probably aren't. However, you are the best we have."

"Why don't you bring someone in from the outside to be the 'Great Leader.'"

"Rick we have a very basic problem; that is having a legitimate government."

Rob continued, "Whoever governs does so at the will of the people. Here in the United States we have a long tradition of electing our government. Just think about it, if all collapsed and your group stands up and says we are now the government. Not only would you not be accepted, but every other clown would say they are in charge. You would win because you will have the most firepower, but that isn't what is needed for a successful future."

Rick shook his head even though it wasn't a video phone, "Rob, what have I let myself in for?"

"George must have asked himself that question almost every day."

"George?"

"George Washington."

"You have got to be kidding!"

Rob quietly replied, "No I'm not kidding, if successful you will have founded a new nation. Well, at least part of a new nation, we are hoping all the survival centers make it.

But right now the smart money is saying yours has the best chance due to locality and population."

"Rob you have to come down here and take charge," Rick stated adamantly.

"Rick you know I can't do that, I am an outsider, plus I have some health issues which mean I won't be able to see this through."

"May I ask; what health issues?"

"Cancer, it is early, but not looking good. It is in the pancreas.

"Damn, Rob I am so sorry." "

Rick not half as sorry as I am, but that is the way it is."

"Before we get maudlin, I need to talk to you about the bank you are going to buy."

"Huh?"

"The bank you are going to buy, that is how this whole operation is going to be financed."

"I only have some millions, not billions."

"Leverage, you are going to buy the Pikeville Valley Savings and Loan. With your forty or so million as collateral we will arrange a loan of two hundred million to buy the bank. Then the Fed will deposit five hundred million in the bank. You will pay off the two hundred million dollar loan. Then use the remaining three hundred million to make loans. You will be allowed to loan seven dollars for every one you have on deposit so you will have over two billion dollars to loan."

"I don't know anything about banking at that level or any level other than writing a check. Heck Marsha even writes those nowadays."

"Not to worry, we will have a president and a support team to run it for you."

"Why do we need that much money," inquired a punchy sounding Rick?

"To buy all the land we will need for our project and help to set up the infrastructure. It will give you power in the Valley like you can't believe. Besides when you set up your own currency after the fall you will need a financial institution to be setup or buy a local bank. That will be the foundation for your treasury when you print your money, and it will be the storage repository for your gold deposits."

"Gold deposits," echoed Rick?

"Well Fort Knox has got to go somewhere. Contrary to the rumors we actually do have twenty six million ounces there."

"Rob could you call me back later?"

"Sure; how come?"

"Because I have to go throw up," replied Rick as he hung up the phone.

## Chapter 35 - Really it is easy - July 2024

Rick didn't go throw up; instead he went out on the wide veranda surrounding the house. He just sat there looking into the distance. Marsha who was in the room when the call was going on could tell it was big. She came out onto the porch with him and just sat quietly. After about twenty minutes, he stirred and asked her to get him a drink.

She asked, "Coffee or iced tea?"

"Double Jack Black straight up," he replied.

"Serious?"

"As a heart attack," was his response.

Rick seldom drank hard liquor much less before noon, so this was serious. Marsha didn't comment, just went and fixed the drink. He sipped it for a few minutes; then proceeded to tell her about the phone call.

“Marsha they want me to run an army, be a dictator, own a multi-billion dollar bank and give me all the gold in Fort Knox. This is insanity!”

Marsha who was having a hard time comprehending what she was hearing gave the time honored response.

“Yes dear.”

Rick looked sharply at her. “Aren’t you supposed to say I’m sorry?”

She giggled as she replied, “That goes with, you are right, I’m wrong, I’m sorry. Weren’t you paying attention in husband class?”

Rick gave a bark of laughter, “Yes Dear,” and the tension started to wind down.

They went in and while Marsha was fixing them grilled cheese sandwiches with salsa on them, he gave her more detail of the phone call.

“Well it makes more sense now that you have told me all,” she commented. “That is the individual points make more sense. The big picture has got me lost, how will we ever accomplish everything. As a group we don’t have the required knowledge to implement each item, much less make the entire project come together.”

"Actually, I don't see that as the problem. As Rob told me; for the bank they would bring a professional team. I would be the owner and Chairman of the Board but they would run it. I would be the public figure head. That is the way every one of us would work. We could question and give our input, but they would run it."

"That is the issue, they would run it. It is going to be very difficult for us to keep control. Another question is do we want to keep control? But then who are they? What are their motives? I would be a lot more comfortable if I knew 'their' long term vision. I'm not for a strongman type of government even if I am the strongman."

"If someone has to be the single person in charge I would rather it be you, than a lot of people."

"Thanks for the vote of confidence, but remember, a good strongman can be followed by a bad one. That is what bothers me."

Just then the phone rang.

It was Rob calling back.

"Feeling better," he asked?

Rick replied, "Yeah with a little help from my friend Jack Black and a lot of help from Marsha."

Rob barked a laugh, "Yeah I have visited him myself recently."

Rob proceeded to recap their previous conversation. Rick had correctly understood what was being said.

Rick then told him about his concerns about a martial law governor being followed by a poor one.

Rob agreed that this was a major concern. He also agreed with Rick that there might be a long term vision for the CSC that they weren't aware of.

They both ended up agreeing that all they could do was pay attention and keep the project moving along.

"Speaking of moving along, I think it is important that we gain the group legitimate standing within the community as soon as possible."

"I agree Rick; could I attend your next group meeting and explain what has been proposed?"

"Sure the sooner the better."

"Okay, put me on the agenda for next Monday and I will be there."

"Rob why don't you come down Sunday night and stay with us, we could have an extended conversation about all of this."

"Sounds like a plan."

"Be here before six so you can join us for dinner."

"Okay, see you around five in the afternoon on Sunday."

Sunday night the three of them had a long conversation. Nothing really new was brought up, but they did get a firmer idea of where they were going and what had to happen.

Monday brought the Valley Group meeting. The General presented well as one would expect from a General. He explained that DHS was very interested in creating CSC's which could support the recovery of a breakdown of society.

He presented it as FEMA writ large. The only difference rather than coming in after the fact they were trying to be proactive.

Paul Kettler's, "Now I have heard everything," spoke for the group.

It also set the stage for Rob to present how they were going to legitimize the group and set the stage for them to be the leaders if the events they were predicting came to pass.

"DHS is going to ask for an advisory group to be established to represent the Valley. The fix is in. The County Commissioners will appoint everyone in this room to be the advisory group. No, you don't want to know how that was accomplished. I will just say it was a carrot and stick approach. Some of the County Commissioners had some things they didn't want to make public, others took a payoff, and one of them actually did it for all the right reasons. Bill you can stand up and take a bow."

"I can announce it now; Bill Wigle saw the possibilities before anyone else. He approached a friend at DHS and presented his thoughts. There was already a project of this nature in the pipeline and Pikeville was on the short list.

Bill then helped vet every one of you to be certain you were the people we needed in the group. He has been in constant contact with DHS. Now we think he can help us more by being our voice in Congress."

To say that took everyone by surprise was an understatement. Rick started a round of applause which all joined in. Bill stood up, but was speechless. Rob came to his rescue.

"What we have here tonight is a group who are risking their lives, their fortunes and their sacred honor. We have here the founding fathers and mothers of a future nation. You are the few, the happy few, a band of brothers. Now I have mangled the Declaration of Independence and Henry V, so I am sure Bill is now comfortable to speak."

This brought some general laughter.

Bill said simply, "It needed to be done and I was the one who did it. But now it is time for me to turn it over to you as a group and Rick King as our leader. For what is coming, Rick has the background to make it happen and follow through."

Now it was Ricks turn to respond, but he had his thoughts in order.

“My background is what is needed. The vision has been seen by Bill, the DHS has set the policy and is providing the support, now is the time for an honest sergeant to work for his living and make it happen.”

General King went on to explain about the working groups at various Universities and think tanks around the country. How each of them would have a role as advisor to them.

How once the plans were laid out professionals from hospital administrators to 3D printing plant managers would come in and set them up. However, this group would be undergoing training to become the nucleus of the new government to bring the country back under control.

Judge O’Malley said, “Why wouldn’t Congress just move here and run the country if the cities fall.”

“Mark, if the cities fall I doubt if any of us will make it out,” said a sober Bill Wigle. “I won’t be moving my family to Washington.”

This remark brought everyone down. A somber group went on to discuss the bank which Rick was going to buy and then was quick to adjourn.

That meeting was the start of the whirl wind. The first gust of that wind was the announcement that Rick King had bought The Pikeville Valley Savings and Loan.

A team led by David Christensen was brought in to run it. Construction was started immediately on some bank owned property for a large expansion. Not only was the bank itself going to move there but there was enough space for a staff of fifty people.

New vaults were put in place two levels below ground. These were large vaults. Some jokers down at the diner told Mary they thought they would be moving Fort Knox there. Mary didn't spread that rumor.

A new subsidiary of the bank started buying land. Hope Popule, a new employee of the bank headed this effort. Within six months she and her team had acquired ninety five percent of the available land in the valley.

The last five percent were holding out for more money than it was worth and those parcels weren't really needed. They then started work on property that wasn't for sale but had been identified as needed.

One such land parcel was spread out over three farms adjacent to the old Watkins land. DHS needed it for a runway they were putting in. The runway would go with the long axis of the valley and would be seventeen thousand feet long.

It could handle any aircraft in the commercial or Air Force fleet. There would be secondary runways but of necessity they wouldn't be as long.

The group all began to accumulate frequent flier miles as they visited the support groups around the nation. They still met weekly but half the members would telecommute from around the country.

The nuclear reactors went in on schedule and without protest. The reactors weren't put out to bid, they were deemed unique items which come from a sole provider, so no announcements were made.

They were small enough to move in the dead of night on flatbed trailers. Of course that was the easy part. Getting them set up and working with the proper infrastructure took another six months.

The next issue to be addressed was housing. Some of the newly arrived higher level executives had contracted the building of new homes. This still left a housing shortage. Rick was forced to open another division of the bank.

The bank loaned itself the money to build tract housing and apartments on some of the land it had purchased. This in turn led to a need for water, sewage and electric services. These were paid for completely by impact fees by the developer.

This included new schools for students who hadn't even arrived yet and health care facilities for the patients that weren't ill yet. The school buildings were Rick's problem.

The school curriculum was Marsha's. She had to have one in place for the current laws, and one that would work for the future.

Many were the night that Rick and Marsha would collapse in bed. Many were the night they had a little left over for each other. Though they were running like crazy, they both seemed to be getting stronger all the time.

## Chapter 36 – Maybe not so easy – April 2025

The Valley group had the hope that they could become independent from outside food. However, when they did the math it wouldn't work. They had come to the conclusion they would have fifty thousand people at the 'Time'.

The studies estimated for a normal diet it would take twenty acres per person. This worked out to one million acres or forty square miles. The valley was long but narrow. They didn't have that sort of land and weren't in a position to start out in other valleys.

If they had to allow two years for things to settle down, and then get crops in where ever they could, they would have to have a lot of food in storage. That had always been the plan but the numbers were amazing.

All of sudden the Federal help they had been shying away from was very welcome. Of course this increased the number of warehouses, and the people to staff them, so that upped the headcount and more food was needed.

How many mules did the army really need became the running joke, but it was also kidding on the square. If they didn't get this right it could kill them.

Something else occurred that Rick hadn't foreseen. He was asked by Rob King to apply for a reserve commission in the Army. His explanation was that it would help later when and if Rick had to take charge of any armed forces they had.

The short term rationale was that a major review was going to be held of the entire U. S. Army sergeants training program. Since Rick had helped establish the current one he would be a good historical resource and have valuable input in the new program.

Rick asked why he had to be in the service. He was told that they wouldn't want to listen to an old civilian. He then inquired why he had to be an officer.

The response was that officers would be doing the review and they wouldn't listen to an old has been Sergeant

Major. This response really got the old has been Sergeant Major on his high horse.

He demanded as much rank as he could get so they would have to listen to him.

All of a sudden Rick was a reserve Colonel in the United States Army Reserve. He was called to active duty. It was arranged for him to attend an abbreviated Officers Candidate School.

There was none of the early wake up, uniform BS. It was to let him know how todays Army differed from his. He quickly found out the old ways weren't acceptable.

No giving the Sergeant a hint that a man had to be taken out behind the barracks. If the officer had to give the hint then it was probably time for a new Sergeant.

He now had to be sensitive to genders and preferences. The up side was that no officers had been fragged recently.

He actually spent several weeks involved with the new training program. To his surprise his every word was hung on to like gospel.

This may have had something to do with the Distinguished Service Cross, Silver Star with one Bronze Oak leaf, Bronze Star with one Silver Oak leaf, Purple Heart with four Oak Leaves.

His tabs were the tower of power; Airborne, Ranger and Special Forces. His parachute device was that of a Master Parachutist Badge with a gold combat device.

Finally he wore a Combat Infantry Badge with a star on it. He had served in the Korean and Viet Nam eras.

One Major said it all when he heard that Rick finished his enlisted career as a Sergeant Major, "That is one bad assed dude!"

In setting up the new courses, Rick had to remind people time and time again that the Armies mission was to break things and kill people.

What Rick had to adjust to was that the new Sergeants had to be able to adapt to rapidly changing tactics based on new weapon systems, which were being provided at an ever increasing pace.

They had a series of weapons and tactics trials. Rick was hated by the Political Correctness people because that was the first thing he threw out the window when he was in command of the exercise and he always won.

Why did they not get that upper body strength was enforced by the laws of physics not the laws of man! They thought that he wouldn't allow any homosexuals in combat.

His question was, "Can and will they pull the trigger? If so I want them."

Rick was happy being a Colonel. He didn't have to put up with the BS as he expressed it. He got a little bent with Rob when he was told that his name had been submitted to Congress and he had been awarded his first star.

"Rob, this is over the damn top," was Rick's expression!

"You need it for what we think is coming," replied an unrepentant Rob.

Marsha was very helpful after pinning his stars on, she kept saluting him. After three days it got a little old!

He did receive some retraining, even a General had better remember, "Yes Dear."

Now he had to attend a five week course at the National Defense University in Washington D.C. The course was the 'Capstone General and Flag Officer course.

It taught General officers that they had to behave themselves because they would be under more intense scrutiny than ever before in their life. The curriculum was heavy on interacting both professionally and personally with General officers of all services.

Vanity led Rick into a trip to Leavenworth, KS where he was measured by Marlow White for a full set of uniforms including full mess dress, both blue and white.

Rick figured if he was going, it might as well be all the way. Rick had learned about this old line military tailor when he attended the United States Army Command and General Staff School for Command Preparation when he was promoted to Command Sergeant Major.

When Rick put on his regular uniform for the first time Marsha was amazed. Rick had his ninetieth birthday last February. Standing in his normal ramrod straight posture one would be hard pressed to think he was sixty.

The frail old man she had fallen in love with was a mature hunk!

Rob King had disappeared into a hospital in March. They visited him several times and the wasted man they found almost had them in tears. On a visit in April Rob asked them not to come anymore.

"It is too hard on all of us and my time is close. Rick, I have had the paperwork submitted to the Society of Cincinnatus, you will be taking my place. There is no secret handshake to learn, nothing behind the scenes.

You will meet a lot of good people that will help you, think of it as networking. Think of it as a social club that works for the good of the service, like pensions and education. However it is the most prestigious club in the military."

"You can only wear your badge on formal Society occasions when in Uniform, but it will give you a social cachet for the next few years."

"Why will I need that," inquired Rick?

"Oh, the combat group we are going to station near here will give you plenty of need. That and another reason, which will be clear later, is why you had to have the star."

"You will be contacted by David Paul. He is the Director with DHS, who will be taking over my duties."

Both Rick and Marsha kept quiet when they heard that. Not that they knew anything about David, it was the fact that Rob just told them this was the end.

They made no false protests. They had both seen too many friends and family die to play the games of denial anymore.

Two weeks later Lieutenant General Robert King, United States Army, Retired died in his sleep. Rick and Marsha attended his funeral and later interment at Arlington National Cemetery.

There were no close relatives in attendance but there were many former subordinates present. Rick in full dress uniform was singled out quickly by a four star general.

The General introduced himself as Chief of Staff of the U. S. Army.

"I thought I knew all the General officers in the Army. Where are you stationed?"

Rick explained that he was a reserve officer who had just been activated and was attached to DHS.

"Oh, I heard about you. I can't tell you conniptions that you have caused. A former Command Sergeant Major bumped to a one star! Eighty some years old! I can tell you the grapevine was going crazy. I hadn't read your service jacket, but looking at your merit badges tells it all.

I would like to introduce you to several people. It will take some pressure off me."

The General turned to Marsha, "You don't mine if I borrow him for a few minutes?"

"He's all yours General. Please return him in the condition you found him."

From there Rick was given a whirlwind introduction to six different General officers who held between them eighteen stars. One of those was the Chairman of the Joint Chiefs.

In each case it was like two strange dogs meeting. Who would be dominating? They had the rank, he had the awards. One serious look at what he did have and while maintaining their reserve he was acknowledged the respect of a true warrior. A brief explanation was given about his call up, promotion and duties with the new Sergeants program, and how he needed the rank to get heard.

It was a specialized call up and wouldn't be upsetting the natural order of things in the Army. Rick would only be on active duty until the Sergeants program review was finished and his pension wouldn't be greatly enhanced.

From the nods and body language Rick was soon comfortable. It turns out the objections were based on the thought that he was taking a permanent advancement slot. Since he wasn't they could have cared less.

When the rounds had been made General Lee (descendent of) took him back to Marsha.

"Thank you ma'am, this will take some pressure off my office. One last question Rick, were you related to Rob King?"

"Distantly, we were both descended from a Rufus King."

"Will you be presenting your paperwork to the Society of Cincinnatus?"

"Rob had already helped me get my paperwork in order. It has been submitted."

General Lee thanked Rick for his cooperation, shook his hand while handing him a business card.

"If you run into any difficulties give me a call, your case is so unusual it will get kicked up to me anyway." He took one last look at Rick, shook his head, made a comment about the wonders of 'Live' medicine and left.

Rick and Marsha had both been running into curious attitudes from people about their apparent age. With the advent of 'Live', people were expected to live longer and healthier lives. They had the feeling that their health and appearance had more to it than the medication, since they never had taken it.

When they returned to Tennessee they had another discussion on their general health and appearance.

Marsha kicked it off by saying, "Rick, is there going to come a time when people catch on that we aren't normal?"

"I don't see how it can be avoided."

"Do you think we should change our identities?"

"Not really, we created and have maintained those false ones in Chattanooga for the Watkins deal, but they wouldn't stand up to a real investigation. I don't know how we would even go about doing it."

## Chapter 37 -Who's in Charge? -April 2025

This conversation started a process that would last for many years.

Marsha mused, "If we could control the records twenty or more years in advance that would take care of it."

"What do you mean?"

"Well, if we were involved in creating birth and death certificates we could be who we wanted."

"Wouldn't it be more complicated than that, what about school records, driver's licenses, school pictures?"

"Yes it would, but we have to start at the beginning. I am going to see about getting a job in the records department at the courthouse now that my major tasks on education are under control."

Their lives were in a spin. They barely had time to adjust to one situation when another would pop up. The Valley group settled down and was actually getting it together.

Each member was interacting in their respective field with the corresponding expert groups. Each member set up a sub-team in their field to aid and guide. No one person could keep it all together.

As Judge O'Malley put it, "This is so much fun it should be illegal. Oh wait I'm the one making the laws!"

One guiding principle was that if it was too long to read, then it was too long to use. There wasn't going to be any, "You have to pass it to find out what is in it."

Another battle that was constant was, "That sounds good, but that is not our culture."

The schools and think tanks had a liberal bias which they were trying to impose on the gun toting, god-fearing Bible belt. The Valley group finally quit arguing and just accepted what they were given then changed it to suit themselves.

Hope Popule was in a realtor's heaven as she bought every property on the market and made offers on those they needed, but weren't listed.

She had signed on with the bank but still got a reduced commission of one percent. So far, she had over five hundred million dollars in transactions and going strong. She wondered if there was a billion-dollar real estate club.

Rick was brought in for a presentation of the financial status of the bank. This was a high level review prior to their first financial audit. On their two billion dollars, they made a profit on the books of fourteen percent. This worked out to two hundred and eighty million dollars.

When Rick asked, "Now who gets this profit if we cashed out?"

The President of his bank looked at him like he was crazy. "Rick you own this bank lock stock and barrel. You would get all of it."

It was Rick's turn to look at the President like he was crazy.

"How can that be?"

“Well you put in the startup capital. The government put deposits in the bank. You loaned the money out, made a profit. The government could ask for their money back, which could create a mess if it demanded it all at once, but that isn’t going to happen.

Now the question is how much to you want to leave in the bank? If you withdraw it, it will be taxed; and taxed heavily.

Rick’s response was to say, “Let me think about it for a few days.”

What he really meant was Holy Cow; I need to talk to Marsha about this! He and Marsha had several long conversations, and he came back to the bank President with a question.

“Can I leave the money in the bank, but buy gold and hold it as reserves?”

“Yes, that would work well. Especially, if after you have the gold in place you let it be known that is how your reserves are stored. It will give the bank enormous credibility. Combine that with the good loans on land and this has to be one of the strongest financial institutions in the world.

“Then let’s proceed on that basis, plan to do that every year until further notice.”

A few days later, the DHS Director David Paul made an appointment to see him. Rick took it as a good sign that Paul elected to call and ask if he could meet him and Marsha at their home, then later if appropriate be introduced to the Valley group.

David Paul came across as low-key and affable. However, there was something about him that left both Rick and Marsha wondered what his temper would be like.

Though he seemed easy going there appeared to be a fury waiting to be unleashed. They agreed they would always treat him as a stick of dynamite waiting to go off. They could work with him, but he would never be a friend or confidant.

He explained that there were several scenarios that could play out.

"One nothing happens and there is no need for the CSCs. Two there could be a partial failure of the country where the cities collapsed but the country side held. Three it went all to Hell and the only things left were the CSCs."

David added, "There are also subsets of the above. We might lose it all on the coasts, but the center of the country holds. There are many possibilities, but we are preparing to some degree for the three. If nothing happens, then a lot of money has been spent for nothing."

“If the second scenario plays out the CSCs will have to coordinate to bring it together. If the last one plays out, it is every group for itself.”

“This has been war gamed to death. The highest probability is the middle ground. So we are planning on the CSC’s being the core of each region as we put the country back together again.”

Rick said, “I am confused about one issue. We are going to a lot of work to come up with simpler laws which will work; education system, government structure and a whole host of other items. If all the CSCs are doing this, it will be a complete confusing mishmash.”

“Ah, you are catching on. Yours is the only CSC doing this. You are the model for all the others. Since the Valley group formed itself, your CSC had a head start. You had people in place to get things moving, so we are taking advantage of that,” replied Paul.

“In the next month, you will have to start visiting each CSC to get an idea of how they are progressing. We will be basing a reinforced company with high mobility at each DHS facility. They will have a Major in command since it will have higher than normal staffing. We are also trying to attach a heavy element but the logistics of supporting tanks or artillery are pretty stiff, and we don’t see how we can do it.”

“Wait a minute I will out rank all the others.”

"That's the idea, Rick we want you to have overall command of the remaining armed forces."

"Oh my God, what have I gotten into?"

"Simple Rick, with your heritage and military background, you are the most qualified person who we know will be absolutely loyal to the idea of the United States of America and all it stands for."

"How will I get around?"

"Why do you think we have those runways at the Ranch? You will have five C21's, as those are the most adaptable in the current fleet, since they replaced the old C17 they have proven themselves time and again as being reliable and versatile. Plus, we are looking into basing some Blackhawks and Apaches here, but the logistics once again are the problem."

Also we are really being selective on the personnel of the reinforced companies. Single where we can get them; but fewer attachments the better. Also most of them will have had training experience, so they can be the cadre for enlarging your forces as needed."

"Okay I will be in command, which scares the hell out of me, but who will be in charge politically of the combined CSCs?"

"We won't know till after the first elections, but that will not matter for a long time to come. We will start out under martial law and hold the elections after things are under control. You will be running things for about the first ten years."

"You have got to be kidding," exclaimed Rick!

"Not at all, as a matter of fact, your nickname in the DHS planning group is not Richard King, but King Richard!"

"Why me Lord," groaned Rick. "I don't understand why you guys are giving this country to me."

"Rick, we don't think we are. The best estimates are a less than one-percent chance that it will come to pass that your group will come into play."

"We fully expect the current military will be able to step in restore order; then restore the Republic. Yes, I do mean the Republic."

"Then why are we going to all this bother and expense, it must be billions by now."

Paul replied, "About fifteen billion at this point. That is chicken feed compared to the multi-trillion dollar budgets that we now have. Since the advent of the 'Live' drug and conquering Alzheimer's health care costs have become a very small part of the budget."

"Social Security used to take a significant portion, now it is almost gone. We as a nation can afford to plan for events like this. If we quit spending money, it might hasten the end. We are in a delicate balance I am told, so must continue the dance."

"Yeah, dance right of the edge of the cliff," Rick retorted.

"That may be the case, but it is the only thing we can do. Rick you have no idea how scared the real powers that be really are. You just think you are in survivalist mode. Some of these guys have retreated to underground fortresses."

"Exactly what do your planners see happening," Rick asked?

"That is the problem. They don't have a clue. All they know is the History doesn't repeat itself, but it does rhyme. We are well overdue for some sort of event that will change the civilized world as we know it. It may be for the better for all we know."

"It could be super computers taking care of all our problems. No death, no work, no problems or it could be the four horsemen of the Apocalypse. Where do you want to put your money?"

"I see what you mean David. Where do we go from here," Rick inquired?

"The next step is for you to become familiar with the other CSCs."

"Where are they, I have never been told."

"They are in the country side like this one; western New York, western Virginia, southwest Georgia, the upper peninsula of Michigan, Arkansas, Utah, and Oregon. The idea is to give them a healthy buffer from the cities."

"You have given up on the cities?"

"Under this scenario yes, with the modern supply chains, they don't keep three days of food on hand anymore. We could never get relief in before the rioting and looting destroys them."

"That is sad. Marsha and I have some very good friends in the Baltimore area. Would there be any problem inviting them to move to our area?"

"Not if done soon enough, and you have a legitimate function they can fulfill."

## Chapter 38 – Back to Basics- April 2025

Rick and Marsha had many long talks about the future. Rick kept coming back to, "I am in over my head Marsha."

Marsha would always come back with, "So would anyone put into this position."

Rick would then continue with, "My concern now is that nothing will happen, and we will look like the biggest fools of all time, even worse than some of those doomsday cults. As a matter of fact, you could make a case that is what we are, except we have Federal backing."

He went on, "It was one thing when it was just you and me wanting to find a place where we could ride out any coming storms. This is more than a level above that. It is like we are responsible for the survival of the entire human race and in fact, there might not even be a survival problem!"

After one such outburst Marsha came back with, "Rick grow up, you yourself made a good case that we have something strange going on with our bodies. We should be dead; instead, we appear to be in our early sixties. We can only go on with what is and that is we might live indefinitely. If that is so, we will probably see the end of the United States of America as we know it. Our government agrees with us."

Marsha continued to explain, "They are just taking it one step further. Instead of preparing for a regime change they are preparing for a massive die off. I for one am glad that someone of your abilities and integrity is in place to see us through these tribulations. Think of yourself as a fire alarm. One of those in a case with a sign which says, 'In case of fire, break glass and pull alarm.' Hope that the glass never needs broken, but it is there just in case. Now quit whining!"

This speech by Marsha left Rick a little red faced because he realized she was correct. He didn't know how to react to that, so he did the one sure thing for almost any situation in a marriage.

He hugged Marsha and said, "Thanks." The hugs lead to a more pleasurable event.

Later Rick had to say, "Hey this world saving isn't such a bad thing!"

That got him hit with a pillow which started the whole process over again. There is much to be said for being younger.

The next morning as they ate breakfast on the veranda the topic of conversation was totally different. Marsha started it with questions about how their bank was doing.

Both were confused and in awe of how they weren't merely well off but now rich by any definition. Changes in the valley were one thing; changes in the check book were another. To be able to live comfortably and not have worry about money issues was one thing. Having so much money you had no idea what to do with it was another.

Most rich people had their money tied up in stocks, bonds or physical assets. Their fortune was a growing pile of gold and property. They now owned almost eighty percent of the valley. Their fortune was in the billions, and they really had no idea how much they were worth, not even to the nearest billion.

Rick pointed out, "It really doesn't matter what we have now. It's what we have later and how we use it. I have been doing some economic homework. I don't want us to have a government that can control money policy like they have, look at the problems we are now facing with trillions in debt. That is the number-one reason the Federal government is backing this project. Even they realize that it can't go on and that a major collapse is inevitable."

"I have read articles on returning to a gold standard, they all say it can't be done. The reasoning is that ultimately the money supply will be limited by the physical amount of gold available to back the money supply. This will limit how the economy can expand."

Rick went on, "Also if there were to be a true emergency where the government had to print more money or borrow it against future revenues it would inflate the money supply over available gold thus leading to the current abuses. No matter how you slice and dice it government always wants more money than is available. It is human nature. We all want more, even those that work in the government. The only difference we have to live within our means, they don't."

Rick continued, "We have several things going for us. We won't have a Federal Reserve to be used as a political tool to control the money supply. The gold will all be in private hands, namely ours. Our bank and others will issue paper gold notes. That is they will look like the money we use now, but they will be actually certificates good for a given weight of gold upon request. I am thinking ten thousandths of an ounce. That way, gold will start out at ten thousand dollars an ounce.

"If there is a world collapse, then people will go out into the destroyed areas and recover gold. This could cause inflation as we exchange it for our 'new dollars,' but I figure that after the collapse, as a survival center our economy will be growing like crazy and the money expansion will hardily keep up with the demand."

"That is why I'm not going to issue all the possible 'new dollars' at first. If we have gold that isn't committed, then we can expand the money supply rapidly if needed. I know that puts you and me in the position of being the Fed, but we know that the newly elected government won't be able to pressure us to issue fiat currency.

"Rick, don't delude yourself, if these things come to pass then you will be in control by martial law for a long time to come. You will end up earning your new nickname."

“My new nickname,” Rick inquired?

“At the dinner the other day I heard you referred to as King Richard.”

“Oh my God, I was hoping that wouldn’t catch on!”

“We don’t always get what we want, Your Majesty.”

“Oh Lord,” Rick groaned, “Why me?”

On a more serious note, Marsha continued. “I know you would rather be a George Washington father of your country type rather than a King, but it may work out for the best. You can set things up and make certain they are in place then abdicate.”

“True,” Rick replied thoughtfully. One thing I want to put in place is a flat tax. Start it out at five percent and lower it if possible. We won’t have any entitlements. People will be responsible for their own retirements.”

“If you are able-bodied and able to work you will work. I remember a trip to Singapore in the 1980s. There were old women sweeping all the sidewalks and curb area. The country was incredibly clean. I found out the government didn’t pay welfare.  They just made a job that they could handle and paid them for it. Each of these ladies would spend the day outside, most of the time sitting in a chair in the shade. If a leaf fell it would be cleaned up, and woe unto a litter bug!”

“There will be those that I call the “Lost. They won’t be able to perform a useful function. We won’t be so uncaring as to not support them, but they and their families will be health and means tested to a fare thee well. Also a sad fact of life is that many life supports that are now in place may not be in the future.

“We don’t have the capability to manufacture insulin so that is almost a death sentence for anyone with type I diabetes. Those with type II will have to correct their life styles or they will also die. I feel for the Type I’s, but not the Type II’s, but the fact is no matter how I or others may feel there is currently nothing pharmaceutically that we can do.”

“Along with no entitlements, everyone will start out with a clean debt slate. If the world collapses our bank will be the only one around at first. I intend to forgive all debt owed to us. It is only a small part of our fortune and why should borrowing from our bank be a punishment for the survivors. I don’t know if I told you this earlier, but DHS has a program in place to track the money on deposit with all local branches.”

“They will all be taken over by us, when and if they fail. At that point, we will stand behind the deposits like we were the FDIC. That way, people won’t lose everything but those with over the 2021 limit of five hundred thousand dollars will share in the pain.”

“Those that choose to live outside the Valley, but within our area of control will pay no taxes. That will encourage people to move out and repopulate the country. As they move further out we will expand the tax boundaries to encourage people to keep moving.”

“The only departments of the Federal government will be the; Department of War, Department of State, Department of Postal Services and the Department of Land Management. There will also be a Supreme Court.”

“The Department of War will be exactly that, our Military. I am going back to its original name to remind people of why it exists.  At first, there will be a very limited Navy and Marine corps as we aren’t near the coasts. There will be no Air Force. The Army and Navy will have their own assets.”

“The Department of State will be very limited in size and scope as there will probably be very few foreign powers to deal with. To serve in State, as all Departments, you will have to be former military. While it won’t eliminate all bleeding hearts it will limit them.”

Marsha got a jab in here with a “Yes, King Richard.”

Rick frowned but continued, “Postal Services will be exactly that, I think David Brin nailed it in a novel many years ago with a book called ‘The Postman’, later a Kevin Costner movie. The main theme was that having the mail delivered tied a spread out, torn up country together. I envision the same here."

"The Department of Land Management will be involved in mapping the remaining territories, taking a census of them. We will also have a homesteader program where we will provide land and startup materials to those who want to try their hand at farming. We will also issue a larger land grant to those who complete military service."

"The Supreme Court will only be a group to interpret our constitution. By charter they won't be allowed to find 'new rights."

"If you are on the government payroll or receiving any direct aid you won't be able to vote until you are on your own. That takes care of that vested interest."

Marsha inquired, "The Military and Police also?"

"Yes, they are serving their country, but they are also a special interest group. I'm trying to limit their powers. "

"Also unions will be limited to a single company or plant. They won't become a big business in their own right. Some companies earn a union, and they can bear that burden, but I'm not going to let unions remain as they are. The unions will also be prohibited from donating campaign funds, along with any other groups. What the individual wants to contribute is fine."

"Also the Constitution will have the Bill of Rights embedded. The right to bear arms will be clarified to say if you want to drive your M4A4 Main Battle Tank down the road the only thing you can be charged with is tearing up public property with the tank treads."

"The same with religion, government can't tell you what to believe, but God can be and will be in our public life. He is anyway, so let's recognize it and get over it. And this bit about the Commerce clause allowing the government to control all trade has got to go!"

"I don't think the social issues will be issues. We will give a bounty for having children. We won't outlaw abortion; it just won't be available unless a panel of doctors and clergy is convinced it is the right thing to do in each individual case."

"I figure when I roll this out under Martial Law, I will be hated by almost every group there is, but that means I have succeeded in being even handed! I am also certain this return to the original idea of limited government will be gradually eroded just like it has this time, but if we get another two hundred year run I will be happy."

Marsha couldn't help adding, "And in two hundred years you will just have to have another revolution."

"Damn Straight."

## Chapter 39 –Lets go Scouting - May 2025

Over the next month, Rick visited the other CSCs. He was impressed with what the government had accomplished, but not so impressed with the other local leaders.

They left him uncomfortable. They all reminded him of Major Watkins. All out for a power grab. At the same time, he realized that he left them very uncomfortable. He made the visits in uniform at David Paul's suggestion. They were all wanted to be. He was the real deal.

He had no doubt that with the Federal help they could control their local areas. The question was what they would do with that control. He expressed his concerns to Paul. Paul told him that they agreed with his assessment, and that he had just passed another test. DHS intention was to replace every one of them with true local control; the problem was identifying the correct leaders.

Rick thought about that for a few days and came back with the suggestion that they should make contact with local volunteer firemen, scout leaders, the civil air patrol and the HAM radio clubs. They had a track record of being involved with the local community because they believed in it, and they had proven that they could make things happen. He didn't limit his thoughts to those groups but expressed the idea that they were the type of people they were looking for. There were probably other groups that met these criteria.

When Rick shared these thoughts with David Paul, Paul got a very thoughtful look on his face. "You know Rick; we were looking at all the official organizations that are part of the local government. We never thought of the volunteers, but as soon as you brought it up, I know this will be the source of the people we need."

"There will be people in the official positions that cross over, but we didn't know how to separate the people that are good for the community from the drones. Unfortunately, the government has become a stereotype for a reason."

"So anyway Rick, how would you identify the key local person?"

"I would get a representative from each of those volunteer groups. I would interview them as to who they thought the local leaders were. I would then come up with a reason to give psychological and skill tests to them to ensure the right mix of people. I would then bring them together in several exercises to see who emerges as the true leader of the group."

Paul continued, "While we are on Leadership issues, there is one that I have been putting off."

"What is that," inquired Rick?

“Paul and Mary Kettler aren’t cut out to be the interfaces with the outside working groups. Paul delights in telling them they are government drones living off the backs of the honest working man. Mary isn’t much better. This doesn’t lead to open communication.”

“I’m not even saying they are wrong. However, they have to realize that the people they are dealing with are the best of the best. The real drones are hidden in the bureaucracy and will never be found. All they are doing is alienating the people who are trying to help them.”

“I wish I could say you are wrong, but I can’t. I will take care of it. I think I may have an idea to make this a win-win.

After Paul from DHS left, Marsha had an amused look on her face.

“What’s so funny,” Rick inquired.

“You, you have been set up again. Want to bet who will be up to his eyeballs in interviews for both the outside groups and Mary and Paul?”

This stopped Rick in his tracks. He had one of his many cups of coffee in hand and almost spilled it.

“You are kidding, right?”

“Nope saw that one coming a mile away.” “

I don’t think you are right, want to bet on it?”

"Sure I could use a break from washing dishes for a month."

"Lawn mowing season is coming up. You can do the first month."

"You got a bet!"

Rick invited Paul and Mary over for dinner the next night. His intention was to have a nice dinner, then bring up the painful subject after the meal was concluded. This wasn't to be.

They were barely in the house before Paul started. "Rick, Mary and I have to get off those committees. They are driving us crazy. I know they are good people, but they just can't see that they aren't really contributing to society."

"Isn't what they are doing contributing?"

"Yeah now, they are practically at the point of a gun. They would be happy to be sitting there doing nothing and collecting a check."

"That may be, but they are now contributing. What do you have in mind?

"We have been paid to attend those meetings. Mary is thinking of opening a day-care center to help with the income."

For some reason, Marsha went into a coughing fit. It couldn't have had anything to do with her trying to imagine Mary running a day-care center for children.

Mary didn't look real pleased at the thought and mumbled something about, "little snots."

Smothering his own laughter Rick stated, "This could help me with a couple of problems. One Marsha and I are gone so often we can't take care of the house and grounds like we should. How about we hire you at the same rate you have been making?

Paul jumped all over that, "That sounds great, what is the other thing?"

"I know you and Mary have been involved in scouting, both Boy and Cub. I would like you to revamp the program for us locally. Also start with the old basics, not the current program."

"What are you looking for?"

Well, you know that Baden-Powell wrote a Handbook for Scouts to fill a need that he had when he was in the field. There were many young soldiers from England, who knew nothing about surviving in the outdoors. It became so popular with youngsters in England it was described as the Scouting Movement."

"It had no organization until King George had two problems which he used to solve one another. One was he couldn't advance Baden-Powell any further in the Military, and second was a huge juvenile delinquency rate, at that time. The young men didn't have enough to do. So the King asked Baden-Powell to set up an official Scouting program."

"I am faced with a similar situation Paul. I won't lie to you. You aren't happy with your advisory groups. They aren't happy with you. Hiring you to take care of the grounds at a fair wage takes care of your income problems and our grounds keeping issues. Revamping the Scouting training and literature will help train our youth for what is to come."

Rick didn't add, "And it will save a lot of toddlers from learning many bad words."

Rick brought out a box of literature; it included copies of the first Boy Scout Handbooks and even a rare copy of Baden-Powell's Handbook for Scouts.

"Use these as the foundation. I suggest you involve the more experienced Scout and Cub Masters and Commissioners, of course don't let Council get wind of this, or they will freak out."

When Rick told David Paul about the changes with Mary and Paul, he was more than satisfied.

Rick didn't complain as he did the dishes all through August as he now had Paul Kettler taking care of the yard. It was July before David Paul called him and told him that teams had done the first local volunteer group interviews. He would be part of the interview team now that people had been tested for skills and mindset.

“Why am I going to be part of the interview process?”

“It is part of positioning you in these people’s mind as the head honcho of the CSCs.”

“Can I get a set of Head Honcho rank badges?”

“I think you are wearing them now Rick”

“I guess, but I thought maybe six or eight stars might be more appropriate for this lash up.”

“Why are you so cynical?”

“Well it seems to me like we are imposing this like a banana republic. We aren’t giving them any choice in the matter.”

“Rick this is one area where we do have more expertise than you. If this played out on its own locally, we would end up with the wrong people in charge, and they would be second guessing you and trying to take over. We are just trying to ensure that we end up with the best we have in charge both locally and nationally.”

“You have more faith in me than I do,” replied Rick.

“Rick the more I work with you the more convinced I am that you are the right person for the job. Besides we have a secret weapon in place to keep you on the straight and narrow."

"What's that?"

"Marsha."

"How ready are the other sites," inquired Rick and also changing the subject.

"About 65% is our best guess. Yours is at 95%. Food and medicines are in place. Raw material stocks are there. Infrastructure is complete. Key professions have been recruited, and most have moved in. About the only thing left are the niceties; like theaters and bowling alleys. Even those are started. If things went to hell tomorrow you could make it."

"Could the other groups make it?"

"Doubtful, though new key personnel have been identified, there is no real leadership that has been generally accepted. But the worse thing is that they don't have any barriers up to keep them isolated."

"We must be okay there, but I haven't been out to look at them."

"Rick the Berlin Wall wasn't as stout as what we have in place. The entire valley has been walled off. Reporters have been all over us wondering why this is being done. If we didn't have the FISA courts on our side, it would be headlines every day. As it is I don't know how long it can be kept quiet. The blogosphere has been chattering for a while, but it has been the conspiracy sites at this point. That will change."

"Where we do have to talk about it, we will present it as an exercise in urban planning. It is a test case for a balanced community. From one point of view that is exactly what it is. From a larger perspective, it is also a balanced country. One of the things we have kept track of is demographics. The percentages of just about any group that you can think of are very close to the country as a whole. Only felons and the hidden groups like pedophiles may be under represented. We didn't move any known felons out, but we didn't invite any in. I don't think they will be missed."

"How is the computer center coming along?" Rick asked.

"You don't rival NSA, but you have a heck of a lot. Literally all of the libraries of the world are included. The whole area is linked with the new ultra-fast fiber optics and the latest Wi-Fi. We have provided beefed-up computers to every business and household at a much reduced rate. Because of this, the kids in this area are cleaning up on all the online games. We have six world record holders in this area. That has become noticeable in the gaming world, but again hasn't made the mainstream yet."

"We are on the verge of the CSC's existence going national. When it does, they will become a Mecca for survivalist's, and we will lose our ability to function as we should. It will become a free-fire zone as the crazy's show up, then if there are real problems later the CSCs won't be able to carry out their mission. We are about at wits end of what to do."

"Short of buttoning down in here and putting up a clear zone outside your walls, there isn't much we will be able to do. That option isn't open anyway. The current administration just about had a heart attack when they were briefed on the CSC's existence. They don't fit in with their equality for all plans. Christ, I don't know how many more of these 'equality for all' plans our nation can survive!"

"Slow down David you are going to have a heart attack. What will be, will be, nothing is worth frothing at the mouth like that," said Rick.

"I know, but we have put so much effort into this, I hate to see it going down the tube. The administration will use any excuse to pull the plug."

Later when he related that conversation to Marsha, she told him, "It might have been more convincing if you haven't been known to froth a little yourself."

A week later the other CSCs, government take overs and public exposure became a moot point.

## Chapter 40 – The Beginning of the End - Monday June 9th 2025

The first hint that there might be a problem came from a phone call from the CDC to their local contact Chris Allen. Chris in turn followed procedure and called the night operator at the town hall. The town hall itself had expanded its original function to being the center for the Valley "government." While having no legal existence, it, in fact was the government center for the CSC.

Its creation was the result of a turf battle between the locals, DHS and the Federal government. A building was being put up at the DHS center, the old survivalist ranch. It was intended to house the Federal government with representatives of all branches with ALL of the federal regulations in place.

For some reason, the local contractor putting up this building kept making mistakes in following the building codes and having to rework the building. The latest was in finding out the EPA required study for environmental impact hadn't been performed properly, and the whole site had to be leveled and brought back to its original condition until completion of the study.

The Federal committee comprised of representatives of each group to be housed there complained bitterly to the owners of the construction company. The owners in turn pointed out, it was the committee who had commissioned the original EPA study and the way it was performed.

The committee stated that they should be allowed to ignore the flawed study as they usually did as they were the Federal government. A suit was brought by a newly formed local environmental group, and a Federal Judge brought it all to a halt. It would probably take many years to sort things out and restart construction.

In the meantime, Rick hoped that it wasn't found out that he was the hidden owner of the construction company; and bankroller of the new environmentalist group. After their victory, this group seemed to go dormant.

Since the Feds wouldn't be moving in soon there was a power vacuum. While running the CSC, the DHS couldn't run the local government. The state of Tennessee had made overtures as they saw a revenue source but the county had firm control over its activities. Thus the expanded role of the town-hall switchboard which followed its own established procedures for a CDC event notification.

A phone tree consisting of the Valley Group was called. Within one hour, the group was assembled and listening to the CDC report being related by Chris Allen.

"There is an event in India that is of concern. A H51A - H1N1 combination type influenza event is occurring. It is a new variant. It appears to have a one-week incubation period, and has a seventy percent mortality rate among the general population. They haven't refined what the rate is in specific age groups yet. The only good thing is that it started out in the country side and is just hitting the cities."

Hope Popule asked, "Should we declare Madagascar?"

"What is that?" asked Mary.

Hope explained, "During the 1918 flue pandemic the governor of Madagascar closed the ports. They lost less than one percent of their population. Samoa which at that time was about the same size and population didn't close their ports. They lost about twenty percent of their population."

"How do you know this?"

"I used to play a computer game called Pandemic. When we closed an area, it was, 'Calling a Madagascar Event'. The term became so common that they now use it at the CDC."

"We don't want to panic people, but maybe this is the time to start a drill. We can turn it real later if needed," observed Marsha.

"Unfortunately, it could be here now with today's rate of travel," observed Mary.

"That being the case let's use our planned twenty-four-hour emergency notice. You either get back or spend ten days in the quarantine area," put in Rick.

Rick continued, "Anyone thinks we shouldn't do this?"

"I don't," replied Jack Nelson, "It will play hell with business. I will have to shut down for days, and I have already spent my advertising budget. People will show up, and I will be closed."

“Well Jack you aren’t required to come into the zone. You can stay on your side of the mountain and keep your store open.”

“Most of my customers will be in here!”

Marsha retorted, “Jack it all boils down to; is the risk to your family worth making the money?”

“Dang Marsha, when you put it that way we better start locking this place down!”

“Any other concerns,” asked Rick?”

After a few moments of silence, he continued. “Okay it is now 4:30 a.m. Thursday June 5, 2025. Marsha, please record that the drill has started at this time and will run for ten days. All work inside will continue. The quarantine centers at the entrance areas are to go active. All employees working outside will continue to be paid, but they will be notified to return with their dependents.”

“All housing that is in a habitable condition is to be opened. Work on those that are close to livable is to be a priority. Assign those not doing anything else to this task. I also declare that we are now under local marital law for the duration of this drill by order of General Richard King under the powers vested in me by the Department of Homeland Security through Executive Order 30532 of the President of the United States of America.”

A chill swept through the group as they suddenly realized what they had just done. Everything they had feared, planned for, and worked to mitigate had just turned into reality. Had they done enough?

Rick dialed the command center and gave his orders. They were terse and to the point. The actions now being taken, and notices being sent out had been through the typical military drill. They had been gamed many times over to ensure they were as good as they could be, short of doing a full drill. This was the drill. Also it could turn out to be the real thing.

After his call, there was an awkward silence as they wondered what to do next.

Mary spoke up, "I think the Lord's Prayer would be very appropriate right now. Our Father who art in heaven….."

It was probably one of the sincerest offering of the time-honored prayer ever given.

After that, things began to happen. The perimeter of the valley was secured. Fences and walls had been long built along the top of ridges and fire lanes cut to keep the perimeter clear. Now portable towers were set up every hundred yards. Cameras and pressure pads were actuated. This was all done according to pre-laid plans.

The main north and south roads were set as the entrances to the valley. Jersey barriers were put into place to funnel traffic to guard stations. The barriers also would prevent anyone shoving through. A lot had been learned about making an area safe in the Middle East sand box.

Outside of the gates, compounds were fenced in. These were varied in size, and each could hold anywhere from ten people to one hundred and fifty. Each had water, power connections, cooking, sanitary and laundry facilities along with sleeping arrangements.

The shelters were based on the US Army "Force Provider" shelters whose early models were intended for one hundred and fifty troops. The updated versions had size variations.

The entire compound area already fenced in, had a medical center and the entire area covered by wireless routers. The idea was that as people arrived after the valley was closed, they would stay in the compound for the incubation period of the disease.

In this case, it was one week. Smaller compounds would be used for families. The larger ones would be populated by sex in most cases. Several would be dedicated to couples who were determined to share their fates together.

Since the basic concept was set on a military version, they tended to look sterile in appearance, but there were some amenities provided. Television, cards, board and video games were available. The intention wasn't to imprison people, but to keep them in isolation until they were known not to be carriers.

There was also a reception center prior to the compounds. Each arrival would be examined by a trained health care worker who was properly masked and clothed. The new arrivals would be given bins to store their personal belongings in while they went to isolation. They were each given several sets of coveralls to wear after showering and delousing if needed. It was surprising how many people who showed up later needed delousing.

No weapons were allowed, so they were supposed to go into storage and would be returned along with their other belongings after they were known not to be carrying the virus. Since the early days of metal detector screening the technology had become very sophisticated and people would be screened as they went through a very normal-looking doorway. There was no need to set anything aside, worry about brushing the sides of the entrance or even go through in single file, or alone.

Each end of the valley could hold up to five thousand people in isolation at one time. After that they would be put into huge fenced in areas with tents, water, sanitary facilities, and with food being delivered. This was a step above primitive camping, but only a step above. They could house another twenty thousand people using this method.

The recall that went out was for two thousand people who were outside on normal business or vacations. Those overseas were at the most risk. The recall was sent out as a

Mandatory Drill. It was well explained that to retain employment in the Valley that these drills would be adhered to.

There were very few residents of the valley who were still independent enough that they could choose not to return and lose their job, but if they did return late, they like all others would spend time in isolation.

The hope was that by making it a Mandatory Drill, they would get everyone back that had a place in the valley, but they wouldn't attract refugees yet. Human nature being what it is they knew that some friends and families of residents would show up for a visit, but that it wouldn't be enough to overwhelm the infrastructure.

All these decisions were part of the preplanning, from business-like meetings. Humans were numbers when the decisions were made, there were no pictures of small children in their mothers arm's looking scared and hungry. After one contentious session about who would be admitted, one grizzled combat veteran was heard to comment that he would rather be under direct fire than do this.

With this many people involved and todays abilities with facial recognition software there would be incidents of families showing up where one of the parents was wanted for rape or murder. They weren't set up to put people in jail. Would they turn the person away and admit the family. What if the family chose to leave together? Was it fair to let children go to a certain death because of their parents?

For this ‘drill,’ they did have a prison compound setup, and the State Police had a presence to take away any with warrants for their arrest. Only those wanted for violent crimes such as murder, rape and sexual predators would be treated under this rule set.

Another series of difficult decisions revolved around those who required special life support methods. Fortunately, with the recent medical breakthroughs, there wouldn’t be many. These day’s people tended to be healthy or dead. Mentally unstable were another group. It was finally decided that all events couldn’t be planned for and that some decisions would have to be made at the time. The worse the situation the more draconian would be the decision.

## Chapter 41 – The Fall - Tuesday June 10th 2025

In the next twenty-four hours as planned over ninety percent of those outside the gates made it back. When the gates were closed there were one hundred and eighty four people not inside. All but one was accounted for as in transit.

The missing person was on a rock climbing holiday according to his family and out of cell phone contact. It was hard to believe but even in this day and age there were still some spots on earth that didn't have cell coverage.

The reports out of India kept getting worse and there was a definite pattern in the reported cases worldwide. In the next three days if one overlaid the new cases to a map of the air routes it was almost a one hundred percent match.

The mass media was still reporting the story as local outbreaks. The Internet was awash with information, some of it even accurate. A few families and groups declared that TSHHTF and hunkered down in survival mode.

Most still were at the, "I'm watching it, but I have got to go to work," stage.

By the fifth day, all of their outsiders were back with the exception of the rock climber, and he was on his way.

On the sixth day, it really did hit the fan. Cases were reported in New York City, Chicago, Los Angeles, San Francisco and Atlanta. All major gateways for foreign air travel.

As usual, the American government was in gridlock. The Executive Branch wanting action out of Congress while Congress wanting action out of the Executive Branch.

Behind the scenes, all the phone lines were in use by special-interest groups. These ranged from the travel industry not wanting a costly shut down to the ‘Close our Borders, America isn’t for newcomer’s crowd.’

At this point, it was too late to keep the disease out. The CDC was being overwhelmed by reports by this time, but they were able to extract patterns. The most frightful was that the virus was showing no signs of natural attenuation. It wasn’t mutating to a weaker version, and there were no signs of resistance in the general population.

With most viral outbreaks, some part of the general population would have a natural resistance. This hadn’t emerged so far. Like the Spanish Flu outbreak of 1918 it was concentrated on the healthy. Most viruses were hardest on the young and elderly, but this wasn’t the case in this outbreak.

On June 15th, the CDC declared a Pandemic and recommended that all interstate travel be halted. This wasn’t implemented because the US Federal government was in disarray. The President, Vice-President their families and most of their staff were all out ill. Continuity of Government plans were attempted, but at this point the spread of the virus was quicker than the plans.

Now on all the news, the recommendation was to stay home. People tried this for several days; then they needed food. They would go to a store, and it might or might not be open depending on the local staff. When a store was open, the crowds were unruly and looting broke out.

By June $19^{th,}$ the major cities were out of food and no more was coming in. Now it turned ugly. This scene was playing out in every city in the world.

One country, Israel declared Madagascar early on. Because of the walls they had erected, it was relatively easy to close their borders. While the Palestine's residents were dying, ill in such numbers, they couldn't attack Israel, even if they had wanted to; an Ultra-Orthodox Jew stated on his blog that this was God's Will, and that he was wiping out all, but the anointed people.

This blog gained worldwide circulation with the End of the World crowd.

Unfortunately, it also gained circulation in the Muslim world. Apparently, someone in power in Iran took exception to this thought and ordered the launch of their nuclear arsenal on Israel.

While in its death throes Israel counter launched on all the major Muslim cities in the Middle East and Northern Africa.

This pulled Pakistan into the fray; they in turn launched against all their perceived enemies, including India. India countered against Pakistan and China. China hit Russia and the United States.

When the United States answered from their remote land, sea and space sites, it was over. The Russian launch took out the major European cities. In the space of ten days, the world population was reduced by sixty percent.

In the next wave of starvation, looting and rioting; the population was cut in half again. Then the winter of 2025 set in. The world population was cut in half again.

By the summer of 2026, it was reduced again as cancers from the bombing took their toll. The pandemic had burned itself out.

There were many stories of tragedy and grief. Few in the world were unaffected. There were stories of triumph over great odds. Mostly, it was human misery and suffering. Since the devastation was so great there was no real record of the events except in the Valley.

There they called it the Dying. Later, Historians would call it The Great Death. Some would claim it was a blessing, in that it gave humanity a chance to start over and be saved from its own self. No one alive during this event would agree with them.

With less than seventy-five million people left alive in scattered locations, the very survival of the human race would have been in question, except for the Tennessee survival center. It was a microcosm of twenty-first century civilization. While far from perfect in its resources both in material and personnel it was enough to become a true center for the restructuring of society.

While these worldwide events were unfolding the actual events were less known to those living through them. Their concerns were local and immediate. Communications were breaking down everywhere, only much later was the timeline of events unraveled.

Even that would be controversial like any historical reconstruction. James Garner in the movie, “Sunset,” said it best, “That is exactly how it happened, give or take a lie or two.” What destruction occurred was fact. The order of occurrence and triggers would always be debatable.

On this fateful day, Rick and Marsha were in the immediate now of the Valley. When the gates were closed, and the refugee centers opened they repaired to their stations. Rick to the Valley Command Center, Marsha to the gates to help with the refugee inflow.

It became quickly apparent to Rick that events were cascading out of any control, and that he was watching the end of a human era. As attributed to Stalin, a human death is a tragedy, millions of deaths a statistic. That day and those that followed the statistics became unbearable billions.

During this time period, for some reason, Rick kept thinking of a day long ago in a jungle where events were also overwhelming and the only way he got through it was to keep moving.

He changed the Valley Survival Center status from a drill to Level One, their highest emergency status. It put the entire Valley under Martial Law. As the area commander, he was now the government.

Everyone on the Valley Council now had a role to play in the emergency government, but Rick still kept the civilian government as an official body. They would meet weekly to discuss what the effects of Martial Law were having and how they would transition back once the emergency was over.

Rick didn't want to become King Richard in fact. He didn't mind the jokes made; he did mind the thought.

Marsha spent her time at the front gate helping with the incoming people. At first, it was very neat and orderly when the residents were returning; they started calling themselves Valley people.

Marsha refused to be called a Valley Girl and got into a snit if anyone tried. With the Valley people, they were dealing with friends or at least people who knew what was going on, and why.

It was when the "Others" started showing up the problems started. Most were scared and confused. A few were trying to get special treatment because they were important. Even fewer were just bad. As is the norm, those few bad caused most of the problems.

The scared and confused were brought into the system; they were interviewed and registered as to names, where they were from, ages, education, skills and what they had brought with them if anything. Everyone went through a delousing procedure without exception. Their goods were fumigated. Pets were put into quarantine.

Family units were kept together. Geographic groups were kept together as much as possible. It was felt if the incomers were with people from near them; they would feel more comfortable.

Mostly that worked but it was also found that the Hatfield's and the McCoy's weren't the only ones having feuds. Once that problem was identified, they were separated as much as possible.

Expulsion was also explained to all incomers. Quickly, it was noticed that the women listened closer to this punishment than the men. The women brought the men under control.

The only actual case of expulsion were two bachelor brothers. They were sent out with no arms, and several days' worth of food. They were told to try it on their own, and if it didn't work out to come back in seven days.

If they acted up again after readmission, they would be expelled for good. They both were at the gate in seven days, and never were an issue again. Any thoughts they may have had about marauding were stopped by the armed drone that followed them the entire time they were outside.

Marsha made friends with one family that was spending their time in quarantine.

She thought they were a lovely young couple. Matt and Janet Wycliffe had an infant girl Susan and a two-year-old boy Robert. Matt was a Marine Captain that was on leave and she a RN. Marsha knew they would be good additions to the Valley.

She made a point of talking to the young couple daily, either through a computer hookup to their shelter or actually yelling through the fence. She thought Robert was adorable, as much as any two-year-old can be adorable and couldn't wait to hold little Susan.

The Wycliffe's were in one of the smaller enclosures. It held three other families. They had all set themselves up to avoid the other groups as much as possible. Sadly, someone brought the disease in with them.

It spread like wildfire through the enclosure. Matt and Janet kept separate from the others as much as possible. It didn't work.

Both Matt and Janet became ill and died. It was heartbreaking when they knew they were ill. Both of them begged Marsha to take care of their children if neither of them survived. She promised she would.

They were among the last of the adults to contract the disease. Their children were now the only ones left alive in the compound. They weren't ill, but were now starving. Since they had been near the sickness, their quarantine clocks started over.

No one was supposed to go into the compound until all had died or the quarantine clock had run out.

Marsha couldn't live with this.

Marsha called Rick and explained her plan. He started to argue and then realized that neither of them could live with themselves if she didn't follow through. He told her he loved her and go with God speed.

Marsha put on a Hazmat suit and went into the compound and bagged up the bodies. She then put the bagged bodies in a wooden container and from there they were transported for cremation, they would burn the box and all.

She then went to the remotest area of the compound and sprayed it with an alcohol solution. She then changed into a new Hazmat suit and then fed the children.

She brought a children's harness to restrain young Richard. It almost broke her heart to hear his cries when she had to leave him. She then proceeded to spray every surface she could get to with an alcohol solution.

After that she returned to the children. Took off the Hazmat suit and picked up both children. As she held Susan for the first time she sobbed her heart out. She now had three weeks in quarantine.

Rick for one of the few times in his life abused his authority. Even though they needed the space, he wouldn't allow anyone else to be put in that compound as long as Marsha was there.

No one questioned his order.

## Chapter 42 – Hitting Bottom - August 2025

The next few weeks left Rick in a daze. Marsha and the children came through their quarantine period without any problems. His world was shaken up by two major events, the end of the world as he knew it, and the beginning of a new family.

Years later he would confess that he didn't know which was more stressful. During the quarantine period the two children had bonded with Marsha. Matt the two year old still missed his parents. Janet would never know any parents but them.

Matt took to Rick, that wasn't the problem. The problem was that Matt was two years old, while Rick was over eighty going on sixty. Rick was in good health for a sixty year old; that was meaningless as he tried to keep up with the toddler.

He could keep up with the little girl as she was smart enough to take an afternoon nap just like him. Matt was a ball of energy from daybreak to lights out. The only mercy was when he fell asleep after dinner that was it. There was no dropping off gradually, the light switch went off and he was gone to the world. Until the sun came up then once again he was on a holy tear.

Rick only had to put up with this until after dinner for an hour or so, and it still pushed him to the end of his rope. It may have something to do with his being at the CSC command center twelve to fourteen hours a day seven days a week ever since events started.

Marsha was at home with the children. Janet was a little angel according to her, other than the fact she woke them both up every night wanting to be fed. Matt, however, came from somewhere else. She loved him to death and tried to keep up with him, but her age was against her.

Then after his first week there he learned a new word, NO! Between hours at work, no sleep this was just about the last straw for Rick. He and Marsha were having their morning coffee along with a serious conversation about the children.

As they talked Marsha was giving Janet a bottle. As Rick continued his litany of complaints he didn't notice young Matthew try to climb up on his lap. He didn't even think about it as he lifted the youngster.

He continued on, but came to a stop as he realized Marsha was smirking at him.

"What," he said in exasperation.

Marsha tilted her head towards Matt.  He was now sound asleep over Ricks shoulder. Rick turned is head to look at the lad.

"It's too late isn't it," he said plaintively.

"Yep," replied Marsha as she cuddled the cutie in her arms. She continued, "We need to hire a Nanny, a Cook, and Housekeeper, and several Maids would be good also. Wayne and Paul have done a good job on the grounds, so that is okay."

"What! Why the staff all of a sudden"

"Because if you haven't noticed it dear, you are now the leader of about fifteen thousand people, and probably the largest concentration of people left on the planet. After things settle down a bit, we will have to pay our social dues."

This thought pleased Rick as much as a root canal, but he realized it was true. He got up to pour himself another coffee, carrying the sleeping Matt with him.

"You are right Marsha, and that brings up another subject. We need some security around here, at least controlled admission to the house, and even the whole farm. That is one nice thing about being the General, I can give orders and it will happen. I will take care of Security if you will hire the rest."

"Yes dear, the staff starts tomorrow."

When you are completely sandbagged sometimes it's best to accept it and move on. That was Rick's story and he was sticking to it.

After some thought Rick decided to have the Military handle security on the perimeter of the Farm, and use a civilian police set up in close contact with the family.

These were the easy problems facing Rick and Marsha. The bulk of the people who had come in at the recall were already residents of the Valley. However they had picked up an additional four thousand people who had tagged along or were smart enough to show up on their own.

Apartments had been started and in many cases completed and were unoccupied. They had enough rooms for everyone. The problem was the apartments were truly empty, no furniture or furnishings of any sort. So while housing was being assigned it couldn't really be lived in yet. Not that a few people camped out in them.

They were so tired of the quarantine quarters that anything was better.

At a staff meeting this was the top of the agenda. The question was; where and how would they get everything that was needed. It was all out there somewhere they just had to go collect it.

A more pressing issue was to find survivors. They had to save everyone they could. While there was a world of food and shelter out there, there was the possibility that some of those left would be too young to care for themselves.

The hard fact was that most would die before they could find them, but that was no excuse to delay. It was the only human thing to do, plus the fact they needed all the genetic diversity they could find.

The preplanning from the think tanks addressed this issue. They would use drones for the initial search for human life. Many drones had been prepositioned for this purpose. These were the huge ones like the Predator versions. These were all about ten feet in length and had a long flying range and time.

Operators were easily trained for this mission. They would have rotating flight crews which would fly the drones twenty-four seven. The take from on board cameras would be computer analyzed for active human sign, such as movement, fire or any lighting. There would also be human observers to react to the software alerts.

The software was set to high alerts, so there would be many false positives for the observers to sort out. It was felt that rather than take the chance on missing someone they would over react.

Once an individual or group was identified the drone would fly low and sound a siren. The operators would then drop a padded canister with a long ribbon flag. The canister would contain a radio which could reach the drone's radio equipment. The drone would then act as a repeater station back to the drone center. As they spread further across the United States they would have to have an airborne system of relay stations.

While they could use the military satellites overhead, none of the portable equipment they had available could reach it yet. This was one item that hadn't been completed in time.

Once they found the needs of the group and found out if they wanted to be brought in, or that the Valley would let them in, a car or cars would be sent. The self-driving cars had oversized gas tanks with a cruising range of a thousand miles. They were communication equipped and each had their own crew, like the drones there were operators and communicators/observers.

While the vehicles were in transit there would be ongoing scanning for active human presence.

As in any group human endeavor a specific language was developed. Along with the special terms came clothing with a patches and badges for accomplishments and rank. Those that worked with drones were in drone ops, the pilots were drone operators or ops, and the observers were called drone eyes or just plain eyes.

The auto flight was car ops, and the drivers were car operators which became cops, and the observers were call talkies. Of course the car operators were never allowed to forget that they were driving self-driving cars. This led to several friendly bar room conversations and a black eye or two.

The entire country was gridded out and the process had started. It was estimated that it would take six months to give a quick look at everything and then another year for a refined search for survivors. This required two fleets of drones, one high flying looking for large signs of life and then the lower more refined search. So now there were LDO's and HDO's, high and low drone operators.

Rick had to wonder if there was an acronym for acronyms. He asked and regretted doing so when he was told there were TLA's and FLA's, three and four letter acronyms. More than that was called a TML's, too many letters.

In meetings they refined the plans for providing employment for the new people and furnishings for the apartments. This was one of those lucky times that one problem would solve another. People who had no employment and were able bodied would be hired to collect furniture, clothes, food and other needs from the outside.

Anywhere outside of the Valley was now called the outside. Teams would go out in convoys with tractor trailers. They would move into a shopping center and load up all the packaged items. Anything open would be left on the shelf. They didn't want to strip any place as loners may show up with needs.

Each box loaded would be given an RFID tag that could be read remotely. While cleaning out a store there would be a team of photographers taking digital pictures for a catalog.

The trailers would be returned full to the Valley. They would be parked, current high need items such as beds and bedding would be unloaded. Samples would be set up in a store. In this case the store was a series of one-hundred thousand square foot warehouses that had been erected for this type of need.

When someone needed a bed and mattress they would go to the store. After picking out the items they wanted a team would retrieve the order from the identified trailers.

The cost of each item would be about one cent on the true dollar cost of the item. The only reason there was any charge was to prevent people from getting new furniture or clothes every week.

The hope was the charges would meet the costs or come close for the retrieval crews.

Food would be free, go to the store and pick it up.

When someone mentioned to Rick that he was setting up a communistic society he went ballistic.

Leaving out all the swear words involved it came down to, "We are redefining the social safety net. There will be no retirement funds or food stamps!"

Rightly or wrongly Rick believed that the food stamp or EBT card program was a national disgrace. If the money being spent on this program was redirected they could have provided American made and grown food to everyone legally in America for free.

Since about everyone coming in now would be undocumented he wasn't worried about that point anymore. More importantly they needed every human alive if possible.

He would like to see the safety net include basic food, clothing, health care and shelter. After that you were on your own. What would have been completely unworkable before the Fall was now a possibility. In his mind the only reason it was unworkable previously were the special interest groups. Free public housing when there was a buck to be made, come on! As far as health care, little was needed now, and the insurance companies and big pharma were out of the picture.

Ricks idea of gun control was proper aiming. It had already been decided that there would be almost no standing army. They would use the Swiss model were everyone had a time of service and took their weapon home with them.

The tradeoff would be the use of weapons in domestic violence versus an armed citizenry that would never fall under a Hitler or Stalin which were the two political extremes. Radical Islam was no longer a fear, but Rick hoped that there wouldn't be a rise of Radical Christianity. It had happened before and could again.

He was prepared to stomp on it hard if it started.

All these thoughts were part of the free flowing conversation he and Marsha were having while holding the young children they were building a new world for. Not bad for a couple of old geezers.

## Chapter 43 – Starting back up - August 2026

The next year flew by for Rick and Marsha. During that time, the Valley expanded to one-hundred and seventy-five thousand residents. That first year took a horrible toll on the outside survivors.

The population of Earth according to the best estimates went from seventy-five million during that first year to less than a million worldwide.

This was due to the last of the influenza. No matter how remote a village was there was some communication with the outside world. When a person from the village visited the outside, there was a high probability they were bringing the disease back with them. This ranged from the Inuit's of the Arctic Circle, to the Indians of the Amazon, to the Pygmies of Africa.

Then there was the fact that the survivors, everywhere but the Valley didn't have access to the Live pharmaceutical. So the remaining population went from robust health to that of pre-Live citizens.

The recovery program worked better than they ever hoped. Once cold weather set in the drones could spot smoke. The crew would then circle in and then sound an alarm siren to alert the residents they were above them.

A canister would be dropped with a bright streamer. It would contain a solid-state radio in its padded case. Once identities were exchanged the Operations Center would do an immediate check on the history of the identified individual or group.

Since it was all computerized it was done while the conversation was occurring. There were only several cases where the people weren't invited to join the Valley. It would be explained why the individual couldn't join them. Fortunately, there were no family groups involved; those not invited were all singles.

Even they were provided with the vaccine, so they wouldn't spread the influenza.

As people were found their name was put into a public database in the Valley. Sadly very few were lost loved ones or friends.

Once the individual was seen to take the vaccine on camera they were allowed into the self-driving car which had been sent for them. The car would have enough food and water for the journey.

There were several encounters that were memorial. One of those was a group of seven children. They were led by a ten-year-old girl. She brought the group together in the town of Springfield. Using a self-driving car programmed to hit every street in town with horn blaring she brought the other six kids together.

Her parents had owned and ran a pizzeria which made wood fired pizza. This was their heat source. She taught herself how to run a forklift and brought in pallets of two-by-fours for fuel from the local lumber company.

One of the boys, a nine-year-old figured out how to start a portable generator from a home-improvement store. This was used to provide battery chargers power. They were siphoning gasoline from cars.

Their leader had them use a lithium battery powered chain saw to cut up the winters fuel supply. She remembered her grandpa telling her that gasoline couldn't be stored for very long, so wanted to be ready for the winter. She also required safety glasses to be worn when cutting the wood.

The local water plant lost pressure to the system for some reason. For rest room facilities, they had portable camping gear gleaned from a sporting goods store. The plastic bags were dumped through the broken window of a basement in a building several blocks down the street. A special note was made in the system about that building.

Clothes and food were plentiful for the group, so they were in very good shape when found. They used paper cups and plates, which ended up in that basement. Five-gallon water jugs were stacked up where they had scavenged them.

The backroom of the pizzeria was converted to a dormitory. Each child had a chest of draws for their clothes. She assembled a first-aid kit for cuts. They had a collection of games, both electronic and board. It was evident that they didn't spend all their time playing.

A small armory of shotguns, rifles and handguns along with cleaning supplies and ammunition was gathered. They had shooting practice three times a week and while not expert, they could use the weapons.

To top it all off, they were continuing their reading, writing and arithmetic lessons, each helping the other.

Rick made note of Linda McDermott's name and intended to keep track of how she performed in the future. This kid was a natural leader.

Each of the children when they came to the Valley was absorbed into a family group. The original families of the Valley had expanded as large as they could reasonably be. New families were being formed within weeks of the individuals coming to the Valley.

Those from the outside had a dose of being alone and didn't like it.

It wasn't all sweetness and light on the recovery. The worse area was in Idaho. Most of the survivalists were just trying to do that. However, some of them had taken a page out of Major Watkins playbook. Before the Fall, they had reconnoitered the other camps, caves and tunnels in the area.

While many tried to maintain security and remain hidden it really was impossible with modern surveillance equipment. When it was evident that the big die off was in progress they all remained in their bunkers. Once they came out, those that were going to die had.

This still left a population of almost one thousand in the area. The strongest immediately set themselves up as warlords. After a few fights, they were too small to call battles; the area came under the control of one strong man, James Bolton.

Bolton promptly reintroduced the practice of slavery and maintained a harem. He must have read too many post-apocalyptic stories. He and his thugs ruled with an iron hand.

Their foot print was so large that it was one of the earliest human centers that the drones picked up. Since it was big Rick had them go slow and scout the place out well. The Idaho group had light planes, so they stayed high and made no contact.

In Rick's military staff meeting where they first discussed this group, there never was a question that they would let this stand. The only question was the how. They called Judge O'Malley in, who reviewed all the facts. He suggested they turn it over to the District Attorney.

The DA's office called a grand jury together who indicted the group in absentia. While under martial law there was no concern about posse comitatus violations. Actually under his authority, Rick could have ordered them taken out, but he wanted to retain as much of the law and order of the old United States as possible.

This wouldn't be a quick raid operation. The enemy had over two hundred armed men. Granted they weren't a trained organized army, but two hundred weapons have a quality of their own.

His staff planned an operation that would occur in several phases. A scouting team was set in place fifty miles from the Idaho base. The slavers set up in Soda Springs, Idaho for some reason. It was a cross roads type town.

While the scouts were doing their work, a series of supply depots were opened along the route to Idaho. They had hopes of bringing back almost eight hundred people. Even with self-driving cars and buses there would have to be rest stops and overnight stops along the way.

It took two months to pre-position food, fuel and set up lodging along the way. One plus from the operation was that they found five more individuals along the way. Each was acceptable to the Valley, and all were overjoyed to join the community.

The whole time the scouts had been reporting back. By the time the last post was set up a battle plan was in place. The slavers had set up large inflatable huts for everyone except the leaders. They had the nicest housing in town for themselves.

They would send out units daily on scavenging trips using school buses and semi-trucks. They had gotten to the point that the scavenging teams would be out for several days. There would be twenty-five people on a team. Five of them would be armed guards; the rest slaves to do the actual work.

The slaves in the compound would do the work. They weren't abused in the form of whippings, torture or sexual abuse. They were just held against their will and forced to work. Their housing and food was the same as everyone but the leaders. The leaders definitely lived a better lifestyle in the form of food and housing. There was some evidence that some of the female slaves were trading sexual favors.

While the scouts were observing one of the slavers was brought out and executed. It was known that it was for rape of a slave because they announced it on the small radio station they had set up, which the scouts were probably the most passionate listeners.

The execution gave Rick pause; it meant that the slavers weren't totally evil, but what concerned him, it spoke of a high degree of organization and discipline.

While observing the scouts were taking pictures continuously of the area and especially the people. In the two months, they were able to build a database of the entire slaver army and the rest of the people. There would be no hiding in the general population for this group.

The attack plan was straight forward. One team would take out the groups that were away scavenging while the main body of troops took Soda Springs. There was no intention of allowing any of the slavers to live. They couldn't afford to have these types loose in the world.

The slavers were careless in their setup. They had security on duty at all road entrances to the area. However, there were no walls or fencing around their quarters.

The guards were set up in nice guard shacks with heating and lighting. This made it easy to see that the night shift would mostly be asleep and would certainly have no night vision.

As much as Rick wanted to lead the attack, he knew he had larger responsibilities. The night of the raid he was in the command post with his staff. They would be listening to the commander on the ground, but wouldn't try to do his job for him.

Each of the four guard shacks had a four-man squad assigned to it. The two main huts the slaver soldiers slept in had ten men and a heavy weapons team. Each of the four houses had a five-man squad assigned.

At the designated hour of three a.m., the go signal was given. The fighting part of the operation took fifteen minutes. It was simple butchery of the slaver army. The closest to excitement was when the team who was taking the leader had to decide quickly who was bad and good, as he had several women in bed with him.

Loud speakers were used to tell everyone to stay in their hut until day break. At first light people started to come out of the huts. As they exited they were directed to an area that had been set up with temporary fencing. There were portable tables and chairs set up, along with a large field kitchen.

Before they were allowed in the area, a picture was taken, and computer comparison performed against the database they had built up. One man was identified as being a slaver. He was led away and kept with several others that had managed to surrender.

The three outside scavenging teams had been captured with no problems or losses. They weren't returning to Soda Springs, but heading towards the first depot along the route. They were bringing no slavers with them.

By noon, all the freed population was fed and clothed then boarded on travel buses. Very few of them had anything but the clothes on their backs. There were no family groupings.

After they left the last of the slavers were executed and left where they fell. A thorough search of the buildings had been conducted so they mounted up and left. They only went as far as the first depot and set up for several days.

A drone was left high up to see if anyone was missed. None were; they waited a week then surveillance was discontinued, and the rear guard came home.

The children with Linda McDermott and the slavers were the best and the worst of the stories to come out of the recovery phase in the old United States and Canada. Many individuals were found and brought back. There were dozens of small groups of ten or less.

None of the groups had any issues like the large slaver group. The fact was that people could walk off if they disagreed with the leaders.

While the people recovery operations were underway, the teams from the Valley were stripping the country like a plague of locust. There were now teams in place, which would move into an area and search every house. They would mark the door of each house that had been searched with an X, using chalk. Many houses had dead in them. They were left in place; there were too many millions to handle.

Special note was made of obvious antiques, but again they were left in place. They would be picked up by another team at a later date if at all. No effort was made to search out weapons, there were too many spots they could be hidden and too many to collect.

If there was something in particular, a member of the search team wanted they would show it to their team leader, and it would be recorded as theirs. A weight limit of fifty pounds per person was enforced. After the first few trips, most people never came close to this limit.

Towards the end of the second year of these efforts, the drones were flown south into Mexico. No life was found. There had been no attempts at controlling travel during the outbreak, so it had spread to the furthest corners.

Ham radio operators were the ones who really brought the world back together. The real enthusiast among them knew how to set up a solar power array to power their rigs. The Elmers among them were able to talk others through the process of setting up repeater networks. Soon most regions of earth were in contact. In the Valley, they were able to make contact with several satellite arrays so worldwide signals were sent out.

By the fifth year, the Valley was self-sustaining with its farming and everyone was housed and integrated in the community. Rick and Marsha talked it over and decided it was time to end martial law.

From lying in bed with Alzheimers to surviving a worldwide disaster they had come a long way. It remained to be seen how long they had to go.

The End

## Epilog

The Imperial Palace, Imperial Planet 7015 CE

*Emperor Charles the 23rd of the Human Empire shifted in his chair as the daily briefing went on. His boredom was evident to those present. The more things changed the more they stayed the same. This revolt, that uprising, another planetary financial collapse to be bailed out made up the norm for an empire of over twenty thousand suns, forty thousand planets each with an average population of five billion people.*

*The head of the Imperial Intelligence Service knew that a bored Emperor could be a dangerous Emperor so he brought up an oddity that had been found.*

*"Chas a project that has been ongoing for the last fifty years has come across a real puzzle."*

*"What's that?"*

*"A project has been to create a common operating system to be able to be backward compatible with previous operating systems. The University of Man main campus felt that too much history was being lost by systems becoming obsolete and discarded. Long story short, they have had success with systems up to fifteen hundred years old. That brings us to within five hundred years of the founding of the Empire. One bright soul came up with a test question. What is the oldest company in the Empire?"*

*"The answer to that is the Tuborg brewery on one of the Monastery Worlds. It was in business at least twenty one hundred years ago, some claim it goes back to Earth, the legendary home of mankind. They included all advertisements in the search so the personals were included. There is an ad that has appeared every one hundred years on the first of December for the last fifteen hundred years! It is in the Imperial Times. It simply says, "Syawla, Imperial Square new year's eve, Reve".*

*"That is odd, some sort of organization?"*

*"We are not certain, it got sent to my shop because the University thought it might be some sort of plot. Though if it is, it is very ineffective since it has been in place seven or eight normal lifetimes with no action. It became a joke in our department so it got passed around and I finally saw it. Personally I think it is a way for the University to request funding for some project."*

*This is where the Intelligences Head fear of a bored Emperor came true.*

*"Brad if they are meeting in the Imperial Square every one hundred years we should have pictures of them. It is the most recorded event in the Empire. All you have to do is compare the virtual identities for those dates of the crowds and you have them! Though I am not certain what you have them for, while it is unheard of, I do not think it is illegal to live eight times the normal human life span."*

*Brad blanched at the thought of the project, there went his discretionary budget. There were almost ten million people present on New Year Eve at the Imperial Square. Even the best of computers would be strained at that.*

*"Well Chas I guess we could do that, they would be interesting lab rats so the rest of us could last that long."*

*"CODS!"*

*"No way do I want to be Emperor that long!"*

*"Well cousin you could always abdicate and go fishing."*

*"You are never going to allow me to forget falling out of that boat are you?"*

*"Nope, not even if we live fifteen hundred years, instead of the normal one eighty to two hundred," Brad retorted.*

*Brad continued, "Still the more I think about it the better this project sounds, it really will give the equipment a workout, and more important shake up the shop as they try to figure out why we are looking for Syawla and Reve, or Always and Ever as it has been pointed out."*

*"Make it so."*

*Brad had no way of knowing that the Emperor had opened a five thousand year old can of worms.*